Survival
of the
Fritters

Survival
of the
Fritters

GINGER BOLTON

KENSINGTON BOOKS
www.kensingtonbooks.com

KENSINGTON BOOKS are published by

Kensington Publishing Corp.
119 West 40th Street
New York, NY 10018

All Kensington titles, imprints, and distributed lines are available at special quantity discounts for bulk purchases for sales promotion, premiums, fund-raising, educational, or institutional use.

Special book excerpts or customized printings can also be created to fit specific needs. For details, write or phone the office of the Kensington Sales Manager: Kensington Publishing Corp., 119 West 40th Street, New York, NY 10018. Attn. Sales Department. Phone: 1-800-221-2647.

Kensington and the K logo Reg. U.S. Pat. & TM Off.

eISBN-13: 978-1-4967-1188-5
eISBN-10: 1-4967-1188-2
First Kensington Electronic Edition: February 2018

ISBN-13: 978-1-4967-1187-8
ISBN-10: 1-4967-1187-4
First Kensington Trade Paperback Printing: February 2018

10 9 8 7 6 5 4 3 2

Printed in the United States of America

Acknowledgments

Many thanks to my supportive friends, including Krista Davis, Daryl Wood Gerber, who also writes as Avery Aames, Laurie Cass, who also writes as Laura Alden, Kaye George, who also writes as Janet Cantrell, and Allison Brook, who also writes as Marilyn Levinson. And then there are the Deadly Dames: Melodie Campbell, Alison Bruce, Joan O'Callahan, Cathy Astolfo, and Nancy O'Neil. Thank you for the critiquing, the laughs, the potluck lunches, and the cake masquerading as salad. Thank you to Inspector Shawna Coxon of the Toronto Police Service for your insight into The Job.

Thanks also to Sgt. Michael Boothby, Toronto Police Service (Retired). If any of the officers in this book don't act correctly, blame me (or my characters), not Mike.

Many thanks to John Talbot and John Scognamiglio for your encouragement and help, and to the Kensington team, especially Paula Reedy for your patience, Kris Noble for the cover design, and artist Mary Ann Lasher for the adorable cat and donut shop on the cover. And many thanks to the rest of the Kensington team working behind the scenes.

Thank you to my family and friends for suggestions, support, and the uncomplaining taste testing.

And last but not least, I raise a mug of coffee to my readers.

Chapter 1

✺

Tom stopped coating hot apple fritters in that tantalizing mixture of cinnamon and sugar. He stared over the half wall separating Deputy Donut's kitchen from our dining area. "One of our regulars is missing."

Naturally, Tom noticed when folks didn't show up for their usual coffee break. Before his stint as Fallingbrook's police chief, he'd been a detective.

"Once a cop, always a cop," I teased.

"You got it, Emily. I might have retired from the force, but . . ." He pointed at his hat. "I'm still the chief and I've got the *fuzz* hat to prove it."

Tom's Deputy Donut hat was a pretend police cap with a fuzzy donut glued on where the badge would be. The rakish way the hat tilted on Tom's short gray hair echoed the tilt of the police hat on the cat silhouette printed on our dishes and embroidered on our aprons. "Not necessarily." I raised my eyes as if I could see the top of my head and my own Deputy Donut hat, identical to Tom's. "Here, we're both chief." In addition to our hats and aprons, we both wore black jeans and white shirts. "Who's missing?"

"Georgia Treetor."

I stopped smiling. I liked Georgia. A lot. "That's strange." The knitters who called themselves the Knitpickers were backlit by morning sunshine slanting in through the front windows, and I couldn't make out features. "Don't I see six women at their table?"

"Not Georgia." The fryer beeped. Tom lifted another basket of fritters out of hot oil. "I see another white-haired woman who resembles her, but she's even smaller than Georgia."

"I'll go check." I carried a carafe of our house blend, a medium roast Colombian, past our glass-fronted display case and the marble counter where patrons sat on stools. The aroma of the coffee almost let me forget the mouthwatering cinnamon behind me in the kitchen.

Greeting other customers in our dining room and topping up coffee mugs, I made my way to the Knitpickers' usual table, one of the two large ones closest to Wisconsin Street. Tom was right. A tiny woman with a dandelion fluff of white hair sat facing the street. Tom had been able to tell from her back that the woman wasn't Georgia.

A twinkle in her light blue eyes, the new woman smiled up at me. "You must be Emily. Georgia told me about you. I recognize the dark curls, bright blue eyes, and friendly smile. I'm Lois Unterlaw. Georgia will tell you I'm her *oldest* friend, but that can't be true." She winked. "I'm not all that ancient. I'm the friend she's known the *longest*." Despite the white hair, she was youthful in her white jeans and flowing periwinkle top. "I just moved back to Fallingbrook from Madison, and she told me to meet her here this morning." She held up a handmade quilted tote, pieced together from cheerful prints in fuchsia, turquoise, and yellow. Knobby ends of knitting needles stuck out of the top. "I brought my knitting. She said I'd fit right in with the Knitpickers."

I shook her hand. "Welcome back to Fallingbrook, and welcome to Deputy Donut." Her hand was barely bigger than a child's. The strength of her grip startled me.

The knitters all began talking at once.

"Where *is* Georgia?"

"She never misses one of our morning Knitpicker meetings!"

"She's never, ever late."

"It's Monday. Maybe she went off for the weekend and was delayed getting home."

"Taking time off from mending dolls at her own doll hospital is one thing, but taking time off from *us*?"

"If she had a trip planned, she would have told us on Friday, wouldn't she?"

"Maybe she slept in."

One of the knitters pointed at me and told Lois, "Emily's the brains behind Deputy Donut."

"Actually, I'm not," I said. "Blame the Fallingbrook police department. They'll tell you that cops eating donuts is a stereotype, but most of them agree that they drink a lot of coffee, and the officers here in Fallingbrook really like my donuts. They made me open the shop so they could buy them every day." One of the four policemen at the next table let out a particularly hearty and contagious laugh. I flashed him a smile.

Lois tilted her head. "What did you do, Emily, drop out of junior high to open this shop?"

"No, but thanks." I lowered one eyebrow in fake skepticism. "I think." I was almost twenty-nine, but saying it would probably make me sound as juvenile as I apparently looked.

"What's your secret to staying so slim, Emily?" Lois was smaller than I was.

I quipped, "Lots of coffee and donuts."

She folded her arms. "I doubt that. You brought your apron strings all the way around to the front and tied them in a *bow*, with lots left over!"

"The secret to *that* is long apron strings." And an unspoken competition with Tom, who worked at staying fit and tied his apron strings in front also, but only in a square knot without excess strings dangling, which was just as well, since he was usually the one operating the fryers.

"Wait until you try the donuts here," another knitter warned Lois. "They're addictive."

"How can you eat donuts and knit?" Lois demanded. "Don't your yarn and needles get all sticky?"

One of the knitters made a pretend huffy face. "Give us credit for a little couth." She cocked her head toward a wall covered in artwork. "The ladies' room is just behind that wall, and it's very nice. We knit, then eat, then wash our hands, and then knit some more."

Lois held both thumbs up. "Georgia's right. I'll fit in for more than just knitting."

The knitters gave one another high fives, a tricky maneuver considering that some of them didn't let go of their knitting. "Welcome to the Knitpickers," they said to Lois.

She studied the wall between the dining room and the hall leading to the restrooms. "You have lovely paintings, sculptures, and wall-hangings, Emily," she said. "And your peach-tinted walls are a perfect background for the artwork."

One of the knitters sat up straighter. "The artists and craftspeople are all local."

Another chimed in, "People can buy what's displayed here through Emily and Tom."

"Tom?" Lois turned in her chair. Tom and his whimsical Deputy Donut hat were visible over the half wall. "Is that Chief Westhill?"

"Yes," I said. "He retired from the police. The two of us own Deputy Donut."

The original five Knitpickers watched me, obviously curious about what else I might say about Tom.

I raised my chin. "He's my father-in-law."

"I remember him," Lois said. "Nice guy."

The rest of us agreed.

A Knitpicker told Lois, "Emily and Tom don't charge commissions on the art in here."

Lois stared admiringly toward a spray of beech leaves sculpted from brass. "That's lovely."

"We get beautiful decorations—for free." I made a sad face. "But people keep buying my favorite pieces and I have to replace them." I opened my eyes as if surprised. "With new favorites!"

Lois ran a finger along the edge of the table. Our tabletops had been made from giant slices of tree, coated with a silky, waterproof finish. "I'll bet your customers like to count the rings to see how old the trees were," she said.

"They do. And they write down the results in the guest book there by the door."

Lois asked, "Do their results vary a lot, Emily?"

"None of our customers could possibly be wrong."

All six women laughed.

Lois patted the arms of her chair. "What a charming and welcoming coffee shop. Even the chairs are comfy." She picked up the handmade copper vase from the center of the table and held it near her face. "I love the scent of chrysanthemums. And these burgundy mums go perfectly with the copper. Are the vases for sale, also?"

"Not from me," I answered, "but the guy who makes them sells them at The Craft Croft, the artisans' co-op down the street."

Lois clapped her hands. "I'll have to get Georgia to take me there. Where can she be? I meant to call her this weekend, but I was unpacking and putting things away in my new house, and she had a big order of dolls to repair."

I suggested, "Maybe our lot's full and she's searching for a parking space." Labor Day was only seven days away. The last week of a perfect summer had brought many tourists to northern Wisconsin. Almost every seat in Deputy Donut was occupied, while out on Wisconsin Street, smiling people were window-shopping and browsing through Fallingbrook's many appealing shops.

"What would you folks like this morning?" I asked. "Tom just made a batch of cinnamon and sugar apple fritters. They're still hot."

All six women ordered them. One woman wanted a cappuccino with cinnamon sprinkled on top, and Lois asked me to make her one like it. As usual, two of the women wanted to share a pot of green tea. One woman asked for decaf Colombian, and the other wanted the day's featured coffee, a dark roast Nicaraguan.

I returned to the kitchen, plated the fritters, steamed the milk to a soft foam for Lois and the other woman, pulled shots of espresso, and combined the steamed milk and espresso in small cups printed with the Deputy Donut logo. Even though the smell of the cinnamon was tempting me to make a cappuccino for myself, I was glad they'd ordered it. Sprinkling it on their cappuccinos made me feel less guilty about not yet having mastered drawing cat eyes, noses, and whiskers in the foamed milk. Usually, I could manage the semblance of a donut. If it turned out lopsided with no hole in it, I could claim I'd intended to draw a fritter.

Georgia still hadn't arrived when I delivered the last of the fritters and beverages to the Knitpickers. The woman who'd said that Georgia was never late repeated it. I heard anxiety in her voice.

Chapter 2

Lois tapped her phone's screen. After a few seconds, she reported, "Georgia's not answering. Maybe she's on her way. Or taking a load of mended dolls to the post office."

The woman with the doleful voice pointed out, "She usually does that in the afternoon."

We told one another that Georgia would be along any minute, probably with an amusing tale about what had delayed her.

Many of our customers asked for fritters or cinnamon-flavored donuts. Chocolate was also popular that morning. I served unraised chocolate donuts drizzled with chocolate glaze, raised donuts with vanilla frosting and chocolate sprinkles, and ganache-filled donuts. Although I had tasted each kind, I wanted to sample them all again. I was a firm believer in what I liked to think of as quality control.

However, I didn't need to perform much quality control. Regular customers and new visitors were generous with their praise. One woman had driven from Pennsylvania to take pictures of the tall and beautiful waterfall that gave Fallingbrook its name. She cradled her ironstone mug between her palms. "Your donut shop warms my heart as well as my hands." She nodded at the hatted-cat silhouette on her mug and then smiled at the expanse of glass between the dining room and our office. "And I love the cat."

A real cat, my black, cream, and ginger tortoiseshell tabby fur baby, was in the office, sitting on the windowsill with her tail curled around her feet. Blinking sleepily, she peered through the glass at the people in the dining room. Tom and I had named Deputy Donut after her. To avoid confusion, I usually shortened the cat's name to Dep.

During a lull in cooking, coffee making, *quality control,* and swapping jokes and stories with customers, I opened the door from the dining room and slipped into the office. Dep's domain had windows on all four sides and a back door so I could whisk her into and out of the office without allowing her inside the dining room or kitchen. We didn't break health regulations, and my cat had the privilege of being both mascot and office manager. Besides, I'd miss her if I left her at home.

She was napping on the couch. She opened her eyes, stretched, hopped to the top of the short, cookbook-filled bookcase, and from there to the cushioned windowsill facing the kitchen. Switching her tail back and forth, she peered in at Tom. He smiled and waved. Dep purred.

The office had been chilly when we'd arrived at six thirty, but now it was toasty enough for my heat-craving cat, and I flicked off the gas fireplace between the windows overlooking the driveway. Dep jumped down to the ottoman, and then up to the windowsill behind the couch, where she could again watch the dining room. She settled down with her front paws tucked underneath her. If she tired of supervising the dining room, kitchen, driveway, and parking lot from her padded windowsills, she could rediscover her basket of toys or climb a carpeted pillar or her cat-width staircase to a multilevel cat-walk circling the room above the windows. She had plenty of food, water, and a clean litter tray.

Planting one knee in the couch, I leaned forward and buried my face in her soft fur. She revved up the purrs. "I'll be back soon," I told her, and let myself into the dining room.

Shortly before noon, the Knitpickers packed up. I held the front door open for them and their crafty totes and handwoven baskets.

Lois frowned at me. "Georgia's still not answering her phone."

"She'll be fine." I hoped I was right. "See you tomorrow!"

I saw them sooner than that.

At five thirty, right after Tom left for the day, I was about to leash Dep and walk her home when a dark blue minivan pulled into the parking lot behind the shop. Lois hopped out. Leaving Dep in the office, I went outside to see why Lois had come back after we closed.

She held up a key. "This is for Georgia's house. She's still not answering her phone. We're going to check on her. Want to come along?"

Dep would be fine in the office with her food, water, litter tray, catwalks, and toys. "Sure." I would have been happier if Lois had come to tell me that Georgia had been at home all day, concentrating on repairing dolls and making tiny outfits for them.

I locked the office door and walked to the van with Lois. The other five Knitpickers were already inside. I crawled into the very back seat with two of them. Keeping my eyes open for Tom's SUV, I pulled my phone out of my bag, and then put it back. I'd have liked Tom to join us at Georgia's, but although he still thought like a detective and a police chief, he had the right to a pleasant evening with my mother-in-law. I could call one of my best friends, a police officer, but that was silly, too. Georgia would be fine. I was thinking it, and the other women were saying it.

About ten minutes after we left Fallingbrook's center, Lois pulled onto a road just inside the town limits. Homes in this subdivision were newer than those close to downtown, but old enough to radiate character. They were set back from the street on large lots surrounded by shrubs and flower gardens, with woods behind them. Tall trees had already dropped a few red and gold leaves on green lawns. Mailboxes near the road and a lack of sidewalks gave the neighborhood a rural atmosphere. It was homey, quiet, and a little isolated.

Lois slowed near a one-story baby blue house with white shutters. On a white sign on the lawn, navy blue lettering spelled out DOLL HOSPITAL. "There's Georgia's house." Lois craned her neck to see around a crimson bush beside a lamppost. "Oh no! Georgia hasn't gone anywhere. Her car's in her driveway." A compact silver sedan was parked in front of the closed garage door.

I suggested, "Maybe she took a taxi to the bus station."

One of my seatmates said, "Maybe someone picked her up. A friend or relative?"

Lois parked behind the silver car, and we all piled out.

No wonder Georgia often bought boxes of donuts to take home. Her front porch was a welcoming outdoor room where friends and neighbors could relax, chat, and enjoy snacks. Underneath its sheltering roof, the deep porch ran the entire width of Georgia's house. Yellow and bronze mums bloomed in white window boxes on the railing. Although the cushioned porch swing and rocking chairs were inviting, we all stood in a bunch at the door.

Lois pushed a button. Stately chimes rang inside the house. Shuffling our feet and fidgeting, we waited. Lois tried the doorbell three more times. Finally, she retrieved Georgia's key from the pocket of her white jeans. "Do you all agree we should go in?"

One of the women asked me, "You used to be a 911 operator, right, Emily?"

"For a couple of years, yes."

"Should we call 911?"

"Probably not." *Unless we discover a reason to . . .*

The key turned, and Lois pushed the door open. "Georgia? Yoo-hoo! Georgia!" Her voice was surprisingly forceful for such a tiny woman.

No answer.

The Knitpickers hesitated, as if they were as nervous as I was, and then, her head up, Lois tiptoed inside. The rest of us followed her into Georgia's comfy living room. Dolls in various states of repair were on the coffee and end tables. Mended dolls wearing intricate outfits were lined up on the mantel above the fireplace, which smelled faintly smoky, as if Georgia had already been enjoying the wood fires that could make late summer evenings in northern Wisconsin especially cozy. Cardboard cartons were stacked beside the front door. The top one was addressed, obviously ready to be taken to the post office. The return sticker said DOLL HOSPITAL.

Lois tried again. "Georgia? Are you here?"

Still no answer.

"Let's check the bedrooms." Lois didn't sound keen on her own suggestion. "There are two."

A woman squeaked, "We have to stay together!"

All seven of us crowded into a former bedroom that now housed a sewing machine, shelves of folded fabrics, jars of buttons, reels of lace and ribbons, and books about dolls, doll repair, costumes, and antique toys.

The closet contained transparent plastic bins. One held batting. Another was full of tiny wigs—blond, red, and brunette, some curly, some straight, some with ponytails, others sporting braids. Boxes were labeled ARMS, LEGS, HEADS, and EYES.

Georgia was not in her workroom.

In Georgia's charming vintage pink-and-black-tiled bathroom, a spare roll of toilet paper must have fallen from somewhere and rolled along the floor, trailing paper as it went. I picked it up and set it on the tank. Every single one of us peeked behind the shiny pink shower curtain. No Georgia.

I probably wasn't the only one who could barely breathe when Lois opened the door to the second bedroom. The comforter on the neatly made bed matched frilly curtains in the same shade of lavender as the roses on the wallpaper. In the closet, blouses, slacks, jackets, and dresses hung from a rod, shoes were arranged on a rack on the floor, and plastic-fronted boxes on the top shelf held folded sweaters. I'd seen Georgia wearing many of those garments.

We returned to the living room and went through it to Georgia's dining room, which was charming with its half-timbered ceiling, varnished wood wainscoting, and yet another fireplace. Yellow mums had been arranged in an orange, mid-century modern vase on a quilted table runner, a patch-work of fall colors on Georgia's shiny dark-stained mahogany table. Two yellow petals lay on a maroon section of the runner.

Heart thumping, I led the others into the kitchen.

Georgia was obviously fond of color. Her kitchen cabinets were glossy red.

However, nothing else looked quite right in that bright kitchen.

One of the four chairs around her table was lying on its side on the black and white checkered floor. On a plate in front of where the chair had been, a fork had speared the remains of a strip of bacon, but its handle was in the congealed yolk of a sunny-side-up fried egg. Beside the plate, a glass tumbler contained an inch of orange juice. A turquoise cloth napkin lay on the floor near the fallen chair.

A donut was in the middle of the floor.

Another donut was even farther from the table.

I recognized those cake donuts dusted with confectioners' sugar and nutmeg. Georgia had bought a half dozen of them on Friday at noon before she and the other Knitpickers left Deputy Donut for the weekend. Feeling responsible because the donuts were cluttering Georgia's floor, I picked them up.

Standing again, I noticed an alcove just off the kitchen, opposite from the back door.

And that's where I found Georgia.

Chapter 3

Wearing blue jeans and a red sweater that I'd seen her knitting in Deputy Donut, Georgia was lying on her back on the floor of the alcove. She was blocking a white-painted door that probably led to the basement stairs.

One of Deputy Donut's distinctive bakery boxes, decorated with the black silhouette of a cat wearing a tilted police cap, was overturned, covering Georgia's face. I yanked the box off and left it, right side up, on the floor. A plastic teen doll was stuffed headfirst into Georgia's mouth. The doll was wearing nothing besides two donuts shoved up almost to her hips like a skirt.

The donuts I'd picked up fell out of my hand. My scream came out only as a gurgle of despair. Behind me, someone moaned, someone cried out, someone gasped, and someone sobbed. Or maybe all of us were making all of those noises. The others were probably trembling as much as I was.

I suspected that my friend, that sweet mender of dolls and of people, was beyond hope or help, but just in case there was a faint chance of reviving her, I knelt, grabbed the doll's feet, and yanked the doll, donut skirt and all, out of Georgia's mouth. Hoping for a pulse, I felt her wrist. She was as cold as the floor.

The back door creaked. I jumped. A breeze blew it open.

It wasn't latched, and the jamb was splintered near the lock.

Had someone run out the back door when we came in the front? Intent on finding that person, but not consciously planning what to do if I did find him or her, I jumped up, opened the door the rest of the way, and dashed onto the back porch. Behind me, tremulous voices discussed the possible merits of CPR.

I peeked behind upholstered wicker chairs. No one was on the porch, which was probably just as well, since the only weapon I was carrying besides the bunch of keys in the front pocket of my jeans was that doll and her stale donut skirt. Although the doll didn't seem like much of a weapon, it had apparently served as one. Its narrow plastic ankles, clamped between my middle and index fingers, felt insubstantial. But not quite inanimate.

I didn't see anyone. The backyard was unfenced, a neat lawn with a few big trees and flowers in the borders. Someone could have been hiding behind a tree trunk, or they could have disappeared into the thick woods behind the yard.

Shoulders drooping, I returned to the kitchen. The six women were standing over Georgia and crying.

"She's *dead*," one said.

"Murdered, most likely," another added between sobs.

I noticed a faint line of powdered sugar mixed with ground nutmeg on Georgia's table. The sugar and nutmeg must have spilled out of the box of donuts, which had probably been on Georgia's table when her killer broke in. I said, "Don't touch anything." My voice sounded like it was several miles away.

Lois wiped her eyes. "Emily, you already moved the donut box, and that . . ." She shuddered. "That doll."

Closing my eyes, I swayed. I'd had what I thought was a reasonable impulse to help Georgia when I lifted the bakery box off her face and removed that doll from her mouth. I'd tossed the box onto the floor, but what was I to do with the doll? There was no way I was putting it back where I'd found it. Gently, I set it beside Georgia's ear. "How about if we split up?"

One of the women shouted, "No!"

I revised my suggestion. "Not completely. How about if four of us go out the back and break into teams of two, and each pair checks a side of the house for footprints or anything that seems out of place?" *Like a murderer crouched in the foundation plantings* . . . "And the other three go back the way we came, through the house and out the front without touching anything, but keeping our eyes open for possible evidence, and then we all meet at Lois's van?"

They agreed. Lois and I took one side of the house. We saw no footprints in the dirt surrounding shrubs next to the house, and no litter in the window wells besides a candy wrapper that could have been there for weeks.

We joined the others at the van. No one had noticed anything resembling a clue about whoever had attacked Georgia.

Surrounded by crying older women, I controlled my shaking fingers and called the police. In what was left of the August evening's sunshine, we wiped away tears, hugged one another, and spoke words that were meant to console but felt hollow. Tree shadows stretched across the driveway.

A Fallingbrook police cruiser raced down Georgia's road and parked. Misty, one of my best friends, got out and strode toward us. Descended from Scandinavian settlers, Misty was tall and fit, with enviably perfect features, a flawless complexion, and blond hair pinned in a ponytail below the back of her police hat. Her dark blue uniform was unwrinkled. Calm and professional, she focused on me. "You phoned in about a deceased person, Emily?"

"Georgia Treetor, a regular customer at Deputy Donut." I pointed. "That's her house. She's in the kitchen. I don't think anyone else is inside, but we didn't check the basement. She's blocking the door." I spread my arms as if about to initiate a group hug. "These are her friends, other regulars."

Misty was not as inscrutable as she probably wanted to

believe. A twitch of empathy crossed her face. "Yes, I've seen most of you there." Her gaze lingered for an extra second on Lois, and then her neutral police officer mask returned.

"It appears that someone broke in through the back door." Tension stretched my words taut and thin, like wires scratching at my throat.

Misty peered toward the house. "Was the front door open like that when you arrived?"

"I opened it." Lois's voice cracked on a sob. "It was locked."

One of Misty's eyebrows rose slightly.

Lois stood as tall as a four-foot-ten person could. "I've had Georgia's key for years. But after we found her, we were . . ." Lois threw me an apologetic glance. "Careful not to touch things, so I guess that's why no one closed it."

Misty turned her piercing police gaze on me. I confessed, "I'm afraid I took a bakery box off her face." I let out a pent-up breath, and immediately had to inhale again. "And I pulled a doll wearing donuts out of her mouth."

Misty lost that inscrutable look again. "A doll wearing *donuts?*"

I explained, "One of those teen dolls, plastic, with long skinny legs."

Lois added, "It looked like the kind of doll that some of us crochet dresses for, ball gowns with big skirts. You insert the doll's feet into the center of a roll of toilet paper, and the skirt covers the roll. It pretties up a bathroom."

"Uh-oh," I said.

Misty asked, "Uh-oh what, Emily?"

"There was a roll of toilet paper on the bathroom floor. I picked it up and put it on the tank."

Misty seemed to be looking into a distant past. "My grandmother was very proud of a doll like that. Did Georgia have one?"

Lois moved her hands as if she were crocheting. "I made it for her. The dress was pink, and the ruffles had black edging.

But until this evening, I hadn't been in her house for over five years, so I don't know if she still has . . . had it."

None of us remembered seeing the doll's ball gown anywhere in Georgia's house.

Misty pinioned me with an icy stare. "I thought that you, Emily, of all civilians, would know better than to touch anything at a potential crime scene."

"I wasn't thinking, and I didn't realize at first, especially in the bathroom, that it could be a crime scene."

"The lab will find *your* fingerprints on the doll. Your prints on the donut box won't surprise anyone, but on the doll?" She glowered at me. "All of you, stay here. I'll have a look. More officers are on the way." She strode to the house and disappeared inside.

Behind us, a hesitant voice asked, "What's going on?"

I turned toward the street. A skinny thirty-ish blonde in black yoga pants, a pale pink knit top, and black ballet slippers walked hesitantly toward us. Her arms were wrapped around her middle, echoing the way one side of her blouse crossed over the other, and her shoulders were hunched as if she were cold. "Why are you all crying? Did . . . did something happen to Mrs. Treetor?"

I didn't know what to say, and apparently all six Knitpickers had a similar problem.

The woman pointed at a white house across the street from Georgia's. "I'm a neighbor." The only makeup she wore was thickly applied eyeliner, giving her a raccoon-like appearance, and her hair was thin and limp. She looked exhausted.

I found my voice. "I'm sorry, but something did happen to her."

She shivered. "I was afraid of that. Will she be all right?"

I shook my head. Lois and her friends sobbed.

The woman tilted her head and studied me. "Hey, aren't you the donut lady?"

My attempt at a smile felt skewed. "I'm one of the owners

of Deputy Donut in downtown Fallingbrook." I didn't remember ever seeing the woman in the shop.

"Don't you bring cakes made of donuts to kids' birthday parties? My girlfriend's kid had a spaceship made of donuts."

"I used to, before we opened the shop. People wanted to buy my donuts and coffee every day." Especially my late husband's police colleagues. I asked the woman, "What did you mean when you said you were afraid that something had happened to Georgia?"

"I saw you all going into her house, and then you were out here crying, and then a police car came, and I kind of pieced it all together."

I gestured toward Georgia's front door. "When the policewoman comes outside again, can you talk to her?"

The blonde picked at a hangnail. "I don't want to get involved."

Lois said, "The police will question *all* of the neighbors." She stared at the house where the woman had said she lived. The front door was open. Lois's sudden fierceness implied, *We know where you live.*

The skinny blonde stayed put, probably because Misty came out of Georgia's house. Misty was scowling. I knew she loved her job, but dealing with cases like this had to bother her, though she might never admit it. She joined us.

I told her, "Here's Georgia's neighbor from across the street. She saw us and was afraid that something had happened to Georgia."

I could tell by the quick upward slant of one of Misty's eyebrows that she understood my hint that the neighbor might know more that she was willing to tell.

The neighbor must have caught my hint, too. "I only *guessed,*" she said.

Hmmmm, I thought. *I wonder.*

Misty took the woman out of our earshot, listened to her, and wrote in a notebook. When they finished, the blonde bowed her head, hugged herself, and crossed to her side of the street. Only the outer edges of her ballet slippers appeared to touch the pavement. She went into her house and shut that gaping door.

And then Misty's reinforcements arrived. Three police cruisers braked quickly in front of Georgia's house. A fourth cruiser, unmarked but recognizable as a police car, blocked the driveway, neatly keeping us from leaving in Lois's van.

Detective Brent Fyne got out of the unmarked car.

Great. He was the only member of the Fallingbrook police department who never came into Deputy Donut.

I really did not want to see him.

Chapter 4

✻

It wasn't that Detective Brent Fyne was hard to look at. He was nearly six feet tall, and although his tweed blazer probably hid a shoulder holster, it didn't conceal his lithe muscularity. He had light brown hair and a square and determined jaw. And gray eyes that were boring into me.

But all he said was, "Em," with no inflection. No surprise, no hint of past friendship and shared grief, no coldness. And no warmth. He walked past us, conferred with Misty for a few seconds, and then turned to the three uniformed officers obviously waiting for his instructions. "You three, get these ladies' statements, and then they can go." He asked Misty, "Show me?" She preceded him inside. They left Georgia's front door open.

The three officers, two men and a woman, all of them frequent Deputy Donut customers, separated us and took our statements and contact information. When they were done, one of the officers moved Brent's unmarked car away from the end of the driveway, and Lois could move her van.

She took us back to the center of town and dropped me off at Deputy Donut. She and the other five Knitpickers waved good-bye, but their spirits appeared as wilted as the mums in Georgia's dining room. Feeling the same way, I went into the office, picked Dep up, and rested my cheek on her head. Then I fastened her halter around her and clipped on her leash. Together, we walked down Wisconsin Street and turned the corner into Fallingbrook's historic neighborhood of Victorian homes.

Breezes teased at red-tinged maple leaves. My eyes stung. Georgia would never see another late August, another Christmas, never awaken to another Wisconsin springtime morning brilliant with sunshine, flowers, and promise.

Dep pounced on fallen leaves and vanquished them. The last six blocks to our sweet Victorian cottage took a while.

Like Georgia's, my front door opened directly into the living room, but my two bedrooms were on the second floor underneath the eaves. Alec and I had painted most of the cottage's interior white, and we'd stripped the woodwork and floors to reveal the antique pine.

Dep didn't wait to be unleashed. She pranced, with me keeping pace behind her, through the dining room and kitchen and into the sunroom where windows on three sides let her observe our secluded walled garden. She hopped up onto a radiator cover that doubled as a windowsill and let me remove her halter and leash. She smoothed the fur around her shoulders with quick flicks of her tongue, and then stretched and hunkered down where she could watch for birds, squirrels, and chipmunks. Her tail twitched. Deputy Donut had gone into jungle kitty mode.

In the kitchen, pine cabinets honored the age of the cottage, but everything else was sleek—a six-burner stainless-steel range with two ovens, a large stainless-steel fridge-freezer, and granite countertops. Alec and I had shared a lot of joy, including the love of cooking.

I sliced Gruyère onto thick homemade bread, broiled the sandwich until the Gruyère melted, and took it to the living room.

No matter what, that room always gave me a feeling of solace. Alec and I had furnished it in colors coordinating with the jewel-toned stained-glass windows above the door and the front window. The rug was mostly red with a royal blue, navy, and cream pattern that the Victorians would have loved. I'd inherited a couch from my great-grandmother and had reupholstered it in deep red velvet that complemented its carved mahogany trim. An overstuffed armchair matched the couch.

The sun was setting, but a few hours earlier it would have gleamed through the stained-glass windows and transformed my collection of glass vases to a sparkling rainbow of gems. I hadn't been able to resist red velvet drapes similar to those that might have graced the room when the cottage was built.

I ate in the deep blue wing chair where Dep and I liked to cuddle. Dep padded in circles on my lap. Why did I suspect that this particular burst of affection was actually aimed at the gooey and delicious Gruyère?

My phone played its strange aliens-from-outer-space tune. I answered.

Misty said, "I'm finally off duty. Can I come over?"

There was nothing quite like good friends. Misty did not need to be told that, especially this evening, I would not want to be alone with my memories. "Great," I said.

I was licking the last vestiges of cheese off my fingers when the front door opened and Misty came in. "Emily, when are you going to learn to keep your doors locked?" Her hair was down, hanging below her shoulders, and damp. She'd changed into jeans, sandals, and a girly blouse, ruffled and printed with pink and purple flowers.

"I was expecting you. Why would I lock you out?"

"I'd have knocked."

"Ha," I teased. "You *didn't*."

"I was just checking." Dep twined around her legs. Misty scooped her up and cooed, "*You'll* fend off intruders and keep Emily safe, won't you, Dep?" She glared at me over Dep's head, but the pointed black and ginger ear sticking up between Misty's blue eyes negated most of the threat in Misty's expression.

I smiled and took my empty plate to the kitchen. "Would you like a sandwich?"

Carrying the purring cat, Misty was right behind me. "I already ate."

I washed my hands. "How about a beer? The sun's just set, but at the moment, the evening's warm enough for us to sit outside."

"Sounds perfect, if I can stay awake. I just worked sixteen hours."

"Did you drive over?"

"Since when did I start driving from my place to yours? It's less than a mile."

I removed two bottles of beer from the fridge. "Since you look like you can barely stand up."

"That'd be a good time to get behind a wheel."

Letting the beer froth just enough, I poured it into glass mugs. "Considering that your fellow officers were probably working overtime and are as zonked as you, who's to know?"

"Someone's *always* out there looking for bad drivers." She gave Dep a kiss and set her on the terra-cotta tile floor.

"That's a relief." The joking did not quite distract me from dwelling on Georgia. I opened a bag of pretzels and dumped them into a wooden bowl handcrafted by one of the artisans at The Craft Croft.

Dep came outside with us. The brick wall surrounding my yard was smooth and tall, and there was no way that a cat could climb it. As a kitten, Dep had discovered that the branches of shrubs wouldn't hold her and that she did not care for backing down tree trunks. She was perfectly safe outside, and so was the wildlife. I'd never known her to catch anything other than leaves, acorns, and bugs.

I put the bowl on a table between two cushioned chaises, and Misty and I stretched out. We preferred to sit outdoors evenings without a light. As night fell, our eyes would adjust. Dep jumped onto my lap.

Misty picked up a handful of pretzels. "I'm sorry about Georgia. She was your friend, also, wasn't she, not only a customer?"

"Yep."

"Look, I understand why you tampered with the evidence. Trying to put things right in situations like that is a common reaction. But I wish you hadn't."

"Me, too. And I'm sorry. I also picked up two stale donuts that were lying on the floor, and then when I saw that doll, I just let them go. I don't know where they ended up."

Birdcalls became sporadic, as if the birds were telling one another good night and falling asleep.

Misty asked quietly, "Are you okay?"

"I guess." Each salt crystal on the half pretzel in my hand was a tiny cube with sharp corners and edges, like miniature knives stabbing at my fingers. "Georgia was in her seventies. When she didn't show up at Deputy Donut as usual this morning, I began to prepare myself that she could have been sick, or . . ." My vision blurred. "I guess I should be glad that Lois came to fetch me, or those seniors would have discovered Georgia by themselves." I brushed at my eyes. "How about you? Are you okay? Seeing Georgia like that can't have been easy for you, either." I popped the pretzel into my mouth. Instead of cutting at my fingers, the salt bit at my tongue.

"We do what we have to. Most of the time, the job is rewarding. Serious crime is rare in Fallingbrook."

The tree above us rustled, the sound of oak leaves turning leathery. I shivered, but not because summer was ending. "Matthias Treetor went missing five years ago," I reminded Misty. "Almost to the day." Georgia's call had been my first real emergency as a 911 operator. I could still remember the panic in her voice when she told me that her son, a popular Fallingbrook grocer, had been missing for several hours and that she'd found his car, empty and locked, parked almost out of sight on a farm lane. She'd also found an empty gas can with *TREETOR* scrawled in black marker on it beside the road near the end of the lane. *If he was going for gas,* Georgia had grated out over the phone that evening, *he wouldn't have left his gas can behind.* "Her son was murdered," I said. "And now she's been murdered, also."

"Thanks to your interference, we can't be sure of it, but Brent suspects foul play. More crime scene investigators should be at her house now, and there'll be a postmortem." She sipped her beer. "Do you have any idea what happened to Matthias's father? Could he still be around?"

"No. Georgia told me he left her right after she had Matthias, about the second time he heard the baby cry. That would have been about fifty years ago. A few days later, police in Illinois contacted Georgia. Matthias's father had died in a collision with a train."

"Did Georgia tell you if Matthias's father had family, like children by anyone else before he met her?"

"I don't think she knew."

"Was Matthias's father's name Treetor, also?"

"I don't know." There was too much that I didn't know, and now would probably never find out, about my friend.

Misty twirled a pretzel on the tip of her index finger. "Did you notice a change in Brent?"

"He was unusually businesslike, which wasn't surprising, since he was on duty."

"He worries me. He always seems to have a new, leggy, and beautiful girl on his arm, but he doesn't seem happy."

I leaned my head back on the soft headrest and gazed up at the sky, that dusky blue preceding twilight. "I'm sure he misses Alec and wonders what he could have done differently that night." *Just like I wondered what I could have done differently* . . . Brent and Alec had been best friends as well as partners, first as patrolmen, and then as detectives.

"Have you talked to him recently?"

"Maybe I said 'hi' to him this evening." Actually, I couldn't remember saying anything. I'd stared back at him, and that was all.

"If you gave him any encouragement, he'd come running."

I recrossed my ankles. Dep jumped off my lap. I immediately missed her warmth. "I admire him, but we're just former friends who've drifted apart, and that's fine with me. He's too much like Alec, too likely to be hit by a bullet some dark and horrible night. If I ever fall for anyone again"— *highly unlikely, considering the way I felt about Alec*—"it will be a man with a nice, safe career, like a librarian."

"Ever hear of protesting too much?"

"I'm just saying what I think." I patted my lap. "Dep, come here. I'm getting cold." Dep turned her back, sat in the grass, and stared toward my rosebushes.

"Brent's the lead investigator in Georgia's case. He'll need to talk to you."

"No problem. No matter how much I sound like one, I'm not a weak-kneed blob of jelly."

"I wouldn't know what one of those sounds like."

"Police officers are supposed to know things like that." My teasing broke the tension. So, what did I do? I went right back to being serious. "Do you think Georgia's death is connected to her son's murder?"

"We don't know. Maybe we never will."

"Why would anyone harm either of them? She was a sweet and considerate lady who owned a doll hospital. She was grateful to me for, she said, caring. All I did was my job—answer a 911 call. And then after Alec's death, talking to her helped me cope, helped us both cope with our losses. How could *anyone* hate her? And Matthias was a nice man, as far as I could tell from shopping in his store. Besides, he coached kids' sports, baseball in the summer and hockey in the winter."

"Crime has a way of not making sense."

We sipped beer, nibbled pretzels, and mellowed. Dep returned to my lap and settled down to a rhythmic and vibrating purr. Misty and I laughed about the comparatively innocent days when she, Samantha, and I had first known one another, about our high school crushes, and about our long-ago plans. Misty had always known she would become a police officer. Samantha had planned to do something in the medical field. I'd changed my career goals about once a week, twice if there was a full moon.

Misty's comments dwindled to "mm-hmms" and then to gentle snores.

The quarter moon sank behind my cottage's chimney. Despite the purring cat on my lap, I was getting cold. I set Dep on the ground, went inside, put on a fleece jacket, fetched a quilt, and spread it over Misty. She didn't stir.

Nicely snug in the thick fleece, I sat down again and picked up a pretzel. Dep leaped onto my lap and pawed at my hand. Since when did my finicky cat beg for pretzels?

I offered it to her.

She turned up her cute little nose, jumped down, and crept into the shrubs at the rear of the yard.

Seconds later, she was back. She again ignored the pretzel. Tail straight up except for a question mark at the tip, she turned around and strutted into her jungle. She even let out a roar of sorts, although to me it sounded exactly like a meow.

She trotted to my chaise, reached up, and batted my shin, and then headed back toward the shrubbery. Turning to face me, she let out a plaintive mew. She barged underneath a fern. Her meows became demanding.

Misty mumbled something and then went back to snoring.

I tiptoed to the fern and called softly, "Dep?" I raised my voice and commanded, "Deputy!"

She meowed again, but her voice sounded strangely distant.

"Come here, Deputy!" She never came when called. Why would I expect her to change?

I trotted past my sleeping friend, retrieved a flashlight from a drawer in the kitchen, and ran back to the rear of the yard. "Dep?"

She meowed.

I got down on my hands and knees and peered under a prickly hawthorn. "Nice new game, Dep," I muttered.

The answering meow was insistent. It seemed to be coming from the other side of the wall, but that was impossible. I stood up and shined my light at the top of the wall. No cat.

I crawled into a brushy cave underneath a sprawling forsythia and aimed my light at the base of the wall.

What was this? An extra row of bricks, jutting out into my yard?

"Meow."

The bottom of the wall was definitely thicker in that spot, about two bricks thicker, but the extra course of bricks was only about three bricks high and four bricks long. I felt one end of it. A hole?

Kitty claws latched into my hand. "Ouch!" I yanked my hand away, which was not the right thing to do, but I managed to detach myself from those sharp claws and shine my light where the paw had been.

I saw no sign of my imperious cat, but there was a square opening behind the outer layer of brick.

"Dep?" I whispered.

Her stripy face with that adorable ginger spot in the center of her forehead appeared in the opening, and then she wiggled backward out of sight and meowed again.

Now I was sure of it. Dep was on the other side of the wall.

A square tunnel just big enough for cats had been incorporated in the base of the wall, probably when it was built. And during the almost six years that I'd lived here, the forsythia had hidden the tunnel.

"Meow!"

And then I heard something else, something that made all the hairs on my body stand straight on end like Dep's when she puffed herself up.

"Help!" The voice was tiny, as if my almost-magical walled garden harbored elves.

Chapter 5

Still on my hands and knees, I backed away from the wall. Twigs snared my curls, but I kept crawling, at the expense of both my hair and the shrubs. Someone—most likely *not* an elf—was calling for help, and I didn't dare waste time. I jumped to my feet.

It seemed like a perfect occasion to ask Misty to come with me, but she was still asleep. I breezed past her.

When some long-ago homeowners had walled in the garden, they'd left no way out except through the house. Although it could be inconvenient, I liked the lack of gates and my garden's perfect seclusion. Alec had approved—unwanted visitors were unlikely, and our new kitten could safely explore. My donut-loving policeman husband was the one who had laughingly christened the frisky little ball of fur Deputy Donut.

Hanging on to my flashlight, I dashed through the kitchen, dining room, and living room. I took a moment to adjust the doorknob to lock the front door behind me, and then I raced down the block, around the corner, and up the next block. The streets were lined with Victorian homes and tall trees. I recognized the cottage behind mine by the gigantic oak looming against the sky.

And then I ran into a brick wall, literally, on one side of

the small house. I ran around to the other side. Same thing. Like my backyard, this one was surrounded by a high wall with no gates, which wasn't terribly surprising. The exterior of this cottage was almost the twin of mine.

I had locked my front door, but this one was standing open. A warm yellow glow lit the living room. I loped to the front porch and knocked on the doorjamb. "Hello! Anybody home?" My voice echoed too loudly in the otherwise silent cottage.

No one answered.

Someone in the backyard had called for help. This was not the time to wait politely for an invitation. I charged into the living room.

The décor reminded me of my house when Alec and I first purchased it. The living room was carpeted and wallpapered. It was perfectly neat except for the off-kilter shade on the lamp shining down on about a dozen large linen-covered books on the floor beside a bookcase that was full except for one mostly empty shelf near eye level.

The floor plan was identical to the one in my cottage, and I had no trouble finding the back door. Like the front door, it was open. Beyond the porch, the yard was unlit. Leaves pattered against one another. Tall ornamental grasses whispered.

I was getting a serious case of the creeps.

I reminded myself that Misty was on the other side of the brick wall. If I needed her, I could shout, and if that didn't rouse her, I could phone her. With her longer legs, she would run here faster than I had, but I hoped I wouldn't have to disturb her.

I shined my flashlight's beam over lawn furniture, flower-pots, and grass.

Bright kitty eyes flashed back at me. Dep pawed at a heap of fabric on the ground beside her. "*Meow!*" She was particularly adamant.

And no wonder.

It wasn't a heap of fabric. It was white pants and a flowing purplish top, with a woman inside them.

I ran to the woman and knelt on the grass. Dep rubbed against my arm.

I shined my light near the woman's face. She was small, thin, and white haired. It took a few seconds to register. I gasped, "Lois?"

She opened her eyes and gave me a sweet smile. "Emily! Can you help me sit up?"

I shook my head. "If you're hurt, you shouldn't move." I placed my fingers on her wrist. "I'll call 911."

"Don't be ridiculous. It's not that bad. I was petting my kitty, and I fell over, that's all."

"You should be checked out." Her pulse was strong.

"I'm okay. I was just winded there for a minute, and then I thought that maybe I'd been hearing someone talking, so I called for help. I thought I shouldn't try to stand up by my-self, but I'm okay." She grasped my hand, bent her elbow, and levered herself to a sitting position. As I'd noticed that morning, she was strong. "There! See? I'm not dizzy."

"Were you? Before you fell?"

"Not the tiniest bit. I just lost my balance, that's all, and toppled over." She knocked one fist against the side of her head. "Skulls are heavy. Hard, too, especially mine." She smiled in a way that was probably supposed to be carefree. "I'm both hardheaded and stubborn."

"You said you'd moved back to Fallingbrook, but I didn't realize that *you* were the new owner of the house behind mine."

"We're neighbors, Emily? That's wonderful!"

"Welcome to the neighborhood."

"Looks like I *fell* for your neighborhood."

I groaned. I hoped that her punning was a sign that she wasn't badly injured.

She moved her shoulders like someone pretending she wasn't quaking. "We should go inside before the damp gets to us."

I pointed at the wall separating her yard from mine. "A friend's asleep in my yard."

Lois whispered, "Then we should be quiet."

"That's not what I meant." Still, I kept my voice low. "She's the police officer who arrived first at Georgia's. She'd be glad to come over. Even better, I have a friend who's an EMT." Samantha would come to my aid even if she was off duty.

"EMT?"

"Emergency Medical Technician."

"Oh, an ambulance driver."

Samantha hated it when people called her an ambulance driver, as if all she knew how to do was drive.

Lois flapped a hand in dismissal. "We don't need that. Don't bother her."

"She wouldn't mind."

"Sure, she wouldn't. She's probably been patching people all day, and can hardly bear *not* bandaging arms and legs and shoving oxygen masks into faces. She's probably dying to look after some old lady who tempted gravity." Lois paused as if catching her breath. "Emily, if you're just going to kneel there like a lump, I'll get up and go inside by myself." She leaned forward and pressed her hands into the lawn. Even if she couldn't walk, she was going to crawl, with or without help from me.

I caved. "Take my arm, but let's go only as far as your pretty lawn chairs. We can sit for a while before we go inside."

"I'm fine. I'm sorry I called out after I fell. You're going to too much bother."

"It's no bother."

We rose together. She was light, and didn't seem tottery.

We made it past her ornate white-painted chairs, mainly because Lois was pulling, and climbed the stairs to her back porch.

Racing through her kitchen before, I hadn't really paid it attention, but now I saw that it was amazing. Her appliances were aqua, authentic 1950s, and appeared to be in pristine shape. The cabinets were spotless and undented white-enameled metal. Dep sauntered to the one underneath the sink, stared down into an empty glass bowl on the black slate floor, and meowed.

Lois touched the handle of that fabulous fridge. "You want a sardine, don't you, Tiger?"

I figured she wasn't speaking to me. "Tiger?" I asked.

"My kitty. That's what I call him."

"Her. She's a girl. I mean the cat is female. Tricolored cats usually are."

Lois put her hands on her hips and squinted at Dep, who was still fixated on the empty bowl. "She doesn't look like a tortoiseshell. She's not all spotted and speckly, except for that darling orange patch on her head."

"Her tortoiseshell coloring is mostly blended into tabby stripes. And she has those funny donut circles on the sides like some tabbies have. She's a tortoiseshell tabby, a torbie."

"Did you make that up?"

"No, that's what they're called, torbies."

Lois insisted, "She's still a tiger."

"How long have you had her?"

Lois patted her shiny black counter. "She showed up after I moved in. She comes inside every evening and I give her a sardine. Then she prowls around the house, checking for mice, I guess, and meows to be let out for the night."

I glanced out at the darkness beyond her back porch. "How does she get into your yard? Isn't it walled?"

"It was, but there was a stone plugging up this clever cat-sized tunnel that goes into the next . . . oh, does the kitty tunnel go into your yard?"

"Yes. I just discovered it tonight."

Lois glanced down at Dep, sitting beside the empty bowl. "So, you knew Tiger was a girl cat because she's *your* cat?"

"I thought so, but maybe she doesn't quite agree with me."

"Let me guess. Your yard doesn't have gates, either, and Tiger doesn't climb walls, so you thought she was safely enclosed in your yard."

"Yes, I did." With one paw, Dep bopped the bowl a couple of inches toward Lois.

"She *was* shut in until I took that rock out of my side of her tunnel. Then she was safely enclosed in your yard *and* my yard. Our houses were built in 1889 by a pair of sisters who lived together until they were in their sixties and then they suddenly couldn't stand each other."

I'd never heard that story, but it explained the brick walls, maybe.

Lois straightened a kitchen chair that, as far as I could tell, didn't need straightening. "I devoured everything I could about this neighborhood and this darling house before I moved in. I'd have liked to live closer to Georgia, but her house is too . . ." She gulped. "Too far out and lonely. You need a car. You can't walk to anything. I thought that if I moved here, she might move closer to the center of town. Like . . . like into the house behind mine." Eyes wistful, she quickly added, "I didn't know you, then, Emily, and I'm happy having you for a neighbor. Anyway, I'm guessing the sisters who built the cottages shared a small pet or two, and that's why they had that wall built with a secret passageway for small animals."

All I could think of, with belated panic, was that Lois's front and back doors had both been open. Dep could have wandered out into the street. I ran into the living room and closed Lois's front door. Obviously, before I let Dep explore my garden again, I would have to block my end of the tunnel.

I went back to the kitchen. Lois was wiping her eyes and

blowing her nose. "I'm sorry about being such a crybaby. It's just that, well, you know, *Georgia*."

I murmured, "I know."

Purring so loudly that she almost *could* have been mistaken for a tiger, Dep rubbed Lois's ankles. Lois started to stoop, then must have thought better of petting the cat so soon after her previous disastrous attempt. She leaned back against her white porcelain sink. "She's such a sweetie that I don't know what I ever did without her." She squared her shoulders. "But if she's your cat, I should get my own." Wiping her eyes again, she turned around and opened that vintage aqua fridge.

Drying blood matted a small patch of hair on the back of her head.

"Lois, did you hit your head when you fell?"

"Maybe. I didn't notice."

"Let me see." The wound didn't look too bad, and the bleeding had stopped. "Do you have ice?"

"Yes." She pulled an old-fashioned aluminum ice cube tray out of the tiny freezer compartment at the top of the fridge.

I removed two cubes, wrapped them in paper towels, and handed them to her. "Hold this to the back of your head to keep the swelling down. I'd clean the wound for you, but I'm afraid I'd start it bleeding again, and I don't see any dirt particles or anything like that in it."

"I don't know where to put the ice. I can't see the back of my head."

"Doesn't it hurt?"

She seemed to be staring inward. "Maybe." I guided her hand and the ice to the spot.

"How long do I have to do this?"

"Twenty minutes."

Holding the ice against her head with her left hand, she took a bowl out of the fridge, removed plastic wrap from it, scooped out a small sardine with her fingers, and dropped it into the bowl.

Dep hunkered down. Head tilted to one side, she gnawed on the treat. She finished it, made a stab at cleaning her whiskers, and headed into the dining room.

"See?" Lois said. "It's like she's checking for intrude . . . I mean mice."

I followed Dep. She investigated the dining room, and then marched into the living room. Mouth open, she sniffed at the books I'd noticed scattered on the floor. They were photo albums. Dep sat down beside them and let out a loud meow.

Lois called from the kitchen, "What is it, Tiger?"

"She doesn't like change," I answered. "Last time she was here, your photo albums must have been on the bookshelf."

Lois's wounded head did not prevent her from rushing, holding the ice against the back of her head, into the living room. The previously white knees of her jeans were grass stained. She stared at Dep and the photo albums as if puzzled. She studied the tipsy lamp, too. "Did you move the lampshade, Emily?"

"No. It was like that when I got here. And your front door was standing open."

Lois glanced at me and then away almost immediately, but not before I saw raw fear flit through her eyes.

Chapter 6

❧

I demanded, "Lois, did someone break into your house?"

"No, no . . ." Her voice trailed away. "I must have left the door open and forgot. It was kind of hot earlier. And . . ." Her chin trembled. "Georgia . . . my best friend." My sympathy swelled for the petite woman standing staunchly in her old-fashioned living room.

Deputy Donut trotted up the stairs toward the second floor.

Lois wiped her eyes. "It was bad enough when Matthias was killed. He was like a son to me. And now Georgia, too . . ."

"And you've been attacked." I pulled my phone out of my pocket.

"No, no, I told you. I left the doors open because it was hot." She must have seen the skeptical tilt of my head. "Maybe it wasn't *that* hot, but I got overheated, taking those books off the shelf so I could dust them. Then before I put the books back, well, I've been flibberty-gibbeting between one thing and another, not really thinking about what I'm doing." She let out a shaky breath. "*Georgia.*" She raised her chin. "Then I thought I heard my . . . *your* cat, and there she was, outside. I bent over to pet her, and I fell. That's all. No big deal. Don't call an ambulance. Don't tell anyone, especially not the Knitpickers. They don't know me yet. They'll think I'm an old fool. Really, it's all very simply explained, but embarrassing."

"Who tilted the lampshade?"

She gave the lamp a dirty look. "I must have. In fact, now that I think about it, I'm sure I jostled it when I stood up. I just forgot, that's all." She straightened the shade. There was an air of defiance in her obviously tense neck.

I didn't put my phone away. "Do you usually throw things on the floor before you dust them?"

"Yes. No. Well, sometimes." She fanned her face. "It was hot. I mean I was hot. And I wasn't thinking, except about . . ." She swallowed. "Georgia." She wiped her eyes again.

"Did you feel faint?"

"No. I told you. I wasn't dizzy, and I wasn't nauseous. I just lost my balance and fell."

If she was bending forward to pet the cat, how did she cut the back of her head? When I'd found her, she was on her right side. And the grass stains on her jeans were in the front and on the right side. Not on the back.

I was almost positive that someone had broken in, pulled photo albums off the shelves, knocked the lampshade askew, chased her into the backyard, and hit her head from behind.

But who, and why?

And why didn't she want me to know what had really happened? Did the attack have something to do with the murders of Georgia and Georgia's son?

"You might as well go now, Emily," Lois said. "Remember, I recognized you as soon as I opened my eyes. I don't have a concussion." Her smile was tentative, but her eyes twinkled with intelligence and humor. "I'm tired. Take Tiger with you. I'll be sure to keep my front door closed—"

"And locked."

"That, too. So, if your kitty comes back, she won't get out. And I suppose you'll want to barricade her secret passageway again."

I wished I could fit through the cat tunnel and keep track of Lois even better than my cat would. Meanwhile, I could use Dep as an excuse to check on Lois, who was refusing to admit she could be in danger. . . . "I don't think I will. As long as Dep can't escape from our two yards and houses, she's perfectly safe."

"Dep? What kind of name is that?"

"It's short for Deputy Donut. Tom and I named the shop after her. She comes to work with me."

"I didn't notice her there."

"She stays in the office. You could have seen her looking through a window from the office into the dining room."

"Well, I didn't. I didn't notice an office. Or Tiger. I mean Dep."

"You were facing the front windows. The office is in the back, next to the kitchen."

"And I was distracted." She ran her fingers through her hair and didn't seem to notice that a blade of grass landed on the carpet. "Wondering where Georgia was." Her eyes watered. Dep trotted down the stairs and joined us in the living room. Lois gave her a fond look. "And your Deputy Donut comes inside and pads through my entire house before she goes outside again. It's like she really think she's a deputy, and she's patrolling! I thought she only worked the evening shift, but now I know where she is all day—Deputy Donut. I'll make certain to look for her when I'm there with the Knitpickers." She twisted the tissue in her hands. "But all of those po—" She broke off. "I mean, now that Georgia's gone, maybe I should go back to concentrating on art." She glanced toward the painting above her couch. It showed a lazy river winding between meadows and reflecting apricot-tinted cottony clouds in a pale blue sky, obviously changing color around sunset.

"That's beautiful." I meant it. "I feel like I'm in the middle of a calm evening. Did you paint it recently?"

"No, I did paint it, but . . . it's one of my favorites."

That was an odd way to answer—or not answer—my question. "Do you have art shows? A gallery?"

"A gallery down in Madison shows my work." She waved a hand toward the stairs. "I have a studio in a room tucked under the eaves upstairs."

"Those sisters built their houses from the same floor plan, didn't they?"

Lois's vigorous nod didn't seem to hurt her head. "Originally, they were going to build a house for the two of them, but after they had their tiff, they needed two houses. They cut costs by building smaller homes and sharing the blueprints."

"How funny that they cooperated that much. Their brick walls send a strong message, and must have cost a minor fortune."

"Labor was cheap in those days." She gave me a sharp glance. "You have a policewoman friend and a former police chief who works with you. Plus, police come to your donut shop a lot. You're not going to tell any of them that I was attacked, are you?"

"Were you? Attacked, I mean?" Was she finally going to admit it?

"No. I just don't want you making things up."

"I won't." I didn't need to. "You know what my EMT friend would say about you not going to the hospital tonight, don't you?"

"An ambulance driver would expect to drive people to the hospital, so she'd say I should go. But I don't need to, and I won't."

"Samantha would say that if you're not going to the hospital, someone should wake you up every hour to make certain you're still conscious."

"That never made sense to me. If I wasn't conscious, what would that person do about it?"

Lois had a way of making me smile, even though the situation wasn't funny. "Probably call an ambulance."

She raised her gaze to the ceiling and lowered it to me. "And they'd take me to Emergency where I could sit up for the rest of the night on some horrid, hard chair while people sneezed and coughed all over me. I'd rather sleep in my own bed, thank you very much."

"They wouldn't consider taking you to the hospital if someone checked on you."

"Feel free to call me every hour." She gave me her phone number.

"It's a deal." Although Lois had tried to get me to say I wouldn't tell anyone about the attack she denied, I hadn't agreed. If Misty was still at my place, I could sound her out. I wouldn't necessarily have to mention Lois's name. I asked, "Will you lock the front door after I leave, and your kitchen door, too, after you let Dep out into your backyard?"

"Wouldn't you rather take her with you, to make certain she gets there?"

I smiled down at the winsome kitty. "I don't have her leash and halter with me, and I don't want to try carrying her around the block. She'd squirm, and her claws are sharp." My hand still stung from its encounter with those claws at my end of Dep's tunnel. "Let her outside, and I'll go out my back door and call her. When she's ready, she'll come."

Lois accompanied me to the front door, opened it, and switched on her porch light.

Near the faceplate where the lock would go into the jamb, wood had been gouged out. Aghast, I pointed. "Someone did break in, Lois." *And someone broke into Lois's best friend's house, too, and killed her.* Panicking, I turned to Lois.

She stared at the spot and flushed. She didn't speak right away, which I found suspicious. Eventually, she said, "That was like that when I moved in. I use the dead bolt at night, though, not that flimsy thing that people can supposedly open with a credit card, so I haven't bothered having it fixed."

"Keep locking your door with that dead bolt, both night *and* day." I tried imitating one of Misty's stern expressions, brows low, chin firm, lips thinned. "Evenings, too."

"Okay."

I went outside and waited on the porch until I heard the bolt shoot into place. On the other side of the door, Lois urged, "C'mon, Tiger, you can have another sardine while we wait for your other mother to get to your yard."

I ran down the porch steps. The evening was still warm, but no one was around. I jogged home.

In my living room, the quilt I'd spread over Misty was folded on the couch, and a note was on it. "I guess you went off to bed. Thanks for the quilt. Misty."

Dep was already waiting outside my kitchen door. I let her in and gave her some of her favorite canned food. She looked at it and left. I followed her into the living room. She jumped up onto the couch and briskly scrubbed her paws and whiskers. "You can't live on a diet of sardines," I informed her. "Cat food is good for you." Apparently, Dep didn't want to hear about it. She rubbed a paw over one ear.

I was uneasy about Lois's safety. What if her attacker had waited for me to go away? Leaving the cat to her activities, which might include eating cat food if I wasn't there to see her do it, I went out onto the front porch and locked the door—with the dead bolt—behind me. Setting my sneakered feet down quietly, alert for potential attackers, I walked to Lois's house.

The light was still on in her living room.

Her sheers were pulled, but I could see through them. The bookshelf that had been mostly empty now held many of the photo albums that had been on the floor. Lois was sitting on her couch underneath the painting I'd admired. She turned a page of an album on her lap. Suddenly she placed one hand on her mouth and stared, wide-eyed, straight toward me.

Could she see me? She was in her glowing living room

while I was out on the sidewalk, in shadows underneath a maple. If Lois recognized me through her sheers, she would probably come outside or wave.

Slowly, she closed the photo album. She eased off the couch and put the album to the left of the other albums. She aligned their spines, and then turned out the light and headed for the stairway, lit by a frilly glass sconce. She climbed out of sight. The downstairs sconce went out and an upstairs light cast stripes through the railing.

I walked home. Everything in the neighborhood seemed peaceful.

I wasn't.

Was someone going around attacking Fallingbrook's older women? Or had Lois been targeted specifically because she and Georgia were friends? Had someone watched Georgia's house and followed Lois's van as she dropped all of us off, and then followed Lois home?

Even if I explained my suspicions to Misty or Tom, they'd say I had no evidence, and that I was basing my theories on hunches, especially if Lois denied it all.

I reminded myself that I was no longer a 911 operator. The safety of Fallingbrook's citizens was not my responsibility. My job was to give everyone in town a place to relax and enjoy one another's company along with the best coffee and donuts in northern Wisconsin.

But I liked Lois. And if someone harmed her again, I would blame myself.

Sometimes I wished I couldn't care. But Alec had cared. Tom cared. Misty and Samantha, and yes, Detective Brent Fyne, too—they all took on other people's problems. They couldn't help it, and I admired them for it. I wasn't as strong as they were, or I would have stayed at 911, but I couldn't help fretting and wanting their advice.

Dep greeted me at the front door and accompanied me upstairs to my comfy Wedgwood blue bedroom.

The light upstairs in Lois's house went out.

I changed into jammies, moved the antique doll—a gift from Georgia—away from the tailored Wedgwood pillow shams, and set my alarm for eleven fifteen. I was still reading when the alarm went off. I called Lois. Her greeting was sprightly. She claimed she had not yet fallen asleep.

At twelve fifteen, I swung my feet over the side of the bed and called her again. This time I must have awakened her. She sounded groggy. I told her my name.

"Don't tell anyone." Her words were slurred.

"Tell them what?"

"That someone hit me."

"When, just now?" I was wide awake.

"No, earlier, when I was petting Tiger. Don't tell. You'll put me in grave danger."

"From what?"

"Matthias . . ."

Hairs on the back of my neck rose. Matthias had been dead for five years.

Chapter 7

❧

"And you'll be in danger, too," Lois added. "Don't tell anyone."

Pulling my comforter tighter around my shoulders, I sat up straighter. "What do you mean? How will you and I be in danger?"

There was a long pause, then a yawn. "Oh, it's you, my neighbor, Tiger's other mother? Emily. What was I saying?"

"That if I told anyone you were attacked, you and I would both be in danger. From Matthias."

Fingernails clicked against her phone. "Matthias? That's nonsense. I must have been dreaming. I've been having nightmares about Georgia." She heaved a deep, grief-filled sigh.

"Lois, what if you weren't dreaming it, entirely? Maybe your subconscious is telling you something, and your conscious is resisting. Maybe, deep down inside, you know you were attacked. We should report it to the police. I'll call them, if you like."

"No! Maybe my subconscious is right about the danger to both of us if we report it." She put a smile in her voice, as if she could be trying to distract me. "Not that I *was* attacked."

"How do you feel? Do you have a headache?"

"No, I'm fine. I just had trouble waking up."

Although skeptical, I let her go, and called again at one fifteen. The phone rang and rang. I was considering throwing on clothes and dashing to her house when she picked up. This time, she was alert. She apologized for not answering quickly. "I wanted to be sure I was awake before I started talking."

I asked her to tell me the date and her address. She answered both questions correctly.

At two fifteen, she sounded okay, but grumpy. At three fifteen, she said, "You know, if I was unconscious, it was only for a few seconds, and the cut on my head is barely a scratch. You don't have to keep calling. You need to get up soon and feed all those cops their donuts, right?"

"I get up at five."

"Okay, call me then."

I slept until my alarm started playing its tune. I was beginning to hate that tune.

I called Lois.

"I'm fine," she told me, "except when I think about Georgia. I'll see you—and the Knitpickers—in a few hours." She made me promise not to tell anyone about what she called her silly little fall.

Despite the many times I had awakened her during the night, Lois was the first knitter to arrive at Deputy Donut in the morning.

I hurried out of the kitchen and gave her a hug. She had dressed in blue jeans and a red sweater. I wondered if she had purposely matched Georgia's last outfit.

"Is the back of my head still bleeding?" she asked.

I ducked behind her and checked. "No. I think I see a small scab underneath your hair."

"Good. I don't want those Knitpickers to worry, so we'll just keep my fall secret, okay?"

"Okay. You do seem fine. . . ." *And I reserve the right to ask for help for you if you need it.*

"I'll prove that I'm fine. I'll make supper for you tonight. Bring Tiger. I mean Dep."

"Sounds great." Visiting her would give me another chance to find out what she knew but wasn't telling me about the previous night. Also, when I was spying through the sheers before bedtime, something in one of her photo albums had appeared to surprise, shock, or maybe even frighten her, and I knew where she'd placed that album. . . . "What should I bring?"

"Nothing. I enjoy creating a meal, start to finish." Her eyes were red and tired.

So were the eyes of the other five Knitpickers when they arrived. We all hugged one another. Each woman was wearing a hand-knit sweater, a couple of them made from the pattern Georgia had used for the sweater she'd been wearing when she died. I asked, "Did you plan to put on similar sweaters today?"

One of them answered quietly, "We didn't discuss it, but I guess we all wanted to pay tribute to Georgia with sweaters we knit here, with her."

The others nodded.

Word of Georgia's death must have spread throughout Fallingbrook. Folks kept pouring in—strangers, neighboring shopkeepers, and people I'd seen in stores, the library, and The Craft Croft.

One of the retired men who stationed themselves at a table near the door most mornings asked every police officer who entered if he or she knew whether foul play had been involved. The answer was always the same. *We don't know. Not yet.*

All morning, whenever she wasn't catnapping, Dep watched us. I could tell she didn't understand why she couldn't wander through the dining room and decide which customers should pay her homage. I was sure she wanted to fish around in Lois's knitting tote in case Lois had hidden sardines in it.

As usual, I helped the Knitpickers with the door when they were leaving at noon.

Lois gave me a smile. "See you and Dep tonight, Emily." I thought I saw a certain wariness behind her eyes.

Our afternoon was busy, too. Even our fire chief, Scott Ritsorf, a lanky blond guy who never seemed to gain an ounce, came in. He was wearing his fireman's work clothes: dark blue chinos, and matching short-sleeved shirt with a badge embroidered in front and the letters *FFD* across the back. Scott had been two years ahead of Misty, Samantha, and me at Fallingbrook High, but I hadn't gotten to know him well until my 911 days. Alec had liked and respected him, and I did, too. He perched on a stool at the front counter, shook my hand, and asked how I was doing.

"Fine."

His sky blue eyes seemed to search mine. Did everyone expect me to fall apart because Georgia's death would remind me of her son's murder, a case that Alec had tried to solve before he was shot?

I asked Scott what I could get him.

"What's good?"

"Everything."

He laughed and ordered a large cup of the day's featured coffee, a subtle medium roast from Mt. Kilimanjaro, and three raised donuts with chocolate icing and toasted coconut on top.

While I was plating Scott's donuts, Oliver Rossimer came in and sat beside him. Oliver was the same age as Scott. At Fallingbrook High, Samantha, Misty, and I had barely noticed skinny, studious Scott, but we'd all had crushes on Oliver. He'd been a football star and had always made the honor roll. His singing voice had guaranteed him starring roles, usually as the heartthrob, in school musicals, and he was elected student council president his junior and senior years. Now he was president of the Chamber of Commerce. He was more handsome than ever, with deep brown eyes and dark hair. Whenever I caught sight of him, I couldn't help a giddy burst of shyness in honor of my girlhood self.

He'd married his high school sweetheart, and they'd divorced amicably a few years later. Samantha and I liked to tease Misty that Oliver would be perfect for her, and she'd tried to convince each of us to go after him. I wasn't interested in anyone, but if I were, I might look at Oliver more carefully, if only because, unlike Alec had been, Oliver was in a safe profession. He sold heavy construction machinery, from an office, in his own dealership. Even if he got behind the wheel or whatever of one of those big earth crawlers or cranes, Oliver would know how to operate it without endangering himself.

Our last customers left at four thirty. Tom and I went into the pantry, the large storage room next to the kitchen. It was bright, with white-painted walls, a window overlooking the parking lot, and a door leading to our small loading dock. We double-checked our inventory of ingredients, and straightened mixing bowls and baking sheets on their stainless-steel wire shelves. Spoons and spatulas dangled neatly from hooks. We tidied the rest of shop for the Jolly Cops Cleaning Crew, who came in around midnight and did the heavy cleaning, including replenishing the oil in the deep fryers.

At five thirty, Tom drove off to deposit the day's receipts at the bank, and Dep and I strolled home through the late afternoon glow. Well, I strolled. Dep pursued falling leaves. She seemed very proud of herself for nabbing one before it hit the sidewalk. When I was a kid, I ran around trying to catch leaves while they were in the air. Whenever I succeeded, I made a wish. I didn't remember exactly what those wishes were, except that they'd had a lot to do with birthday and Christmas presents. If Dep shared that human superstition, what would she wish for? Sardines, probably. Or maybe she'd want to be transformed into a real tiger.

Lois must have been watching for us. She opened her front door the second we stepped onto the porch. She offered me a seat in her living room. "I'll go get the appetizers."

I unleashed Dep. "I can come to the kitchen." Dep bounded toward the back of the house.

"Stay there. I work best by myself." A meow came from the kitchen. Lois laughed. "Tiger expects her sardine."

I stood still, listening. The fridge door opened. I tiptoed to the bookshelf and pulled out the photo album that had seemed to shock Lois the night before.

The fridge door closed. Lois murmured. Dep meowed.

I flipped pages.

Near the middle of the book, I found a pair of pages missing their photos. The prints weren't completely gone. Bits of paper backing were still glued to the pages.

In the kitchen, the oven door squeaked and a plate clacked onto a counter. I shoved the photo album onto the shelf and slipped into Lois's overstuffed wing chair.

Lois came in carrying a warmed Brie, a dish of hot pepper jelly, and a basket of homemade crackers. She set the tray on the coffee table. "Help yourself. I'm having a Bloody Mary. Would you like one, too?"

I reached for the cheese knife. "Yes, please."

A minute later, she brought out two tall glasses filled with tomato juice and ice, with stalks of celery sticking out above the salt-rimmed tops. She handed me a glass, took hers to the couch, and sat down.

She'd been generous with both the vodka and the hot sauce. The drink packed a punch, in a good way. I licked salt off my lips. "This is the best Bloody Mary I've ever tasted."

She thanked me. "Usually, I cook only for myself, so it's nice to have someone over. I was widowed when I was twenty-two. We'd been married less than a year." She jumped and patted her mouth. "I'm sorry. I should have asked if you had someone you wanted to bring. Last night, you said 'my cat' and 'my house,' and I assumed you live alone."

"I do." I slathered melted Brie on a cracker and topped it with a dollop of hot pepper jelly. "I'm a widow, too, but I was married four years before Alec was shot while on duty. He was a detective. I was nearly twenty-six when it happened." He'd been thirty-seven. Three years had passed, and I was getting used to the dull ache of loss.

"Emily, I'm so sorry." She turned the worn wedding ring on her finger. "I see you also still wear your wedding ring."

"I don't know if I'll ever take it off." *Alec* . . .

"They say time heals all hurts. It's been over fifty years, but I'm far from healed. The pain has become more distant, though." She made a brave attempt at a smile. "I would have married again, if I'd ever found anyone I liked as much, but I never did. So, my advice to you might sound a teensy bit off." She tilted her head as if asking if she could continue.

I nodded.

She seemed to take time to choose her words. "Loving again is a testament to the love you felt, still feel, and will always feel for your husband."

"He told me the same thing. He said he wanted me to always be happy, and if anything ever happened to him, I wasn't to feel I was betraying him if I fell in love with someone else." I was tense, like a turtle who couldn't pull its head all the way into its shell. "I suppose it could happen, but I'm not about to go looking for it."

"You're not tempted by online dating sites?"

I jerked my head up. "Are you?" Maybe someone she'd contacted through a dating site had attacked her last night.

"Not at all," she said. "I'm happy living by myself." She smiled. "But I do enjoy visits from your cat." She brushed one knee with a hand. "Do you have family in the area?"

"I grew up in Fallingbrook, so I have friends that I've known most of my life. I don't have brothers or sisters. I was a surprise—a welcome one—when my parents were in their late thirties. They've retired to Florida, but they come back when the weather here heats up enough for them." I grinned. "They won't be back before June."

"Humph," Lois said. "*Madison* was too far south for me."

"I know what you mean. I like cool weather and four dis-

tinct seasons. And the scenery." I nodded toward the painting on the wall above the couch. Since the night before, Lois
had replaced the relaxing river with an angry sky—storm
clouds piled above a blood red setting sun. It was startling,
but I managed to say calmly, "You changed your painting."

"I like to rotate through my collection. The colors in the
other one go better with my couch, but I'm thinking of redecorating and reupholstering, and I'm trying out different
paintings as a focal point."

Maybe she had a painting that wouldn't be as disturbing
as this one. But I only told her again that I admired her skill.

We finished our drinks and she led me to the dining room.
The table was elegant with a starched white linen tablecloth
and matching napkins, silverware that was actually silver,
bone china with a blue forget-me-not pattern, and delicate
crystal glasses. She brought us cold cucumber soup. She followed that with baked salmon, spinach risotto, and butter-
nut squash roasted with pecans. The salad was baby greens
tossed in raspberry vinaigrette. The two of us drank a signif-
icant amount of a bottle of Vinho Verde. And as if all that
hadn't been enough, she served perfect crème brûlée and gave
us each a small snifter containing two fingers of brandy. She
offered coffee, but I passed. "It would keep me awake."

She threw me an impish grin. "Good, then you could call
me every hour." She patted the back of her head. "See? I told
you. It was nothing." She swirled her brandy and stared
down into it. Finally, she looked up at me. "Did you tell anyone about my fall last night?"

"No. Did you?"

"Certainly not! But, Emily, if I tell you something, will you
promise not to tell anyone else?"

I shifted uneasily on my dining chair. "I'm not sure I can
promise that."

"Well, would you at least *consider* not telling?"

"Yes, but . . ."

"As I might have hinted before I was fully awake in the wee hours this morning, if we call the cops, both of us could be in serious danger."

"Yes, but aren't you in danger whether you call the cops or not? Someone broke into your house, chased you into your backyard, and attacked you."

"He or she didn't chase me. He or she found me out there." *Either way was bad news.* "I can use some advice, and I don't know who else to turn to. You seem trustworthy and honest."

"And I have friends in the police force."

"I suppose if you need advice about my problem, you could pose a question as if it's theoretical."

"They might fall for that." I quirked one eyebrow up to show I was joking.

She laughed. "Yes, I guess they probably wouldn't." She was silent for a while, and then she took a rather large sip of brandy. "Okay, here's the thing. Someone did hit me last night. I truly do not know who it was, or if it was a man or a woman. Do you believe me?"

"Yes." The night before, I'd doubted a lot of what she told me, mainly because she wasn't a good liar. This time, she seemed to be telling the truth.

"I was outside, and it was dark. He or she came from behind, grabbed my arms, put his or her hand over my mouth, and whispered that if I told anyone what I knew, I'd be the next old woman to be found dead." She shuddered. "Then he or she hit me with something hard, and you were right. I probably was unconscious, but not for long. When I woke up, I was lying on the ground, someone was saying something in your yard, and Tiger was butting my chin with the top of her head and meowing."

"Lois, that could have been the person who . . . killed Georgia. And her son, five years ago. You have to tell the police what you know. Otherwise, the murderer might keep killing people. He or she obviously came looking for you, and knows where you live."

Lois closed her eyes, rubbed away tears, and then spoke so quietly that I had to strain to hear her. "It's possible that I might know who killed Matthias." Before I could respond, she asked in a rush, "But how can I turn in my own ... I mean ... someone I know?"

Chapter 8

Everything in Lois's house went quiet except for the ticking of the grandfather clock out in the living room. I was squeezing the delicate stem of my brandy snifter so tightly that I was afraid I might snap it. "What do you mean?" I finally asked. "Do you know who killed Matthias Treetor?" Alec and Brent had worked hard to solve that case and hadn't succeeded. And now, five years later, was my new neighbor going to tell me who the murderer was?

If only Alec could be here . . .

I knew I should call Brent, but I sat still and quiet, waiting for Lois to speak again and knowing that the slightest move toward calling the police could make her go silent.

"No," she said firmly, as if my expression was revealing my thoughts. "I don't know who killed Matthias, or anyone else."

I tried to look empathetic. "But you said something about not turning in your . . . I mean someone you knew."

"What I remember would be called circumstantial. *Very* circumstantial. You see, I often paint from photographs. And that one evening, just around sunset, I was snapping pictures of a pretty scene, and a car came racing out of the valley. I was focusing on the scenery and didn't look at the car or think anything about it being there, even later that night when Georgia told me that Matthias was missing. But I remembered that car a week or so later, after Matthias's body was found." She took a long, tremulous breath. "He'd been buried near where I'd seen that car, in that river valley."

That river valley. I should have recognized the Fallingbrook River and that particular valley, several miles southwest of town, in her painting. "Was the painting that was hanging in your living room last night based on one of the pictures you took that evening?"

She bowed her head. "Yes."

"Did you see the driver of the car?"

"No, I didn't even look at the car. It just got in the way of the scene I wanted to capture. In my photo, the sunset was reflecting off the windshield." She lifted her head, but the corners of her mouth continued to droop. "I couldn't see the driver. But a few days later, I was talking to someone, and that person's car might have been the one I saw the night that Matthias went missing."

I tried to still the wild clamor of my heart. This could be a real break in the case. "Whose car was it?"

Those blue eyes flashed with stubborn determination. "No one who could ever kill another human being. I'd stake my own life on it." That was hardly reassuring, considering that her life seemed to be in danger.

I tried a smile. "Any chance that you're too trusting?"

"Who wants to live in a world where no one can be trusted?"

"Not 'no one.' Most people can be trusted. But there is or was at least one killer around Fallingbrook. For our own safety, for the safety of our friends and relatives, for the safety of all of Fallingbrook, if any of us knows anything that could help put this killer behind bars, we should give the information to the police."

She gazed at me steadily. "I couldn't agree more. But what if the thing we *think* we know, like what they call a 'false memory,' would put an innocent person in prison, and the real killer gets away with murder, and then he—or she—is free to harm others?"

I spoke softly. "Like the person who attacked you last night." Why had Lois added that "she" as a seeming after-thought? To throw me off and hide the fact that the car she thought she recognized belonged to a man? Or because she actually believed the car belonged to a woman?

She leaned forward, tilting her snifter. "Could be." Her brandy trembled, catching the light and projecting it on the ceiling. Muscles bunching, Dep stared up at the rippling reflections as if she were calculating how to leap up and catch them.

I tried another tack. "Did you get more than one photo of that car?"

"I can't remember. I don't think so."

"Don't you think you should show it to the police?"

"I can't."

"They won't throw you in jail for waiting five years."

She waved the notion away. "That's not it. I doubt that I still have the photo."

I didn't want to admit that I'd spied through her sheers the night before and had seen her expression when she'd spotted something about one of those albums, and I definitely was not going to admit that I'd snooped through her photo albums before dinner and had found pages that were obviously missing photos. I prompted, "What happened to it?"

"I don't know. I've moved twice in the past five years. I got rid of things both times."

Interesting. "You have photo albums in the living room. Should we go check?"

"Okay." The idea did not appear to thrill her. "Bring your glass." In the living room, she gestured for me to sit on the couch. We set our snifters on colorful quilted coasters on her end tables. "Georgia made the mug rugs," Lois told me. "Aren't they sweet?"

"They're adorable. When she was at Deputy Donut with the Knitpickers, Georgia often knit tiny garments for dolls. They were awesome. I'm not surprised that she also made teensy quilts."

"She was a perfectionist." Lois bit her lip and turned away. Was she hoping I'd forget about looking through her photo albums?

I got up and removed the photo album I'd peeked into, handed it to her, and sat down beside her. "If nothing else, old photos are fun." She was probably thinking I was terribly nosey. She didn't know the half of it.

She opened the book to the first page. "These will be boring. They're mostly scenes I was thinking of painting."

"They're pretty," I said. "Did you copy many of them?"

"Several." She turned the pages slowly, as if hoping that I'd lose interest and go home.

Sounding altogether too chirpy, I praised the photos.

Finally, she came to the pages near the middle where it was obvious that someone had torn out photos in a major hurry, leaving shreds of paper stuck to the pages. There were three blank pages, one more than I'd discovered in my quick examination. "Oh!" Lois managed to sound surprised.

I leaned closer. "Last night, your albums were scattered on the floor. Did the intruder steal some photos?"

"Someone did."

"Wasn't me."

She gave me a halfhearted smile. "I know. You wouldn't do a thing like that."

"I told you that you're too trusting. But you're right. I didn't steal anything. I was panicking, running through your house in search of whoever had called for help."

She paged quickly through the book, and then slapped her hands down on the two facing blank pages. "He or she ripped out every single photo that I took of the valley that day, including the one of the car." Her voice shook.

I closed my eyes, leaned back, and allowed myself a few

seconds of intensely missing Alec. Even though the physical evidence was missing, he'd have known what to do.

He would tell me to call Brent. As soon as possible. I could do it, I supposed, without Lois's consent, but she might stop talking to me. Maybe while I wheedled more information from her, I would think of a way of convincing her that we should call the police.

I opened my eyes and asked, "Could the car have been in other photos that were on these three pages, maybe in the distance? Like either near where Matthias's body was later found, or somewhere else, not anywhere near it?" Dep jumped onto my lap and settled in, purring.

"I don't remember noticing the car in other photos. And now it's too late to get a magnifying glass and have a good look at them."

Dep's fur was warm and comforting under my hand. "Were you using a digital camera?"

"Yes. I went to those machines that print them. I like to keep pictures in albums, from habit, I guess."

"Did you also keep the digital files?" Dep revved up her purring.

"My computer crashed a couple of years later, with the files on it."

"But you must have put them on a portable drive at one time, so you could print the images at those machines."

She picked up her snifter and stared down into the amber liquid. "I might have them on a thumb drive, in one of the many boxes I haven't yet unpacked."

"You could give those unpacked boxes to the police and tell them to look for a thumb drive containing photos. They could be important evidence."

"I can't do that!"

"Why not?"

"I wrapped things like thumb drives in lingerie to protect them."

I burst out laughing. "To protect the thumb drives or the lingerie?"

She made a fake frown. "The thumb drives, of course. And all those fragile trinkets that I seem to accumulate."

"Maybe it's time to unpack your undies?"

She sat up straighter and pretended to be very stern. Her eyes were twinkling, though. "It's not like I'm doing without. A few years ago, I met a . . . potentially interesting . . . man who invited me to dinner. Before our date, I bought an entire wardrobe of frilly and lacy lingerie, just in case. It was a nice dinner, but 'in case' never happened." She gave a rueful shrug. "So, I hold on to the undies and never wear them, in case 'in case' ever does happen. Not that I think it will."

"Could the potentially interesting man be last night's attacker?"

"Not likely. He lives down in Madison. He's a professor. Emeritus. Art History. He bought one of my paintings. He's very calm. A real gentleman. Would never hurt a flea."

She was definitely too trusting. "Did he buy a scene of the river valley where Matthias was buried?"

"No. I painted that scene only once. He bought a waterfall. Not the one that Fallingbrook's named after, one closer to Madison."

"Does he still have the painting?"

"I have no idea. I never talked to him again after that nice dinner. We hit it off okay, but a week or two later, I heard he was going out with a younger woman, like someone in her *early* sixties." Again, that mischievous twinkle. "He was approaching eighty."

I stroked Dep. "Can you describe the car you saw the day that Matthias went missing?"

"It was black. Kind of sporty, with one of those spoiler things on the back. There were probably other cars around Fallingbrook that looked like that one, and I might not be remembering it right. Or if it's the car I think I remember, maybe someone besides the owner was driving it. After all, *I* was driving a borrowed car that day."

"What?"

"Georgia." She bowed her head and pinched her lips shut for a second. "Georgia and I. We often traded. She had a small sedan, still has it. Had it. How are you supposed to talk about someone who isn't here anymore, but should be?" She sniffled. "My van was newish then, and I often lent it to her because she sometimes has . . . had . . . big boxes of supplies to pick up. She didn't really need a van, but lending it to her justified owning the sort of vehicle I'd always wanted so I could haul big paintings around." Her tears were about to overflow.

"But that could mean . . ." I couldn't go on. I wished I hadn't opened my mouth.

Not that Lois wouldn't have figured it out, anyway. She wiped her eyes. "Yes. If the person who was driving that car was Matthias's murderer, he saw *her* car that evening and assumed that the gray-haired woman was Georgia. We both had gray hair then, not white, yet. Besides, the sun would have been in the driver's eyes, so he—I'm just saying 'he' because it's simpler than saying 'he or she' every time—probably didn't get a good look at me." She sighed. "And then he waited five whole years before he went and killed the wrong one of us." She gulped at her brandy. "That burns."

I wasn't sure if she was talking about the brandy or about someone murdering Georgia because of something he or she thought Lois knew. I said softly, "After he killed Georgia, he might have figured out who was driving her car that evening, and that's why he came after you last night. You're not safe, Lois."

"Maybe I am, now that he stole the pictures. Maybe he had a good look at the photo of the car and realized that I couldn't possibly have seen the driver."

"Not at that angle, but what if he thinks you saw him after he passed you?"

"But I *didn't*. Maybe he looked in his rearview mirror and could tell I was still snapping pictures of the valley."

"Maybe he'll think you snapped a photo of his license plate?"

"Well, if he thinks that, he now knows I didn't keep it, because it wasn't in my photo album." She closed the book so forcefully that a puff of air brushed my face. "I decided that the driver of the car can't be anyone who knows me, or he would have stopped to talk to me, then and there." She shook her head as if to clear fuzz from her brain. "I was probably mistaken about whose car it was."

"You should tell the police everything you've told me."

She shook her head vehemently. "Too dangerous."

"Think of it from the viewpoint of the person who threatened you. He can't come back here. If he does, he risks being identified."

"And I risk being dead."

"I know Brent Fyne, the lead detective on Georgia's case, the man who arrived at Georgia's in the unmarked police car. He worked on Matthias's case, too. He's fair and honest. You can trust him."

She set down her empty snifter and folded her arms. "He didn't find Matthias's killer."

And if he had, if Alec had, Georgia might still be alive.

"Maybe the leads you give him will prevent other deaths." Like Lois's, but I didn't say it. I was sure she was thinking it, anyway.

"As I told you, the sunset was sparkling off the windshield, and I couldn't see the driver. Weeds hid the license plate. On top of everything else, the car was making a cloud of dust. No one could identify it, at least not positively, from the picture."

"Maybe the driver had a totally innocent reason for being there, like he'd been fishing. So, if the police can figure out who he was, they can question him about what he might have seen in the valley that evening." Lois was going to have to talk to the police. And I was going to have to stop avoiding Brent, at least for a while. "If you can find the picture, the police could get the state forensics lab to enhance it. They might prove that your friend was *not* driving the car. Let me call Brent, Lois."

She exhaled and then slumped down as if the air in her lungs had been the only thing holding her up. "Okay."

I could barely hear her.

Chapter 9

Brent picked up right away. "Hi, Em. I was about to call you."
He paused, then added quickly, "About Georgia Treetor."

"Um, good," I managed. "I've been talking to her friend
Lois." What had she told me her last name was?

"Unterlaw? One of the women who was with you when
you discovered Ms. Treetor's body?"

"Yes."

"She's on my list to call, too."

"Does that mean . . ." I didn't want to finish the sentence
in Lois's hearing. It was bad enough that her friend was dead.
Although I knew she suspected that Georgia had been murdered, Lois shouldn't have to hear it spelled out in harsh,
cold words.

As I'd hoped he might, Brent finished the question for me.
"Does it mean we're investigating her death as a homicide?
Sorry, I'm afraid we are."

Lois was watching me. I tried to keep my expression neutral. "Lois just told me something that I—*we*—think you
should hear. Want us to come to the station?"

Lois made an exaggeratedly frowny face.

Brent asked, "Where are you?"

"Her house."

"I've got her address. I'll be there in five minutes." He
hung up.

There, I told myself, *that wasn't so bad.* Brent and I could talk to each other without allowing our grief to overwhelm us. In the kitchen, I washed the dishes. Lois lovingly dried them and put them away. We didn't talk. She was probably planning what to tell Brent.

I always tried to avoid thinking about the evening that Alec died. However, knowing that I was going to have to spend more than a few minutes with Brent, I couldn't help reliving that devastating night.

Like Alec, Brent was a kind man, funny and smart. Where Alec had been wiry, quick, and given to pranks, Brent was a gentle giant. He was sturdy, thoughtful, and fond of saying witty things in a deadpan voice and with a perfectly straight face. Alec had caught on to Brent's jokes immediately, and I had learned to.

But that one night just over three years ago, I'd traded shifts with a new 911 operator so I could go to dinner with out-of-town friends the only evening they were available. Alec hadn't been able to take time off to join us.

That night, when I wasn't working the phones at 911 but should have been, Alec and Brent were shot.

Brent had been only grazed. His arm bandaged, he'd come to Alec's and my home to tell me news that would shatter me and change my life forever.

Alec had not survived.

I'd been too desperate, too much in shock, to recognize the anguish that Brent must also have been feeling. As if all of my joints were frozen in place, I'd stood facing Brent, and I hadn't allowed the man's sympathy and compassion anywhere near me. Feeling like I'd sprouted a coat of thorns and barbed wire, I'd moved to put the dining table between us. I'd wailed, "I should have been at work tonight! I should not have traded shifts with the new guy! I could have made the calls faster, gotten police backup to the scene sooner, sped the ambulance, and saved Alec."

"Don't let the what-ifs get to you, Em," Brent had said. "Didn't they tell you that during training?"

"Yeah, but I didn't know it would be my own husband."

Brent had stayed calm despite my near hysterics. "I radioed headquarters that we'd been shot even before a citizen phoned 911. When police headquarters hear 'officer down' they really move. Neither you nor your substitute could have done anything more quickly than it was done."

"We were only married four years. It's not fair."

"I know."

His gentle tone had undone me. I'd turned away and told him I wanted to be alone.

He'd remained still and silent for a few seconds before saying, "If you need to talk, call me. Any time." Then he'd let himself out.

I hadn't called. Two weeks later, I could no longer stand working at 911, and I'd quit.

Brent had phoned. "You save lives, Em," he'd said.

"Not the most important one. Don't try to talk me into going back. I won't. I can't. Ever."

Then I'd started making donuts, lots of donuts, more donuts than I could ever eat. For some reason, replicating Alec's favorite treat was consoling. Partly as a sop to my conscience for being short with Brent—had he thought I wished he'd taken the fatal bullet instead of Alec?—I'd boxed up three dozen donuts and left them at the police station.

The next day, one of the officers called and asked me to create a castle of donuts to serve as a cake at her twins' fourth birthday party.

That castle of donuts caused quite a stir. Before long, most of the three- to nine-year-olds in Fallingbrook demanded birthday cakes made of donuts stuck together to resemble forts, robots, or princesses, and the adults loved the coffee I brought to the parties. Actually, they liked the donuts, too. Folks in Fallingbrook, especially members of the police force, badgered me to open a coffee and donut shop.

Brent had been the only dissenter. He'd phoned. "They'd take you back at 911, Em. You're the best they ever had. I'm not just saying that. I mean it."

Except for the night I traded shifts so I could go out and have fun.

During the next few months, Brent had often called to ask how I was, but I'd kept my answers short, and our correspondence tapered off. Eventually, he stopped contacting me.

The last time I'd seen him, other than when he arrived at Georgia's to investigate her death, was at the trial of the man who'd killed Alec and injured Brent. After the verdict, Brent had sought me out. Hands clenched at my sides, I'd thanked him for helping convict the shooter.

"If you ever need to talk, Em," Brent had murmured, "I'm always available."

My response had come out before I could think about it or stop it. "Me, too. If you ever need to talk." Brent was good at keeping his thoughts and emotions hidden. But surprise had flickered through those gray eyes before he became expressionless again, and I'd blurted, "You don't always have to be the one that others lean on. You're allowed to ask for help, too."

He'd stared at me for a second as if wondering what to say, and then his phone had beeped, and he'd apologized and taken the call.

And I had fled the courthouse.

Neither of us had accepted the offer to talk. I had Misty, Samantha, and a donut shop full of knitters, cops, and caring citizens to talk to, if I wanted to, but my years of happiness with Alec had been no one else's business, and neither was the depth of my grief.

And if Brent wanted to tell someone his troubles, he had his colleagues on the force, and, according to Misty, his leggy girlfriends.

My hands were still in the dishwater when the doorbell rang. Was it Brent? Or last night's attacker?

Lois tossed me a towel. "Come help me answer."

Fortunately, her door had a peephole, and Brent was standing far enough back for me to see him. In his jeans, black T-shirt, and sneakers, he could almost pass as a civilian. However, the tweed blazer, which probably hid a shoulder holster, and his wary policeman-like bearing gave him away. Even through the distorting lens and in the dim light on the porch, I could tell he was exhausted.

I opened the door. Ordinarily, I might hug an old friend, or at least offer a hand to shake, but what did one do when the old friend had almost become a former friend, and was here to question me and a new friend about a murder?

Dep had no doubts about socially acceptable behavior. Mewing, tail straight up, she marched to Brent and began rubbing cat hair onto his jeans. He looked down. "Deputy Donut?" A question in his eyes, he returned his gaze to me.

Feeling stiff and artificial, I locked the door. "Yes." I cupped a hand around Lois's elbow. "Brent, this is Lois, my new neighbor. Dep found a secret passage between my yard and hers, so we've been sharing her."

Brent backed slightly and clapped a hand over his heart. "A secret passage?"

He was defusing the situation with humorous fake surprise, and I couldn't help smiling. "Only big enough for a cat."

Lois offered her hand to Brent.

He shook it. "You have something you want to run past me?"

"When did you last eat?" she answered.

He rubbed his chin. He had at least a day's growth of beard. "I don't remember."

"Come on through to the kitchen. We didn't finish the salmon, squash, and risotto."

He glanced at me. Was he afraid of being poisoned? Maybe he thought Lois could be the murderer he was seeking.

"It's delicious," I said.

He followed us into the kitchen. Lois told us to sit at the table while she rustled up his dinner. Dep jumped onto Brent's lap. Lois set a plate in front of him. Dep inched her face dangerously close to his salmon.

Plucking her off Brent's lap would have invaded his personal space. I ordered, "Dep, get down."

Like she ever obeyed when she didn't want to.

Lois opened the pretty aqua fridge. After giving me some reproachful cattitude as if to inform me that she wasn't following *my* orders and it was solely *her* decision to abandon Brent's lap and his salmon, Dep landed on the floor and daintily accepted a sardine from Lois, who then sat at her kitchen table and watched Brent eat.

He finished his meal with only a little intervention from Dep. He thanked Lois, took out his notebook, and gave me that steady look that could unnerve a criminal.

Actually, it could unnerve someone who wasn't a criminal, also. I apologized for tampering with the scene and the evidence.

Brent shrugged. "It's a normal reaction. We're taught to uncover faces and remove obstructions to breathing. Most people would have done the same."

"You wouldn't have."

"I would if I thought I could save someone."

"But I couldn't save her, and my tampering meant that, when you arrived, you couldn't be certain it was . . ." I threw an apologetic look at Lois. The unsaid word hung in the air, anyway. "Murder," I managed in a hoarse voice.

"Were you certain?" he asked me.

"Yes."

Lois wiped her eyes. "It certainly looked that way."

Brent studied her bowed head for a second before turning back to me. "Em, you said there was something else that you two wanted to tell me."

I described hearing Lois's call for help, running around the block to her house, and finding the front door open, a lampshade knocked awry, photo albums scattered on the floor, and Lois, injured, lying on the lawn out back.

Brent questioned her about the attacker. Her story was consistent with what she'd told me. She didn't know who it was, or whether it was a man or a woman, and whoever it was had threatened Lois with death if Lois told anyone about being attacked. "And I'm fine," she concluded. "It was barely a scratch."

I corrected her. "She was knocked unconscious."

Lois shrugged. "Only for a few seconds."

Brent was watching her intently. "Did you see a doctor about it?"

She shook her head. "It was nothing. Besides, Emily insisted on calling me every hour all night to make certain I was all right."

Brent flashed me an unreadable look. "And were you?" he asked Lois.

"Of course."

Brent was quiet for a while, writing in his notebook. He raised his head and asked Lois, "Do you have any idea why this person attacked you?"

She nodded. "He or she must have heard me outside and wanted to keep me from discovering him or her ripping pictures out of my photo album." She told him about taking photos and seeing a car the evening that Matthias Treetor went missing. "At the time, I didn't know he was missing, and I didn't really look at the car, but it ended up in one of the pictures. Later, after Matthias's body was found near where I'd been that evening, I looked more closely at that photo. Because of the glare on the windshield, I couldn't make out who the driver was, but I thought I recognized the car. However, that car's owner would have stopped to say hello. But he didn't, so it couldn't have been who I thought it was."

I remembered that the grave had been barely more than a shallow scraping in dead leaves on the forest floor, as if the murderer had been in a hurry. And I doubted that many murderers would stop to chat in the midst of fleeing the site where they'd buried a victim.

I suspected that Brent was thinking the same thing, but he only asked, "Who did you think it was?" His manner was calm, his voice steady.

Lois glanced at me and twisted her mouth. "I'm sure it wasn't him, but the car looked like one my great-nephew had at the time."

Brent asked, "What's his name?"

Suddenly I knew.

Chapter 10

❧

Randy Unterlaw had been two years ahead of Misty, Samantha, and me at Fallingbrook High. If the three of us thought about studious Scott at all, we admired him, and we'd all had crushes on Oliver, but most of the girls we knew had never tired of watching and talking about Randy. He'd been good-looking in that bad boy, I-don't-care-what-anyone-thinks way. Girls salivated over him, partly because of his looks and his devil-may-care attitude, but also because he had his own car from the moment he turned sixteen. Girls could go—or fantasize about going—on dates with him, and none of their fathers or mothers would have to drive, saddling their daughters with embarrassing and inconvenient chaperones. I hadn't seen him or thought about him since around the time that Scott, Oliver, and presumably Randy, also, had graduated.

"Randy Unterlaw," Lois told Brent. "He's my great-nephew. He's the only family I have. He lived with me during his teen years after his mom's latest husband became difficult. Randy's a good boy." With an earnest look on her face, Lois scooted forward on her kitchen chair. "Matthias was like a caring older brother to Randy, and Randy was terribly broken up when Matthias was killed. And Georgia was like another great-aunt to Randy. He's broken up over her, too. He would never have hurt either one of them. Or anyone."

Brent stared down at his notebook.

Anyone? I remembered Randy being hauled, frequently, into the principal's office because of fighting with other boys. Randy had been expelled or suspended a few times, which only made him more intriguing to many of the girls. Maybe Lois was an older version of the girls who thought they could rescue bad boys. Lois would be loyal to family, besides.

Brent looked up at her again. His expression was neutral. "Can you describe the car you saw the evening that Matthias Treetor went missing?"

This time, she added a crucial detail. "One of the fenders was white."

No, I thought, *noooo.* During his high school years, Randy had owned a series of memorably dented old cars with mismatched panels. My heart almost broke for Lois. She obviously loved her great-nephew, but he could be a murderer. And he could have attacked her last night.

She explained her theory that if Matthias's murderer had been driving that car, the murderer might have mistaken Lois for Georgia. "We traded vehicles that day."

Brent asked. "What kind of vehicle did Georgia own at the time?"

Lois didn't hesitate. "The one that was in her driveway Monday evening."

Brent frowned. "Silver compact sedan, similar to about a million others in Wisconsin."

Lois folded her hands on the table. Her knuckles paled. "If all the driver of that black car with the white fender knew about me was that I was driving a silver compact sedan, it's no wonder it took him five years to track down Georgia's car." She shuddered. "Except it was really *me* he wanted to track down."

I added a theory. "Maybe he had a good memory for license numbers, and it took him five years to find that number."

Brent frowned. I thought he was going to tell me to butt out, but he didn't say a thing.

I should have been the one frowning. My cat was stretched

out on his leg, her eyes closed in utter bliss, like Brent was her favorite person. Then I realized why Brent was frowning, and it wasn't completely due to Dep's claws. I admitted, "That doesn't explain why, after he killed Georgia, he came to Lois's house, attacked her, and stole the pictures she took the day that Matthias Treetor went missing."

Brent laid a gentle hand on Dep's back. "No, it doesn't."

I suggested, "He would have thought that by killing Georgia, he had eliminated the only witness, right?"

"You'd think so," Brent answered.

"So why would he go to a different part of town to search for photos that he thought belonged to the woman he had just killed?" Picturing our quick trip through Georgia's house, I half-closed my eyes. "If he searched Georgia's house for those pictures, he did it neatly. Nothing seemed out of place." Except in the bathroom, where the spare roll of toilet paper trailed across the floor, and in the kitchen, where, in addition to Georgia's body, there were signs of a break-in and a struggle.

Lois sighed and tapped her fingers on her handwoven place mat.

Brent remained quiet, observing her as if waiting for her to say something.

I imitated his watchful silence.

"Maybe . . ." Her voice cracked. "No, I can't even think it."

"What?" Brent asked gently.

"Maybe Georgia told the person who attacked her, before he . . . maybe she told him that we sometimes traded vehicles before I moved down to Madison."

I asked, "Who else would know about that?"

Lois looked suddenly happier. "A lot of people. We never kept it a secret, and we drove all around Fallingbrook in each other's cars." The pleased look drained from her eyes. "If Georgia didn't tell her murderer about us trading cars, he found out about it later on Monday, from someone else. It's horrible! It should have been me."

"It shouldn't have been anyone," Brent said, and I could tell he was thinking that if he had caught Matthias's murderer, he might have prevented Georgia's death. And maybe he was remembering the night when his best friend was killed and he was only grazed.

I wanted to remind Brent how hard he and Alec had worked to solve Matthias's murder. Knowing Brent, he had never stopped trying to tease out a solution to the case. But I only said, "Lois, even with your sheers closed, the painting that was hanging over your couch yesterday was noticeable. Anyone could have seen it. Maybe your attacker was walking past and recognized the scene, and he came in hoping that the photographer he'd driven past that day lived in the house with the painting. He could have seen the photo albums from your porch. And then he broke in to search through those albums in case you still had the photo you based the painting on. But he heard you and ran outside to attack you so that you wouldn't see him and be able to identify him later."

"I moved the painting out of sight too late," she said. "I guess I knew that."

Brent handed Dep to me and stood. "May I see the painting? And the photo albums?"

Lois pressed three fingers against her mouth for a second, and then clamped her hands together at her waist. "Let me pull the drapes in the living room. I don't want whoever threatened me to see me talking to a policeman."

"I'm not in uniform."

"Doesn't matter," I said.

Brent stared at me, wordlessly demanding an explanation.

"It's not like Fallingbrook's a huge place. Lots of people must know who you are." I didn't add *and you can't help looking like a cop.* He would say I thought that only because I knew he was. True, but that wasn't all. He carried himself with the authority of someone used to getting things done the way he thought they should be done.

Lois called from the living room, "Okay, you two can come in now."

Brent pulled a phone from his pocket. "Go ahead, Em. I'll be there in a minute."

In the living room, Lois opened the photo album to the ravaged pages and laid it on the couch. I could hear Brent's voice in the kitchen, but not what he was saying.

He strode in. "Lois, someone's going to keep their eyes on your house tonight after I leave. But don't be afraid to call 911 if anything seems the least bit off."

"Or scream out your back window for me," I suggested.

"Just call 911, Lois." Brent examined the album that Lois had opened. "I'd like to find the photos that match these torn bits. Preferably in someone's possession."

Wouldn't we all.

Using his phone to shoot pictures of the nearly bare pages, Brent asked us, "Did either of you tell anyone else about Lois's attack?"

I told him, "I didn't."

"No way!" Lois exclaimed with great vigor. "It's too embarrassing. I shouldn't have let it happen."

Brent eyed her. "Don't blame yourself, Lois. You were the *victim*. You did not bring it upon yourself. Both of you, please continue keeping the assault and the theft of the photos secret. Let's assume that threat was real. Besides, if the thief knows we're looking for the photos, he or she might make certain that we never find them. Please don't tell anyone, not even your great-nephew, Lois."

"I won't. Randy would worry and coddle me like I was an invalid."

Brent glanced at the photo album. "Do you have the photos' original digital files, Lois?"

"Emily asked me the same thing." She threw me a warning look as if she were afraid I would blab about frilly lingerie and disappointing suitors. "I don't know. I have more boxes to unpack. If I find the files, I'll let you know. Otherwise, you'll probably produce a search warrant and turn my house upside down."

"We wouldn't turn your *entire* house upside down. We'd only commandeer your computer and all of your unpacked boxes."

"Good luck with *that*." Apparently, she'd already caught on to his poker-faced sense of humor. She started toward the stairs. "I'll get the painting."

"We'll come up," Brent said.

She looked down from the second step. "It's a mess. Unpacked boxes . . ."

Brent gestured for me to go ahead of him. "Messes don't bother me."

Brushing one hand along the polished, satiny railing, I climbed the stairs. "You just moved in, Lois. You can't be expected to have everything unpacked yet."

We stopped at the top. "Mess?" Brent repeated. "Most people's houses aren't this neat, even if they've lived in them for years."

"Give me time." She showed us into the front bedroom, now an artist's studio.

Brent took a deep breath. "My grandfather was an artist. I love the smell of linseed oil."

Lois smiled. "Me, too. It's probably addictive. Maybe even a controlled substance." She raised her chin as if challenging Brent.

He merely grinned down at her. I wasn't surprised that he understood her humor.

I pointed to about twenty cartons stacked neatly along one wall. "Are those the only cartons you have left to unpack?"

Lois turned her mouth down in synthetic regret. "I wish! The basement's almost full of boxes. I didn't do the world's greatest job of labeling them."

So much for quickly checking for labels like LINGERIE and THUMB DRIVE. . . .

Although there were many paintings on the walls and leaning on furniture and on other paintings, Brent zeroed in on the one of the river valley. He moved it to an easel under a strong light. He seemed particularly interested in the bottom left corner. Finally, he focused on Lois. "How closely did you copy the photograph?"

"I'm . . . not sure. I painted that nearly five years ago, and I used several photos. You've been there. Does it look like the valley where Matthias was found?"

"Yes." He pointed at a dark splotch deep in the valley, near the river. "Could this black thing be part of the car you saw?"

She peered at it. "I don't know. I didn't see where the car came from. Suddenly it was chugging up the hill toward me, and it was close. I was parked on the shoulder of—County Road G, I think."

He nodded and pointed at the bottom left corner of the painting. "The track winds through trees, so you wouldn't have seen the vehicle part of the time it was heading uphill, but maybe the photo caught a bit of black paint that looks like a shadow here." He made a rueful face. "Or maybe it really was a shadow."

I pointed. "Is the black splotch near where Matthias was found?"

Brent's wave took in the entire painting. "*All* of it's near where he was found."

We trooped downstairs. Brent peered through the peephole. "Good. An officer is parked across the street."

Lois gasped, "No!"

"Plainclothes. Unmarked vehicle. And by 'unmarked' I don't mean it's one of those cruisers with markings that show up when lights shine on them. It's just a regular car with no markings." He shot me one of his amiable grins. "And good brakes, new tires, and a powerful engine. Alec would have approved. I'll walk you home, Em."

"Didn't you drive?"

"Did you?"

Never expect a cop to give a direct answer. "Dep and I walked." I fastened her halter around her and attached her leash.

Lois opened the door. I showed Brent the splintered door-jamb. This time, Lois said nothing about the damage being there when she moved in.

Brent told her, "Try not to touch anything your attacker might have touched. I'll bring the fingerprint tech over here tomorrow morning, first thing, okay?"

"I suppose." She smirked. "I won't wash the cutlery and glass you were using."

"Okay." His voice was totally flat. But he was smiling.

Lois said, "Emily, if I'm late tomorrow morning, tell the Knitpickers not to worry."

"Nitpickers?" Brent asked.

" 'Knit' with a *K*," Lois explained. "Haven't you ever been in Emily's donut shop in the mornings and seen the group of women knitting beside one of the front windows?"

The tops of Brent's ears reddened. "Um, no."

Lois demanded, "You haven't noticed or you haven't been there?"

The tips of my ears were becoming hot. I had a very good guess about why Brent never went to Deputy Donut. He probably thought that if the shop didn't succeed, I would go back to being a 911 operator. But I would never return to 911. And one person boycotting Deputy Donut was not going to put us out of business, either. Tom and I were doing well. Besides, I loved working there. I thought Tom did, too, but part of Tom's motivation could have been to keep me safe, for the sake of his late son.

Brent wouldn't have seen my reddening ears. He seemed to be avoiding looking in my direction, "I've never been there."

Lois tilted her head. "I've only been there two mornings, but I gathered that the entire police department goes in and out of that shop, not all together, but in twos and threes. I don't know whether to feel safe or raise my hands and confess to crimes I've never heard of. You have to stop by Emily's shop, um . . . Detective."

"Call me Brent."

"Brent. Emily and Chief Westhill make the best donuts in the whole world."

"I know. I remember her donuts from before she and Tom opened that shop."

"And from while Alec was alive." I was feeling more comfortable speaking of Alec to Brent now that he'd mentioned Alec and his approval of powerful cars. I told Lois, "Alec liked making donuts. He came up with many of the flavor combinations we're using."

My comment failed to put a stop to Lois's interrogation. She thrust her face up toward Brent's. "So. You know how good their donuts are. Why don't you drop in?"

I tried again. "I suspect Brent doesn't take many breaks. Thanks for dinner, Lois."

Brent thanked her, too.

She aimed a forefinger toward him. "You work too hard. You'll burn out. You should take breaks. And stop missing meals."

"Yes, ma'am." He followed me onto her porch.

Chapter 11

Lois hadn't turned on her porch light, probably because she didn't want anyone to see a detective leaving her house. Brent and I stood outside her closed front door until the lock hit home. Brent gave me a satisfied nod, and we started down the porch steps.

I tried not to be obvious as I glanced at cars parked along the street. Underneath the quarter moon and the streetlamps, leafy shadows danced over everything, and I couldn't make out anyone inside the vehicles. I also couldn't tell which one was the completely unmarked car. I hoped that the person who had attacked Lois was not around, and that if he was, he was no better at recognizing new tires in the dark than I was. Maybe he—or she—would never venture anywhere near Lois or this street again.

I looked up at Brent. "Georgia's doorjamb was splintered much like Lois's was. And Lois's front door was gaping open. So was her back door. And Georgia's back door was un-latched."

"You're a good witness. The report you gave us about Ms. Treetor's house meshed with what we observed there."

"Thanks, but I wonder if I missed something." I spoke slowly, thinking it through. "There was only one breakfast plate on Georgia's kitchen table, but she still had four of the six donuts she bought from me the Friday before. Is there any chance she had a breakfast guest? Did you check her calendar, the one on her computer or phone? Or maybe she carried a paper one."

"We did, and although she made notes of many appointments and meetings and the dates she'd promised repair work on dolls, she appeared to have nothing scheduled at breakfast on Monday morning."

"Not even a name?"

"No."

"And they're sure she died Monday, not Saturday or Sunday?"

"Yes."

Silent except for our quiet footsteps, we passed several houses.

"Do you believe Lois?" Brent asked me. "About not knowing who hit her?"

"I didn't last night when she was pretending she merely lost her balance and fell, but tonight, I thought she was telling the truth. Did you?"

"Why didn't you call the police last night?"

"I didn't understand how closely the attack on her could have been connected to Georgia's death. And Matthias's. It was only shortly before you called this evening that she told me about seeing a car she thought she recognized the night Matthias disappeared." For late August, the evening was surprisingly warm. The air felt soft on my face. "And Lois asked me not to call. She was sure she'd be safer if we *didn't* call the police."

"Mmp."

"I managed to wear down her resistance after she told me about seeing that car."

"Do you know her great-nephew?"

"I knew who he was in high school, but I doubt that I ever said more than about ten words to him. He was a couple years ahead of me."

Brent muttered, "And maybe light-years behind."

"What? Oh. He did seem to be in trouble a lot of the time. I haven't seen him for years, though. Maybe he's grown out of picking fights. Lois seems very fond of him."

"Mmp."

Conversing with a donut might have been as enlightening. We turned the corner and were on my block before he spoke again. "What's this about a secret passageway?"

I explained about the cat-sized tunnel, and Lois's and my conjectures about why it was built.

"Can you show it to me sometime in daylight?"

"Sure. It could come in handy if Lois and I wanted to pass illicit objects back and forth to each other."

"Mmp." This time I heard a smile in the comment. Perhaps it rated as progress.

He came right up onto my porch with Dep and me. Since I hadn't left a light on, the porch was dark under its sheltering roof. Brent shined a light on the door while I unlocked it. Dep pranced inside. I was nearly ready to close the door, leaving Brent on the porch, when he spoke again. "Em?"

"Yes?"

"Be careful."

"You, too."

"I mean it." Did he think I didn't? "Your new neighbor's friend was murdered and your neighbor was attacked. Being around her could be dangerous."

"I—"

He interrupted me by holding up one hand as if he were back in the days of being a traffic cop, if he ever was. "I know. You think you can and should protect her. You probably can't and you definitely shouldn't try."

"I—"

"Just be careful, Em. For Alec's sake."

Heat rushed to my face. "*Don't.*" I shook my head and gazed sightlessly toward my feet.

I was being rude.

Contrite, I looked up into Brent's eyes again. There was

nothing resembling a smile on his face, and he looked totally worn-out. "Sorry," I mumbled.

"S'okay. Call me if you think of anything else or need help. Good night, Em."

"Thanks for coming so quickly to hear what we had to tell you."

"Thanks for calling."

I backed inside, threw the dead bolt, and listened to his barely audible footsteps going down the porch stairs. I crouched and let Dep out of her halter. "What did you think of all that, Dep?"

"Mmp," she said.

"No. Not you, too, you little traitor." I picked her up and kissed her cute black, cream, and ginger forehead.

"Me-*ow!*" I understood that demand. It meant, *Put me down and go into the kitchen and feed me.*

I obeyed.

Leaving her contemplating her bowl as if she couldn't decide whether or not to eat, after all, I turned out the kitchen lights and went upstairs.

In my bedroom, I glanced at the mirror. My curls were rowdy and my eyes, although as bright blue as ever, looked almost as tired as Brent's. I mumbled, "Mmp."

I wasn't as good at imitating Brent as Dep was.

After the previous night's fractured sleep, I drifted off immediately and didn't hear a thing until the alarm went off at five. *At Deputy Donut,* I reminded myself, *I won't be alone. I'll be surrounded by friends and customers.* I hopped out of bed.

Lois showed up only about an hour late for the morning get-together of the Knitpickers. Before she sat down, she whispered to me, "Has that detective—Brent—been in here yet this morning?"

"No. I thought he was going to be at your place."

"He left five minutes before I did, and I thought he might have come here."

"Nope."

She leaned closer. "Is he married?"

"I don't think so."

"Why are you rolling your eyes like that?"

"He . . ." I smoothed the tuck in my apron over the strings tied at my waist. "He's a ladies' man. I can't imagine him settling down."

"Except maybe with you."

The tips of my ears were getting hot again. "I'm not . . ." I almost said *ready.* "I'm not *interested.*" Lois, of all people, should understand.

Apparently, she didn't, or she was being purposely obtuse. "You don't notice the way he looks at you?"

What I was noticing was that the other Knitpickers had quieted and were watching us, obviously trying to eavesdrop. "Ladies' man," I whispered. "And now he has *you* under his spell, too." Everyone was betraying me. First my cat, and now Lois. I raised my voice to a normal speaking tone. "What can I get you?"

She winked. "Not a man."

I rolled my eyes again.

"What's your special coffee today?"

"Kona, from Hawaii, a light roast. It tastes like freshly ground coffee smells. Don't tell anyone, but it might be my favorite."

"I'll try it. And what donut do you suggest?"

I glanced back into the kitchen. Tom was dipping donuts in frosting. "Tom's making a new flavor—penuche donuts."

"That sounds swoon-worthy."

Apparently, it was. When the other Knitpickers saw her expression of nearly terminal ecstasy when she bit into the donut, they ordered them, too.

Police officers must have praised the new donuts when they went back to the station. Misty came in after lunch and bought a dozen of the rich brown-sugar confections for colleagues who didn't have time for an afternoon break. She also bought six unraised cake donuts dusted with nutmeg and confectioners' sugar. "Brent asked for these." She studied my face.

Although I had nothing to hide, I made certain there were no thoughts or emotions on my face that anyone could read, not even a best friend. Not even a best friend who was a *cop*. "He interviewed my new neighbor last night while I was visiting her."

"New neighbor?"

"Lois. She's the one who was driving the van Monday night, the latest member of the Knitpickers."

"Georgia Treetor's long-lost friend? Petite woman with a whole bunch of white hair and a scared look on her face?"

"I didn't notice the scared look."

"You're not a police officer."

"Don't boast. Anyway, while Brent was at Lois's place, she was campaigning for him to eat donuts."

"It must have worked," Misty said.

"Or it has something to do with his investigation. The donuts in Georgia's kitchen Monday afternoon were unraised cake donuts dusted with nutmeg and confectioners' sugar."

"Those donuts." She hitched up her belt. About a ton of tools and weapons were attached to it. "Do you remember her buying them?"

"Yes. She bought six of them Friday before she left at noon. She usually buys—bought—half a dozen donuts on Fridays for her weekend breakfasts. She said it was a long drive back into town, and our donuts stayed fresh."

"It's only about five miles. Did you put the six donuts she bought on Friday in a box?"

"Yes."

"Can you think of anyone else who bought at least four donuts like that on Friday, and had them boxed?"

"No. But let's ask Tom and look at Friday's receipts."

Tom didn't remember anyone else buying at least four of those donuts, either, and the only record we had was for the six donuts that Georgia had bought at noon on Friday. We checked the rest of the week's receipts, too. I concluded, "It seems that Georgia bought the donuts that were found in her house."

She picked up her boxes and headed toward the front of Deputy Donut. "I'll tell Brent. If you think of anything else, call him?"

"Sure." I helped her with the door. "Or you."

"Not me. Brent." She gave me a sly look. Probably knowing how close I was to childishly sticking out my tongue at her, she laughed and then strode away with her donuts.

Scott and Oliver came in for their afternoon break and sat at a table together. Dep stared at them for a second and then went back to burnishing a paw. Scott and Oliver both ordered chocolate donuts filled with marzipan cream, shredded coconut, and chopped dried cherries. Scott, forever skinny, ordered two of them.

Another man about their age came in. He looked familiar, but I couldn't quite place him. His gaze locked on me. He walked to the counter and squeezed between two barstools. "Emily?"

I recognized his voice.

Randy Unterlaw had lost that uncaring bad-boy attitude, and there were flecks of gray in his dark brown hair, but he was still great looking—tanned, a smile lurking in his dark eyes, and noticeable bodybuilder muscles under his white dress shirt. When did bad boys start wearing dress shirts?

Maybe when they wanted to cover poorly done tattoos on their wrists. I remembered that tattoo. According to rumors, he'd inked it himself in junior high, with a needle and an ink pad, and it had certainly looked that way. In those days, the tattoo had been a word, all capital letters, each one with a period after it: B.A.D. I wondered if he'd added to it since. Whatever, he wasn't about to show it off. He pulled his sleeve down and covered all but the period after the *D*. His aftershave or cologne was a little strong and reminded me of mouthwash. I preferred the fragrance of our donuts, which, with him nearby, I could barely smell.

"You probably don't remember me." He sounded almost apologetic. "You've been kind to my great-aunt, and I came to thank you."

"She was here earlier. And I do remember you, from high school."

He still had a wicked smile. "You remember terrible things, then. I was only good at getting into trouble." If he hadn't reformed, he was playing the part well, white shirt, men's fragrance, and all. He flicked a glance toward the kitchen, and the smile was gone. "I heard about your husband, Chief Westhill's son. It must be hard."

I didn't flinch. "It is." Since his high school days, Randy had learned how to look sympathetic.

He drummed his fingers on the counter. "The house you and your husband bought—bet you didn't know that I was renting it at the time."

"No, I didn't." He'd kept it neat and clean. "Sorry for dislodging you."

"No problem. And now Great-Aunt Lois has its twin. It's sort of like coming home. A lot like. I've been out west until recently." He tugged his sleeve down again. "Wrangling horses at a dude ranch in Wyoming."

He was making me wistful. "I hear that's a beautiful area."

"Absolutely."

"And a dude ranch must be fun."

"Totally." Those deep brown eyes twinkled, and I could easily imagine all of the dude ranch's female visitors, from eight to eighty-eight, developing galloping crushes on him.

"Emily?" I hadn't heard Tom come up behind me. "Can you have a look at the mixer?" He asked Randy, "What can I get you?"

I turned toward the kitchen. In her special kitty-cat room, Dep was about twice her normal size, and glaring at Randy.

My heart made a series of odd thumps and bumps. Dep was demonstrating a hefty dislike for Randy. Dep had been nearby when someone clobbered Lois. Did Dep know that Randy had hurt the "mother" who fed her sardines and called her Tiger?

Tom delivered an Americano and plain unraised donut to Randy, who was sitting with Scott and Oliver at their table.

Tom returned to the kitchen. "The mixer's fine," I told him.

He muttered, "That Unterlaw kid was always trouble. Had to arrest him a few times back in the day. I don't think it's a well-kept secret, but you should know that he and another boy, a kid whose father owned a gas station, put each other in the hospital when they decided that fists weren't enough and went at each other with pocketknives. Far's I could tell, Randy was the one with the hair-trigger temper, the one who started the fights. Just wanted to warn you."

"Thanks, Tom. I hadn't heard the details, but I remember him. He seems different now." Oliver and Scott were talking to him like they were all old buddies.

Tom grunted.

"The newest Knitpicker, Lois Unterlaw, is Randy's great-aunt. She seems very fond of him. She just moved into the house behind mine."

"I don't have to warn you to be careful," Tom said. "I know you will be."

I laughed. "And I don't have to tell *you* to be manipulative. I know you *are*."

He grinned. "Am I that transparent?"

"Not all the time."

He looked toward the door and frowned. "And there's another one to be careful around."

Chapter 12

❦

The rotund blonde didn't look particularly dangerous. Her shapeless dress was several sizes too big and looked like she might have made it herself from blue denim, with frills of golden lace around the neck and elbow-length sleeves. Her most noticeable feature was her scowl, which marred an otherwise pretty face with a peaches and cream complexion.

Her gaze went from table to table, as if she was looking for someone in particular.

"Why did you say we should be careful around her?" I asked Tom.

"Litigious." He concentrated on golden oil shimmering in the fryer in front of him. "Causes trouble."

"Who is she?"

"Imagine her seven years younger and about two hundred pounds lighter."

"I can't."

"Does the name 'Honey' ring a bell?"

Honey, Honey, Honey . . . Finally, it dawned on me. "Honey Bellaire, Fallingbrook's most notorious Bridezilla?"

But Tom had turned away and was heading toward our industrial-sized stainless-steel fridge. It was as if he didn't want Honey to see him. She took her time about choosing a table, and then she sat facing the door. Because the street was more interesting than the kitchen? Or because she hadn't found the person she was looking for and wanted to watch the door? Maybe, despite Tom's turning his back, she knew he was Fallingbrook's former police chief, and she was hoping he wouldn't notice her.

It was no wonder I hadn't recognized her. About six and a half years ago, she had been about a hundred (not *two* hundred as Tom had said—he wasn't unobservant, but he did like to exaggerate) pounds lighter and about to marry the man of her dreams. Then, the day before her wedding, she'd become seriously ill and had been hospitalized after eating lunch meat she'd bought at Matthias Treetor's grocery, Taste of Fallingbrook. She had postponed the wedding until she could rent the same hall, an entire year later. Unfortunately, during that year, she outgrew her dress. Meanwhile, the man of Honey's dreams found a new dream girl, but neglected to tell Honey. He simply did not show up at the rescheduled wedding.

Gossip had run rampant in Fallingbrook while she was planning those weddings. People found many of her Bridezilla antics hilarious, as long as they weren't in the direct line of her ire over the lack of perfection in everything from her gowns (neither size had been shiny enough), to the flowers (she'd insisted on lilies of the valley in February), to the bows on the backs of the chairs (they had to be starched, unwrinkled, and whiter than white).

I'd never met her or talked to her, and there was no reason for her to know my name or that I'd been married to one of the detectives who had undoubtedly scrutinized her after Matthias was killed. She'd made no secret that the tainted meat had ruined her life, and she had continued to blame Matthias, even though it was announced early on that the meat packer was responsible for the food poisoning. Matthias had taken all of the meat from that packer off his shelves and had contacted everyone who had bought some to tell them not to eat it and to return it for a full refund.

Apparently, Honey hadn't paid attention to him or to the

frequent warnings on the news. No sensible person should have eaten any of the meat or blamed Matthias. But who said that Honey, aka Bridezilla, was sensible? She'd sued Matthias. She'd lost.

I went to her table. "What would you like?"

"Two unglazed cake donuts and a coffee." Her voice had raspy edges. Her cologne was even more overpowering than Randy's.

I tried to speak without breathing in very deeply. "What kind—"

Glaring, she interrupted me. "Unglazed cake."

I tried again, politely. "And the coffee? Cappuccino, espresso, Americano? Our featured coffee today is Kona."

"*Coffee* coffee. Nothing fancy and overpriced or foreign with a funny name." She grabbed a sugar cube out of the cute Deputy Donut sugar bowl and popped it into her mouth.

I went behind the counter to the coffee machines and poured a mug of our house blend. I figured that the mild Colombian would meet her definition of "*coffee* coffee," even though it had originated in a foreign country, while our Kona was grown in Hawaii. However, we did charge a premium for the Kona, so she might categorize it as fancy and overpriced. And maybe as having a funny name, besides.

Tom had told me to be careful around her. I wasn't about to go anywhere alone with her, but I sort of hovered after I served her coffee and donuts. I was sure that Honey wouldn't blurt out any murder confessions, but maybe she would say something that would give her away, and I could pass it on to Misty. Or, I supposed, to Brent.

Honey bit into one of the donuts. "It's not very greasy." From her tone and her frown, it was a complaint.

I acted like it wasn't. "The secret is heating the oil to the correct temperature. If the oil isn't hot enough, the donuts soak it up like sponges."

She took another bite. "It's not very sweet."

Again, I pretended it was a compliment. "Good."

She made a face like someone catching the scent of a startled skunk. "I can taste *nut*meg."

This time, I was sure it was not a compliment, but I didn't apologize. "Most people like nutmeg in their plain unraised donuts."

"That's probably why I'm tired of it."

"Did you like nutmeg once?"

"I guess."

I persisted. "Did *our* donuts make you tired of it?"

"How could they? I've never been in here in my *life*, before today."

"A friend could have brought you some." *Georgia, for instance.*

"Is it true that Georgia Treetor used to come in here a lot?" *Had* Georgia shared donuts with this peevish woman?

"Yes, she was here most weekday mornings."

"That woman!" Honey dumped three sugar cubes plus most of the contents of the Deputy Donut cream pitcher into her coffee. Stirring, she clanked the spoon against the mug. *Bang, bang, bang.* "I took a doll to her for a simple repair. Simple." *Bang, bang, bang.* "All she had to do was sew up the side." Honey ran a thumb and forefinger up the puckered seam of her dress. "That was all. But she took it upon herself to restuff the doll, too. I told her there was no way I was paying for that extra work, and she said she never thought of charging me for it, but you ask me, she would have doubled the price if I hadn't said something about it." *Bang, bang, bang.* If she hadn't set the spoon down, I'd have been tempted to take it away from her. She put the mug to her lips. "Burning hot. You could scald someone. They could sue."

Our coffee was never scalding, and she'd poured so much cream into hers that it couldn't be more than lukewarm. Maybe I needed to carry an instant-read thermometer in my apron pocket. At times like this, I could whip it out and take the coffee's temperature.

My own temperature was considering rising.

Honey stared toward the table that the Knitpickers occupied on weekday mornings. Six police officers were enjoying one another's company there. They didn't seem as carefree as they had before Georgia's murder, but their camaraderie and mutual trust were obvious. Most of them were only drinking coffee, but a couple of the slimmer men had ordered donuts.

Honey swiveled her head to study the tables closest to her. "I heard that lots of cops hang out here. I don't see many." Six officers having a break at the same time in a town the size of Fallingbrook weren't a lot? She crooked a finger, beckoning me closer. Standing, I wasn't much taller than she was, seated, but I leaned down. She whispered, "Do you know if any of the men sitting near the front window are single?"

Two of them were, but their marital status was their business. "Sorry."

She pointed at Scott, Oliver, and Randy. "How about those three hotties over there? Oh! I know who the tall one is—the fire chief!" She licked her lips. "Yum, yum, yum. Is he single?"

"I don't know." Actually, I did know. He was.

"Then how about the other two? It's not like they're short, except compared to the fire chief."

Oliver was divorced, but for all I knew, he was dating someone, and Lois hadn't said anything about Randy's love life. It didn't matter. I wasn't about to spread tales about my customers. "I don't know about them, either."

"You *should* know." Honey looked at my left ring finger. "Oh, you're married. I guess it's not important to you, then."

"No, it's not."

"You should have a TV in here, to give people something to do." Honey was the queen of shifting subjects.

I wanted to say that folks who visited coffee shops often wanted to talk to friends. However, Honey had arrived alone, and I didn't want to hurt her feelings. Not that she seemed particularly worried about hurting other people's.

"Like, maybe there's more news," she said around a mouthful of donut. "Maybe they caught that doll doctor's murderer. None of us can feel safe until they do." The flesh of her neck rippled as she made an elaborate shudder. "I'm scared, even locked in my own apartment."

I edged closer. "Do you feel like someone in particular is threatening you?"

She glowered at me. "Who knows? I live alone. That doll doctor lived alone. For all we know, someone's out to get all the women in this town who live alone."

"I hope not!"

She eyed my wedding ring. "*You* don't have to worry."

"I don't. What else can I get you?"

She waved a pudgy hand in dismissal and gulped down more of the "boiling" coffee.

In the kitchen, I quietly told Tom, "Honey complained that Georgia did too thorough a job repairing a doll, and would have charged too much if Honey hadn't told her not to."

Tom turned the corners of his mouth down in a way that showed he was about to say something sarcastic. "That woman's brilliant. When there are murders, she lets everyone know the grudges she held against the deceased. She blamed the son for her own stupidity, eating lunch meat long after it had been recalled."

"That's kind of extreme." I held up a finger like a TV lawyer about to make the final convicting (or acquitting) point. "Maybe it's a ploy. A real murderer would never admit to such things. Maybe she's the real murderer, trying to look naïve and innocent."

"Maybe." His tone implied that he thought it unlikely.

"She's never been here before. Why today?"

"Why is *everyone* here today?" Waving a slotted spoon, Tom answered his own question. "When something happens, people like to unburden themselves, and our shop has become known as the place to gather and talk."

"That's good, isn't it?"

"You bet."

"We'll hear people's secrets."

"Who's going to reveal their deepest secrets in a donut shop full of cops?"

He had a point.

Anyway, one of the six police officers at the front table was keeping his eyes on Honey. Apparently, Tom wasn't the only one who had her on his radar as possibly being connected with the murders of Matthias and Georgia. Or maybe the officer was curious about the way Honey was gazing at his table. The six police officers sauntered out and turned left, toward police headquarters.

Scott waved at me and followed them. He was probably going back to the fire station. Randy and Oliver walked out together, planning, if I heard them correctly, a golf game.

They must have mellowed since high school. I couldn't imagine them hanging out together then, the student council president and the kid who was always in trouble. They'd both been popular, though, in their own ways. Maybe fighting had been as much a social activity for Randy as being president of various organizations had been for Oliver.

Randy and Oliver turned right. Honey got up and headed for the front door. She turned right, also.

At four, I turned the sign in the front door from OPEN to COME BACK TOMORROW and locked the front door to allow customers to leave, but no new ones could come in. Just before four thirty, the last group of regulars called out their good-byes and let themselves out. I double-locked the door.

Tom and I finished tidying. In the office, I logged on to the computer. Despite Dep's roving around on the keyboard, I put in an order for sugar and flour. Tom came into the office, gave Dep a hug, set her down, said his good-byes, and went out to the lot in back where he always parked.

Tom wanted me to steer clear of Randy, but there were other ways of learning about him. I phoned Lois. "How are you?" I asked.

"Fine. How else would I be?"

"Concussed."

She made a rude noise. "You saw me this morning. How much more did you think I could have deteriorated this afternoon?

"Not a whole lot."

She laughed.

"Want to come to my place for supper? It won't be as luxurious as what you served me last night."

"That doesn't matter. I'd love to."

"I have to shop, first." I told her to come at six thirty.

As always, Dep transformed the walk home into an exercise of pouncing on imaginary prey, and then after we arrived home, she settled in the sunroom, where she could watch for anything exciting that might come into the backyard, like more leaves.

I went out to the driveway beside the house. Alec had planned to build a garage so that potential thieves couldn't keep track of when we weren't home. We'd had two cars then, and both of us had driven to work most of the time. I hadn't built the garage, but now I usually walked to work, and my car seldom left its parking spot except in rainy weather or when I needed groceries.

I loved the car. Alec had talked me into buying a sports car like the ones he always owned. Its power was wasted on me. I had no intention of bombing around town at speeds that might feel comfortable to a police officer. However, cars had always fascinated me, and if I could have afforded and maintained them I would have owned an entire stable of antique and vintage cars. I liked imagining my neighborhood when the homes were new and some residents still traveled by horse and carriage while others terrified their friends with noisy Tin Lizzies that could attain dizzying speeds approaching all of forty-five miles per hour. The speed limit in our neighborhood was now a comparatively sedate thirty-five.

When Matthias Treetor owned Taste of Fallingbrook, I had shopped there whenever I wanted special delicacies, but after Matthias died, the gourmet grocery was closed for about a year, and I'd started shopping at a supermarket on the outskirts of Fallingbrook. And then Alec had been killed, and I'd had no reason to return to Taste of Fallingbrook and no one with whom to share the surprising sorts of treats that I'd found in the shop when Matthias owned it.

It was time for me to stop avoiding everything that reminded me of losing Alec. Taste of Fallingbrook was closer than the supermarket, and might be the perfect place to quickly purchase ingredients for a dinner worthy of my foodie friend, Lois.

I parked in the lot behind the small grocery. There was only one other vehicle in the lot, a dented SUV that might have been black but looked beige under its coat of dust. The SUV was parked in front of a green door with NO ADMITTANCE hand-painted on it in white. Matthias had let customers use that door to go to and from the parking lot. I walked around to the street side of the store.

The awning stretching across the front of Taste of Fallingbrook had faded from hunter green to uneven shades of kelly green, and there was a long tear near one end of it.

I walked into the grocery. And almost walked out.

Chapter 13

Taste of Fallingbrook just wasn't the same as when Matthias owned it.

For one thing, it smelled wrong. Not bad, exactly, but not like a squeaky-clean supermarket, and not like I remembered Taste of Fallingbrook from five years ago—a mingling of spices, baked goods, and fresh lemons. About the strongest aroma I could single out was coming from plastic bags at the checkout.

For another thing, Frederick Aggleton, the man who had bought Taste of Fallingbrook from Georgia about a year after Matthias died, was scowling as if I'd spoiled a wonderful day. Matthias had always smiled and welcomed me.

I tried sunny politeness. "Good afternoon!"

The response was gloomy. " 'Noon."

I would have thought a grocer might want to be neat and clean. Aggleton's salt-and-pepper hair looked greasy, like it hadn't been washed recently. He wore gray polyester trousers and a rumpled plaid shirt. His shoes were scuffed. His apron had probably originally been hunter green like the awning, but now it was faded and stained, and threads were escaping from the embroidered Taste of Fallingbrook logo. Didn't he care how he presented himself, or his store?

As far as I could tell, I was the only customer, which I found disconcerting at five forty-five on a Wednesday evening.

I picked up a basket and headed toward the back. I was hoping to find freshly prepared shish kebabs that I could quickly marinate and barbecue, like the ones that Matthias used to sell. And if Taste of Fallingbrook also carried a selection of salads—Matthias and his employees had made theirs—the only other stop I'd have to make would be at Cookies and Bakies for dessert.

There were no shish kebabs.

The "steaks" looked like gristle marbled with fat. I picked up a package of two boneless, skinless chicken breasts. Remembering Lois feeding Brent the night before, I put a second package in my basket. Maybe Misty would show up. Or Samantha.

The deli counter was nearly empty. Except for a few containers of limp-looking coleslaw, there were no salads. Fortunately, I found some crisp romaine and a tin of anchovies.

I took my purchases to the cash register.

Barely speaking, Aggleton ran them past the bar code reader. "New in town?" he finally asked me.

"No."

"Haven't seen you in here before."

"No." Now I was the nearly silent one.

"You should come in more often."

"Yes."

"Not enough people know about this store."

"Oh?"

"I got a bum deal when I bought it. From the mother of the previous owner. He was dead."

I made a noise sort of like Brent's noncommittal grunts.

"His mother said this place had lots of customers. Even had financial records to prove it, but they musta been whadya call it. Forged. No one comes in here." He pounded on a box with a see-through top. "Look at these donuts. Hard as rocks. People coulda bought 'em fresh, but they go to that fancy-schmancy place that caters to cops while my donuts go stale. It's not like I don't sell coffee, too." He waved toward a carafe containing a murky dark brown liquid that smelled like it had been sitting undisturbed on its hot plate for about a week. "They pay twice as much for coffee and donuts as they'd pay here."

And our coffee and donuts have to be worth ten times as much. I didn't say it.

His hand hovered over the cash register. "You'll come back and shop here again, won't you?" The request was plaintive. "I have a store full of really good things. Tell your friends."

"Okay."

"I can't keep running this place at a loss, you know. No one could."

"Is it that bad?"

He pinched his thumb and forefinger together and shoved them almost into my face. "I'm this close to bankruptcy. And I got a wife and kid to feed."

I backed away. "That's sad." Maybe "mad" would describe his mood better. His face was red and he was breathing heavily.

"It's a crime, is what it is."

So is homicide. Wondering if his anger at Georgia had boiled over into a murderous rage, I paid for my purchases, put them into colorful cloth bags that Georgia had made for me, and went outside. A scrap of torn awning flapped in the breeze.

I hadn't been sincere when I promised to shop at Taste of Fallingbrook again, but maybe I needed to reconsider. Learning more about this angry man could be useful.

Leave it to the police, Emily. I could almost hear Alec saying it, with Brent, Misty, and Tom backing him up.

However, I had very good reasons for wanting to keep my ears and eyes open for clues about Georgia's killer.

Alec had not solved Georgia's son's murder. No one would say that I was duty bound to carry on my late husband's work, but I wasn't sure I could help trying.

And perhaps more important, a murderer was very likely

in or around Fallingbrook, and none of us were safe until he was caught.

When I was talking to Honey Bellaire earlier that afternoon, I'd wondered if she could have murdered Matthias and Georgia. Honey had been angry at them both, but Frederick Aggleton seemed even angrier. The thought that he could be a murderer did not make me any fonder of the idea of buying food from him, but it shouldn't hurt to snoop around his store.

Unlike Taste of Fallingbrook, Cookies and Bakies tempted me to linger, inhaling the scents and admiring the colorful cookies and bars. I finally chose lemon cookies shaped like birch leaves and frosted in lemon icing.

At home, I checked the chicken breasts I'd bought. They were fresh. I marinated them in olive oil, garlic, ginger, and the zest and juice of two limes while I washed and cut the romaine. I assembled Caesar salad except for the dressing, Parmesan, anchovies, and the croutons I'd made and stored in the freezer.

The doorbell rang.

Lois looked adorably girlish in a buttoned-up fisherman's cardigan, tight blue jeans, and espadrilles. Her jaw dropped when she stepped into my cottage. "This is how I imagine redecorating my living room!"

I picked Dep up and cuddled her. "No one says you can't." If Lois decorated in the scarlet and royal blue that I'd used, though, she might want to hang something besides that ferocious orange sky above her couch. That painting wouldn't go with the Victorian reds I'd chosen. Besides, could anyone truly relax in a room dominated by that disturbing painting? However, her tranquil river scene wasn't very peace inducing, either, considering what must have happened in that valley shortly before she snapped the pictures of it.

Lois admired my dining room and my sleek, modern kitchen, too.

"Yours is perfect," I told her.

"I'm not doing a thing with it as long as those aqua appliances continue working. Then, when I need replacements, I'll have them repainted aqua—Randy knows of an auto body shop that repaints things like major appliances and patio furniture. And then maybe I'll update my kitchen, but it will still have to go with the appliances, even though they're not Victorian."

Outside, we sipped Chardonnay while standing over the barbecue. The chicken smelled delicious. Dep twined around our legs.

"Four chicken breasts?" Lois asked. "Who else are you expecting?"

"I never know when Misty or my EMT friend Samantha will show up. And if they don't, we can have seconds or I'll have leftovers. Do you like anchovies, or should I leave them off the Caesar salad?"

"I love them. We'll cut back on salt tomorrow." Lois's grin was diabolical.

It was warm enough to eat outside at the table on the flagstone patio underneath my sturdy timber pergola.

We finished most of the bottle of wine while we ate and chatted about everything besides Georgia, Matthias, and violence. Dep stayed near us, even though the tunnel to Lois's yard was still open and Lois and I refused to give her anchovies. We were willing to compromise our own health with a pinch or two of salt, but we drew the line at possibly harming our favorite kitty.

The sun hadn't set, but after my house began shading us, the evening cooled rapidly. We went inside to the living room for lemon cookies and liqueurs. "We'll cut back on alcohol and sugar tomorrow, too," Lois said.

She hadn't mentioned Randy all evening. I enjoyed Lois's company, but I had hoped to learn more about Randy over dinner. As casually as I could, I asked, "Did you look for those digital photo files for Brent?" Maybe she'd already given them to him.

"I forgot!" She pulled a thumb drive out of her pocket. "I unpacked some boxes, and I think this drive might hold my photos from five years ago."

"Let's go upstairs and load it on my computer."

Dep ran past us and then stood at the top of the stairs, meowing down at us. I was certain she'd have led us the rest of the way if she'd known exactly where we were going. I guided Lois into the front bedroom. Dep whisked in ahead of us, jumped onto the couch, sat down, thrust one back leg almost straight up, held on to it with both front paws, and licked it vigorously.

The room served as both an office and a guest bedroom. The couch converted to a double bed, and its matching upholstered chair was comfy for reading. Guests would not be able to hang much in the closet, however. Closets in Victorian houses tended to be small, which didn't make sense considering the bulk and length of Victorian gowns. I kept my out-of-season clothes in this one. Like most of the other rooms in the house, the walls in my guest room were painted white. Unlike the walls in Lois's front bedroom, mine were almost totally devoid of art, mostly because I hadn't gotten around to choosing much.

Lois rubbed her toes in the soft nap of the blue and cream rug. "Another gorgeous rug." It was patterned like an oriental rug, but that was as close as it got to the real thing. Still, it was pretty, and went well with the dark blue couch and chair. Dep toppled over on her side, acted like she'd done it on purpose, jumped down to the floor and then up to the desk. From there, it was only a short hop to the sill of the dormer window. Switching her tail back and forth, she gazed into the branches of the maple tree in the front yard.

I turned on the computer, inserted Lois's thumb drive, and pulled out the desk chair.

Lois remained standing. "Where will you sit?"

I tugged the upholstered chair to the desk. "Here. I'd give you this chair, but it's kind of low."

She glanced down at me as I sank into the chair and peered over the keyboard to the monitor. "For you, too, but thank you. Being able to see the pictures might help." She sat in the desk chair.

Sure enough, the drive she'd brought contained photo files, hundreds of them. They weren't organized by date, so we couldn't zero in on August five years ago. Eventually, we found a folder labeled LAKES AND RIVERS, with a sub-folder marked FALLINGBROOK RIVER.

Lois was practically bouncing up and down in that desk chair. "That's it! I remember now. Maybe we can prove that Randy wasn't driving that car, that it wasn't Randy's car, and that I was remembering it wrong."

Right, even though the initial "remembering" was only about ten days after she saw the car....

The first photo in the group was very similar to her painting. Down in the left corner, between trees, we could see the dark splotch that Brent had asked about. Could it have been a black car? We enlarged the photo on the screen until it blurred. A few pixels were lighter, possibly a gleam off metal. Or a brighter spot among the shadows.

We clicked on the next picture. It was almost the same.

In the next one, Lois had turned to her right. She'd snapped many pictures from that angle, and then she must have heard the car and turned to her left again.

There it was. A black car was heading toward her, with the sun reflecting off the windshield, dust billowing around it, and a front license plate hidden by tall grasses. I clicked the next picture. It showed the dirt track, empty except for the tan-tinged haze of dust settling after the car passed.

Lois inched the desk chair closer to the computer. "Apparently, I remembered correctly about taking only one photo of that car."

"Does it look like the one Randy was driving back then?"

"Maybe. He was always trading one old thing for another. He often had mismatched fenders and panels, and the section over the driver's side front wheel looks lighter. It seems to me that it was actually white, like I told Brent last night. But I'm sure Randy wasn't the only person in Fallingbrook who was driving a patched-up but not repainted car at the time."

"Probably not. I don't think I saw Randy after he graduated from Fallingbrook High, so I have no idea what car he was driving five years ago."

"I do. He came to say good-bye before he left for Wyoming, and I remember telling him that he should have had that fender painted black before he moved to a new community. Just having fun, you know? Not really criticizing."

"How'd he take it?'

"Fine. We've always teased each other. He laughed at me for owning a seven-passenger minivan even though I lived alone."

"Did he know that you sometimes traded vehicles with Georgia?"

"Sure. He often borrowed my van, and offered to let me drive whatever rattletrap he owned at the time. Ha. I wasn't about to go around in something held together with wires and duct tape. It would break down in the middle of nowhere, and then where would I be? But he said his cars were always in good mechanical condition and safe to drive. They just wouldn't win any beauty prizes. He's a good kid, with a sense of humor. You'll help me, won't you, Emily?"

"Help you what?"

"Figure out who the murderer was. You used to work at 911, your husband was a detective, your father-in-law was our police chief, you know Detective Brent, and one of your best friends is a policewoman. You must know something about solving crimes."

"Not enough." And Alec, Tom, Brent, and Misty would tell me to stay out of criminal investigations. . . .

"Well, I'm an artist, and, if I do say so myself, pretty observant. We're both intelligent and spunky. We should be able to uncover the truth."

And what if she didn't like the truth we found? I didn't ask her if Randy still had his temper. "We can keep our eyes and ears open, but we can't interfere."

"We wouldn't do that."

Right. "And we have to stay out of danger."

"We will. That's settled. We'll keep our eyes and ears open, we'll use logic, and we'll figure out who was driving a car similar to Randy's."

"That person might not have murdered Georgia. Or Matthias, either."

"Exactly."

Her "logic" was making me dizzy. I pointed at her thumb drive. "Did you unpack your frilly undies?" I asked with pretend formality.

"Yes, and they're so lovely I draped them in my front window for all the world to appreciate."

"I'll come over with a camera later."

"No need. I already snapped a photo so I can immortalize it in oils." Making delicate strokes with an imaginary paintbrush, she spoke dreamily. "I like it. A window, a makeshift clothesline with pretty undies pinned to it, sheer curtains blowing in a breeze . . . And when it's finished, I'll give it to you to put up on some of your bare walls." I could tell she was kidding.

"Thanks." I clicked back to the photo showing the car and enlarged the license plate. Blurry weeds. Not very helpful.

I moved the cursor to the windshield in front of the driver's face, and zoomed in, but neither of us could make out anything about the driver. We could see a slice of the steering wheel, which could have been gray or black, but no hands or face.

The only part of the front passenger seat we could see was the top corner beside the door. The seat belt was hanging, slightly twisted, from the doorpost. If anyone was sitting in the front passenger seat, he or she was slumped toward the driver. And was not wearing a seat belt. I couldn't help a shudder. Had Matthias been transported in that car shortly before Lois took that photo?

"We can't prove that the driver's not Randy." I heard the disappointment in her voice.

"We can't prove that it is, either."

"True."

Dep sat up, leaned closer to the window, and made a noise halfway between a chirp and a bark.

Lois smiled at the cat. "I thought she was a tiger, but maybe she's part dog and part bird."

"Bird dog," I suggested. "She makes that noise when she sees a bird or a squirrel in that tree." I pointed at the monitor. "Do you want to call Brent about these photos, or should I?"

"Does he need to apply for a search warrant before he comes?"

"He would if you weren't freely giving him the evidence. Lending it, I mean."

"So, if I don't want to lend the drive to the investigators, they'd have ways of getting it from me?"

"Yep."

"And Brent already knows that the thumb drive might exist, so he's going to want it, eventually, and we can't lie and say I never found it, can we?"

Did the car look too much like the one she remembered Randy owning before he moved out west? "I'm afraid not."

"You phone them, Emily. You seem to know the number by heart."

I'd learned it when Alec was alive. I didn't know either of my parents' cell phone numbers, but the police department's number was burned into my memory.

Brent promised to be at my place in ten minutes.

Chapter 14

✵

Lois said, "I wonder if Brent's had dinner. Or anything to eat today. You fixed extra, and it's really good. He should appreciate it." Her eyes gleamed.

I burst out laughing. "You're a matchmaking schemer."

"Who, me? I just don't like to see a good man go hungry, that's all. Anyway, you said you weren't interested in him. He's a ladies' man, or something like that."

"I'm not. But he was a friend once."

"Aha."

"There's nothing to 'aha' about." I changed the subject to a more important one. "Did you make a copy of your thumb drive?"

"I didn't have time. Besides, I wasn't sure it contained files that Brent would want."

I opened my desk drawer and pulled out a new, blank drive. "I'll copy the entire drive. It could be years before they return the original drive to you."

"That long?"

"Yep. If you're lucky, they might copy the important files and give your drive back sooner, but you never know, especially in a major case like this." *A murder. Possibly two. And maybe more, if we don't catch the murderer. Or murderers.*

First, as Alec would have, I copied Lois's Fallingbrook River pictures to my hard drive in case I ever wanted to examine them more closely. Then I started copying all of the files from Lois's thumb drive onto my blank one. The doorbell rang.

Lois shooed me downstairs. "I'll keep track of this. You go let your detective in. Offer him something to eat."

Brent was dressed almost the same as he'd been the night before, in jeans and a tweed blazer, but it was a different blazer, more blue than gray this time, and he was wearing a light blue T-shirt under it. And, undoubtedly, his service revolver in a shoulder holster.

Apparently, Dep recognized his voice. She ran downstairs so quickly that her little kitty paws actually thumped. She wound figure eights around Brent's ankles. He picked her up. The way he nestled her against his right side reminded me of Alec holding her the exact same way, keeping her away from his weapon. *Alec.*

I asked Brent, "Have you eaten?"

"I'm okay."

"That's not what I asked. We grilled chicken—"

He glanced toward the back of the house. "We?" Gently, he put Dep on the floor as if he were considering reaching for his gun. I knew he wouldn't, but he looked ready. Then again, he always seemed ready for anything. Alec had, too, and Misty did. And Tom still did, even though he was retired. Apparently, that constant alertness was an occupational hazard for police officers.

"Don't worry. I'm not harboring any murderers or would-be attackers. No one's here besides Lois and me."

I saw last night's warning in the steady gaze of those gray eyes. *Just be careful, Em. For Alec's sake.*

I went on as if he hadn't spoken volumes while not saying a word. "And there's Caesar salad if you don't mind anchovies." If I remembered correctly, he liked them.

"I haven't eaten. And anchovies are great. But first things first. How about that thumb drive?"

"It's upstairs. Lois is using my computer to look at the images."

His jaw tensed. I knew what he was thinking. We'd tampered with evidence. Again.

I felt the blood drain from my face, and I had to work at not looking stricken. "We didn't delete or change any of them. We weren't going to bother you if the images hadn't been the ones you needed, so we looked at them first. Lois is sure that some of them match the prints that were torn out of her photo albums."

"Checking on possible evidence is never a bother. Lead the way?"

I scooped Dep up and cradled her in my arms all the way to the second floor. Brent followed us, but stopped in the doorway of my combination office and guest room. "You haven't changed the color since I helped paint this room before you and Alec moved in."

Undoubtedly having heard us coming, Lois had filled the screen with the picture of the car driving up the dusty track.

"I like the white," I said. How inane. "It's nice and bright." Even more inane. Dep must have thought so, too. She squirmed. I set her on the floor. She hopped up onto the desk, and from there onto the windowsill again. She wouldn't see many birds now, at dusk, but that didn't deter her from gazing at the tree.

Lois rolled the desk chair back. Lights on the two thumb drives were flashing madly. The copying was still going on.

I couldn't tell if Brent noticed. He bent forward and stared at the sunlit black car on the screen. After a long silence, he asked, "Are there more?"

"Not of the car, unfortunately," Lois said, "but there are more that I took that day, including the one I used for the painting I showed you last night." She clicked back to that picture and pointed to the lower left corner. "It has that black splotch that might be the car, but I can't tell more than we could from the painting."

Brent smelled like sunshine and fresh air. I straightened, farther from the screen and from him. "It's very much like your painting," he told Lois. "Mind if I take the files to the forensics guys so they can try to enhance the images?"

"Okay." Her voice was unusually soft as if she could barely force the word out.

"We can make copies for you," he offered.

I pointed at the two thumb drives connected to my computer. "We already are." The lights had stopped flashing. Duplicates of Lois's files should now be on the drive I was planning to lend her. "Evidence can be held almost indefinitely, so I thought she should have a copy now. Forensics might take a long time."

The slight tilt of Brent's head could have been agreement.

Lois clicked back to the image of the car and pointed at the windshield. "They can't just wipe the reflections off the windshield and reveal the driver, can they?"

Brent studied her as if wondering if she truly regretted that reflection's existence or was asking for assurance that no forensics tricks could reveal the driver's face. "I'm afraid not."

She rolled the chair away from the desk and folded her arms. "It couldn't have been Randy. He would have stopped to talk. Besides, I saw the car and didn't even think of Randy. So, there was no way it was his car. I'd have recognized it."

Her pallor and obvious shortness of breath were giving her away. She wasn't as confident as her words implied, and maybe, despite her denial, she was scared that her great-nephew might be a murderer.

But I had to give her credit. If she'd truly believed that Randy was driving the car coming toward her that evening, she probably would have flagged him down to say hello. And if, five years later, she still thought the driver was Randy, she might not have told us about possibly having seen him. But she had.

I showed Brent the list of files on Lois's drive and pointed out the subfolder labeled FALLINGBROOK RIVER. "This is where the photos are." I clicked on the subfolder, showed him the thumbnail images, and then ejected Lois's drive.

Thanking me, he took a small evidence envelope out of his pocket. The envelope's flap had a perforated section with a numbered receipt printed on it. He wrote on the receipt, signed it, detached it from the rest of the flap, and handed it to Lois. Then he slid the drive into the envelope, sealed the envelope, and dropped it into his jacket pocket.

I headed toward the top of the stairs. "Now you can help with the leftovers, Brent."

"They're good," Lois told him.

I stood back to let her lead the way. Dep scooted past all of us. At the foot of the stairs, Lois turned toward the front door. Dep planted herself at Lois's feet and looked up toward her face. "I'll be off now," Lois said.

Brent reached for the doorknob. "I'll walk you home."

She glanced at me. "No! Your dinner's been delayed enough."

"Stay while Brent eats," I suggested. "And then we can both walk you home."

"Don't be silly. It's only eight thirty. I'll be perfectly safe."

I countered, "You were attacked about this time two nights ago."

Brent was still holding the doorknob. "Would you like a patrol car to pick you up?"

She glared at him. "No! A detective walking me home would be bad enough if the person who threatened me has been hanging around watching to see if I *did* contact the police."

I offered, "How about if I walk you home while Brent eats?"

Brent quickly put a stop to that idea. "Then I'd have to send someone to pick you up, Emily." I figured he was calling me by my full name to show how serious he was about our not wandering around outside at night when a killer could be loose. "Let's both walk her home."

"You're going to too much trouble," Lois complained. "If my great-nephew's home, he could pick me up."

"It's no trouble," I answered.

"I could use a walk," Brent said.

All of us, except Dep, headed toward Lois's house. Brent positioned himself closest to the street. I made certain that Lois was between us, making it more difficult for someone to leap out of nowhere and attack her.

I watched for shadowy figures near hedges and picket fences, and I also peeked into houses where lights were on but drapes weren't drawn. I wasn't looking for anything inside those houses. I was merely curious about others' décor. Brent seemed to be keeping track of everything—cars that were parked and cars that were moving, license plates, a family dawdling along the sidewalk across the street, a couple snuggled on a porch swing, a lone cyclist, a teenager, humming and weaving down the street, his baseball cap backward and his hands and eyes on his phone. "Hey, kid," Brent called. "You're on your way home for your helmet, right?" The kid raised a lazy hand and kept going.

Lois's lights weren't on. Saying he'd check her back door and windows, Brent turned on his phone's flashlight and went inside first. Lois and I stood in the dark beside the door until Brent returned, pocketing his phone. "Everything looks fine."

Lois thanked him. "Now will you please go eat? I don't want to be responsible for the starvation of one of Fallingbrook's finest."

He saluted. "Yes'm."

"And can you manage the porch and front steps if I don't turn on the light? Sorry, but I feel unsafe with a policeman here."

"No one will recognize me as a cop if I fall down the stairs," Brent deadpanned.

"Unless your gun goes off," I teased.

"How do you know I'm carrying?"

"Aren't you?"

Lois opened the door. "*Would* you two get going?"

Neither of us fell down the stairs, or even tripped. Out by the street, I looked back at Lois's sweet cottage. There were still no lights on inside, but one of the sheers in her front window twitched.

The kid on the bike was gone, and so was the couple from the porch swing. The family, with two grade-schoolers who were apparently collecting fallen leaves, had not traveled very far. A car passed slowly. Brent didn't seem to notice it, which made me pay it more attention. I didn't recognize it or the driver. I asked, "Is someone still watching Lois's house?"

"Not constantly, but we're keeping an eye on it." At my door, he said, "Listen, Em, if you're busy, I can grab a bite at home."

When would that be? Probably not for hours. "Help me eat the leftovers, and save your bite for another day."

"Who can resist an offer like that?" He followed me inside and locked the door.

"Come into the kitchen," I said. "Lois and I ate outside, but now it's too chilly." I was babbling. Maybe I shouldn't have let Lois plan my guest list.

In the kitchen, Brent perched on a barstool. I set a plate of chicken and the salad bowl, now only half-full, on the granite countertop in front of him. "Wine?" I asked.

"I'm working."

"Overtime?"

"Yep, and thanks. I keep skipping lunches." He tasted the chicken. "This is delicious."

I felt silly, standing on the other side of the counter as if we were in Deputy Donut and I was about to hand him a bill. I put the rest of the cookies on a plate and then slipped around the counter, pulled the other barstool farther from his, and sat down with my feet on the footrest. "Have you made progress in Georgia's case?"

"We found fingerprints on that doll's legs, and they matched some in our database."

"Mine," I guessed. "They'd be in the database from when I applied to work at 911."

"Mmp."

"I'm really sorry about touching that doll."

"Don't worry about it, Em. It was an understandable reflex."

"Were other fingerprints on that doll?"

"Gloves."

"What about that donut box?" I knew they could use a chemical, ninhydrin, to cause fingerprints on paper to show up in, of all colors, purple.

"Your prints, Chief Westhill's, and Ms. Treetor's."

"What about the rest of Georgia's house? Like around the back door where he or she broke in?"

"Gloves."

"Could you tell by the size of the fingers of the gloves whether the person wearing them was a man or a woman?"

"Don't you think a woman could wear gloves that were too large for her?"

"I suppose, though they might make her too clumsy to accomplish much."

"Mmp."

"Did the fingerprint guy find prints in Lois's house this morning?"

"Hers, yours, mine, her great-nephew's, and someone wearing gloves."

"Aha. Randy wouldn't have needed to wear gloves. No one could have been surprised that his prints were in that house."

"He'd need gloves if he wanted to make it look like someone besides him had broken in."

I glared at Brent. "Why do you have to be so *right?*"

"It's my job." I detected a slight twinkle in his eyes.

"Did any of Georgia's neighbors have surveillance cameras?"

"No. A few businesses on the main streets near her neighborhood had cameras. We're looking at the videos."

"Need help?"

"I wish I could say yes, but . . ." Instead of finishing the sentence, he popped another piece of chicken into his mouth.

I said it for him. "I found her, and touched that doll, so that makes me a suspect."

"Mmp."

"Do you suspect me?"

"No."

At least he was clear about that. Still, had he been about to say *but,* as in *but someone else in the department does?* If they did, I wasn't sure I blamed them. My fingerprints were on that doll and on the donut box. Besides, I had probably touched Georgia's back door when I ran out of her house. And my prints were in Lois's house, too. But so were Brent's, and no one was going to suspect him of murdering Georgia and attacking Lois.

He declined coffee. We both ate a couple of cookies, and then he received a text message and said he had to go.

I opened the front door. A car door slammed. Samantha, not in her EMT uniform, but wearing jeans, a sweater, and sneakers, ran up the walk to my porch. With her head down, probably so she could watch for cracks in the concrete that might trip her—an EMT would be teased forever by her colleagues if they had to take her to the hospital—she didn't notice us on the porch until she was close to the top of the steps.

She didn't jump, much. "Hey, Brent! Hi, Emily."

"Come in, Samantha," I said. "Have you eaten?"

"Yes. I know it's late. I can only stay a minute. I just wanted to check on you. How's the investigation going, Brent?"

"Well enough that I have to go. See you two." He ran

down the stairs and turned left, toward downtown Falling-brook. I wondered if he'd walked from the police station or, for some reason—Lois's protection, maybe—had purposely not parked near my house.

Samantha followed me inside. Like nearly everyone else except Lois, Samantha was taller than my five-foot-nothing. Shorter than our stately friend Misty, Samantha was solid muscle. She worked out regularly because, as she told it, she was totally scared that she might accidentally drop a patient on his head. She looked like a rosy-cheeked Victorian picture of health, but she hated her round face, especially the cheeks. She said they made her resemble a chipmunk, to which Misty and I always replied, "That's a stretch." And then Misty and I always elbowed each other and giggled. Samantha wasn't as elegantly beautiful as Misty, but she was very pretty, and she didn't look fragile enough to break, like I did. The three of us together often attracted attention, maybe because we were often laughing too hard to walk or talk. That evening, Samantha's glossy brown hair was streaked with brilliant ruby stripes.

"I like the red," I told her.

"I'm certain that it cheers and distracts my patients better than last week's cobalt. So!" Humor shined from her dark brown eyes. "When were you going to tell me about you and Brent?"

"There's nothing to tell. Georgia Treetor was a frequent customer at Deputy Donut, and her best friend, Lois Unterlaw, was here for dinner tonight. Lois brought some evidence—possible evidence—that might pertain to Georgia's murder. Brent's the lead detective on the case, so he came over and picked up the possible evidence. But come back to the kitchen. I still have some cookies from Cookies and Bakies."

"Yum." She followed me through the living room and dining room. "Is Lois Unterlaw related to Randy Unterlaw? Remember him?"

"Lois is his great-aunt."

"I haven't seen him in a while, which could be surprising. When we were in high school, didn't he regularly need an ambulance or cause someone else to need one?"

"He was in Deputy Donut today. He seems to have become a normal, law-abiding citizen. He was hanging out with Scott Ritsorf and Oliver Rossimer."

"He must have had a personality transplant. Remember our crushes on Oliver Rossimer? He's still gorgeous."

"All three of them are."

"I think I chose the wrong profession. The way to a man's heart is not through IV drips."

"It could be, if you saved his life."

She batted her extravagantly long and curly eyelashes. "I can hardly wait. Meantime, you're serving delicious donuts and coffee to gorgeous guys, day in and day out."

"And to make things worse, I'm not even interested."

She tilted her head. "Uh-huh."

"Who doesn't like eye candy?"

In the kitchen, she noticed that I was putting only one place setting into the dishwasher. "I thought you said that Randy's great-aunt ate with you."

"She did. After we were done, she made me feed Brent. Here, help me finish these cookies."

"You could do worse than Brent."

"You're welcome to him."

"Me?" She made a dramatic gesture, one hand to her heart and the back of the other hand against her forehead. "My heart will always belong to Oliver."

She didn't stay long. Both of us needed to get up early in the morning. Telling me to be careful, especially around Randy, she left.

Chapter 15

Tom hummed while he rolled out dough with his favorite rolling pin, an oversized marble one. We'd been in Deputy Donut's kitchen for over a half hour. Thanks to our preparations the day before, we'd already made dozens of donuts and decorated them with frostings, glazes, sprinkles, coconut, and mini chocolate chips.

It was almost seven. Breathing in the fragrances of fresh coffee and warm donuts, I unlocked the front door and then went to the back of our neatly arranged dining area so I could peek through the window into our office. Blinking, Dep stood up. I couldn't help smiling. She looked warm, sleepy, and adorably cuddly.

Behind me, the front door opened. Dep fluffed up into the perfect vision of a fierce and intimidating kitty cat. Who had caused that reaction?

I whipped around.

It was Misty.

How strange. When Misty came in, Dep usually leaned against the office window as if trying to get closer to her.

Then I saw what must have confused Dep. The defeated expression on Misty's china doll face made her almost unrecognizable. Her uniform was crisp and her hair was neatly tied back, but her shoulders were tense, her eyes were grim, and her smile was strained. Setting her police-issue boots down hard with each step, she strode to me. "Brent's been demoted," she said.

"Demoted!" I couldn't help sounding shocked.

"He's no longer the lead detective on the case."

I tilted my head, undoubtedly dislodging my Deputy Donut hat. "The . . . Georgia Treetor case?"

She nodded.

"Why?"

Misty just watched me. Dep's fur had settled down to almost normal. She gently pawed at the glass, opened her mouth, and let out a plaintive *meow*.

I asked in a voice so small it almost squeaked, "Because Brent's former partner's widow is the person who found Georgia's body?"

Misty still didn't speak. She was obviously waiting for me to say more.

"And she left her fingerprints where she shouldn't have? I mean *I* left my fingerprints where I shouldn't have."

Misty scrunched her mouth to one side.

I again apologized for moving that doll.

"It's not that, entirely." Misty's voice was soft with compassion. "The chief called in the state DCI to help."

That made sense, I guessed. The Wisconsin Division of Criminal Investigation undoubtedly had more resources for investigating homicides than local police forces had, but the Fallingbrook police department had its own detectives. Maybe I was biased, but Brent was at least as good as anyone in the DCI, and probably better. He had investigated Georgia's son's murder. He understood the web of relationships between the Treetors and their friends, family, associates, and possible enemies. However, calling in the DCI for serious crimes in Wisconsin was not unusual, and a voice in my head reminded me that Matthias's murder was still unsolved. I asked Misty, "What does Brent think about it?"

"You know him. Poker face, saying it's totally normal, which it is, but I'd be frustrated and seething." She obviously tried to control a teasing smile. "I talked to Samantha last night."

I settled my Deputy Donut hat more firmly on my head. "And she told you that she saw Brent leaving my place. He had come over to pick up some evidence. That's all."

"And had dinner with you?"

"Not *with* me and Lois. After. Lois fed him at her place the night before, too. Lois likes to feed people."

Misty became serious again, almost forbidding. "You'll be careful around her?"

"Sure. Not that it's necessary."

"It is. You've known her since Monday, right? And this is Thursday. Four days."

"She and Georgia were *friends*."

"Did you ever hear that from Georgia?"

She had a point. I winced. "I don't remember Georgia ever mentioning her."

"And Lois had a key to Georgia's house, right?"

I held up a cautionary finger. "The murderer *broke into* Georgia's house."

"We can't be certain. Even if we were, it doesn't prove that Lois wasn't the murderer."

"Someone attacked Lois later that night."

"So she said. While I was asleep in your yard. And no one witnessed the attack."

"Attackers generally prefer to do their attacking when there *are* no witnesses."

She ignored my sarcasm. "What did you hear that night?"

"A tiny call for help, more like a gasp."

"No thumps or thuds?"

"No. You were snoring."

Misty gave me a haughty look, as if she were peering over half-glasses, a look she probably gave drivers who claimed they'd been under the limit after she'd clocked them at twenty miles over.

I quickly added, "Dep was doing some insistent meowing, though, and you know how loud *she* can be."

A distinct *mew* came from the other side of the glass.

Misty smiled at the cat. "We weren't asking *your* opinion, Dep." She turned back to me. "I wish you'd gotten me up when you heard that call for help."

"I do, too. Too bad Dep can't tell us what happened. She was probably crouching in her secret passageway, watching everything."

Misty gave Dep a thumbs-up, but she had a warning for me. "Even if Lois didn't murder Georgia, she might have said something that led one of her friends or relatives *to* Georgia."

"You mean Randy Unterlaw. Do you know when he left Fallingbrook and when he came back? Could he have left town *before* Matthias was murdered, and come back *after* Georgia was murdered? And he wasn't here at the time of either murder?"

"I'm afraid not. He left Fallingbrook during the week after Matthias went missing, but before his body was found, and returned about a week before Georgia was killed. Why are you trying to exonerate Randy? *You're* the one whose fingerprints were found at the scene."

"I didn't murder anyone. I don't need to be exonerated."

"Innocent people are sometimes convicted."

"I have an ironclad alibi for Matthias's murder. I was working that afternoon when he was in his store. I didn't take long breaks, and I was the one who answered the call from Georgia after he closed his store for the evening and didn't show up at that preseason meeting for potential hockey players and their parents. If no one else remembers that, 911 should have records." *Should.* I wondered how long they kept recordings and logs of calls and, if they still had them, if they could retrieve them.

Misty hooked her thumbs in her belt. "Okay, I'll play devil's advocate. Where were you Monday morning?"

"Here, from six thirty on."

"What about before?"

"Before Dep and I walked over here? Home alone."

"Did anyone see you or talk to you at home or on the way over here?"

"No. Well, maybe someone saw us walking here between six twenty and six thirty, but I wouldn't know who."

"See?" She looked kind, but also concerned. I would be, also, if she or Samantha were possibly in trouble.

"Not really. Can you think of a good reason for me to do away with one of my best customers? Or a motive for Randy?"

"No, other than Randy was known for his violent temper way back when. Remember?"

"Yes. He seems very nice now."

"Huh. '*Seems.*'" She glanced at our menu board. "I see you're featuring a medium roast from India today. Can I have a large to take out?" She pointed at the top shelf of our display case. "And two of those fudge donuts with fudge drizzle. I need chocolate to cheer me up. Know why?"

"Dep scared you by puffing herself up?"

"No. Guess which detective from the DCI has been parachuted in over Brent's head."

I nearly dropped an entire tray of donuts. "Uh-oh. Yvonne Passenmath?" Misty and I had been appalled a couple of years before when the DCI hired Yvonne Passenmath as a special agent. It was a relief that the woman was no longer on the Fallingbrook police force, but in our opinion, she wasn't clever enough to be a detective, especially on an elite team.

"'Fraid so."

"And she probably still hates both Tom and me."

"It wasn't your fault that Alec chose to date you instead of an unpleasant policewoman five years his senior. And her charges about Tom being biased and unfair when he promoted Brent and Alec instead of her were unfounded. Her police work was about as sloppy as her uniform always was. Brent and Alec *deserved* the promotion."

"And if I hadn't gone along with Lois and the Knitpickers

on Monday, and if I hadn't tampered with the scene, Brent would probably still be the lead on the case."

"Maybe." Glancing toward Tom in the kitchen behind the half wall, she leaned toward me and lowered her voice. "Our new chief must have political aspirations. I suspect that he doesn't want to fail at solving this. He's spinning his decision to bring in the DCI to make it look like he's doing the only thing that a conscientious police chief can do. And then, if agents from the DCI don't catch the murderer, no one can blame him. Very convenient." It was the first time I'd ever heard her criticize her boss. But then, until Tom retired, Tom had been her boss, and everyone, police officers and citizens alike, had loved Tom and found him to be fair. Everybody, that is, besides Yvonne Passenmath.

"Someone had better catch the murderer, if they're suspecting me!" I said it in a joking tone. No one could possibly suspect me of murder.

Right. My fingerprints alone weren't enough, but Yvonne Passenmath would probably love making my life difficult as punishment for "stealing" Alec from her. Alec had not been the least bit interested in Yvonne. And anyone would agree that no reasonable person could accuse Tom or me of the murder merely because our donuts and box were at the scene.

Misty was watching my face as if figuring out what I was thinking. "The police will catch the murderer, even if Brent and I and a few of our friends have to give Yvonne answers that she'll happily take credit for." Misty lowered her eyebrows into an exaggerated frown. "By 'our friends' I mean our friends in the police department. That fuzzy donut on your hat does *not* entitle you to investigate murders."

I tried to keep a straight face but ended up laughing. "Don't worry. I'm already in enough trouble for interfering with the scene. I'll stay away."

But later, when Lois came into Deputy Donut with the Knitpickers, I noticed that she looked drawn and worried. There had to be something that the two of us could do to prove that neither Randy nor I was a murderer, something entirely safe, like look at old photos. But we'd already done that.

Deputy Donut quickly filled up. Was it my imagination, or were some of the police officers paying me more attention than usual? I dashed around, bringing them coffee, donuts, and gooey, delicious cinnamon rolls. The officers were all friendly, as if they were going out of their way to show that I had their support. Some of them left larger than usual tips. A cynical person might suspect they were trying to be buddy-buddy so that I would confide in them, like confess to a murder. But I had nothing to confess, and I wasn't cynical.

I picked up a fresh carafe of our house blend and was about to go around the tables refilling coffee mugs when a skinny woman opened the front door just enough to slip into the shop. She took one look at the police officers at a nearby table and edged backward, as if she'd changed her mind about coming inside. Then she apparently spotted me behind the counter and stared for a second. Straightening her back slightly, although her shoulders were still rolled forward as if she planned to duck out of sight at any moment, she walked toward me. I'd seen that gait recently. She seemed to let only the outer edges of the soles of her ballet slippers touch the floor. She also appeared to be doing some deep breathing, as if she needed extra oxygen to give herself courage to approach me. She wrapped her arms around her middle. Even though she was wearing a baggy turquoise T-shirt instead of a neatly fitted shell pink wraparound top over her black yoga pants, I recognized her.

The evening we'd found Georgia's body, this woman had come across the street and asked us if anything had happened to Georgia.

Chapter 16

✿

Wraith-like, as if she wished she could be invisible, Georgia's neighbor slipped between tables and chairs to the counter. She bent toward me and murmured, "I need to tell you something about Monday morning."

I wanted to signal some of the police officers to come listen to what she had to say, but I'd seen her avoid them. I set the carafe on the marble counter. "Okay."

She whispered, "When I got up that morning, there was another car in you-know-who's driveway, sort of like hers— small, old, and the color was sort of grayish, at least by streetlight. It was very early, and I wasn't quite awake." She glanced over her shoulder, turned back to me, and whispered, "I wondered if you-know-who had a boyfriend stay over. Or maybe a doctor was making a house call. And then when I finished my morning workout, I happened to look out again, and the car was gone."

"What time was this?"

"My alarm went off at five, so it was a little after, and then he was gone by about five forty-five. The sky was just beginning to get light."

"He?"

She tightened her arms around the baggy T-shirt. "I meant the car was gone."

"Did you see the driver? Know for sure that it was a man?"

"I might have seen a shadowy form near her trash can when I first looked out, but I wasn't sure."

"Where was the trash can?"

"Beside the garage."

Lois and I had checked the other side of the house. I wondered if any of the Knitpickers had looked into the trash can. Probably not, if the lid was on. I'd reminded everyone not to touch anything. By now, investigators would have sifted through everything in and around Georgia's house. I asked, "Man, or woman?"

"I wasn't sure if I saw a person, so I don't know." Was she shivering from cold or from something else? The coffee shop was nice and warm.

"Did you tell the police officer, the tall blond woman, about the car and the shadowy figure?"

"I didn't think it was important, and besides, it slipped my mind."

Alec had taught me that multiple excuses could be a sign that the person giving them was not being entirely honest.

I must have succeeded in keeping my skepticism from showing. She confided, "And then, last night, I told my husband about you-know-who's death, and he said that when he backed out of our garage early Monday morning, he saw that extra car tear out of you-know-who's driveway and race down the road. He said it was being driven too fast. He stayed back, and wasn't following the car on purpose. Then, way ahead, he thought he saw it turn into the parking lot of the mall where his office is." She smiled proudly and upgraded her voice to a murmur. "He's a dentist." She went back to a conspiratorial whisper, "And when he went to park in his usual spot, the car that had been in you-know-who's driveway was in my husband's spot, and my husband had to park in the next one."

"Was he certain it was the same car?"

"Pretty sure. There weren't a lot of cars on the road at that time of morning."

My pulse sped. If it was the same car and if she was telling the truth, her information could help catch a murderer. "Did he notice the license number?"

"No."

"Did he see anyone in or around the car?"

"No."

"Which mall?"

"I don't think it has a name. It's the one that's about a mile south of our place, down on Packers Road."

"And your husband's usual spot is near his office?" At a mall, there was a good possibility that there were surveillance cameras, and some of them might be aimed toward her husband's office. Even if there were several dental offices, her information could help narrow down the search.

She shook her head. "He doesn't park in front of his office. He parks in front of the post office because it has a surveillance camera. He figures his car is safer there."

Even better. I tried not to look excited. "Did you or your husband tell the police?"

She glanced up at my patently fake police hat. "No. I'm telling *you*."

"They'd rather hear it from you. And your husband."

She hunched her shoulders forward again. "He's at work now, but we can tell the police about it tonight." *Would they?* "Anyway, since then, no one has parked in my husband's regular spot. That car was there only that one morning."

I double-checked. "Which morning?"

"Monday. I always add a new yoga pose to my routine on Mondays, and that was the day I did that."

"Did your husband notice the color or model of the car?"

"Gray or silver, he said, a small older car, you know, one of those nondescript ones. It wasn't dawn yet, and he didn't pay a lot of attention. The car's driver was gone."

"And it wasn't Georgia Treetor's car, but another one?"

"I told you. An extra car was in her driveway. The extra one went away. Hers stayed."

Was she telling the truth? I put on what I hoped would pass as an admiring smile. "Your husband puts in long hours."

"A patient woke us up that morning, calling in horrible pain. My husband never lets them suffer long if he can help it." She had clear, pale skin, sort of like mine, the kind that betrayed even the slightest blush, but I didn't understand why thinking about her husband's admirable work ethic and dedication to his patients would have turned her face red.

Did she or her husband murder Georgia and then concoct a convenient story about a gray or silver car? Or was the dentist a murderer and she was doing her best to protect him? It wasn't working—she'd caused me to suspect both of them. I thought of pretending I needed a new, caring dentist, and asking the dentist's name, but I was sure I could find out who he was. I knew where she lived, and if she'd been truthful, I knew approximately where her husband's office was. If he really was a dentist. How many dental offices could be in one mall?

Her story wasn't consistent. First, she said she'd seen the extra car after her alarm went off, and later in the conversation, she said that a patient had awakened her and her husband. Both things could have happened, I supposed.

I asked, "Would you like a donut?"

She hesitated.

"It's on the house."

"No, thanks. My husband's a *dentist*. We don't eat sugar." With that peculiar gait that seemed to make her knees bow as if she were a patron of Randy's dude ranch, she left. She passed the outdoor patios flanking our front door, and then turned right, but she didn't walk up our driveway. If she had come into town in a car, I didn't see it.

A couple of police officers left immediately after she did, but they only glanced to the right, and then they turned left, toward the police station.

I topped off coffee, served donuts, cappuccinos, and lattes, and stopped at tables to chat. As soon as I could take a break, I ducked into the office and sat at the desk. Dep jumped into my lap and purred. I phoned the police station and asked for Brent. He wasn't in. I left the number for my cell phone, which I kept in my apron pocket, and also the number for the Deputy Donut landline.

By noon, when the Knitpickers packed up their knitting, Brent hadn't phoned.

I could learn more about the so-called dentist without interfering with the investigation, and then I could give Brent more details. . . .

Helping the Knitpickers with the door, I gestured to Lois to wait. The others started down the sidewalk between our outdoor eating areas. I whispered to Lois, "Can you pick me up here at four thirty this afternoon? I have an idea."

"An adventure?" But those pale blue eyes were wary.

"Definitely. We're going to visit a dentist."

Shaking her head, Lois covered her mouth, but not before I saw her quick grin. Her reluctance was obviously fake. I added, "We'll have to drive there. If the dentist closes at five, I won't have time to go home for my car, first."

She patted my arm. "I'll be here with the van at four twenty-five." Nothing beat having a friend who not only wouldn't scold me for a little harmless snooping but who was also eager to participate.

Scott and Oliver again met for their afternoon coffee break, and gave me smiles that would have made my heart turn cartwheels when I was fourteen. As usual, except for the briefcase he was carrying, Oliver looked like he'd come from a golf course. He was in a white polo shirt and khakis. Scott was wearing the dark blue chinos and shirt he wore in the fire station. Oliver ordered a medium-sized mug of our Indian coffee and one unglazed unraised donut. Scott ordered a large house blend coffee and two grape jelly-filled donuts.

Oliver asked, "How can you eat all that stuff?"

Scott quipped, "One thing a fireman knows how to do is burn things. Including calories."

I laughed.

Oliver opened his briefcase and handed me a flyer. "The Chamber of Commerce is sponsoring a presentation about fire safety. Scott's giving it." Scott blushed, but Oliver went on. "We're trying to get all the business owners in Fallingbrook to attend. Citizens, too. It's tomorrow night. Sorry for the short notice."

Scott cleared his throat. "Emily and Tom designed this place with fire safety in mind. They're probably the last people who need to attend the presentation."

Scott was right about our planning. Tom had made certain that we followed every fire safety recommendation, and then some. He had also insisted on installing hidden video cameras aimed toward our front and back doors and another one pointed at the counter near our cash drawer. If we opened the drawer and reached all the way back, we could push a button that sent a distress signal to 911. The police, emergency medical, and fire departments were only blocks away. Deputy Donut was probably the safest shop in all of northern Wisconsin. I smiled at Scott. "Tom and I are always happy to learn new things." Scott blushed again. I offered to set a pile of flyers on the counter near the cash drawer where patrons would see them.

Oliver accepted. "It's at the high school gym. How about if I pick you up here at six thirty tomorrow evening, Emily?"

I forced butterflies down. It was almost like a date—with my high school crush. I could hardly wait to tell Misty and Samantha. Except in my heart of hearts, I knew I wasn't really interested in Oliver, or in anyone. And I wished he had asked one of my friends, instead. On the other hand, he was giving me an opportunity to introduce them to him. Now all I had to do was convince them to attend the presentation, also. Unless they had to work, they would, if only to tease me about going to it with Oliver. Trying not to blush, I smiled at both him and Scott. "That would be great."

"Glad you can make it, Emily," Scott said in an uncharacteristically dry and unenthusiastic way.

I set some of the brochures on the counter where people would see them when they paid their bills.

Brent didn't return my call, and he didn't show up in Deputy Donut, either.

Randy Unterlaw did, again in a dress shirt, light blue this time, worn untucked over jeans that fit him perfectly. I was sliding a tray of fresh donuts into the display counter. He came straight to me.

Chapter 17

❦

I asked Randy what he'd like.

"What's new?"

"Tom made cranberry-orange-walnut fritters. We have one left. And the chocolate donuts with orange icing are going quickly, too."

"They both sound good. Give me one of each. And a coffee."

"Drip?"

He grinned. He really was handsome. "Who're you calling a drip? Can I have a latte instead?"

I grinned back. "Sure."

"Do you deliver?"

It wasn't the first time that a male customer had asked a question that could be taken more than one way. I gave my stock answer. "I'll bring them to your table."

"No, I mean, does Deputy Donut deliver outside the shop? Like down the street or across town?"

"Coffee is really best served fresh."

"If you didn't have to go far to make the deliveries, would it be fresh enough?"

"Almost, but why wouldn't people come here?"

He flashed that delectable grin. One of his front teeth was chipped, which didn't make him any less adorable, even though I thought I remembered how he'd chipped it—tumbling down the concrete steps in front of Fallingbrook High. After that, very few fights started at the top of the steps. " 'Cause I have this really cool idea. Did you see the article about Deputy Donut in today's *Fallingbrook News?*"

"No, but a reporter came here and interviewed us a couple of weeks ago."

"It said you started out taking donuts to kids' birthday parties." He tilted his head in a cute way, like he was unsure of himself or his facts. "Did you make cakes out of stacked-up donuts and things like that?"

"Yes, then we started the shop, and now people come here and pick up their cakes made of donuts."

Looking beyond me, Randy pulled his left shirt sleeve down, but I could still see the tattooed *D* and the period after it on his wrist. "What if you delivered in a cop car?"

Tom spoke from behind my shoulder. In his quiet sneakers, he had crept up behind me. "I don't think the police department would approve." I was surprised, given that we were speaking to Randy Unterlaw, that I heard a smile in Tom's voice. Maybe Tom was starting to notice that Randy had grown up and was no longer the hot-tempered boy from twenty years ago.

Randy put on a very respectful face. "No, Chief Westhill, here's my idea. You buy an old police car, or just a vintage car, and paint it to look like a cruiser, but with 'DEPUTY DONUT' on the side. And maybe a donut on top instead of a flashing light?"

I couldn't help a big smile. "I love it! I love old cars."

Tom complained, "Emily would want to be our delivery person so she could drive the antique car, and then I'd be stuck running around in here like she does." He was only pretending to disapprove. I could tell that he liked the idea.

"I might let you drive it sometimes, Tom." I managed to say it with a completely straight face.

Randy paid for his coffee and donuts and sat at Scott and Oliver's table.

Brent didn't return my call. Maybe Yvonne Passenmath had sent him out into the countryside where phone reception was spotty or nonexistent. I found a moment in the kitchen to tell Tom that Yvonne Passenmath was now investigating Georgia's murder. His comment could not be repeated in polite company. I teased, "Does it make you want to leap in and investigate on the sly?"

"No." Even wearing that silly hat with the fuzzy donut on it, Tom could be fierce and intimidating. "It certainly does not. Civilians do not *do* that."

"It's all my fault! I should have known better than to touch anything in a possible crime scene. And now Brent, just because he was Alec's partner, has to pay for my actions."

"Have a donut," Tom said. "I need one, too." He shook his head. "Yvonne Passenmath! How is she going to solve a murder? She never came close to passing the exams for detective while she was on the Fallingbrook PD. Alec and Brent aced them."

"I need to leave at four thirty, but I'll be back about an hour later for Dep, and will tidy up then, so leave it all for me."

"Okay." He turned toward a vat of hot oil. "Passenmath, of all people," he grumbled.

Fortunately, he must have been too distracted to ask why I had to leave early. Even though the reconnaissance mission I'd planned was going to be perfectly safe and innocent, and there was no way that anyone could think we were interfering in a murder investigation, Tom might try to stop Lois and me from going on it.

At four thirty, I locked the door behind the last customer, took off my apron and hat, and closed myself inside the office.

Brent hadn't phoned our landline, either. Lois's van was already in the parking lot.

"Mew!" Apparently, Dep expected me to clip on her halter

and leash and take her with me. I picked her up and kissed the top of her warm, furry head. "I'll be back for you in about an hour."

I set her down. Keeping her at bay, I eased out the back door and locked it. Then I ran to Lois's van and hopped in.

She started it. "Where are we going?"

"Actually, I hope you'll know."

Lois revved the engine. "Well, I don't. A dentist, you said, but you didn't say who or where." With luck, Tom wouldn't come out to investigate her race-car noises.

"I mean, I hope you'll know of a mall about a mile south of Georgia's place. Supposedly, there's a dentist there, and a post office, and I don't know what else."

"Why are you so excited about seeing a *dentist?*"

"Did you notice that the woman who lives across the street from Georgia's house came into Deputy Donut this morning?"

She steered down the driveway. "Yes, I did." She turned right, on a route that would eventually take us toward Georgia's neighborhood, several miles south of downtown.

I told her what the woman had said about an unfamiliar, small gray car starting out in Georgia's driveway early Monday morning and parking in the mall where the woman's husband had his dental office.

"And she said there's a post office there, too?" Lois asked. "We should *definitely* check that out. That's probably where Georgia usually took her packages. Georgia told me that the lady at the post office thought it was strange that a tiny person like Georgia borrowed a '*great big*' minivan, and then thought it was even stranger when Georgia told her that the artist she borrowed it from was just as small as she was, and just as old. As if! I mean, hadn't that postmistress ever heard of power steering and power brakes?"

"Do you know that postmistress?"

"Never met her. I never went to that post office. But anyone who knew about our trading vehicles could be responsible for the attack on me. And maybe for Georgia's death, too. And Matthias's. Ah, what am I thinking?" She sounded disgusted with herself. "It would have been over five years ago that Georgia told a postmistress about us trading vehicles. Post office employees could have changed a dozen times or more by now." She pressed harder on the gas pedal. "But it won't hurt to see what we can find out."

I patted the small backpack on my lap. "I always have a notebook and pen with me in case I think of new flavors for donuts. I'll watch for small silver or gray sedans like Georgia's neighbor described and take down their license numbers."

"And then we'll . . . do what? Turn the numbers over to your detective?"

"He's not *my* detective. Besides, he's no longer the lead detective looking into Georgia's death." I described my conversation with Misty.

"He was demoted because of you. In my book, that makes him *your* detective."

"I don't think much of your book." I logged on to my phone and searched for post offices. "Okay, I found all three of Fallingbrook's post offices. There's the one downtown that I've gone to all my life except when I was away at college, another one in the east end where the new subdivisions are, and there's also one on Packers Road, about a mile south of where Georgia lived." Casually, I asked, "Does Randy still drive that black car with the white fender? Or did he have it repainted while he was out west?"

"I don't know what happened to that one. He came back with a small gray car. And you're *not* to think it's the one that the dentist's wife told you about."

"*If* she was telling the truth."

"Right. Besides, there are oodles of cars like that. See?" She pointed at cars coming toward us. "There are three in a row, and at least one behind us."

Lois had a surprisingly heavy foot. She turned onto Packers Road. It broadened into four lanes bordered by car dealers, furniture stores, and chain restaurants. After several stoplights, my phone directed us into the parking lot of an L-shaped mall housing a podiatrist, a drugstore, a real estate agent, the post office, a pizza place, a dry cleaner, and a health food store. And a dentist, Dr. Jierson, whose name was printed across a giant three-dimensional molar hanging over his office's front door.

Lois grimaced. "I hope that thing's fastened securely."

A big, shiny black car with the license plate TOOTHY was parked in front of the post office. Although we saw seven grayish and silverish sedans in the parking lot, none were near the post office or next to TOOTHY. I jotted down the license numbers of all of them.

"Now what?" Lois asked.

"It's almost five. Guessing that the post office closes before the dentist does, I think I need stamps before I need dental work."

She stared at me for a second. "Oh, I get it. You're joking. If things get dull, I might need stamps, too. But no thanks to dental work. Or to walking underneath that sign."

She parked in front of the health food store, at the far end of the mall from the dental office and out of sight of the post office, and then we walked. The video camera high above the post office door was so obvious that I couldn't help wondering if it was real. Maybe the non-sugar-eating Dr. Jierson was fooling himself about the security of his parking space.

Inside, the post office appeared to be newly renovated in neutral, easy-to-clean surfaces. Luckily, the ceiling was acoustical tiles, or our footsteps on the speckled brown tile floor would have been deafening. We were the only customers, and no one was behind the one and only sales window. I followed Lois to the window and stood behind her right shoulder.

Nobody came. Lois pushed a button on a bell attached to the desk. I didn't know if anyone else heard it, but we certainly did. Lois jumped.

A woman in a back room hollered, "Coming!"

Wiping a hand across her mouth, Honey Bellaire, aka Bridezilla, aka the woman who had complained to me about Georgia Treetor, came to the sales window.

Chapter 18

Honey's eyelids drooped as if she had no interest in post office customers. Her gunmetal blue skirt was rumpled and her white blouse was several sizes too big. She had a spot of mustard on one cheek. Wincing, she shifted from foot to foot. "I've been standing all day, and these are not the most comfortable shoes. I was just sitting down, taking a load off and having an early dinner. I work Thursday nights at the movie theater, with no time to eat between." Her wiry blond hair stuck out in odd ways.

"Sorry—" I began.

She waved a hand past her face. "I'm so used to it that I've gotten to expect it. What can I do for you? I'm about to close."

"Stamps, please," I said. "Five for first-class letters."

She reached toward something beneath the counter, and then stopped moving, her hand in midair. "Hey!" she said. "You're the woman from the donut shop, aren't you?"

"Yes."

"You like working there?"

"Love it."

"Get lots of free donuts?"

I handed her a ten. "My partner and I try not to eat all of our profits."

"You and your partner work for yourselves? Lucky you."
She counted my change and handed me the stamps. "I bet
you don't have to put in long hours, like I do."

"Ouch, you poor thing. How long?"

"I'm often here by six thirty, sorting mail. Some days, like
when I went to your donut shop, I'm done at noon, and some
days, like today, I work until five." She turned and looked at
the clock on the beige wall behind her. "Eight more minutes."

Trying to look innocent, I suggested, "At least starting that
early, you don't have to worry about a parking spot."

Honey pointed to her left. "When they built that new leg
of the mall, they didn't add more parking. I know for a fact
that there used to be parking where they built that section.
Before that, we had plenty for our customers." She gestured
toward the back wall. "We've got our own spots behind,
near the loading dock, or I might have to quit working here."
She seemed to examine our faces for sympathy, so I tried to
show some. It must have been enough. She added, "The businesses in that new section don't have parking behind. It's a
crying shame. Most of the people who work in those shops
and offices are okay with it, but that dentist, the guy that
owns that big black car out there, he gets bent out of shape if
he can't have the spot he's parked in right now, which isn't
that close to his office, anyway. Can you imagine?"

I nodded in what I hoped was an appearance of solidarity.
"Does that happen often?"

Lois turned around and gave me a startled look, possibly
because my voice warbled between deep throatiness and a
squeak.

"Not *usually,* but he stormed in here Monday morning as
soon as I unlocked the front door at nine. He claimed he had
come to work early, like *six* if you can believe it, and he
couldn't park in his favorite spot because a car was already in
it! What does he expect at six in the morning? People from

those new apartment buildings around the corner sometimes park in our lot all night, and the police can't seem to do a thing about it. But by the time that dentist was asking me, the car he was complaining about was long gone, so I have no idea what the big fuss was about. He wanted to know if I knew the other car's driver." Her voice became shrill, which made me miss her raspier tones. "Why does he have to have a favorite spot, let alone a spot in front of *us* instead of in front of his own office? The lot wasn't anywhere near full. Then he wanted the car's license number. How would I know that? That dentist didn't bother memorizing it. Why should I?" She stared off into the distance for a second and then leaned forward and confided, "But I think I *did* talk to the driver. Don't tell that dentist."

Lois and I shook our heads, which could mean nearly anything. I asked, "Did the driver explain why he parked in the dentist's spot?"

Honey scowled. "I'm not sure he did park there, but there weren't many other people around at that hour, so maybe he did. Anyway, he didn't need to explain. It's not like the spots are reserved. But you ask me, that guy was almost as *out there* as that dentist." She twirled a finger near her ear. "He pounded on the door just after I got here. It wasn't even six thirty yet. I finally went and opened the door just a crack, and told him we were still closed. He said he just had a simple question. But you ask me, the question was just plain weird. He wanted to know if I knew anyone who would lend him a minivan."

Lois went still.

I stopped breathing.

Lois recovered first. "That *is* a strange question." She sounded like someone was strangling her.

"Thing is, I knew the answer, sort of. You know that doll doctor who died, the mother of that grocer?" She stared hard at me. "I was talking about her when I was in your donut shop." She'd had nothing good to say about Georgia then. I wanted to get out my phone and record her, but that would have been a super-efficient way to make her stop talking.

I nodded.

Honey leaned forward and put her elbows on the counter. "A few years ago, that doll doctor had a friend with a van, and sometimes they traded when the doll doctor needed lots of cargo space, like she often picked up big boxes of supplies here, and she mailed oversized packages. I never understood why she didn't buy her own van. Figures that a selfish person like her would take advantage of her friends." Lois stiffened visibly, at least from the back, but she didn't say anything, and Honey went on. "She and her son took enough advantage of the rest of us. Surprising that she even had a friend." Honey straightened, fished keys from her pocket, and turned them in drawers and cabinet doors that were out of our sight underneath the counter. "Now, what was that friend's name? Something like 'Glow.' Gloria? Whatever, the friend moved away a few years ago, to Madison, I think, or was it Milwaukee? Anyway, that doll doctor was very excited because this woman was moving back to Fallingbrook. Chloris? Chloe? No, that wasn't it. Funny, I remembered her first name—I never knew her last name—early Monday morning when that man came to the door, but now the first name has slipped my mind. I told him I thought she might have moved back to town, but I didn't know if she'd go around lending her minivan to complete strangers." She pointed at her head and looped her finger in circles again. "I mean, *really!*"

I asked, "Did you know the man?"

"Of course not, or I'd have said, wouldn't I?" She glanced toward the front windows, and then returned her attention to us. "A handsome guy. No wedding ring. Dark hair and eyes. His Packers cap was pulled down low over his forehead, probably to hide his hair, but I could tell it was messy, like he'd just gotten out of bed, and he hadn't shaved for at least a day, either." She fanned herself. "A really hot guy, you know what I mean?"

Lois didn't answer.

I said, "Yes."

Honey stroked her left wrist. "He had a tattoo on his arm. It looked like someone had scratched it into his skin with a rusty nail or something."

Lois could have become a statue.

I asked, "What was it?"

Honey stared at her wrist. "I couldn't see much of it, but it looked like letters, maybe a word or a sentence, but homemade and not very neat. He kept pulling his sleeve down like he thought he could cover it, but that just made it more noticeable, especially since his other sleeve was rolled up almost to his elbow."

I asked, "What kind of shirt was it?"

Her eyes wide, Honey stared at me like she couldn't figure out what cave I'd crawled out of. "Long-sleeved. I just said."

"What color?"

"White, you know, like a man would wear with a suit, but he didn't have on a jacket, and he was in jeans. He looked real nice." She gazed past me again, as if searching for the man or his car in the parking lot.

From where she was standing, she shouldn't be able to see Lois's minivan near the health food store. I didn't think it would be a good idea for Honey to connect Lois to the minivan. Then again, maybe she already knew who Lois was because she had followed Lois into her backyard on Monday night and had clobbered her. . . .

I looked up at the very obvious video camera behind Honey. Imagining Detective Yvonne Passenmath studying me in a videotape, I quickly looked away. "Did the man come inside?"

"No, I told you, we weren't open. I answered his question and he went away. Too bad I couldn't think of something to say to keep him here, cute guy like that." She dusted her hands together. They were pudgy, with short fingers and no rings. "That's life, isn't it? A great guy comes along, and you get all tongue-tied until he leaves, and *then* you think of all the clever things you shoulda said."

"You didn't think he was too 'out there'?" Lois's voice sounded strained.

"Sometimes you just have to take the bad with the good. And the good was very, very good. Yum."

Honey's cologne was not as strong as it had been the day before in Deputy Donut. I asked her, "Did he smell good, too?"

"Yum, yes. Masculine, but subtle."

Subtle? Maybe it was all relative. I needed to know one more thing. "Did he get into the car that was parked in the dentist's spot?"

"No idea. I had to get back to work. Before I turned around, he headed off in that direction, and there weren't many cars out there at that hour, just the dentist's barge of a car and that small gray one. Y'know, if I could remember the name I told him, maybe I could find that woman who used to lend the doll doctor a minivan, and if he contacts her, she might help me hook up with him. Wait—I've nearly got it." She tapped her lips with an index finger. "No, I'm sure the doll doctor didn't say 'Grandma Moses,' but it was something like that. An artist, you know. I wonder if the doll doctor was already dead when that man showed up here, and he was an undercover cop. Yeah, that's probably it." She bobbed her head up and down. "He pounded hard on the door, like a cop would. And that would explain the weird questions, too."

Her guess had to be wrong. The police didn't know about Georgia's death until early Monday evening after Lois and I and the other Knitpickers found her. But I still suspected that Honey might have killed Georgia, and I wasn't going to blurt information that might help the crabby woman wriggle away from charges that the police might make against her. "You're sure you told the man the name of the artist who had a minivan?" I hoped she didn't notice that I was focusing on what might seem, to her, an odd detail.

"Just her first name, *if* I remembered her name right, and now I'm thinking that I probably didn't. I wonder if he'll ever come back. He was dreamy, and I love cops, don't you? Hunky and fit. And those uniforms! Mmmmmm."

Lois and I made unintelligible mumbles.

As if we'd agreed with her, Honey nodded. "I told him I thought the van was dark blue, but if it's still around, it would be kind of old, you know? I said the woman had probably traded it in on a newer one, but if she was still painting giant-sized pictures, she probably still had a van of one sort or another."

Shoulders back, head up, Lois headed toward the door.

Honey turned around and looked at the post office clock. It was about a minute until five.

"Thanks for the stamps," I said. Hurrying toward the door, I spotted another surveillance camera, aimed, it seemed, right at me. I quickly looked down at my feet, and when I left, pushing the door open with my rear end, I checked out the interior of the post office. At least three cameras had been pointed toward us when we were at Honey's window—the one above and behind Honey that I'd already noticed, and one on each side wall.

According to Honey, the tattooed man questioning her on Monday morning hadn't gone into the post office. However, if the inside cameras worked, they might have captured a recognizable image of him. And there was definitely a camera on the outside, above where the man had, if I understood correctly, stood while he was talking to Honey. It should have recorded him walking toward the door, and, a few minutes later, away from it. If it was true that the dentist tried to park his car in view of the camera, and if the camera was aimed the way the dentist believed it was, the camera should have recorded the arrival and departure of the small grayish car, too, and its driver. Now I really needed Brent to return my call.

I caught up with Lois.

She muttered between thinned lips, "I know what you're thinking. But that man could not have been Randy."

Chapter 19

✺

I patted Lois's arm. "Let's get away from the mall and its video cameras before we discuss who Honey was describing. Want to check out the dental office?"

"That TOOTHY car is gone."

"In case someone's there?"

"I suppose, but I don't want to walk underneath that sign."

The chains holding it creaked. Very reassuring. We edged around it.

The door to the dentist's office was locked, but a woman at the reception desk inside looked up, waved, opened the door, and smiled. Her teeth were, not surprisingly, perfect, and so was her straight, raven black hair. She looked too young to have a full-time job. "Dr. Jierson is gone for the day, but if you need an appointment, I'll be glad to make you one. If you're in pain, I can call Doc and he'll be back in, say, ten minutes. Fifteen, tops."

"It's not an emergency," I said. "I'm thinking of switching dentists. I had a toothache one weekend, and my dentist told me to go to Emergency. I waited for hours." I pressed a hand against my jaw. "It hurt."

Swishing her long hair back and forth, the woman shook her head. "Dr. Jierson would never do that to a patient. He comes in early, misses lunch, or stays late. And he'll come in on weekends, too."

Lois said with great sympathy, "I suppose you have to work extra hours when he does."

The woman lifted one shoulder. A tiny flush crept across her cheeks and the bridge of her nose. "I'm only the receptionist. I can't help with the difficult cases. I make certain everyone's comfortable, hand toys to kids, and things like that. People, especially kids, can get pretty worked up about visiting the dentist. Dr. Jierson wants everyone to see it as a pleasant experience. And most visits to the dentist are painless." She was very earnest. It was still hard to believe she was over sixteen.

"He sounds great." And I sounded phony. "Does he have a card?"

"Absolutely." She went to her desk and returned with two molar-shaped business cards. She displayed her perfect teeth in an apparently sincere smile. "Here you go." She handed each of us a card.

We thanked her and left. As we hurried past the post office, I kept my face averted from those cameras. I noticed that Lois did, too.

A sidewalk led away from the parking lot, toward the back of the row of stores. Lois and I looked at each other and then detoured down that sidewalk.

It ended near a pharmacy at a smaller parking lot behind the stores. Like a couple of spies, we peeked around the pharmacy's corner.

A small gray sedan pulled out of a parking spot next to the post office loading dock. The driver had wiry blond hair. Honey. We jerked our heads back.

"Did she see us?" Lois asked.

"I don't think so."

"Is she coming this way?"

"I hope not."

We speed-walked to the main lot, but Honey's car didn't appear, and we guessed she'd gone the other way, behind the new section where Dr. Jierson's office was. After we shut ourselves inside Lois's van, she snickered. "I think I know why Dr. Jierson works those long hours."

"You're bad," I told her. "He's married. To a yoga enthusiast."

"I'm sure *that* makes a difference." Staying far from the post office and its video cameras, she drove through the parking lot.

Without turning my head, I glanced at the post office and the parking spots in front of it. "I wonder if the gray car parked in the dentist's spot early Monday morning was actually Honey's."

Lois turned north on Packers Road. "Me, too. And if it came directly from Georgia's driveway."

"I suspected that Mrs. Jierson could have been lying about the car in Georgia's driveway, and about her husband following it here, but now we've heard from two different sources about a small gray car being in the mall parking lot early Monday morning."

Lois tapped the steering wheel. "That doesn't clear Dr. and Mrs. Jierson. Honey could have parked in TOOTHY's spot many mornings. Maybe she usually moved her car before TOOTHY arrived, but he came in early on Monday. He could have seen Honey's car in his spot, so he and his wife cooked up a story about a car in Georgia's driveway that morning as a cover-up for what one or both of them did to Georgia, and they described Honey's car."

"It's hard to imagine Mrs. Jierson getting the better of Georgia. She isn't much bigger than Georgia was."

"But she's a lot younger. And she might be fit, though she looks skinny, not muscular."

I agreed. "And Dr. Jierson must also be younger than Georgia, and most likely strong, with strong hands." But would he stuff something into a victim's mouth? He might be afraid to call attention to a mouth, in case people would be reminded of mouths, and then teeth, and then dentists, and then suspect him because he lived across the street from the victim. Did either or both of the Jiersons have a reason to murder Georgia? "Lois, could Dr. Jierson be Georgia's dentist?"

"He wasn't five years ago, but she might have switched. Your detective can find the answer to that question."

"He's not my—"

But she wasn't listening. Her voice hardened. "It can't have been Randy who asked Honey about borrowing minivans. You know why?"

"Because if he wanted to borrow a minivan, he would ask you."

"And besides, if he was the one who drove out of that valley the evening that Matthias disappeared, he would have recognized me, even though I was beside Georgia's car. He wouldn't have killed *Georgia* five years later." She wiped her eyes. "Whoever killed Georgia must have found out from her that she borrowed a minivan the day that Matthias was killed, and that the minivan's owner was using her car. But by the time she told him that, it was too late. He'd broken into her house and attacked her, and he couldn't leave her alive to contact the police. It's all so horrible. Who would do a thing like that?"

"Before our talk with Honey Bellaire, I suspected Fred Aggleton, the man who bought Matthias's grocery from Georgia after Matthias was killed."

Slowing, Lois gave a go-ahead gesture to the driver of a car exiting another mall. "Ugh, yes, he's been grousing for years that Georgia ripped him off. And he tried to buy the store when Matthias was alive. He tried for years! He wasn't offering anything near what it was worth, and Matthias always turned him down. Then, after Matthias died, Georgia had to keep lowering her price. She ended up selling it to Ag-

gleton for peanuts. And in the four years since Aggleton
bought it, he ran it into the ground. I was shocked when I
went in there recently."

"That's not the only thing that doesn't make sense," I said.
"Why would a murderer or anyone else go to a *post office* to
ask about borrowing a minivan?" I scooted as far forward
as my seat belt would let me. "Lois, you're going to like my
theory."

"I hope so."

"Suppose that *Honey* murdered Georgia, and then drove
to work and, not expecting Dr. Jierson that early, parked in
his favorite spot. But after Dr. Jierson complained about her
car, she realized that he might report seeing her car in Georgia's driveway."

"Aha!" Lois crowed. "Honey sorts the mail and could easily know that he lived near Georgia, and that he could have
seen her car at Georgia's."

"So, to protect herself, she concocted a story about a
strange car and a fictitious driver."

"Yes!" Lois banged so hard on the steering wheel that she
honked the horn. "But Honey knew Georgia. Why did she go
after Georgia instead of me?"

"You said that the car was going fast and stirring up a
cloud of dust, and the sun would have been in the driver's
eyes. Maybe Honey had time to recognize Georgia's car, but
didn't get a good look at you."

"And then, maybe after she broke into Georgia's, she told
Georgia that she'd seen her near where Matthias was buried.
And Georgia could have said that she'd never been to that
spot until after Matthias's body was found, and then, because Honey had sometimes seen Georgia with my van, she
figured out that *I* could have been the one who saw her fleeing from the crime." She took a deep breath and let it out
noisily. "What I don't understand is how she managed to describe Randy so well."

"That's the part of my theory that you'll really like. Honey could have driven around Fallingbrook looking for a car resembling hers, and she saw one near Deputy Donut, maybe even in our lot. So, she came inside, her first visit ever to Deputy Donut. Randy was there. I know she noticed him. She asked me if he was married. She undoubtedly memorized his looks and the way he pulls his shirt sleeve down as if he's trying to hide that tattoo. She left shortly after he did. She probably watched him drive away in his small gray car, and came up with a story about him parking in the dentist's spot. When we came into the post office, she could hardly wait to tell us her story and describe Randy. Rehearsing, probably, in case the police ask her."

Lois braked as the car ahead of us slowed. "But Honey knows you work at Deputy Donut. When she was going on about trying to hook up with him, why didn't she simply ask you to introduce her to him?"

"Good question." I squinted at the pickup truck and car ahead of us. Three vehicles waiting at a light on Packers Road qualified in Fallingbrook as a rush-hour traffic jam. "Maybe she didn't want to remind me that she'd seen him at Deputy Donut. She asked me about nearly every man in the place between the ages of twenty-five and forty. She probably hoped that I'd forgotten that she'd seen Randy. Then I wouldn't realize that she could have purposely memorized his appearance so she could describe him as the driver of the 'mystery' car, one that was actually hers."

I saw the tension ease out of Lois's hands. "You're right. I do like your theory."

Unfortunately, my theory didn't explain why the car leaving the burial site five years ago resembled Randy's, or the coincidence of Matthias's murder just before Randy left town and Georgia's right after Randy came back. I didn't say any of that to Lois, who was quite capable of thinking of—and worrying about—it herself. I left another message for Brent to call me. I put away my phone and said to Lois, "I wonder what kind of car Honey was driving five years ago."

"That would be good to know. She's big enough to overcome a smaller, older woman. When Matthias was killed, Honey wasn't as big as she is now, but she was probably more fit, and could have done some sort of surprise attack on him, and even buried his body."

"Supposedly, it wasn't much of a grave. Almost anyone could have scraped it out in a few minutes."

"I heard that, too." The light turned green and Lois drove across the intersection. "It's hard to believe Honey's dedicated enough to go to work at six thirty."

"Maybe she did it on purpose, for an alibi. She probably knew that Dr. Jierson would complain if anyone parked in his spot, and would remember that it was her car. They can't pinpoint the time of death to the exact minute. She could claim she was at work when Georgia was killed. And it was her bad luck that the Jiersons saw her car in Georgia's driveway. But then when Dr. Jierson didn't seem to realize that the car in his favorite spot was Honey's, she came up with a better idea than making certain that her car was noticed early at work. She went out looking for a car like it and found one."

Lois turned off Packers Road onto Wisconsin Street. We were almost in downtown Fallingbrook. "Choosing Randy as her scapegoat was a mistake. She doesn't know that Randy would not have asked about minivans, or that he would never have attacked and threatened me."

"Could Honey have been the person who attacked you Monday night? She's kind of, um, pillowy. If she pulled you back against her, wouldn't you have noticed? You said you didn't know if it was a man or a woman, but if it had been Honey, wouldn't you have known for sure? Besides, Honey wears a strong perfume, though from what I've seen, rather *smelled*, her fragrance wears off toward the end of the day."

"I was so scared that I didn't notice if the person was a beanpole or a walking mattress or if he or she smelled like flowers or turnips. He or she was taller than I am, but just about everyone is, and I don't think he or she did pull me close. I didn't notice much besides my neck being clamped in what I thought must be the crook of an elbow. I was too terrified. Do you think she recognized me just now as the person she attacked?"

"Don't ever go to that post office alone."

"I won't. And I won't go to the movies without at least three bodyguards, either."

"And keep your door locked with the dead bolt, and your phone with you at all times."

"I will." She drove into the lot behind Deputy Donut. We said our good-byes, and I went inside.

Tom had done all of the tidying and left a note that we didn't need to order supplies. I leashed Dep. We'd barely gone a block when a dust devil swirled leaves around in a mini-tornado on the sidewalk in front of us. Dep stopped and stared at it, and then at where it had been. I urged, "Come on, Dep. Look at the sky in the west." Ominous clouds churned, shades of charcoal that were almost purple, but edged in green. "You know you don't like to be out in the rain."

The first drops splatted as we sprinted to the shelter of our front porch. Distant thunder rumbled.

Inside, I released Dep from her halter. As if a dust devil were chasing her, she skittered sideways toward the kitchen.

I went upstairs. I'd been distracted the night before and had left my computer on. With an electrical storm brewing, I needed to power it off and unplug it.

In my guest bedroom and office, I sat at the desk and began shutting down web pages.

A picture I'd never seen before filled the screen.

About five years younger than he was now, Randy was pointing at his wrist and the tattoo on it: B.A.D. His smile was huge and warm, full of affection for the person taking the picture.

Behind Randy, a car was packed almost to the roof, with barely enough room left for the driver.

The car was black except for the fender near the front wheel on the driver's side.

It was white.

Chapter 20

✼

The man in the picture was definitely Randy. As far as I could tell, the car was identical to the one that had rushed out of the Fallingbrook River valley the evening that Matthias disappeared.

Lois must have found this picture on her drive last night while she was copying files. She must have heard Brent and me coming up the stairs, and had quickly loaded the photo we already knew about, the one in which the sunset reflecting on the car's windshield hid the driver.

Maybe Lois meant to close the photo file, but she'd only minimized it. If I had noticed the tiny icon indicating that another picture was open, ready to be enlarged for viewing, I would have dismissed it as one of the others that we'd examined. But this picture was dated three days later, and it wasn't one of the photos that I'd copied to my hard drive.

Lois must have known that the car in both pictures was the same car. She'd told me she wasn't sure after all these years, but comparing the two pictures must have convinced her.

I'd been wrong about her. She wasn't as sweet and honest as she'd appeared. Defeated, I slumped down in my chair.

She should have shown Brent this photo linking Randy to the getaway car.

She wanted to prove that Randy wasn't guilty of murder, but hiding a clue pointing to guilt wasn't the same as unearthing evidence to show that someone was innocent. On the other hand, maybe she had hoped that Brent would find the incriminating photo, and she wouldn't have to betray her great-nephew by being the one who showed the picture to the police.

I'd promised to try to help clear Randy's name. It was looking more and more difficult.

Brent had said he would take Lois's thumb drive to the police department. If the investigators were thorough, they would look carefully at all of the pictures on her drive, and I wouldn't have to tell them about this one.

Thunder boomed, close. I jumped. Afraid that a bolt of lightning might take out my computer and everything on it, I saved the telltale photo on my hard drive, and then powered off the computer and unplugged it.

A zigzag of white tore through the sky beyond the houses across the street. Thunder crashed and rolled. Rain poured down the window. Alec had tried to show me the beauty of extreme storms when viewed from the shelter of our sunroom, but I still found them scary.

I could almost hear him assuring me that I'd be fine if I stayed inside.

Alec.

He would also tell me that I shouldn't trust law enforcement to discover the photo I'd just saved. He would say I had to tell them about it.

What I really wanted to do was crawl into bed and burrow my head under pillows.

I didn't want to keep bothering Brent, but I had to tell him about the Jiersons and Honey, and now I also had to tell him about the picture of Randy smiling in front of his packed car only three days after Matthias went missing. Lois had told me that, several days after she saw the car driving out of the Fallingbrook River valley, she'd talked to the person she originally thought might have been the car's owner and had seen the car.

This time, Brent answered. He apologized for not returning my calls.

"No problem. I learned some things today that I thought you should know."

"I'll be right over."

"But it's pouring. And there's lightning."

"So?"

"Be careful." I was talking to a dial tone. "Be careful for *Alec's* sake. Lightning can kill." I put the phone down and went to the kitchen.

Dep twined herself around my ankles. "Meow."

"Sorry, no sardines. But I *am* hungry, and Brent might be, too. What are we going to feed him?"

"Mmp."

"No, we'd have to go to Lois's for sardines." And I wasn't sure I could look Lois in the eye. I followed Dep into the sunroom.

She jumped onto the windowsill and stared out at the rain. "Mmp."

"It'll stop, and then you can go pester Lois for a sardine."

The doorbell rang. His hair, jeans, and nylon jacket wet and his grin boyish, Brent balanced a water-splattered pizza box on a six-pack of beer. "On the chance that you haven't eaten, I gathered up a dinner of sorts before I called you," he said. "I'm off duty, finally." He'd found time since the evening before to shave. A powerful-looking black SUV was parked in the driveway behind my car.

"I haven't eaten, and the smell of that pizza is making me ravenous. Thank you." I gestured for him to come in, locked the door, and carefully lifted the pizza box out of his arms. Good thing I did. Mewing, Dep nearly tripped Brent as he walked through the living room.

"The sunroom's a good place to watch storms," I said. "Want to eat there?"

"Great."

In the kitchen, we set the beer and pizza on the counter.

Brent removed his wet jacket. His light blue oxford cloth shirt did not appear damp, and as far as I could see, he wasn't carrying a firearm. I hung his jacket in a drying closet that Alec and I had designed. Outside, it looked like a normal closet with pine doors. Inside, a heater, vents, and a fan maintained low humidity, and a tiled floor sloped to a drain. I turned on the heater.

Brent had brought my favorite beer, and he knew where to find the beer mugs. He poured a couple of beers while I got out plates, napkins, and a pie server. The pizza was from San Remo, the restaurant that made the best pizza ever. Inhaling the wonderful smells, I opened the box. Either Brent had remembered my favorite toppings, or he'd guessed right, or they were his favorites, too. In addition to heaping yummy cheeses on their pizzas, San Remo chopped their toppings into tiny pieces that caused the flavors to mingle in a delicious way. I saw morsels of tomatoes, black olives, mushrooms, onion, and bacon, and I smelled oregano and the yeasty crust. I slipped a large slice onto each of our plates. Brent carried the mugs to the sunroom. I brought the plates and napkins.

We sat together on the two-seater couch—I was *not* going to call it a love seat, and besides, there was plenty of space between us—where we could look out through three walls of windows at the torrent sluicing down the glass and puddling on the lawn outside. From her spot on the radiator cover, Dep made derogatory comments about the storm.

I bit into the pizza and couldn't help a moan of pleasure. I quickly covered it with a statement. "Misty told me they brought in the DCI and Yvonne Passenmath."

"That's why I can be off duty tonight. We were in meetings all day, and if anyone is going to work long into the night, it can be her."

"Constructive meetings?"

"Mmp. Bringing her up to speed."

"Which means you've just lost a day in the investigation."

"*I* didn't say that."

"You didn't have to."

"Mmp."

I had a new reason to help solve Georgia's murder. Yes, I wanted to prevent Randy from being unjustly accused if he truly was innocent, but now I also wanted to help Brent find the actual murderer. *We* would show the police chief and Yvonne Passenmath that Brent should have remained as lead investigator. Alec might even have approved of that reason for my poking my nose into a murder investigation. Although Alec had never divulged facts that he wasn't supposed to, he had discussed general theories and possibilities with me. He'd said I helped him work out problems. I'd replied that putting his theories into words was what had really helped him see the issues clearly, and then he had solved the cases himself. Or with the help of the man sitting beside me.

Brent asked, "Why'd you call me?"

"If I tell you, you'll be working."

"Tell me after we eat, then."

I gobbled two of those delicious slices, and Brent ate four. Outside, the rain let up and the thunder diminished. The last shreds of clouds drifted away. Beyond the shadow of my sloping roof, sun glittered on drops of water clinging to leaves and grass. Dep jumped down from her perch and stood beside the door leading to the backyard. "Me*ow!*"

I opened the door. She stalked to the patio. At its edge, she touched a blade of grass with one delicate forepaw. She lifted the paw and shook it. "Me*ow!*"

Brent said in a teasing voice, "Do you have a leaf blower? I could dry a pathway for her."

I attempted to sound serious. "No. We'd have to use a hair dryer."

"Let's not, then." He helped me put the dishes into the dishwasher. Reluctantly, it seemed, he opened his ever-present notebook. "Okay, what did you learn today?"

I told him about Georgia's neighbor coming into Deputy

Donut and describing the car that she and her husband claimed they saw, first in Georgia's driveway, and then at the mall where her husband had his dental office. "Maybe you've already interviewed them, and you know all of this already," I said. "Misty talked to Mrs. Jierson at Georgia's on Monday night."

"Mrs. Jierson didn't tell Misty more than her name and address. This is all new. Sorry, but I'd better call it in so Yvonne can send someone to interview these folks."

He left a terse message. I noticed that he didn't mention me as the source of the information, but Yvonne Passenmath would probably find that out, courtesy of Mrs. Jierson.

Chapter 21

I said, "There's more." I described Lois's and my trip to the mall and told him about our conversations with Honey and with Dr. Jierson's receptionist. I explained my theory that Honey could have murdered Georgia. "And then, because Dr. Jierson saw her car, she searched for one like hers, discovered Randy, and described him to us."

Brent looked skeptical.

I defended my theory. "Honey knew about Georgia and Lois trading vehicles, and that Lois was moving back to Fallingbrook. All Honey had to do was find out where Lois lived, wait until dark, break into Lois's, attack her, and rip those photos out of the albums."

"But what about the car that Lois thought was Randy's, leaving the scene of Matthias's burial? Are you saying that Honey Bellaire owned a car matching Randy's five years ago, also?"

"That does sound like too much of a coincidence. But Randy *might* have been there innocently, fishing or something."

"If so, there was no need for him or for anyone else to steal those photos. It's the theft of those photos that makes the driver of that particular car a person of interest."

"You're right." *And I have more to tell you about Randy and that car. . . .*

"You should have stayed out of it, Em, all of it."

"Mrs. Jierson volunteered the information. I said she should tell the police, but she acted like telling me was enough, and I guessed that she wasn't going to tell you what she told me."

"You were right, unless she left a message today while we were in meetings. Let us do the investigating, Em. Civilians snooping around can put themselves in danger. You can add to the risks for law enforcement, also." He said it gently, and I pictured Misty running into trouble because of something I did. Or Brent. Or other men and women on the force.

I admitted, "I learned more at the mall." I described Dr. Jierson's receptionist corroborating that the dentist worked long and unusual hours.

Brent wrote it all down. "And that's it?"

I said reluctantly, "I learned one more thing today."

"Thank you, but please tell me you'll stay out of the investigation from now on."

"I will." *Unless I have a good reason not to.* "I did stay away from suspects after we left that mall. The other thing I discovered was here, on my computer."

One of his eyebrows twitched up slightly, and then he went back to being poker-faced.

I explained, "I didn't turn it off last night after Lois copied those files onto a drive for herself. This evening, I discovered that Lois had been looking at another picture from a different folder on her thumb drive. The picture is time-stamped three days after she photographed the river valley. It shows Randy standing in front of a packed car. I'm almost certain that it's the car Lois photographed the evening that Matthias Treetor disappeared. The picture should be on the thumb drive Lois gave you last night."

"That's at work."

"I can show it to you." Dep was still outside. I opened the sunroom door and called her. My funny cat hadn't ventured off the patio. She condescended to join us inside, and then she plunked herself on the mat inside the door and licked her front paws as if she could not bear any raindrops that she might have collected while trying her hardest *not* to touch the grass.

Brent and I laughed and went upstairs. For once, we got there before Dep did. Seconds later, though, she was perched on the windowsill and staring out at the maple tree.

I loaded both of Lois's pictures of the black car with the white fender, and then gave Brent the chair while I stood behind him.

He studied both photos. "Do you mind if I e-mail the picture you found this evening to myself, to make certain that we have it at work?"

"Go ahead."

After he sent the picture, he stood and rested a hand on the monitor. "The techs will go over the photos—all of Lois's photos—more carefully, but to me, it looks like the same car in both pictures. Do you think a print of the second photo was stolen from Lois's album along with the ones from three days before?"

My guest room seemed too small for both of us to stand facing each other. I took a step back, away from him. "I think she said that all of the prints from images she took that day were missing from the albums. I don't know about pictures she took later, and I didn't look through the album beyond the pages that were missing pictures."

Dep jumped off the windowsill and sat at Brent's feet. He looked down at her. "Now that the investigators have her digital images from around that time, it might not matter. Could Lois have removed the photos from her albums herself, and hidden them?"

"Anything's possible. But I went back to check on her Monday evening. I didn't ring her doorbell because I could see her through the sheers in her living room window. She was looking at that album, and she seemed shocked by what she saw."

Staring up at Brent's face, Dep meowed. He bent and

scooped her into his arms. "Shocked by missing pictures, or by pictures that she later removed from the album?"

"Missing pictures, I'm guessing, or she never would have admitted to me that pictures were missing, and we wouldn't have known to ask for that thumb drive."

"Makes sense."

"Do you have surveillance videos from the mall south of town where the post office is? I saw three cameras inside the post office and one outside. You might have videos of that gray car and its driver. The driver could be Randy, as Honey described, or it could be Honey."

Dep squirmed. Brent put her down on my ivory and cobalt rug. "We should have videos. I'll go over them."

I started toward the doorway, but stopped and turned toward Brent. "The evidence against Randy—it's all circumstantial, isn't it?"

"You got it. Even if all you've told me tonight leads to him, it's not enough for a charge, but it might be enough for a search warrant for those stolen photos. He's probably tossed them by now. It won't be the first time I've searched through garbage."

Dep batted at my leg. I picked her up. "Lois told me that Randy thought of Matthias as a sort of big brother, and that Georgia was like another great-aunt to Randy. They were like family to him. He wouldn't have killed them."

"Mmp."

"I guess you're right," I conceded. "People do murder family members." Now I was interpreting his *mmps.* I wasn't sure we were helping the English language evolve in a useful way.

"Mmp."

Dep struggled. Putting her down, I asked, "Will you keep an open mind about possible cover-ups by Dr. Jierson and his wife, and by Honey Bellaire?"

He grinned down at me and tapped his head. "My mind is always wide open."

I leaned against the doorjamb. "And you won't rule out Fred Aggleton, the man who blames Georgia for the failure of the grocery store he bought from her? He says she ripped him off, yet Lois told me that he got that store for a very low price."

Brent tilted his head as if asking me a question, but he didn't say anything, not even *mmp*. Dep meowed up at Brent. He lifted her off the floor.

I asked Brent, "Didn't you know about that?"

"I did."

There was something expectant in his gaze, like he thought I knew something that I hadn't mentioned. I felt myself blush as if I truly had concealed evidence implicating Randy.

Wait. Alec had told me something in his oblique way, something about one of the suspects in Matthias's murder. I dredged it up from the depths of my memories from five years ago, memories that had, like everything else, been overwhelmed by Alec's death two years later. "Wasn't there someone besides Honey that you and Alec looked at in Matthias's death, but you didn't find sufficient evidence about him?" I asked. "Something to do with a Little League team coming in only second in the state? *Only* second! I remember Alec being disgusted by one father's attitude. The father blamed Matthias for the loss, insisted that Matthias took a pitcher out of that final game too soon, and if he hadn't, the Fallingbrook team could have gone on to the regional finals."

Brent continued to watch me, but I thought I caught a slight but encouraging nod. From the security of Brent's arms, Dep meowed at me. What did she want me to do, grab her away from Brent? At this rate, we were never going to make it out of my combination guest room and office.

I asked, "Didn't that father say something like Matthias should be taken out and shot?"

Dep meowed at me again. Brent smiled. " 'Relieved of his misery' was the wording I heard." Brent held Dep out toward me.

I grasped the warm kitty and cuddled her. "Right. Now I remember."

"Do you remember who that father was?"

Dep wriggled. I set her down again. "Alec didn't tell me. *Randy* doesn't have children, does he?"

"Not that I know of."

"Dr. Jierson?" I was having problems imagining Mrs. Jierson being motherly.

"Nope." Dep threatened to climb Brent as if he were a piece of her playground equipment. I was about to grab her, but he picked her up again.

I pushed myself away from the doorjamb. "The bridegroom who jilted Honey?"

"Nope."

Frederick Aggleton had mentioned having a kid. "Frederick Aggleton?"

"Mmp."

"So, Aggleton had been putting in lowball offers for Taste of Fallingbrook for years, offers that Matthias always rejected. For some reason, Aggleton thought he should own that store. Then Matthias had the gall to give another young pitcher a turn, and Aggleton had two grudges against Matthias. I remember Alec saying that the person you guys found with the strongest motive also had an alibi. Wasn't it something about a vacation?"

Scratching Dep between the ears, Brent paused, probably deciding how much he could tell a civilian. "His alibi wasn't watertight, but we had no actual evidence against him. It was like Honey Bellaire. Both she and Aggleton had griped about Matthias Treetor, and Bellaire even sued him, but there was no firm evidence tying either of them to the murder." Although Brent's attention was making Dep purr, she stared at me under half-closed eyelids and meowed.

I ignored her. "Now they're both complaining about Georgia Treetor, and she's been murdered."

Brent eased Dep to the floor. "That, too. I promise I won't rule anyone out, Em."

"Including me."

"Including you."

"Great."

He reached toward me as if to pat my shoulder, but seemed to think better of it.

Dep meowed at me, and all of a sudden, I remembered her acting this way when Alec was alive. The only way we'd been able to stop her ping-ponging between us was to hug each other with her in the middle.

Blushing, I ducked around Brent and hurried down the stairs. Brent followed. Dep got there first and strode purposely toward the back of the house. "Meow!"

I said, "Dep must be desperate for her sardines from Lois." Maybe Brent would think that's what Dep's attention-getting upstairs had been about. "You wanted to see Dep's secret passageway. Do you have time now?"

"Sure."

I started toward the dining room, then stopped and whirled to face Brent. "I just thought of something else. But you're probably already investigating it."

"What?"

"They say to follow the money. Georgia inherited from her son. Do you know who inherits from her?"

Brent's eyes held a hint of apology.

I asked, "You can't tell me, can you?"

He gave his head a slight shake.

"Maybe Lois knows."

"I would feel better about you hanging out with her if I was sure she can be trusted. You don't know her very well."

I folded my arms. "I feel like I do." *Too trusting*, I'd told Lois, *you're too trusting*. Did that apply to me, too?

Apparently, Brent thought so. "Monday night, she lied to you about how she got her injury, and last night, she easily could have told me about that possibly incriminating photo of her great-nephew with his packed car, but she didn't. I'm seeing a pattern. Be careful around her."

"She's at least forty years older than I am. I think I can take care of myself."

"I'm not saying she's dangerous, necessarily. I'm saying she might be dragging you down the wrong pathways in her attempts to prove that her great-nephew is not guilty of murder."

"I know, but I can't just . . ." I nearly said that I couldn't abandon a friend, but three years ago, I'd let the ties of my friendship with Brent unravel and fall apart. Brent was probably thinking the same thing. I covered it with a quick comment. "I mean, Lois's best friend was just killed, and she hardly knows anyone here, just Georgia's friends, Randy, and me."

"She was in Madison for less than five years. She must have other friends up here besides Georgia."

"I suppose."

"And like her great-nephew, Lois left Fallingbrook shortly after Matthias was murdered, and returned shortly before Matthias's mother was killed."

Lois, a murderer? I shook my head.

A demanding *Meow* came from the sunroom.

Brent grinned. "Let's go see Dep's secret passage."

The grass hadn't dried completely since Dep's first attempt to walk on it, but she picked her way across the yard. We followed.

Dep disappeared underneath shrubs. "It's right in front of her," I told Brent.

He looked slightly dismayed, but the next thing I knew, he was crawling on damp earth—I wasn't going to call it mud, exactly—underneath the forsythia. I stayed back. He was swallowed by dripping foliage. He made a few surprised exclamations, one of them about a drop of cold water on the back of his neck.

Beyond the wall, Lois crooned, "Have you come for your

sardine, Tiger?" I assumed that Lois was talking to Dep, not Brent.

But Brent was the one who answered. "No, I'm not," he said in an exaggeratedly deep voice.

Lois quavered, "Who's there?"

Before Brent could scare her even more, I called out, "Emily and Brent."

"Have you two eaten?"

"Yes," I said.

Brent didn't answer.

"Would you like dessert?" Lois asked. "I baked a cake."

"Yes!" Brent was still using a theatrically dangerous-sounding voice.

"Wait there. I'll give Tiger her sardine, and then I'll bring it over."

Apparently, Lois still did not want anyone seeing a detective visiting her.

Or, a voice said in my head, *she doesn't want a detective snooping around inside her house.* It was probably bad enough that he was crawling around on the other side of her wall.

Chapter 22

✣

Brent crawled backward out of the bushes next to my wall and stood up. Twigs and leaves were stuck in his hair and mud covered his jeans from the knees down. I did not point and laugh. I might have smirked, though.

With a rueful look, he showed me the palms of his hands. They were muddy, too. "Is your outdoor faucet where it used to be?"

"You can come inside for warm water and soap."

"Not yet, I can't." He lowered his voice to a murmur. "Please don't tell Lois about that picture you found today. I'd like to give her the chance to mention it."

"Okay." Maybe she hadn't tried to hide the photo from us. Maybe she'd forgotten it. Last night, she didn't remember until after dinner that she'd brought her original thumb drive with her.

I dragged the hose, spitting cold water, to Brent, and then went inside and brought him a handful of paper towels.

He'd hosed the mud off his jeans. They were drenched from the knees down. My smirk threatened to flare up.

He dried his hands. "I'll eat that cake out here."

"It's almost dark."

"I don't want to drip all over your house. I know how hard you and Alec worked refinishing those pine floors."

"A few drops won't matter, but . . ." I eyed his sopping

pant legs. "Try stretching out on one of the chaises. They're used to rain."

"They certainly are. They're also quite *wet*."

"If you're lucky, Dep will sit on you."

Blinking, Dep emerged from underneath the shrubbery.

Brent turned that boyish grin on me again. "Maybe I'll just stand here and drip."

"The chairs under the pergola are almost dry." Like the table they matched, my outdoor dining chairs were cast aluminum, painted gray, and too smooth for water to have collected on them.

I ran upstairs, grabbed a beach towel from the linen closet, and trotted back down. Expecting Lois, I opened the front door. She was trying to ring the bell while hanging on to a plate that was almost completely hidden by a fudge-covered layer cake.

"Is it your birthday?" I asked.

"It's nobody's. Well, it has to be somebody's, plenty of somebodies', but no one that I know. I just felt like making one. Where's Brent?"

"Outside. His pants are wet—"

"*What?*"

"He hosed himself off after examining Dep's tunnel."

Those blue eyes brimmed with laughter. "*That* explains it. Sort of."

"Bring the cake outside." I slung the towel around my neck and gathered cutlery, plates, napkins, and a candle. Outside, I gave Brent the towel, set the almost-dry patio table, and lit the candle.

The cake looked almost as fudgy as the icing. Lois cut it in generous slices. We sat down, and Brent wrapped the towel around his lower legs. "I hope no one wants me to jump up and chase a criminal," he deadpanned.

I gave him a fake serious look. "You'll be surprised how quickly I can whip that towel away."

"Ooh!" Lois said.

Ignoring her, I praised the cake.

Brent warned, "Lois, I'm going to ask a personal question. You don't have to answer it."

It wasn't a normal lead-in to asking for a recipe. Had he given up waiting for her to confess that she hadn't shown him that photo of Randy smiling beside his packed car?

Lois flicked a glance at me, and I could have sworn I saw amusement in it. Remembering our jokes about frilly undies hanging in her front window, I couldn't help smiling.

"Okay," she said.

"Do you have a will?" Brent asked.

The amusement died from her eyes. "Yes. You want to know who my beneficiary is, don't you?"

Brent shifted in his seat as if more than the wet jeans made him uncomfortable.

Lois put down her fork. "I might as well tell you, since you'll find out anyway, and it's who anyone would guess. Everything I own goes to Randy. But I'm not a wealthy woman."

Brent just stared at her.

She leaned back and folded her arms. "I'm *not*."

With both thumbs, Brent rubbed his temples. "Do you know what Randy's current financial situation is, Lois?"

"No. He used to live hand to mouth, but he might have put some money away working on that ranch out in Wyoming. He knows if he starts running low, he can borrow from me, interest-free." She glared at Brent.

I read sympathy in the way he leaned slightly toward her.

Slowly, she defrosted. "No," she whispered. "Don't tell me. Did Georgia will anything to me?"

Brent didn't answer. He glanced at me. I thought I saw a plea in his eyes.

I stood. "I'll give you two some privacy."

Lois put out a hand to stop me. "Don't go." Candlelight glittered on tears welling in her eyes.

I squeezed her shoulders and sat down again.

"I'm sorry, Lois," Brent said. "Georgia must have loved you very much."

"Best friends. Closer than some sisters. We were all each other had, that and our two boys, her son Matthias and my great-nephew Randy." Lois wiped her eyes. "Are you saying I'm in her will?"

"Very much so," he confirmed.

"But she wasn't wealthy, either. Both of us would have given Randy nearly anything. Randy wouldn't kill. Not for money. And if I didn't know that Georgia had named me in her will, how would he know?"

I thought, *if Randy was not Georgia's direct beneficiary, he could have signed as a witness to Georgia's will.*

Brent pushed his chair away from the table. The chair's metal feet screeched on the flagstones. He winced. "Sorry, Em." He turned back toward Lois. "I have another question for you, and again, you don't have to answer. I just need some background."

Lois pinched her lips together.

Brent apparently took it as assent. "When did Randy leave Fallingbrook for Wyoming?"

"Five years ago. I don't know the exact date, but it was about this time of year."

"Why did he go?"

"He had this offer to work at a ranch. He loves animals, especially horses."

"Did he have the offer before he left?"

"Yes. For him, it was a dream come true. But he almost didn't go."

Brent picked up his fork and seemed to study it. "Why not?"

"He didn't think he should leave me."

I sat on my hands, which was probably an odd way of preventing myself from leaping into the conversation, but it worked.

Brent turned the fork and examined its back. "Didn't you go away about then, too, Lois?"

"Yes. The art department at the University of Wisconsin offered me a teaching position in Madison. I hated to leave Georgia, but she knew I'd always wanted to share my love of painting with others. I thought there might be better job opportunities for Randy in Madison. He was at a disadvantage here where so many people remembered the trouble he'd gotten into as a boy. They wouldn't know what a hard worker and considerate person he is. But when I asked him if he wanted to come with me to Madison, you should have seen the relief on his face when I told him I wouldn't *need* him there. He'd already been offered the job at the ranch, so it turned out well." Her voice became quieter. "It turned out for Randy and me, but I should have asked Georgia to come with me. She'd probably still be alive if I had."

Brent said quietly, "We can't know things like that, so there's no point in torturing ourselves by second-guessing."

"Except we can't help it," I muttered.

"True," Lois said.

"Mmp." Brent asked Lois, "Was Randy living with you before you both left Fallingbrook?"

She ducked her head. "No. I'd told him he could stay with me after he graduated from Fallingbrook High, as long as he didn't drink and didn't get into fights, but he did both. I kicked him out." She raised her head. "Tough love, you know. I should have done it sooner. He stayed out of trouble from that day to this." She glowered at me. "He has. I'm sure of it. He got his act together, and he didn't have to come back and live with me. He was managing on his own."

I nodded toward my kitchen, bright and welcoming beyond the darkened sunroom. "He told me he was renting this house when Alec and I bought it seven years ago."

"It was *this* one?" Lois asked. "I didn't remember what street it was on. Though I think in those days, he had a roommate or two to help pay the bills."

"They kept it neat and clean." I threw Brent a glance. *I know that doesn't prove he's not a murderer, Mr. Super-Detective Brent Fyne.* A niggling voice in my head reminded me that Randy had implied he'd been renting this cottage by himself, but according to Lois, he'd had at least one roommate. Her version sounded more plausible for someone living "hand to mouth." But if she was right, he'd let me believe the wrong thing. It wasn't exactly a lie, but it was a sign that trusting everything he said might be foolish and could be dangerous.

Brent asked Lois, "What made you come back?"

"It was only a five-year contract. And I'm seventy-two, and wanted to paint full-time again." She quirked a corner of her mouth up. "That is, when I'm not sitting in Deputy Donut with the Knitpickers. Painting is a solitary activity. It's good to get out and talk to people. I enjoy being with Georgia's friends."

Brent asked her, "Why did Randy return to Fallingbrook?"

"He knew I was coming home. The two of us have a strong bond, and I'm sure he's afraid I'm about to need help, even more than the lawn care he's been doing and the snow clearing he will be doing. I suspect that he was coming back to keep an eye on both me and Georgia. Plus, he wants to return to school and work toward a career, in law enforcement if he can. He has this great need to serve others. And although he never said so, I think he left a sweetheart behind in Fallingbrook, and he's come back because of her, too."

If Lois and Randy were as close as she claimed, why didn't she know for sure about this so-called sweetheart? But I didn't butt into Brent's interview, and he didn't ask her about the possible discrepancy. I was sure he'd noticed it.

And so, apparently, had Lois. "I don't ask him about his love life, and he doesn't ask me about mine." Winking at me as if thinking about frilly undies, she stood up. "I should go. Shall we split this cake three ways?"

Neither Brent nor I hesitated. In the kitchen, she cut off

rather large wedges for Brent and me and left a sliver on the plate for herself. We wrapped them all.

"I'll walk you home, Lois," Brent said. "Is it okay if I leave my piece of cake here and pick it up later, Em?"

I pretended to think about it. "I'll have to come along, or I might have my cake and eat yours, too." I removed his jacket from the closet. The heater had dried it.

He put it on. "Thanks, Em. That's nice and warm."

"What is?" Lois demanded.

"His jacket," I answered.

She opened her eyes extra wide. If Brent hadn't been looking at me, I'd have made a rude face at her.

We left Dep sitting on the stairs to the second floor and went out onto the porch. Brent watched as I dead-bolted the door.

At Lois's, he again checked her back door and downstairs windows while she and I waited just inside her front door. Lois didn't seem to mind. Maybe she wasn't worried about what a detective wielding only his phone as a flashlight might find inside her home. I really, really wanted to ask her about the photo of Randy standing in front of his packed car. Instead, I mentally urged her to tell me about it. I thought she might do it while Brent was out of earshot, but she stayed quiet, probably listening, as I was, to Brent's progress through the back of her house.

He returned to us and held up a thumb. "All clear."

He and I left. After a half block, I could no longer hide my disappointment. "I thought for sure that Lois would remember to tell us about that photo of Randy with his car."

"Do you think she forgot?"

"I don't know."

"Don't you think she'd have told us about it last night if she was planning to tell us at all?" His gentle voice prevented him from sounding critical, of me, at least.

"I suppose so."

He probably understood that I wasn't happy about it. "I

know," he said. "She seems like the sweetest person imaginable, but it could be an act."

"One thing she told us turned out to be true. Misty warned me that Lois might have made up being Georgia's friend, since I'd never heard that from Georgia. But if Georgia wrote Lois into her will, that proves they were friends."

"Georgia willed everything she owned to Lois."

"When did she write that will? Not before Matthias died, I'm guessing."

"A couple of years later."

"So, it was when both Randy and Lois were gone from Fallingbrook." I reached for a falling leaf and missed. "It could be a coincidence that both Randy and Lois left town shortly after Matthias's death—"

"Murder."

"Okay, *murder*. They left town shortly after his murder and returned shortly before Georgia's." We turned onto the street that connected Lois's and my streets.

"In police work, we're skeptical about coincidences."

"And *I'm* skeptical about Mrs. Jierson's story about the car she and her husband supposedly saw in Georgia's driveway. Why would a murderer park in the victim's driveway where his car could be easily seen and identified?"

"It was seen, but not very well identified. They didn't get the license number."

"But they probably could have. Any passerby probably could have."

"Let's hope we find someone who did. But to answer your question about why someone would park in plain sight—criminals aren't always clever. And I know you'd like to prove that your friend's great-nephew is innocent, Em. You want to suspect that the dentist and his wife made up the story about the car because *they* murdered Georgia. At the same time, you want me to believe that Honey Bellaire left that car in Georgia's driveway while she murdered Georgia, and then drove it to the mall where the post office and Dr.

Jierson's office are. Those two scenarios are mutually exclusive." He zipped up his jacket as if he were chilly.

We turned onto my block. I explained, "They're two different possibilities. I think the one about Honey Bellaire murdering Georgia, driving around Fallingbrook to find a car like hers, and then throwing suspicion on Randy is more likely than one or both of the Jiersons killing Georgia and then making up seeing a strange car in Georgia's driveway." I was cold, too, and glad I wasn't wearing wet clothes. Luckily, I was almost home. Brent could warm up in his SUV.

"Your Honey Bellaire theory is not bad. I can't quite pick it to shreds."

"Thanks." He wasn't the only one who could speak in a deadpan voice.

"Any time, Em. Unfortunately, we can't charge on guesses."

I held up an index finger. "You might be able to after you review the surveillance videos from the post office."

"We have videos from some of the businesses on Packers Road. I'll try to get around Passenmath's decrees that we look at the ones north of Georgia's first. But you might not like what we find."

"A video showing Randy, you mean? You won't find that."

Boy, it was easy to bait him into making one of his noncommittal grunts.

He came inside with me and picked up his wrapped cake.

When he reached for the front door knob, Dep blocked the door. "Meow."

"Stay," Brent told her.

I laughed. "She's not asking to be let out. She's trying to keep you in."

He looked down at the cat. "Sorry, Dep, but after everything I learned from your two servants this evening, I'd better go to work."

I picked Dep up. "I should have waited until morning to tell you."

"You did the right thing. I'll just pass it on to whoever's on duty tonight. Those DCI agents are keen."

He reached toward me. I braced myself, ready to back away, but he merely gave Dep's head a knuckle-rub. "See you, Em. See you, Dep."

As I locked the door behind him, I shouted, "Thanks for dinner!"

I wasn't sure he heard me until the answer came back from the other side of the door. "Any time."

San Remo pizza, beer, and a chaser of fudge cake. Not, perhaps, the most balanced of meals, but I'd be willing to repeat it about, say, three times a week.

Chapter 23

✲

The next morning at Deputy Donut, I was tempted to ask Lois to go to the fire safety presentation with us so that Oliver and I wouldn't look like we were on a date, but I restrained myself. Halfway through the morning, though, Lois beckoned me to the Knitpickers' table. She didn't need another blackberry fritter or a refill of the day's special coffee, a rich, dark roast from Sumatra. She nudged the Knitpicker next to her. "Tell Emily what you were telling me."

The woman put her knitting down and paused, taking a dramatic, deep breath. "Georgia had an argument with people in her neighborhood. Georgia wanted Fallingbrook to put in sidewalks so that children could walk safely to the school bus stop, but the dentist who lives across the street from her led a faction claiming that sidewalks would lower their homes' resale values. He said it would look like just another city block."

Not with those wide, expansive lots, it wouldn't. But all I said was, "The anti-sidewalk folks must have won. There are no sidewalks on that road."

"The town fathers are still making up their minds. And now, without Georgia to lead the pro-sidewalk coalition, our elected officials, who have been leaning toward the anti-sidewalkers, might support the dentist and his friends."

Lois tapped a knitting needle on the table. "And remember

the way the dentist's wife hesitated crossing the road, like she was nervous? And her question was strange. Not 'what's going on?' but *'Did something happen to Mrs. Treetor?'* "

The knitter on her other side nodded. "I noticed that particularly."

I had, too, but Mrs. Jierson had claimed, believably, that she'd guessed after seeing the six Knitpickers and me hugging one another and wiping our eyes, and then seeing Misty arriving in a police car.

I patted Lois's shoulder. "Thanks for telling me."

At noon, the Knitpickers left. Scott and Oliver must have been preparing for the presentation. They didn't show up for their afternoon coffee break. Maybe Randy was helping them. He didn't come in, either.

After Tom and I finished tidying up for the evening, Dep and I walked home. I grabbed a quick meal of raw veggies and sliced cheddar, and then drove to Taste of Fallingbrook. I was kind of hoping that it wasn't open, but it was. I parked in the lot behind the store and walked around to the front.

Misty was driving a cruiser past Taste of Fallingbrook. She stopped and lowered her passenger window. "What's up?"

I waved toward the grocery. "I promised Fred Aggleton that I'd shop here."

She wrinkled her nose. "Check the best-before dates."

"Okay. Are you working tonight?"

"No. Want to get together?"

"Yes, but I'm not sure you'll want to go where I'm going."

She waved her hand in front of her face as if clearing cobwebs. "Huh?"

"Scott Ritsorf is giving a fire safety presentation."

"He's a sweetie."

"I know. But here's the thing. The Chamber of Commerce is sponsoring it, and I somehow managed to agree that Oliver Rossimer could take me to the presentation. *Wah!*"

"What do you mean, *wah?* I remember when you'd have given your eyelashes to go somewhere with Oliver."

"Me, too, but I don't know why I said I would now, after all these years. I'm not ready to date, and I don't want to lead anyone into thinking that I am. But if you and Samantha go, also, I can introduce him to both of you. And we can all sit together."

"The sacrifices we have to make for our friends. When is it?"

"Seven. He's picking me up at six thirty."

"That's in forty-five minutes!"

"I know."

"Don't sound so glum. I'm just going off duty and was about to take this hunk of metal back to the police station and change out of my uniform. But how about if I come into Aggleton's store with you? No telling when he might slip you some tainted meat."

"That was before his time, and besides, the food poisoning wasn't Matthias's fault."

"I wouldn't put it past *Aggleton*." She radioed headquarters that she'd return her car five minutes late, and got out.

Even scruffier than the last time I saw him at Taste of Fallingbrook, Aggleton didn't seem particularly pleased to see us.

I pasted on a fake smile. "You said to tell my friends about your shop, and this is one of my friends."

Although he was standing, he had to look up at Misty to give her the full force of his glare. "You spend your working time shopping when the citizens of this town are paying you to keep our streets safe?"

She hitched up her gun belt. "Those two activities are not necessarily mutually exclusive." She could be very threatening when she wanted to. Apparently, she wanted to.

"Okay, ladies, I know why you're here. I saw you plotting for ten minutes outside." It had been more like two, and we hadn't been plotting. "The woman who sold me this store died recently. I did not kill her, and I did not kill her son, and I can prove it." He reached between the table holding his cash register and the counter where people set their purchases. He pulled out a slightly curling light blue poster board with brochures and scraps of paper stuck to it, some flapping loosely, others dog-eared. It looked like a grade school project that had seen better days. "This is my alibi for when Matthias Treetor went missing and was killed. See here?" He pointed at a receipt pasted to the upper left corner of the poster board. The receipt was so faded that I couldn't read it in the dim light. "After Matthias Treetor pulled that stunt with the pitcher in the state baseball finals, I wasn't about to let my son play either baseball or hockey with Treetor coaching. When Treetor failed to show up for that organizational meeting for hockey here in Fallingbrook, and was getting himself murdered, I was buying gas fifty miles away, taking my son to a town where a much superior hockey team was forming." He pointed at a postcard. "Read this."

The printing was irregular, in pencil. "Dear Mom, Dad and I are in Wisconsin Dells. We're having a lot of fun."

I couldn't help asking Aggleton, "You didn't clear the trip with the boy's mother before you left? She didn't find out where you were until this postcard was delivered?"

He sneered. "You got it all wrong. I phoned her while we were on the road. But kids like to think they're the first to tell someone their news. And just in case you think all we did was buy a postcard, look at these. Here are the kid's ride ticket stubs and the brochures we picked up at the hotel. And down here, see? It's the receipt for our hotel. We didn't get back until after Treetor had been missing for two days."

"Impressive," I managed.

Misty asked, "Did you show this to the police right after Treetor's body was found?"

"Not right after. I showed it to them when they came around my house asking where I'd been that week. Seems that someone, probably Treetor's mother, let it be known that I'd been trying to buy this store. I might have been, but I didn't want it badly enough to kill for it. And now, with it losing money all the time, I don't want it at all." He folded his arms and turned up the wattage of the glare he was aiming at Misty. "I knew you'd be back now that the guy's mother is dead."

"I'm a street cop, not a detective."

"As if that'd stop any cop from arresting an innocent person." He turned his back on us. One apron string was safety-pinned to the apron near a hole where the string must have once been sewn. He retrieved another, less ratty poster. This one was orange. "I had the smarts to keep everything from the trip I made with my son last week. And don't look at me that way. I wasn't planning anything about that Treetor woman. I've always kept souvenirs, receipts and ticket stubs. See? We bought gas Thursday afternoon after three in Fallingbrook." Georgia had been in Deputy Donut Friday morning. "See? Selfies, time-stamped on Friday outside Lambeau Field. And on Saturday, we were at Lambeau Field again for a Packers game. Here are the ticket stubs. Two, one for me and one for my son. And here's our hotel receipt. Thursday, Friday, Saturday, Sunday, and Monday. When we arrived home on Tuesday, I heard that the Treetor woman had been found dead. So, Madame Policewoman, you can take all that information back to your station and tell the others not to come around here bothering me."

She gave him an easy smile. "I'll tell them that, but detectives don't take orders from patrol cops. Someone might bother you anyway. I'm sure your display will impress them." She turned to the door and I followed.

"Hey!" Aggleton called. "I thought you were going to shop!"

I smiled as sweetly as I could. "We were, but I just looked at the time. I don't want to be late for the Chamber of Commerce's fire safety presentation. Are you attending, Mr. Aggleton? It's for everyone, especially business owners. It's at seven in the high school gym."

"Hardly." He flicked a gaze toward the ceiling, and then back at us. He looked guilty, as if he'd disconnected the sprinklers up there and hoped that no one would figure it out.

At her cruiser, Misty said, "I'll call Samantha. If she's not working tonight she can join me, watching you blush every time Oliver looks at you."

"Thanks." I was becoming expert at Brent-like deadpanning. I hurried into the parking lot behind Taste of Fallingbrook. "Mmp," I mumbled, but my *mmping* was still vastly substandard. I drove to Deputy Donut and parked in our lot in back. With all that rushing around, I was five minutes early. I went around to the front of Deputy Donut and admired how inviting it looked with outdoor patios on both sides of the front door and flower boxes on the wrought-iron railings surrounding the patios.

I was happily deadheading asters when I heard a strange, coughing engine sound, and then a squeaky *Ah*-ooo-*gah!*

Chapter 24

❧

Wearing a pale blue polo shirt and khakis, Oliver piloted a Tin Lizzie to the curb.

I climbed into the passenger seat. "A Model T! The other day, I was thinking about how these things must have startled horses on the streets of Fallingbrook."

"Like it?"

"It's great. Where did you find one in such pristine condition?"

"It wasn't like this. It was almost unsalvageable. I restored it. I'll probably sell it and restore something else."

"How did you learn to restore cars?"

He turned right on Wisconsin Street. "I taught myself. My father owned car dealerships. I hung around their maintenance departments until they put me to work when I was twelve. By the time I graduated from high school, I was managing three maintenance departments."

"How did you find time? You were student council president, and involved in clubs, sports, and the theater department, plus you were always on the honor roll."

"You have a good memory."

"Many of us looked up to you."

"I noticed. I was able to do all those things because I don't need much sleep and I like to be organized. I never, ever waste time. I don't watch TV except for the late news. I don't play video games or read novels. I have a part-time house-keeper and hire help for home and lawn maintenance. That way, I can concentrate on what I need and want to do, like restore cars. After I finished my business degree at college, I went to work for my father and became manager of all five of his maintenance departments."

"Five at once?"

"I had assistant managers. When my father died three years ago, cars and pickup trucks were beginning to seem small and less challenging. I sold three of my father's dealer-ships and bought the construction equipment business, but I kept two dealerships. Plus, to keep my hand in with the tech-nology in each new generation of vehicles, I run the two car dealerships I kept. I'm in charge of sales and all the rest of it."

"Even with not sleeping and being organized and not wasting time, it's amazing that you can do all that and run your heavy equipment dealership, too."

He tapped his forehead. "Assistants. As I learned way back in grade school, delegating allows me to do what I want, including playing golf. You'll see, when you become successful enough. You might have to take some chances, be a risk taker. Open franchises, license your product and recipes, hire more staff. You wouldn't have to work such long hours. Play your cards right, and you won't have to work at all. I'm retiring in ten years. I've got it all planned down to the last penny."

I liked working at Deputy Donut. "I figure that if you love the work you do, it doesn't qualify as work. Certainly not as drudgery."

"I would have never accepted a life of drudgery."

Some people, I thought, *don't have a choice.* Oliver and I were lucky.

He stopped for a light. "I love my work, but I won't mind being free to do other things. Travel, for instance. Wouldn't you like to have time to travel?"

"I suppose so." I tried to imagine what I'd have thought at

sixteen if anyone had told me that I would one day have this conversation with Oliver Rossimer. At sixteen, I'd have taken his question about traveling as almost a marriage proposal. I smiled just thinking about being that young and imaginative.

"Too many people think they can wait until they retire to do all the things they want to. Some, like my folks, don't live long enough."

"I'm sorry about your folks. Mine stay in Florida except during the hottest weather. Then they come back here."

"To each his own. Though there are some good golf courses down there, if you don't mind alligators getting in the way."

Picturing alligators prowling the greens and deliberately blocking shots with wide-open mouths or outstretched claws, I couldn't help laughing.

"It's true," Oliver said. "Alligators are everywhere in Florida, even on golf courses."

The light turned green. People in other cars smiled at us and at the Model T puttering along below the speed limit. The ride was bone jarring, but fun, and I pictured myself wearing a long dress, boots with hundreds of tiny buttons, and a wide-brimmed hat tied on with a lacy scarf.

Fallingbrook High hadn't changed much, at least from the outside, in the eleven years since I'd graduated. The parking lot had never been big, but Oliver found a space close to the door leading into the gym. I hopped out of the Model T. A red SUV labeled FIRE CHIEF pulled up several rows back, and Scott, in his firehouse uniform of navy pants and shirt, loped toward us. "Sorry I'm late," he said.

Oliver touched the gold watch on his wrist. "We just got here." He held the door open for me, and then there was a shuffle as both Scott and Oliver tried to let the other one go inside first. Scott won, and followed us in.

The gym smelled the same way it had over a decade ago—rubber from basketballs and sneakers, and a nose-prickling aroma of sweeping compound that had been whooshed over the shiny hardwood floor by the world's widest dust mops.

Considering that the presentation wasn't due to start for twenty minutes, and custodians were unfolding chairs on the gym floor, there were a surprising number of people sitting in the chairs that were already set up.

A table, with three chairs facing the audience, was next to the podium. I asked Scott, "Need help bringing anything in?"

He gave me one of his lazy grins. "It's just a couple of cartons. I'll get them. I wanted to scope everything out first." He strode out.

Oliver pointed at the table beside the podium. "I'll be in front, so sit wherever you like, Emily."

I slipped into an aisle seat, four rows back, in the section of seats to the right of the aisle. Then I sat there wondering if Dep was worrying if I was ever coming home again. Probably not. She knew she was in charge. Whenever she heard me step onto the porch, she probably believed she had commanded me to show up that very moment.

Hearing familiar voices behind me, I turned around. In jeans and a white cotton sweater, Misty was holding the door for Scott and Samantha, who were carrying large cardboard cartons. Samantha had also changed out of her uniform and was wearing a denim skirt, a red sweater, and red patent flats.

I moved so that Misty and Samantha could have the seats closest to the aisle.

Samantha sat beside me. "Misty said you came with Oliver. Was she joking?"

I did my best to look insulted. "Why would it be a joke? Never mind. Don't answer. Oliver brought me here in his Model T."

Samantha crowed, "Hoo-whee!"

Misty flapped one of her hands as if she were trying to shake off hot coals. "What's it like to live a dream?"

I asked, "Do the dreams of kids count after we're adults?"

"You betcha!" Samantha was no sluggard when it came to fervor.

"I might have outgrown my dreams about Oliver," I confided, "but I don't know if I can ever outgrow dreams of flivvers."

Samantha crossed her eyes. "Sooo romantic."

"I thought she said 'livers,' " Misty retorted.

I fixed her with a frown. "No, you didn't."

She reached across Samantha, gripped my wrist, and nodded toward a slim, round-shouldered woman carrying an outsized tote and wearing black yoga pants, a tight black top, and ballet slippers. "Isn't that . . . ?"

I knew of only one person who walked like that, as if she were tiptoeing, but on the sides of her feet instead of on her toes. I completed the sentence for Misty. "Georgia's neighbor from across the street. Yes. I wonder if the man with her is her dentist husband, Dr. Jierson."

Misty squinted toward him. "Could be. He looks like a dentist."

Samantha giggled. "I don't see a drill."

"Perfectly groomed," Misty explained.

"Men in lots of professions wear suits and ties to work," I pointed out.

"But dentists aren't necessarily among them," Samantha contributed.

Misty stared at him. "Look at his fingernails. They're short, even for a man, and I bet you won't find a speck of dirt underneath them."

With her thumb and forefinger, Samantha pinched her nostrils closed for a second. "You can carry your police officer observation talents too far sometimes, Misty."

"You're just jealous. All *you* have to do is figure out if someone is sick or injured enough to warrant medical care or transport to the nearest hospital, preferably with you at the wheel driving at excessive speeds and cackling as you leave us poor cops behind in the dust."

"I never cackle."

"What's that sound I hear when you're speeding past, then?" Misty demanded.

"Her siren," I answered. "Both of you probably chose your professions because they allow you to blast sirens."

Samantha and Misty gave each other high fives. "You could have, too," Samantha said.

"It's not too late," Misty added.

I thought about Randy's idea of using an old police cruiser for deliveries from Deputy Donut. Even if the car had a siren, though, turning it on would probably be illegal. Pity. I brightened. I would be able to tease Misty by *threatening* to turn on a siren and strobe lights.

Mrs. Jierson sat at the left end of the front row, lowered her head, and pawed through the enormous tote on her lap.

The immaculately groomed, short-nailed man walked to the podium. Unlike Mrs. Jierson, he walked loudly, setting each hard-soled loafer down solidly. "Short-man walk," Samantha commented. The man shook hands with Oliver and Scott.

Misty leaned toward us. "Dentistry is perfect for short men. Their patients are lying down and can never tower over them."

"Watch what you say about short people," Samantha warned. "Emily and I might gang up on you."

"How?" Misty asked. "By standing on each other's shoulders?"

"Not possible," Samantha said. "Not both at once. I'll stand on Emily."

Misty demanded, "Are you threatening an officer of the law?"

"Don't worry," Samantha soothed like someone talking to a beloved pet. "If Emily and I injure you, I'll drive you to the hospital. Very fast."

I nodded enthusiastically. "Sirens blaring."

People kept arriving. I recognized Deputy Donut customers, the head librarian, the woman who owned the clothing boutique next to Deputy Donut, several people whom I'd seen in The Craft Croft, the owner of the diner across the street, the woman from the sewing shop, and the twin brothers who owned the bookstore.

Oliver and the man we'd guessed was Dr. Jierson helped Scott arrange smoke and carbon monoxide detectors, fire extinguishers, brochures, coloring books, and stickers on the table beside the podium.

At precisely seven, Oliver gestured for Scott to take a seat at the tables. The well-groomed man also sat. Shoes hitting the floor at least as hard as the shorter man's had, Oliver strode to the podium. He welcomed us and introduced Dr. Jierson as the vice president of the Chamber of Commerce. Strangely, Oliver didn't mention Dr. Jierson's first name.

Dr. Jierson made another welcoming speech.

Misty sighed loudly. Samantha elbowed her.

Finally, Dr. Jierson introduced Scott, but before he yielded the podium, he announced, "We're going to be passing a petition around. If you care about Fallingbrook, you'll want to sign it."

Chapter 25

❧

Relaxed and smiling, Scott began his spiel.

Mrs. Jierson leaped to her feet, reached into her tote, and yanked out a clipboard. White sheets of paper were clamped to it, and a pen dangled from a twisty pink cord. She shoved the clipboard underneath the nose of the man next to her. Pale and visibly shaking, she dropped her tote. It landed on the floor with a thump.

What was inside it, a firearm? Too bad Brent wasn't in the gym, although Misty was, and she was staring at Mrs. Jierson. But then, so was almost everyone else.

Interrupting Scott with a loud, "Sorry," Mrs. Jierson sat down.

The man next to her hunched his shoulders and studied the clipboard.

Oliver seemed to be pondering something over our heads or in the back of the gym. Dr. Jierson was studying his undoubtedly immaculate fingernails. Was anyone paying attention to Scott? I concentrated on what he was saying about smoke detectors, fire extinguishers, and unattended cooking and candles. Even so, I was aware of that clipboard's progress along the rows of chairs. Recipients looked at it for at least a few seconds. Some whispered to neighbors. Others flipped pages back and forth, most of the people scribbled on the paper, and everyone passed the clipboard on, sometimes bumping other people with it and then apologizing.

The petition came to me. It called for Fallingbrook to refuse to build sidewalks where none presently existed. It waxed eloquent about frugality and retaining the town's charm and beauty. The first person to sign it was Dr. Jierson, with an address on Packers Road, which had to be the mall where his office was, not his home. The second signer was the name I remembered seeing on his receptionist's desk, at the same address. The third signer was "Mrs. Dr. Jierson," also at the Packers Road address. Did the Jiersons have first names? I glanced through all three pages but didn't recognize any other names.

I tucked the pen into the clamp and handed the clipboard to Samantha. "Don't sign it," I whispered. "Tell Misty."

Samantha raised her eyebrows as if she were about to launch into a debate about whether I had the right to tell her what to do, but she whispered to Misty, who got up, crossed the aisle, and placed the clipboard in a woman's outstretched hand. Without taking time to read the petition, the woman signed it and passed it on. Maybe I should have held on to the clipboard until everyone left the meeting, and then given it to Mrs. Jierson, signed only by some of the audience members. I hated to think that Georgia might have been killed because someone hoped to preserve real estate values by lobbying against sidewalks that might prevent serious injury or worse to children. And even if the Jiersons and their anti-sidewalk coalition hadn't actually killed Georgia, I couldn't admire them for reinvigorating their opposition to the sidewalks even before the Medical Examiner released Georgia's body.

Oops. I was supposed to be watching the front of the room, not the audience to my left.

Both Oliver and Dr. Jierson were craning their necks to see Scott, and I wondered why they'd opted to sit beside the podium rather than facing it. Both Oliver and Dr. Jierson had dark hair and eyes, but Oliver was taller. I suspected they both worked out. But while Oliver's face was handsome, Dr. Jierson, who wasn't much older, seemed to have no expression other than permanent vertical ridges between his eyebrows. Maybe the frowny look came from spending his life peering into people's mouths. Or maybe he couldn't help the wrinkles because of the way his eyebrows dipped toward the center of his otherwise smooth face. Or it was the thought of sidewalks ruining his large green lawn. Then again, if I had the sort of crick in my neck that I suspected he had at the moment, I wouldn't be happy, either. Oliver was farther from Scott, so maybe his neck wouldn't be in quite as much pain. And while he wasn't exactly smiling, at least he wasn't glaring at a spot near Scott's nose. Watching Oliver was much pleasanter than watching Dr. Jierson.

I still wasn't paying Scott the attention he deserved. I concentrated on him again, and then I realized that I was mainly admiring his looks, warmth, and wry sense of humor, and not listening carefully to his words.

Samantha nudged me. "It's almost like old times again, isn't it?"

I grinned and whispered. "Randy should be here."

Misty frowned and shook her head. Because she didn't want to be distracted from listening to Scott? Or because she didn't approve of Randy? Worrying again that Lois's photos had increased Yvonne Passenmath's suspicions of Randy, I felt sorry for Lois, torn between loyalty to the boy she'd helped raise and her desire to help put Matthias's and Georgia's murderer or murderers behind bars.

I contrasted Randy with Dr. Jierson. Randy's eyes tended to be alive with laughter, but except for Dr. Jierson's scary eyebrows, his face seemed to show no emotion, as if in his attempts not to make grimaces that went with the eyebrows, he had scrubbed all expression from his face. But despite his

almost-robotic yet demonic looks and his desire to keep
sidewalks from marring his neighborhood, I didn't believe he
was a murderer.

I was certain that Honey Bellaire had concocted her story
of Randy's visit to the post office early Monday morning.
Randy would have had no reason to ask about borrowing
minivans. Honey must have murdered Georgia. The police
would discover that it was Honey's car that was parked in
Dr. Jierson's spot early Monday morning, and that it was
Honey's car that Dr. Jierson followed from Georgia's driveway to the mall where his office and the post office were. The
police would prove that Honey had seen Randy driving a car
like hers and had followed him into Deputy Donut so she
could describe him as the driver of the car that had been at
Georgia's.

*Dr. Jierson needs a doll doctor to paint a more human
look on his face.* My head jerked up out of a nod. I'd made
that comment about Dr. Jierson in the beginnings of a dream,
not aloud, but I was embarrassed, anyway. I'd drifted off
while Scott was demonstrating how to tell when a fire extin-
guisher needed recharging.

"You two!" Samantha whispered.

Misty's eyes snapped open. "Sorry."

"It's hot in here," Samantha muttered. "I hope no one
faints."

"At least you're here to give mouth-to-mouth," I teased.

"If it's Oliver, I might have to fight you for the privilege."

"No thanks!"

Misty shook her head. "Sh."

Scott was watching us and I was sure I detected a twinkle
in those blue eyes. He and Misty, both tall, slim, and blond,
would look great together, as would Oliver and Samantha.

Both Misty and Samantha knew Scott because they were
all first responders and frequently encountered one another

at emergencies, but I wasn't sure that Oliver knew my long-time best friends. I would change that.

After Oliver thanked us all for coming and Dr. Jierson made certain he knew where his petition had ended up and had nodded at his wife to retrieve it, the audience began gathering belongings and clattering chairs.

"Come to the front with me," I said to Misty and Samantha. "You know Scott, and I'll introduce you to Oliver."

Misty stared at Dr. Jierson. "I've talked to that dentist's wife, but not to him."

"I don't know him," I said, "but maybe Oliver will introduce you."

When we arrived at the front, however, Oliver was finishing signing the petition. Dr. Jierson grabbed the clipboard, turned away, and shepherded his wife toward the door. Why was he in such a hurry? Was another patient in pain? Maybe his wife had told him that Misty was a police officer and he didn't want to stick around and possibly have to talk to her. Guilt could do that to someone, guilt about an affair with his receptionist, perhaps. Or about murdering the woman who lived across the street from him . . .

I introduced Samantha and Misty to Oliver. "They also went to school here," I told him. "They were in my grade."

He was as charming as he'd been then. "I remember you both. All three of you. You seemed to be observing everything around you, all of the time."

Especially the best-looking guys. But I didn't say it with Scott right there. We hadn't spent much time ogling Scott, which, looking at him now, and knowing him better than we had then, seemed like a major omission on our part. "What do kids know?" This time, I did say it aloud, and nearly clapped my hand over my mouth. Our old high school gym seemed to be transforming me into an underconfident ninth grader. Hoping that neither Oliver nor Scott had somehow latched on to my thoughts about our having been remiss in not having dreamed about Scott as much as we'd dreamed about Oliver, I searched for a different topic of conversation. The custodians who had set up the chairs were nowhere to be seen. "Who's putting the chairs away?" I asked Oliver.

"The Chamber of Commerce." He glanced toward the door. Dr. Jierson had disappeared. "I guess that means me," Oliver said. "Sorry to delay you, Emily."

"No problem. I'll help."

"Me, too," Samantha said.

Misty and Scott pitched in, and it didn't take us long. With Scott and Samantha carrying Scott's cartons, we all left. Oliver set the alarm and locked the door.

In the parking lot, we all admired Oliver's Model T.

Oliver suggested, "The night's young. Why don't we all go out for a drink?"

It was a perfect opportunity for the matchmaking I'd hoped to do. I smiled at Oliver. "That Model T is lots of fun, and I already had a turn. Why don't you ride with Oliver, Samantha, and I'll drive your car?" Maybe I was being too obvious. . . .

"I came with Misty."

I offered, "I'll ride with Misty. Okay, Oliver?"

"Sure. Come on, Samantha. Meet you all in ten minutes at the Fireplug Pub?"

The rest of us agreed. Scott went alone in his fire chief SUV, and I followed Misty to her sporty convertible. "I could drive your car if you want to ride with Scott," I told Misty.

"Nice try." She started the car. "But you're not driving this car. And technically, Scott's not allowed to take passengers who aren't firefighters."

"I'll bet there are exceptions for police officers."

"Only in emergencies." She let Oliver get ahead, and then followed him. "You don't mind possibly giving Oliver to Samantha?"

"He's not mine to give. Was I rude?"

She laughed. "A little. He took it well, though."

"He should. Samantha would be quite a catch." I squinched my mouth to the side in remorse. "But I should have told him I'm not ready to date."

"He could have caught the gist."

"I suppose. Hey, did you know that the fire chief is following you?"

"Yep."

"You two would make a great couple."

She shrugged and shifted gears. "He kept looking at *you*."

"Probably because when I wasn't drifting off, I was watching that clipboard."

At the Fireplug, a popular pub in downtown Fallingbrook next to the firehouse and only a block from Deputy Donut, I didn't have to pair people off. Oliver scooted into the booth first, followed by Samantha, talking nonstop about the Model T. I sat across from Oliver, and Misty sat across from Samantha. Scott fetched a chair and sat at the end of the table, adjacent to both Misty and Samantha. Score.

I insisted on paying for the first round of drinks, which didn't exactly break the bank. Misty, Samantha, and Scott were all due to begin shifts at ten, and opted for nonalcoholic beverages. After I downed my small glass of craft beer, I pointed out that I had to be at work at six thirty in the morning. Oliver offered to take me home, but I told him my car was at Deputy Donut, and I could easily walk there.

Then my plans fell apart. After Misty let me out of the booth, Scott insisted on walking me to Deputy Donut. He told the others to stay there, and he'd be right back.

I could hardly keep up with him and his long-legged stride, but I really wanted him to return to Misty quickly, so I put an extra hop into every other step. Somewhat breathlessly, I thanked him for the presentation. "You did a good job."

He laughed. "I saw you fighting sleep."

"Sorry. It wasn't your fault. That gym was hot, and I do get up most mornings around five." Beside my car, I asked him, "Want a ride back to the Fireplug?"

He hesitated, then shook his head. "I should get some exercise after all those donuts I eat." He started back toward the almost, sort of, kind of double date that I had engineered.

Chapter 26

❧

As usual, the Knitpickers took Saturday off from their morning meetings at Deputy Donut.

Scott showed up late in the afternoon for his first meal of the day—our featured dark roast Peruvian coffee and two battered and deep-fried sausages. For once, Oliver didn't join him. I hadn't talked to either Samantha or Misty since I'd left the Fireplug the night before.

I asked Scott, "How did the rest of last night go?"

"Fine, but we missed you."

"Was Oliver okay?"

"Sure. Why wouldn't he be?"

"I was afraid he would feel like he had a date with me, and that I kind of dumped him before the evening was over."

"*Afraid* he would think it was a date?"

"Well, you know, you were here when he said he'd pick me up, and it wasn't really a date, but I wouldn't want him or anyone else to think I'm . . ." I rubbed at a bead of water on the shiny woodgrain table. ". . . available. I'm just *not*."

He studied me for a second, then asked gently, "Because of Alec?"

Other customers were at nearby tables. I spoke quietly. "I know it's silly, but I still feel married to him."

Scott's crooked grin was irresistible. "Don't worry about it, Emily. I think Oliver was happy to show off his Model T, and you and Samantha were very appreciative. Besides, he was the one who suggested going out for a drink. It was more like a group of people having fun together than a date. You didn't dump him. You gave him more admirers for his car."

"Thanks, Scott. I was worried when he didn't come in this afternoon like he sometimes does. I didn't mean to be rude."

A glint lurked in Scott's eyes as if he knew I'd been match-making. "You weren't."

I wanted to ask him how he liked Misty, but it wasn't something I could just blurt out. I thanked him and went off to chat to other customers.

Randy came in and joined Scott, but neither of them stayed long.

About four, Tom and I were mixing yeast dough so it could rise during the night. Tom turned his head and smiled broadly. "Look who's here."

It was Brent, dressed for work in a navy blazer, gray slacks, a light blue shirt, and a red-and-blue-striped tie.

Wiping his hands on the towel hanging over his apron strings, Tom hurried to the sales counter. "*De*tective Fyne, sir, how are you doing?"

Brent grinned. "Okay."

"Aw, come on," Tom urged. "Say it."

"I'm *Fyne*."

"Fine, Fyne. What can we get you? First visit's on the house, for a *Fyne* detective like you."

Brent just shook his head and looked past my father-in-law to me. "Is he always like this?"

I finished drying my hands and joined them at the counter. "Never." It was nearly true. Tom had been more lively before his only child had been killed, and although I believed he loved working at Deputy Donut, he was fairly quiet, making donuts and other pastries while keeping his eye on the shop and everyone inside it. But he had always liked Brent. I hadn't seen them interact at the police department when Tom was chief, so I didn't know how much they'd teased each other at work in those days. Police officers tended to joke with each other in ways that the rest of us didn't always understand. I gave Brent a patently fake evil eye. "You must be a bad influence."

From the office came a rather loud *Meow!*

We all laughed, and Brent backed up until he could smile at Dep in her window. "Your boss is calling me, Em. Think I could have a coffee in your office so I can obey the summons?"

"Sure," I said. "What would you like?"

Brent looked a little scared, the typical expression of someone who was unsure of all the latest terms for coffee and didn't want to make a mistake around people who might consider themselves experts. "You choose. Just don't put stuff in it, flavors or dairy products or sweeteners. I like to taste the coffee."

"Will you be working late tonight?"

"Not sure."

We had just enough Kona beans left from Wednesday for one mug of coffee. I ground them, and then, hoping to make the best coffee he had ever tasted, I brewed it in our one-cup French press. Tom's and Brent's voices were low, and I couldn't make out all of their words, but I definitely heard "investigation" and "Passenmath."

I poured heated water from our always-hot spigot into a mug to warm the mug, pressed the French press's plunger, replaced the hot water in the mug with delicious-smelling coffee, and turned around.

Brent was gone. Tom was heading toward his unfinished dough.

The mug in my hand was steaming. "Where's Brent?" I asked Tom.

"He wasn't kidding about visiting Dep."

The office windows looked into the kitchen and the dining room, but if Brent was with Dep, he had to be in the corner of the office where there were no windows. I carried the coffee into the office and closed the door. Brent was sitting on the end of the couch nearest the kitchen. Dep was purring on his lap. Wondering who had named coffee tables and how often they were used for coffee, I set the mug on the one in front of the couch. "Can I get you a donut?"

"No, thanks." He leaned forward and picked up the mug without appearing to disturb Dep. "Do you have a sec, Em?"

"Sure." I sat on the other end of the couch.

He looked up at the catwalks surrounding the walls above the windows. "Dep's one lucky cat."

"Yes. Tom built those."

He sipped at the coffee. "Perfect." Again, he studied the kitty playground near the ceiling. "Are there surveillance cameras up there?"

"No. Imagine what Dep might do to them. Think there should be?"

"Not necessarily."

"We have three outside, one above the front door, one above this door . . ." I pointed at the door leading from the office to the parking lot. "And one above the other back door, the one that goes straight from the loading dock into the storage room beside the kitchen."

"And inside?"

"One in the ceiling, aimed at the counter where the cash drawer is." I nodded at the desk in the corner between the kitchen and back walls. "The video files from all of the cameras are on the computer, and are kept for a minimum of ten days, depending on how much the motion detectors keep them recording. Do you need to see any of our videos?"

"No. Do you have recording equipment in here?"

I tilted my head. It seemed like an odd question. I pulled my phone out of my apron pocket. "I could record with this if you like."

"That's not it. I don't want what I'm about to ask you to be recorded."

What he was about to ask me? My face heated, and so did

the tips of my ears. The conversation was becoming seriously weird. Not only that, he was holding his Deputy Donut mug in front of his mouth as if he were a master spy who didn't want anyone reading his lips. "It can't be." For good measure, I added, "And from where you're sitting, no one can read your lips unless they're using binoculars or come up onto the back porch. But if Tom looks up, he can read mine. If he can read lips."

Almost anyone could have read Brent's lips at that moment. He'd pinched them together, which made him look strained. The tops of his ears reddened. "It's nothing draconian, but I don't want our discussion getting back to work, specifically to Detective Passenmath."

"I haven't seen her in years, which is fine with me."

His lips relaxed into an almost-natural grin. "I'd like to talk to Lois Unterlaw, but off the record for now. I don't want to bring her to the station and throw her to the wolves there. She'd freak, right?"

By "the wolves," he probably meant Detective Yvonne Passenmath. "Probably."

"I can't quite picture Lois murdering her best friend and her best friend's son, but as you know, I'm not ruling anything out. However, if Passenmath gets her claws into Lois or finds out that Lois tried to hide that photo of Randy and the car from me, there's no telling what might happen. I want to get Lois to tell me about Randy and the car and her photos, and I figure I'm more likely to get helpful answers if I have an informal conversation with her. Possibly the best way to do that would be if you were present. Could I impose on you to invite her to your place this evening, and I can talk to her there? The three of us have been getting together lately, so maybe she can endure my questions without clamming up. I know this will be out of the ordinary, but I think it's important, especially to her."

"Okay. I'll invite her over." Somewhat to my surprise, my ears were getting hotter, not cooler. "And I won't tell her why."

"Thanks, Em." He gulped down the rest of the coffee, set the mug down, and stood up. "Can I go out the back so I won't trail cat hairs all over your dining room?"

"Sure."

"Thanks for the coffee."

"Thank Tom. I'd have charged you," I teased.

"Next time. See you tonight. How about seven?"

"I'll let you know if there's any change." Like if Lois couldn't make it. "Don't eat dessert before you come over. I'm afraid it will be only donuts."

"Who doesn't like donuts?" He went out the back. I locked the door.

Tom and I finished the dough for the next day, tidied the kitchen and dining room, and upended chairs on tables to make cleaning the floor easier for the Jolly Cops Cleaning Crew. I packed an assortment of donuts into a box and then gathered Dep while Tom armed the alarm system. After he drove off in his usual way, like a police officer racing to an emergency, I figured that Dep and I could step off the back porch and walk down the driveway without having to flatten ourselves against Deputy Donut or the clothing boutique on the other side of the driveway.

It was another nearly perfect early September evening, warm with a hazy sky and maybe a little too much humidity. Strolling home with Dep, I hoped that Brent's proposed meeting wouldn't upset Lois, but I was almost sure that it would, no matter how hard Brent tried to seem encouraging and not accusing.

I called her as soon as Dep and I were safely inside the house and I'd removed Dep's halter and leash.

"I'd love to come for donuts with you and Brent this evening, Emily," Lois said, "but I expect Randy to drop by, so why don't you and Brent come over here?" She let out a girlish giggle. "Better yet, why don't you two simply enjoy the donuts and each other's company alone together?"

I stuttered an answer about not being interested in Brent

that way. "And besides, I brought home too many donuts for two people. I'd end up tossing the ones we didn't eat."

"I can't let that happen. Bring him here at seven, then. And Dep, too, or let her meander over her own way." I still hadn't blocked the cat's secret passageway. Maybe I wouldn't, as long as Lois lived in that house.

I called Brent and told him the change in plans.

"Randy might show up? Even better. I'll walk to Lois's with you."

He arrived at my place at ten to seven. He had removed his tie and undone the top button of his light blue shirt. I leashed Dep, and the three of us walked to Lois's.

Smiling, wearing a red tunic over black jeans that almost matched mine, Lois welcomed us all. I handed her the box of donuts.

"Coffee, anyone? Or liqueurs? Or do you know what really goes with donuts, besides coffee?" She didn't wait for us to answer. "Milk."

Brent must have expected a long night. He again wanted coffee.

Unleashing Dep, I opted for a small glass of milk, and then Brent and I followed Lois to the kitchen. She started the coffee, I arranged donuts on a platter, and Brent poured milk for Lois and me.

Lois fussed over Dep and gave her a sardine. The coffee didn't take long. Lois poured it into one of her forget-me-not-patterned bone china cups and handed the cup and saucer to Brent. "Let's go enjoy this in the living room," she suggested.

I picked up the platter and a stack of paper napkins. "I thought you didn't want anyone to see a police officer in your house. Your sheers are, um, sheer."

She carried the two glasses of milk. "He can sit with his back to the window."

Knowing from Alec and Misty that police officers preferred to sit with their backs to walls so they could watch entryways,

I checked Brent's face. He thinned his lips, but gave me a nod.

"Take the wing chair, Brent," Lois said. "Except for the top of your head, you'll be invisible to people outside."

Dep galloped upstairs. Lois and I sank into her couch.

Across the coffee table from us, Brent bit into a raised donut with fudge frosting. "Mmmm."

Lois's hand hovered over the plate as if she couldn't decide between a blueberry fritter and a strawberry donut with pink icing and darker pink sprinkles shaped like tiny strawberries. "See, Brent? I told you they were wonderful." She settled on the blueberry fritter.

I took a maple-bacon donut. When Tom first floated the idea, I'd been skeptical, but the combination of salty bacon bits and sweet maple glaze was delicious.

Dep trotted downstairs, made a beeline for the wing chair, and hopped into Brent's lap.

Knowing that Randy might show up, I'd brought lots of donuts, but Brent wiped his hands and face after the first gooey chocolate delight and said in a conversational tone, "Lois, when we looked at your photos at work, we noticed that several are missing. Your camera automatically numbers them, and there are breaks in the sequence."

She didn't look concerned. "Not every photo turns out. I delete the ones I'll never want."

"Right away?" he asked.

"Usually. There's no sense in cluttering my hard drive with junky photos. They take up a lot of space. But sometimes I do it later, when I go back and notice that something's poorly focused or I missed the shot I wanted, like the dog that had been sitting still suddenly jumped up and all I captured was his tail. With my camera, that is." She winked at me. "That was good, Emily. I'm going to have another one, and this time I *am* going to have the pink one with the cute strawberry sprinkles." She cupped a hand behind her ear. "What's that noise?"

Something buzzed again near Brent. "My phone," he said, "vibrating."

He checked the screen, sighed, and gave me a look that I couldn't quite fathom. It was some combination of apology, regret, and reluctance mixed with stubborn determination. "I'd better take this." He touched the screen. "Hey, Yvonne, what's up?"

Chapter 27

No wonder Brent had given me that look. He hadn't wanted Detective Yvonne Passenmath to know about his "informal" chat with Lois, and now, during that chat, Passenmath was calling him. If he was afraid that I might think he had engineered receiving a call from the detective while he was talking to Lois, he was wrong. Alec had trusted Brent, and so did I.

However, I worried that this interruption could cause problems. If Lois had been on the verge of confessing that she had purposely not shown Brent that photo of Randy and the packed car, Passenmath's call might give Lois time to change her mind or make something up. Brent might conclude that Lois was covering up Randy's crimes.

Etiquette probably dictated that I should leave the room and give Brent some privacy. However, he had not moved from the wing chair, so he apparently didn't mind my eavesdropping. Besides, for the sake of the sweet woman sitting next to me, and for my sake, too, I wanted to hear as much of this conversation as I could.

"What do you mean, 'missing'?" Brent's voice was harsh, with a core of iron.

I tightened my grip on my glass of milk.

Lois paled. She whispered to me, "Is someone missing?"

I set the glass down and raised my palms to show that I didn't know.

Tears welled in her eyes. "Randy hasn't shown up. Has he disappeared?"

I patted her hand.

Brent said into the phone, "I e-mailed it to you." He glanced at me again. "Want me to resend it?" I couldn't hear Passenmath's response, but Brent asked, "Isn't it among the originals? Files can be recovered if they haven't been written over. We can use the copy I e-mailed to myself. . . . Yes, I understand. . . . Yes, I'm doing that. . . . Right now. . . ."

I heard a shrill comment, a question I guessed, judging by the rising tone at the end.

Brent spoke more loudly. "I need to finish here, first." With a wink at Lois and me, he pointed at the platter of donuts.

Lois eased back in her seat in apparent relief.

Still with the phone to his ear, Brent frowned. "I don't think that's necessary. I'll bring in my *notes* later, and we can go over them and then decide whether we should. . . . No, I don't know when I'll finish. By ten, for sure."

Smiling at me, Lois pointed at the donuts. She obviously wasn't worried about Randy or about what Brent was saying. She probably hadn't picked up on the unheard part of his conversation.

I thought I had.

On Wednesday evening, Brent had e-mailed himself the photo of Randy standing in front of his white-fendered black car, and by now, Brent must have also made certain that Passenmath and the other investigators saw that photo. This afternoon at Deputy Donut, Brent had told me that he wanted to talk to Lois before Yvonne Passenmath found out that Lois had omitted telling Brent about the photo.

However, from his side of the conversation, I guessed that the investigators had gone through the photos on Lois's original thumb drive, and had discovered that Lois had deleted the photo of Randy in front of the packed car.

And if I was guessing right, Detective Passenmath wanted Brent to bring Lois to police headquarters for questioning.

The chain of command in police departments was important to law enforcement, and an officer who did not immediately follow orders might be suspended or fired. Brent was taking serious chances with his career by postponing obeying this detective who had been brought in over his head. Passenmath had been micromanaging Brent since she took over. There was probably very little hope that she would give a subordinate leeway to conduct an interview his way.

However, I was certain that Brent was right about having a better chance to learn everything that Lois could tell him by talking to her here instead of interrogating her at police headquarters.

Brent ended the call. "Sorry about that." He reached for another donut, a raised one with a vanilla glaze. Apparently, he wasn't going to talk about Passenmath's call.

"I wonder where Randy could be," Lois said. It seemed that she didn't want to talk about whatever could be "missing." Maybe she had an inkling that Brent and Passenmath could have been discussing the photo that inexplicably was not on her portable drive.

"Is he definitely coming over?" Brent asked.

She looked down at the strawberry donut in her hand. "He didn't say for sure. I could call him and ask."

"It's not important." Brent probably didn't want Lois to tell Randy that a detective was at her place. "These evening get-togethers are great, but you two are feeding me too much."

"Didn't you hear the new rule?" I asked with a straight face. "Cops are immune to the calories in donuts."

"Ha," Brent said. "That's why so many of them take their breaks at your shop."

I wanted Lois to admit, right then and there, that she'd deleted that photo from her flash drive. I stared at her as if I could tell her without words that the longer she took to tell Brent about it, the harder it would be to appear innocent of withholding evidence. And if Brent thought she was lying about this, just as she'd lied about being attacked on Monday evening, he might never believe her again, about anything.

"Your donuts are superb, Emily," Lois said. I guessed that Brent would believe she was telling the truth about that, at least. "I'm getting myself another glass of milk. More coffee, Brent? More milk, Emily?"

We turned her down, and she went to the kitchen. Dep trotted behind her. I heard her murmuring to Dep in the kitchen.

"Sorry, Em," Brent muttered.

I frowned and gave my head a slight shake to show I didn't quite understand.

"I might have to do this by the book, after all."

"The department has a comfortable interview room, doesn't it, for people who haven't been arrested. Can you use that?"

"For sure."

The doorbell rang. Carrying her glass of milk, Lois hurried into the living room. "That'll be Randy!"

A study in reflexes and preparedness, Brent leaped to his feet and whipped around to face the door. Was he afraid that Lois's Monday night attacker had returned?

Her glass in hand, Lois stared through the peephole. "It's a woman." She sounded deflated.

Honey Bellaire, here to threaten and attack Lois again?

Before I could warn her, she opened the door.

Wearing thick-heeled shoes, Yvonne Passenmath clumped in. She did not look pleased.

Her face was red, she was scowling, and I doubted that she'd combed her hair since first thing that morning. I gave her the benefit of the doubt, however. Those of us with curly hair often had trouble keeping it neat, especially on humid days like this one had been. Her white blouse and her pantsuit, the same shade of brown as her hair, were rumpled, as if she'd brought only one outfit to Fallingbrook and had been wearing it day and night. I knew that my dislike of the woman was making me unfair.

She glared for a few seconds at Brent, and then looked past him at me. "You! I might have known you'd be involved in this."

I had a feeling she wasn't talking about Georgia's case. Yvonne had to know that I was one of the people who had discovered Georgia's body. By "this," she must have meant Brent's unwillingness to haul Lois to headquarters. The milk in her small glass sloshing, Lois sat down on the couch beside me.

I said, "The three of us often get together for dessert." I pointed at the coffee table. "Would you like a donut?"

Yvonne snapped, "I'm on duty. And although technically, Detective Fyne is not on duty at the moment, I'm going to have to ask him to—"

The doorbell interrupted her.

Lois made no move to answer it, and neither did I. Brent stood like a statue beside the wing chair.

Detective Yvonne Passenmath stomped to the door. I didn't know who she expected, police backup, maybe? She didn't bother with the peephole. She flung the door open.

With the mischievous bad-boy grin that always reached his eyes, Randy strode inside. He obviously hadn't shaved before he came over, but he'd recently applied aftershave or cologne. It was stronger than ever. He was carrying a white plastic bag from Fred Aggleton's store, Taste of Fallingbrook. The bag wasn't completely opaque and seemed to contain lumpy pinkish fabric.

Lois managed a faint, "Randy . . ." There was a hint of warning in her tone.

Randy stretched his right hand toward Yvonne. "Randy Unterlaw. I'm Lois's great-nephew."

Yvonne let her fingers graze his. "Detective Passenmath, DCI."

Randy's eyes opened in apparent surprise, but he offered his right hand to Brent. "Detective Fyne," he said. "Am I interrupting something?"

Brent shook Randy's hand. "Call me Brent."

Yvonne glared at Brent, and then the twitch of a smug smile crossed her face.

What does the proprietor of a donut shop do in an awkward situation? I offered, "Would you like a donut, Randy?"

Flashing me one of his adorable grins, he chose a plain unraised donut sprinkled with a blend of confectioners' sugar and nutmeg. "Great! And you have my favorite kind."

Yvonne stared at him like she was mentally preparing to snap handcuffs on him.

What was she thinking? If Randy was the one who had shoved plain unraised donuts sprinkled with confectioners' sugar and nutmeg onto that doll's legs, would he have admitted that they were his favorites?

In a few bites, he demolished the donut. He held out the plastic grocery bag. "Aunt Lois, did you make a baby dress and leave it in my car? Only it looks too small for a baby."

Lois jumped to her feet and waved her hands like someone trying to stop a runaway train. "No, no!" She reached for the bag, but Randy didn't seem to notice her frantic gestures.

He pulled a pink and black crocheted dress out of the bag. The dress was sized to fit the top of a teen doll, with a *Gone with the Wind* style of skirt that would cover a roll of toilet paper.

Judging by the way Lois's legs seemed to buckle, making her fall backward onto her couch, that dress was the one she'd crocheted for Georgia, to match Georgia's pink and black bathroom.

Chapter 28

❧

I caught a glimpse of reddish-brown smears on the tiny, hoop-skirted dress. Bloodstains?

I didn't remember seeing blood in Georgia's kitchen when we discovered her body. Maybe this wasn't the dress that might have gone missing from Georgia's house.

Passenmath's eyes became like black marbles, shiny and unforgiving. "Where did you get that thing?" she snapped.

Randy shot her a smile that looked totally innocent. "It was in my car. Aunt Lois sometimes makes things like it, so I thought that maybe she left it there and would want it back."

Lois's face became greenish. "I must have left it in your car." Her voice was wispy. Dep jumped onto the couch and rubbed her head against Lois's arm. Lois didn't seem to notice.

Passenmath ordered Brent, "Bring this man in for questioning."

"That's not entirely feasible." Brent's face was almost totally expressionless. "I arrived on foot."

"On foot!" Passenmath's cheeks bulged as if steam were building behind them.

Brent pulled out his phone and called for a patrol car. Maybe Misty would show up and tilt the balance toward normal.

Holding the white plastic bag in one hand and the crocheted dress in the other, Randy looked totally bewildered. "Why?" he asked. "What's going on?"

Passenmath barked, "Drop those two items, raise your hands above your head, and then do *not* move."

Without a word, Randy obeyed. He still looked baffled. His shirt sleeve slid down, revealing both the *A* and the *D* of his B.A.D. tattoo.

Randy and Lois both seemed incapable of speech. I asked the question that they probably should have been asking. "Is Randy under arrest?"

"Not yet," Passenmath retorted, "but he will be if he doesn't cooperate, and so will you, Ms. Westhill." Without taking her eyes off Randy, she bobbed her head toward Lois. "And you, too, Ms. . . . *um.*"

Although she was threatening to arrest all three of us, I had to speak in Randy's defense. "Randy can't have murdered Georgia. If he had, he would not have taken that dress out of that bag when two detectives were watching."

"I told you to be quiet, Ms. Westhill." She hadn't, but I decided not to argue. Besides, Brent had laid a quelling hand on my wrist.

I'd have expected Passenmath to be pleased that Brent looked ready to subdue me. Instead, she snarled, "Don't manhandle the suspects, Fyne. Next thing you know, they'll be charging you with police brutality."

The *suspects*. Brent squeezed my wrist and then let go.

"Will someone tell me what's going on?" Randy begged. His hands were still above his head. The arms of a less fit man would be shaking.

Passenmath's voice was hard and cold. "You're either coming willingly for questioning about the deaths of Matthias Treetor and Georgia Treetor, or I'll arrest you."

Dep jumped off the couch and stalked toward Lois's dining room.

Randy closed his eyes tight for a moment and then opened them. "Matthias and Georgia? I would never—"

Lois stood up. "Randy did *not* kill either one of them. I know because *I* did. *I* killed them, both of them."

Randy's nostrils flared, his face reddened, and his mouth distorted. He obviously had not entirely discarded his famous hair-trigger temper. "You did not, Aunt Lois. I didn't, either, so there's no need for you to make false confessions. We both . . ." His voice cracked. "Loved both of them."

Passenmath took a few steps toward Randy until she was almost nose to shirt pocket. "And you and your aunt are both coming to headquarters for questioning." Without taking her eyes off Randy, she demanded, "Fyne, call for another couple of patrolmen and another cruiser." As soon as Brent ended the call, Passenmath accused, "I suppose you don't have your cuffs with you, Fyne."

"We haven't placed anyone under arrest."

Again, I couldn't stand by quietly and allow injustice to happen. "Besides, it's not necessary."

Passenmath growled, "You want to come, too, Westhill?"

"Sorry, Detective Passenmath." My singsong response bordered on sassy. Passenmath glared.

Lois asked Passenmath, "May I get my purse and lock up before I go, Detective?"

Brent answered, "Tell me where to find your purse. I'll get it."

"It's on the kitchen table," she said.

Passenmath widened her stance. "Check it for weapons before you give it to her."

Brent strode out of the living room, leaving Randy, Lois, and me skewered by Passenmath's glare. I couldn't believe this was happening—to Randy, to Lois, and to me. I was innocent, and I was certain that the other two were, also.

His mouth thin, Brent returned and handed Lois her purse. "Your back door and windows are locked."

"Thank you, Detective Fyne." Why was Lois being formal? Was she blaming Brent, or trying to show Passenmath that she didn't expect favors from Brent despite the evenings that the three of us had spent together recently? Maybe she had caught on that our apparent friendship with Brent was making Passenmath angrier and more difficult.

Two uniformed officers, neither of them Misty, arrived. Passenmath directed each of them to take one of the Unterlaws to police headquarters. All of us, including Dep on her leash, went outside. It was only dusk, but streetlights were on. A small gray car was parked behind Lois's van in her driveway. It looked a lot like Georgia's car, and had to be Randy's. Sympathy for both Randy and Lois pricked at my heart. They would be worried and uncertain. Under Brent's careful scrutiny, Lois locked her front door.

"I'll meet you there." I wasn't sure if Brent was addressing Passenmath, Randy, or Lois.

"No need." I heard derision in Passenmath's voice. "You're off duty and on foot."

From Lois's front walk, Brent and I watched Passenmath help the officers place Randy in the back seat of one cruiser and Lois in the back seat of the other. Passenmath got into an unmarked car and attempted a fast U-turn, but the street was narrow, with cars parked on both sides, and she needed two back-ups before she roared off.

The two cruisers, their drivers waving lazily at Brent, followed at a more sedate pace.

Brent shoved his hands into his pants pockets. "I'll walk you home, Em." He sounded as dejected as he looked, and as I felt.

"Despite what Passenmath said, won't she expect you to hurry back to headquarters?"

"I'll see you safely home."

"And then, will you do whatever you can to prevent . . . innocent people from being arrested for crimes they didn't commit?"

"Yes'm."

"You don't have to walk me home. I have my guard cat."

He made an amused sort of grunt.

I could tell he was distracted, probably thinking about how to handle the interviews at police headquarters, if Detective Passenmath let him participate. I couldn't think of a non-sarcastic way of saying that if Randy had murdered Matthias and Georgia and had also attacked Lois, the streets of my neighborhood were now safe. I pointed out, "That doll dress had stains on it, like bloodstains. I didn't notice blood when I found Georgia."

"It was there."

"Oh." With Dep leading the way, we walked silently.

Brent kicked a pebble off the sidewalk into the grass strip beside the street. "I suppose it won't hurt to tell you this, but please don't spread it around. The doll stuffed in Ms. Treetor's mouth didn't kill her. She had already died. She was hit on the back of the head."

"Like Lois."

"Exactly."

"Did you find the weapon?"

"No. Forensics figures it was a rock, probably about the size of a baseball, but with at least one bulbous protrusion. We searched Georgia's yard and the woods behind it."

I remembered Mrs. Jierson's story of the shadowy man near the trash can in Georgia's driveway. "Her trash can, too?"

"Everything."

"And I guess you couldn't search Lois's yard, because if her attacker saw investigators there, she'd be in danger."

"The attacker would have merely seen a soil-sampling crew. They were thorough, though. Among the rocks they delivered to the forensics lab is the one that had probably blocked Lois's end of Dep's secret passage."

Although I heard a smile in Brent's voice, I answered seriously, "I'm certain that Lois's attacker left by her front door, unless he was good at scaling walls."

"The soil-sampling crew didn't find the right sort of stone in Lois's front yard, either. It could be anywhere—her neighbors' yards, the Fallingbrook River, or just by the side of a road with others like it. I doubt that we'll ever find it, and even if we do, it's not like it will be registered to an owner or have his or her name and address carved on it."

I couldn't help a gasp of something resembling laughter.

Brent came up onto my porch and watched me unlock the door. He placed his hands on my shoulders and turned me toward him. I resisted looking up into his face. "I'll do the best I can for your friends, Em."

"Thanks." I sounded breathless.

He put his arms around me and pulled me close, only for a second. "Stay safe, kid. Lock yourself in."

Dep defused the suddenly awkward situation. "Meow!"

Brent and I both laughed. Still not looking up at him, I escaped into the house and locked the door.

In my living room, I stood still, listening. Brent's footsteps diminished into the distance.

Purring, Dep wound herself—and her leash—around my ankles. "Sorry, Dep," I murmured. "I should set you free, shouldn't I?"

"Mmp."

I cooed in a lovey-dovey voice so she wouldn't know that I was ordering her about, not that ordering her about would cause her to obey. "Oh, stop it with the 'mmps,' Dep." I bent down and unsnapped her halter. She galloped toward the kitchen. I turned on lights, even though I had no plans to gallop.

Feeding Dep, I moved like a robot, working with only my right hand while holding my left fist over my mouth.

How was Lois doing? I should have insisted on going with her.

No, I shouldn't have. Passenmath would probably have found an excuse to lock me up, and Brent wouldn't have been able to stop her.

Brent. We hadn't hugged each other in years, since before Alec died, when we were casually affectionate with each other—a hug on greeting sometimes, or saying good-bye. Brent and Alec hadn't been afraid of showing their fondness for each other with back-slapping buddy hugs. It had all seemed natural and easy, and I'd never given it a second thought. Alec and I were a couple, and Brent was our friend, and so was whoever he was dating at the time.

But now, after three years, when I was alone, I found Brent's brief—extremely brief—embrace disturbing. Had someone told him that I'd gone on what might have appeared to some folks as a date? No, even if someone had told Brent that, he wouldn't have used it as an excuse to make a pass at me. He wouldn't make an unwelcome pass at me, period. We had been friends at one time, and we were cautiously renewing our friendship, and that was good. It was also enough. Why did people say "just friends" as if being friends wasn't as important as, say, being a couple? Friends could be the best and most supportive people in our lives. And it seemed to me that couples could break up more readily than friendships. Some friendships, anyway.

I hoped that Brent and I could return to the easy relationship we'd once had, with neither of us leaning too much on the other. Maybe the hug was because he was afraid I would be angry at him if Randy or Lois was arrested. Maybe the hug was a final good-bye because this case was going to make it impossible for us to stay friends.

I removed my hand from my mouth. "I'm not going to worry about it, Dep." I would worry about Lois. I would worry about Randy. I would not bother my head with wondering whether or not Brent and I could return to our once easy friendship.

Dep continued eating her dinner.

I should have told Lois to call me when she got home. Maybe she would.

And Randy was either very good at acting innocent, or he wasn't a murderer. And neither was Lois. Brent would make certain that both of them were treated fairly.

But what if he couldn't? Passenmath would be making the important decisions, and she seemed determined to believe that Randy was the culprit she was seeking. And maybe Lois, too.

I hoped that Lois and I could stay friends.

Chapter 29

When we opened Deputy Donut at ten on Sunday morning, Lois still hadn't called, and there was no hope that the Knitpickers would change their schedule and show up on a weekend.

Maybe I'd slept through the ringing of my phone. I could hardly bear to think about Lois's pain and fatigue if she'd been interrogated for hours by Detective Passenmath. I hoped Brent had been allowed to stay with her. He would have lowered the hostility levels.

I served the day's featured coffee, a rich but light roast from Costa Rica, to a pair of police officers. I asked them if progress had been made on the Georgia Treetor case. They shrugged. One of them bit into Tom's latest creation, a raised blueberry donut with lemon icing. The other said, "Haven't heard a thing."

Hadn't heard a thing, or hadn't heard a thing he was allowed to say? I stared into his warm brown eyes. He didn't blink.

Shortly before noon, there was a lull. I joined Dep in the office and checked my cell phone. Lois hadn't returned my calls. I tried her. No answer. I left a message inviting her to dessert that night.

In the afternoon, Tom made raised donuts filled with raspberry jam and dusted with powdered sugar. They disappeared rapidly.

We closed at four thirty as usual. Lois had not responded. I boxed a half-dozen deep-fried treats and then walked Dep home. I reminded myself that if Lois didn't show up, I was not supposed to gobble our dessert by myself.

The evening was cool, perfect for sautéing green pepper, garlic, and tomato bits in extra-extra-virgin olive oil, tossing the veggies with fettuccine, and topping it all with a snow-drift of freshly shredded Romano cheese.

I didn't hear from Lois, and she didn't show up.

I didn't want to call the police station and ask for Brent. I'd probably agitate DCI agent Yvonne Passenmath.

But I was worried about Lois. Was she still at police head-quarters?

I tried Brent's personal phone.

"Hey, Em, what's up?" His deep voice came across as kind and sympathetic.

Disregarding my resolve not to lean on him, I wailed, "I in-vited Lois to come over for donuts for dessert, and she hasn't returned my calls. I'm afraid she's been attacked or hurt again, and I want to go to her house to look for her, but . . ." *The last time I searched for a missing Deputy Donut patron, I found her. Dead. I can't face that again.*

"Don't go anywhere. I'll be at your place in ten minutes, and we'll figure out what to do. Okay?" He sounded tired.

"Okay. And you can help me eat these donuts."

He didn't laugh. Without a hint of a grin in his voice, he said, "See you in ten."

He was at the door in less than ten minutes, which was fortunate. My pacing was about to trample a furrow in my beautiful ruby and cobalt rug, from one end of my living room to the other. I suspected from his outfit—sneakers, jeans, dark blue T-shirt, and navy blue casual jacket—that he was not on duty.

As soon as he stepped inside, he said, "I'm sorry, Em."

Suddenly I was cold all over. "What? Where's Lois?"

"Last I knew, she was at home. I drove her there last night shortly before midnight and went inside with her to make certain everything was as we'd left it."

"Randy's car was at her place. He didn't walk her home." I stated it as a fact.

"Yvonne was still questioning him. And I'm really sorry, Em—shortly before you called me just now, we charged Randy with the murders of Matthias and Georgia Treetor."

To steady myself, I gripped the carved mahogany at the back of the red velvet armchair. "*No.*"

"Sorry. When I left work, the chief was writing a press release. If you hadn't called me just now, I'd have come over, anyway, to tell you."

"Should we go to Lois's and break the news?" *And check to see if she's all right?*

"I can go by myself."

"I'd like to go, too, but I don't have a key, so I don't know what we'll do if she doesn't answer her door."

Someone pounded on my door *and* rang my doorbell. Holding up one finger signaling me to let him answer, Brent peeked out the peephole. "It's Lois," he said in a strangely flat tone. He opened the door.

Lois's eyes were red. Her dandelion froth of white hair was tangled and uncombed. Tears ran down her cheeks.

Brent stood back and let her in.

She curled her hands into fists as if she were about to pummel him, but she rolled her fists into the lapels of her purple hand-knit cardigan, instead. "Why?" she demanded, looking straight at Brent and not bothering to wipe her eyes. "*Why?*"

I took her elbow and guided her to the wing chair. She was almost lost in it. Dep jumped into her lap. Lois wormed her fingers into Dep's fur, but her eyes were still on Brent. "Why?" she asked again, more hesitantly.

Still wearing his jacket, he eased into the couch opposite

Lois and leaned forward, his forearms on his knees and his hands clasped together. "I believed him and didn't think we should arrest him, but the evidence piled up. First of all, during your interview with Detective Passenmath and me, you admitted that you had once given Georgia Treetor a doll dress like the one that Randy showed you last night."

Lois's hands stilled on Dep's back. "I made lots of those dresses."

"How many were mostly pink with black trimming like that one?" he asked.

She slumped back. "I told that surly female detective that I don't remember, and I *don't*. I made doll gowns to cover toilet paper rolls for years, and I must have had other friends whose bathrooms were similar. Besides, I sold those dressed dolls at my church's bazaars, year in and year out. That color scheme was popular for bathrooms when I was a girl, and Fallingbrook has many houses from that era."

I again pointed out that if Randy had taken that gown off the doll and stuffed the doll into Georgia's mouth, he wouldn't have allowed two detectives to see it.

Brent lowered his head for a second, and then looked up at me. "Passenmath decided he did that to deflect suspicion from himself."

I plunked myself down on the opposite end of the couch from Brent. "That's too weird."

He explained, "It was clear that when Randy came in, he didn't expect to see any detectives in Lois's living room, let alone two. And he didn't know who Passenmath was until she introduced herself. She figures that he knew the bag was translucent enough that she might have seen the dress and guessed what it was, so he quickly made up a story about finding it in his car."

I brushed a small drift of flour off one knee of my black jeans. "That doesn't explain why, if he'd murdered Georgia, he brought that dress to Lois."

"Passenmath thinks that's just one more sign that Randy is unhinged." Brent's jaw tensed up.

Lois made a despairing noise in the back of her throat. "He's not."

"I agree," I said. "Lois, does Randy shop at Taste of Falling-brook?"

"I doubt it."

"Do you?" Brent asked her.

"Not since Matthias's death. Anyway, Matthias used paper bags. He said they were better for the environment. Randy didn't get that plastic bag from me."

I had another idea. "Brent, if Randy parked somewhere with his car window open, could Fred Aggleton have thrown that dress into the car?"

Brent stretched his legs, barely missing kicking the coffee table. "Randy told us the dress was in the bag, and shoved deep underneath the front passenger seat. Someone would have had to open the door."

I burst out, "Passenmath obviously believed that, but *not* that Randy wasn't the one who put the dress into his car. She's cherry-picking which of his statements to believe."

Brent's only response was a quick and unreadable glance at me. He focused on Lois again. "Lois, is Randy one of those people who leaves his car unlocked?"

"Probably. He's fairly easygoing about possessions."

"Aha," I said.

Brent leaned back and folded his arms. "Unfortunately, there are more clues pointing to Randy. When we finger-printed your house the day after you were attacked, Lois, the prints we found were yours, the previous owners', a couple of Emily's, some of mine, and lots of Randy's."

Lois nearly exploded. "Randy helped me move in! Of course his fingerprints were there."

Brent stayed calm. "We all accepted that, at first."

I asked Brent if Randy's fingerprints were found in Geor-gia's house.

"No, but her killer wore gloves."

Lois sagged back into the wing chair. "Emily touched things there, like that doll's legs and feet."

Brent nodded. "You and five other women testified that you saw her touch them after you discovered Georgia, who appeared to be deceased."

"I could have gone to her house early Monday morning, before work." My statement came out more sarcastically than I meant it to.

Brent flicked a steely glance at me.

"Emily's not a killer," Lois asserted. "But it just goes to show you that fingerprints can be somewhere quite innocently."

Brent conceded, "Randy's fingerprints in your house, Lois, would not have been enough for a homicide charge."

Lois turned Dep over on her back and cuddled her in her arms like a baby. "It was those photos, wasn't it? The car that looked like his, coming out of the valley, and the one Passenmath made me tell her about last night, the one of him in front of the car that I had to admit was his. I never should have shown you the first one." Dep flipped herself upright and scrambled off Lois's lap.

"Or deleted the second one from your flash drive." Brent managed to sound supportive.

Lois brushed a tear from her cheek. "I know that now. But it's all circumstantial. Even if Randy was driving his car out of the Fallingbrook River valley the night that Matthias went missing, it doesn't mean that Randy had anything to do with Matthias's death. It couldn't have been Randy driving, anyway. As I told you before, Randy would have stopped to say hello."

"He waved at you," Brent said.

"*What?*" Lois ran both hands through her hair, which only made it stick up more. "I didn't see him wave."

"You said you weren't looking at the car," Brent reminded her.

"I wasn't. But if it was Randy, why didn't he stop?"

Brent thinned his lips and stared at her, daring her to draw her own conclusion, I guessed, like the one I'd thought of before. A fleeing murderer would not stop to chat.

Lois answered her own question. "Maybe he was late for a date or appointment. What makes you think he waved?"

"The forensics guys enhanced and enlarged the photo. Let's go up to your computer, Em. Now that I know what to look for, I can show you two what the forensics team found."

As usual, Dep beat us to the top of the stairs. I sat in the desk chair, turned on the computer, and loaded the photo.

Behind my right shoulder, Brent tapped near the driver's side of the windshield. "Enlarge that portion, Em, please."

I did.

He pointed above where the top of the steering wheel would be. "Center it on this spot and try enlarging it more."

The picture blurred. It was beginning to look like an abstract painting. "There," Brent said. "See? His left hand isn't on the steering wheel. He raised his arm."

"Maybe to pull down the visor," Lois suggested in an unusually aggressive tone, "not to wave."

"Doesn't matter," Brent said. "Look at his wrist. See those dark marks?"

Lois was behind my left shoulder. "I don't see anything."

I could barely make out the dark marks. I turned around in my seat and looked up at Brent. "Want me to play with the brightness and contrast to bring them out more?"

"There's no harm in trying. The forensics guys thought they saw a tattoo. Letters or a word."

Lois didn't utter a sound.

Brent and I tried different ways of temporarily editing the photo until the dark marks were clearer. I rummaged in my desk and found a magnifying glass, only slightly scratched. I held it up to the screen. "I see where someone might have thought they were seeing a tattoo."

I stood and gestured for Lois to sit in the desk chair. She sat and peered through the magnifying glass. "You'd have to have a wild imagination and want to believe you're seeing Randy's tattoo so you can close your case and go back to Milwaukee or wherever you—I mean she—came from."

Brent said mildly, "The forensics guys got a clearer picture, and it did look a lot like Randy's tattoo. Can we go downstairs again, Em? Your donuts are calling to me."

Lois followed me downstairs.

In the living room, she again sat in the wing chair. I went to the kitchen and poured three glasses of milk. I managed to fit the glasses, three dessert plates, and a stack of pretty cloth napkins on a tray. I set the tray on the coffee table and then returned to the kitchen for the platter of donuts. Lois chose an unraised orange donut with orange icing.

Brent came downstairs with Dep draped around his neck. He stared at me for a few seconds, and then sat on the couch. As if she'd planned a ride down a playground slide, Dep slithered off Brent's shoulders and landed on his lap. He leaned forward and helped himself to a raised donut with bits of candied ginger sprinkled on dark chocolate icing. I gave Lois and Brent each a plate and a glass of milk, and put the napkins on the coffee table next to the platter of donuts.

"This is delicious, Emily," Lois said. "Thank you." Then she confronted Brent again. "So, you're telling me that Randy was arrested for killing two of his favorite people because someone enlarged a bunch of pixels until they were completely fuzzy, and then made up something that might implicate him? It won't hold up in court, and meanwhile, the actual murderer is free to kill again."

"There's that dress you crocheted," he reminded her. "There's blood on it, O positive, Georgia's blood type."

Lois waved her hand in dismissal. "That's the most common type."

Brent agreed with her. "We've sent it for DNA analysis, but that could take a while. Clues added up, and the first thing this morning, a judge approved Detective Passenmath's application for a warrant to search Randy's car. Investigators found several objects in it linked to Georgia's murder and the attack on you. That was enough for Detective Passenmath, for any of us, to arrest him. I'm sorry, Lois, but the evidence is fairly conclusive."

Lois looked about to chomp on the insides of her cheeks. "What *objects* did they find in his car?"

"A chisel," Brent answered, "with a blade that matches the size of the gouges near the locks on your front door and Ms. Treetor's back door."

Lois frowned, obviously unconvinced. "So? It's probably not an unusual size."

"It's not," he said. "But no chisel blade will be exactly like another, and they'll be able to tell for certain if it was the chisel the killer used. Also, there were other things in the bag with the chisel. There was a rock with a protrusion that matched the dent in Georgia's head. It has O positive blood on it, and also AB positive, which I'm guessing is your blood type, Lois."

Lois started to shake her head, then got up, turned her back on us, and blew her nose. "That's my blood type, but it's impossible. My boy is not a killer."

Brent continued to sound soothing. "Again, we'll compare the DNA."

She folded her arms. "I don't have to give you a DNA sample."

His answer was mild. "You're correct. We might not need it to convict Randy, anyway."

She turned pale. "Why not?"

He closed his eyes and took a deep breath as if he didn't want to tell her. Finally, he opened his eyes and said with obvious reluctance, "The pictures that were missing from your photo album were in that bag. I've obtained a warrant for your album so we can determine if the vestiges of paper and glue in the book match the ones missing from the pictures, but based on the photos I took of your album, I'm almost certain they do."

"Noooo," Lois moaned, almost as if she were beginning to accept the horrible truth. She sat up straighter. "May I see the warrant, Brent?"

He handed it to her. She studied it. "Mind if Emily takes a look?"

"Of course not," Brent said.

I didn't take long to assure Lois, "It looks legit to me, for all I know. You can trust Brent, Lois."

She bowed her head and sniffled. "I'll give you the album, Brent." I could barely hear her.

I asked Brent, "What kind of bag were the things in?"

He gave me another penetrating stare. "A white plastic grocery bag from Taste of Fallingbrook."

"Frederick Aggleton's store." I couldn't help showing my dislike of Frederick Aggleton.

Lois sat in the wing chair again. "That man! He always wanted to buy the store when Matthias owned it, but he never offered what it was worth. Then he beat Georgia down in price until she sold it to him, and have you been in there, Brent? It's nothing like it used to be. He's run it down and made customers feel unwelcome, and now it's bringing in hardly anything. Right, Emily?"

"Yes. He complained to me that he might have to go bankrupt. He also showed Misty and me a couple of collages that are supposed to prove he's innocent."

"*Supposed* to?" Brent repeated.

"You don't have to stay in a hotel to have receipts saying you paid for three nights there. It's all a little too convenient, as if he planned his so-called alibis before killing Matthias and Georgia. Aggleton could have put that bag of evidence in Randy's car."

Brent picked up a pineapple fritter. "Why would a store owner murder someone and put the evidence in a bag from his own store?"

I had what I thought was a convincing answer. "Because no one in his right mind would do that, and besides, he was going to shove them into the first unlocked car he saw, so it didn't matter what bag they were in."

Brent bit into the fritter.

I held up an index finger. "I just thought of something else. Randy wears a strong cologne. If *Randy* attacked you, Lois, wouldn't you have recognized his fragrance?"

Suddenly Lois looked happier than she had since she'd arrived at my place that evening. "Emily's right. Randy always has on the same aftershave or whatever, but when I was attacked, I didn't notice *any* fragrance."

I added, "Aggleton wasn't wearing cologne when I talked to him."

Brent pointed out the obvious. "Cologne can be washed off."

Looking defeated again, Lois said she should go.

Brent offered, "I'll walk you home."

"Why?" she demanded. "My dangerous great-nephew is locked away."

"I can get that photo album from you." He followed her outside and patted his jacket pockets. "Em, I think I left something near your computer. I'll come back for it in a few minutes."

He was between Lois and me, so he didn't see her give me a watery smile. Her great-nephew had been charged with murder, and the man staring into my eyes might have been instrumental in that arrest, and I was sure that Lois liked me, yet she was still hoping to pair me off with Brent.

I had a feeling that his coming back later had nothing to do with any sort of romantic interest. I suspected he wanted to tell me something that might sadden Lois even more. We said our good-byes, and I locked the door.

I almost tidied the living room instead of going upstairs to my computer, but Brent had spent extra minutes upstairs alone with Dep after Lois and I came down. I asked Dep, "Is there something upstairs that he wants me to see?"

"Mmp." She raced me up the stairs. As usual, she won.

An unfamiliar thumb drive was plugged into my computer. The screen was blank. I moved the mouse. A grainy black and white picture appeared on the screen. I could see several cars, including the passenger side of a small gray or silver sedan, in a parking lot at night. The sedan looked a lot like Georgia's—and Randy's. The only illumination came from above, as if a surveillance camera shared a pole with a light fixture.

A largish right-pointing arrow was in the middle of the picture.

Brent had loaded a video on my computer.

Chapter 30

✣

A good citizen would not view the surveillance video that a detective had, inadvertently or not, left on her computer. I told myself that it wasn't like I was tampering with evidence. Besides, it was *my* computer.

I clicked on the arrow.

At first, nothing moved except seconds ticking away on the time stamp at the screen's lower right corner. If the camera's clock was right, this video began last Monday, the day that the police believed that Georgia was murdered, at eighteen minutes after five in the morning.

A man came into the upper right corner of the picture and walked toward the camera. He wore jeans, a light-colored long-sleeved shirt, and a white ball cap pulled low in front. The insignia on the cap was the Green Bay Packers' G.

It had to be Randy, with his bowlegged gait, a sort of swagger from side to side that I attributed to horseback riding. Randy tugged his left sleeve down as if to hide that tattoo, got into the small grayish sedan that I'd already guessed was his, backed out of the parking space, and headed away from the camera. The picture was too grainy for me to read the license plate. A number was painted on the pavement where the car had been. I couldn't tell for sure, but I thought it said 406.

The video stopped and restarted, same camera on a pole in

a parking lot, at six forty that same morning. The sky was light. Several cars had left the parking lot. Headlights came toward the camera. Because it was mounted high, showing a wide view, I couldn't see the driver as he swung the small gray car into the space it had left more than an hour before.

The driver got out and locked the car. Even from the back, I could tell it was Randy by the way he walked. His right sleeve was rolled up to the elbow, but it was his left sleeve that he pulled down past his wrist. He disappeared near the top right of the picture.

The video, again from that same camera and showing the small silver or gray car, restarted at seven Monday evening. The sun was still up. Wearing his jeans, white shirt, and Packers cap, Randy came from the middle of the right side of the picture, got into his car, and drove away.

He parked the car in spot 406 again at ten on Monday night, and went toward the middle of the right of the picture. A white plastic grocery bag dangled from his right hand. I couldn't read the words on it, but I guessed they were "Taste of Fallingbrook."

So. This was what Brent had wanted me to see. Randy had driven somewhere around the time that Georgia was murdered, and had again gone off in his car around the time that Lois was attacked. That was all circumstantial, but there he was, carrying the bag that might have contained the chisel, the photos, the bloodied rock, and maybe the doll dress, also.

The video continued. At one on Tuesday morning, Randy again came into the picture at the top right of the screen. Neither of his sleeves was rolled up. Again, that bulging white plastic grocery bag dangled from his right hand. He unlocked the trunk, opened it, leaned forward, flung the bag in, shut the trunk, and locked it with a key. Tugging at his left sleeve, he went back the way he came.

The video stopped, and a new one started. This camera appeared to be mounted in the lobby of an apartment building. The timer started at five on Monday morning, and sped through the minutes until eighteen after five. No one appeared in the lobby. Then the timer changed to six forty. Again, the action was sped up. People left the apartment lobby by the front door, but no one came in, and the timer stopped at seven.

About twelve hours later, at five to seven in the evening, Randy, dressed as he had been in the morning, except that both sleeves were rolled down, entered the lobby from where the elevators probably were. He went out the front door. He came back inside shortly after ten that night. He was carrying the bulging white bag. Knowing that the words on it were "Taste of Fallingbrook," I could read them.

And then the video, still black and white, changed to a location I recognized—the parking lot in front of the post office where Honey Bellaire worked. At the beginning, the time stamp said it was six twenty Monday morning. A small silver or gray sedan pulled into a spot in front of the post office. This time, I thought I could read the license plate. His Packers cap pulled down low, Randy got out of the car and walked off to the right of the screen.

Moments later, Dr. Jierson, TOOTHY license plate and all, pulled into the spot next to Randy's car. The dentist got out, slammed his door, and strode toward his office. TOOTHY's lights flashed twice as if Dr. Jierson had locked his car remotely. The young-looking receptionist opened the office door, and Dr. Jierson went inside. The giant molar over the door was shining so brightly that it was hard to be sure, but it appeared that Dr. Jierson embraced his receptionist. Through the glass door, I saw her pale arms on the back of his dark jacket, and then they both moved farther inside, away from the windows and door.

Randy came from the right and pounded on the post office door. Because of the height of the camera, I couldn't see any of his face except for his unshaven chin. Beneath the Packers cap, his hair was messy. His right sleeve was rolled up past his elbow, but the cuff of his left sleeve almost covered his wrist. Before he tugged it down, I saw the *D* and the period after it.

I didn't realize that I'd said, "No," aloud until Dep let out a questioning chirp.

Just as Honey had described to Lois and me, she opened the door from inside, only slightly. I could see the edge of the door and the top of her head. She stood talking to Randy through the crack for about two minutes. Then she retreated into the post office, and the edge of the door disappeared. Randy returned to his car, folded himself into the driver's seat, lifted a bulging white bag from the passenger seat, bent over, and tucked it underneath the passenger seat. He straightened and turned the key in the ignition. He grabbed a watch off the dashboard, slipped it onto his left wrist, looked down toward his wrist, tapped the face of the watch once with his index finger, moved the watchband slightly as if centering the watch on the back of his wrist, shook his hand as if to settle the watch more comfortably, put the car in reverse, and backed out of the parking spot. He turned north on Packers Road. It was six twenty-nine on Monday morning. Georgia was probably already dead.

The video corroborated Honey Bellaire's story, and although Dr. Jierson might have lied about his reason for going into work early that morning, perhaps he and his wife had not made up the story about the small sedan in Georgia's driveway.

The videos, combined with Honey's description and the Jiersons' report of a silver or gray sedan that didn't belong in Georgia's driveway, firmly implicated Randy.

Bowing my head, I let sorrow overwhelm me. What had Georgia possibly done that had made Randy kill her? Had she threatened to report him for murdering her son? Or had he learned that Lois was Georgia's sole heir? I felt sad for Lois and horrified that I'd believed Randy had reformed since high school.

I wanted to figure out what had caused Randy to kill two people whom he supposedly thought of as family.

Most of all, I missed Georgia.

Tapping on my front door sent Dep flying downstairs, with me following at a mere trot.

I peeked through the peephole. Brent. I let him in and shut the door. Dep purred and twined herself around his ankles.

I asked, "Did she give you the photo album?"

"With no problem, other than a few tears. It's now safely locked in my car. With Randy in custody, there's no rush to take it to headquarters." He studied my face.

"I found a video on my computer," I told him. "I watched it."

"Shame," he said, poker-faced. "*Now* will you be more cautious and less trusting, especially around Lois?"

I raised my chin and looked up into his eyes. "I'm sure she had nothing to do with the murders of her best friend and her best friend's son."

"Me, too, but what if Randy gets out, either legally or illegally? Being around Lois could be dangerous."

"I'll take that chance. Meanwhile, you probably want your thumb drive. It's upstairs. Come on up. I have some questions."

At my computer, I started the video again. I pointed at Randy when he appeared on the upper right corner of the picture. "When he comes and goes from this direction, there's no sign of him in the apartment building lobby." I edged my finger down the screen. "But when he comes and goes from about here, he seems to have come from the apartment building lobby."

"The building's front door is closer to where he parks his car. When he's coming from farther away, he's coming from the direction of the back door. Vandals broke the surveillance camera back there last June, and the building's owner hasn't replaced it."

"And Randy probably knows that. It's curious, though,

that some of the time, including when he takes that plastic bag inside around ten on Monday night, which would be when he returned home after attacking Lois, he uses the door where the surveillance camera *is* working."

"He could have been distracted." Brent shut down the video and disengaged his thumb drive. "Did you make a copy?"

"No. I wouldn't want either of us to get into trouble."

He gave my shoulder a quick squeeze.

I hurried downstairs. At the front door, Brent asked, "Are you okay?"

I picked Dep up so she wouldn't try to run off with Brent. "Yes. I'll probably never get over Georgia's death. I didn't know her son well, but it's sad, and I feel sorry for Lois. And Randy wasn't that bad in high school, plus I thought he had grown up. I liked him." I snuggled my face into Dep's warm fur.

"Were you dating Randy?"

My head shot up. "No! Why would you think that?"

"Your defense of him. Plus, Lois told us she thought he came back to Fallingbrook because of a woman. He denied it, but I thought maybe you were that woman."

"Impossible. Alec was still alive when Randy left for Wyoming." I didn't mean it to come out sounding quite that angry.

I thought I read apology in Brent's eyes. "I assumed that if it *was* you, you and he had begun corresponding in the past year or so."

"I doubt that I gave him more than a few seconds' thought after he graduated from high school until he showed up again. He's been in Deputy Donut a few times, and he seems nice, but I'm not interested in him other than as a customer. An ex-customer now, I guess."

"Sorry for suggesting it, Em. I know how you feel about Alec. I miss him, too."

I looked down at Dep again and said softly, "I know."

"If Randy has a girlfriend, I'd really like to talk to her. Last night when we were questioning him, I thought he was going to tell us about someone he might have been with some of those times his car left his apartment building's parking lot, but he said there was no one."

"Maybe he has a thing going with Mrs. Jierson. *That* would serve her husband right."

Brent grinned. "And undoubtedly complicate our investigation."

"Is there any chance that the man going to and from Randy's car from the back of Randy's building could be Frederick Aggleton?"

"Who did it look like to you?"

I hung my head. "Randy. Aggleton's thinner, and so is his hair, but he could have been wearing a wig and some padding."

"And Randy's left arm. And driving Randy's car."

"I suppose you're right," I conceded. "Poor Lois."

"Do you think that, without telling her about the videos, you can help her get a grip on reality?"

"Maybe, but I'm not sure I want to try. She believes in Randy. He's losing everything. Maybe he shouldn't lose the affection that he and his aunt share. And neither should she."

Brent opened my front door. "You might have to accept that Randy's guilty, Em."

I looked past him, toward the glow underneath the streetlight in the otherwise dark night. "I'm trying to."

"Take care, then." He let himself out.

"At least he didn't hug me again," I informed Dep, although she'd been there to see the non-hug. "And I won't blame him for doing his job and not stopping Detective Passenmath from arresting Randy. Those videos are incriminating."

Chapter 31

❧

I woke up in the morning with a sense of failure. I had promised to help Lois exonerate Randy. I'd known all along that we might not succeed, but after I became reacquainted with Randy, I'd believed that Lois was right, and that her great-nephew could not be a killer.

Still, he *was* innocent until proven guilty, and there would be a trial. Unfortunately, the evidence that I knew about was persuasive, and Detective Passenmath and her colleagues, including Brent, were sure to find more. If the DNA tests on the blood on both the rock and the crocheted dress were conclusive, Randy could spend the rest of his life in jail.

As usual on nice days, Dep and I walked to work. I established her in her windowed playground, and then opened the door to the dining room. Tom must have been at work for a while. Smelling the yeast in the rising dough and the crisp sugary aroma of donuts coming out of the fryer made me almost forget that I'd polished off a spinach and cheddar omelet only about a half hour before.

I went into the kitchen and put on a clean apron. "Expecting lots of business today?" I asked Tom.

"It's Labor Day. We could get extra tourists enjoying the last day of their vacation. Besides, you know how it is. When there's news, the place fills up. You heard, I suppose. They made an arrest." He didn't have to name the case. Georgia's murder was Fallingbrook's only recent major crime.

I folded the tuck in my apron over the bow in my apron strings. "Randy Unterlaw, one of our customers."

"Are you surprised they charged him?"

"Yes. It seemed to me that he'd grown out of acting on his anger."

Tom spooned another donut out of the hot oil. "We always hope that people can change for the better. The truth is, they seldom do."

"But children mature into adults."

"Most of us don't change a lot from the kids we were." He shook the spoon at me. "And don't say that I was a grade school bully. I was a child prodigy, developing my law enforcement skills."

"Right." I didn't believe for one second that Tom Westhill had ever been a bully.

"I liked Randy's vintage car idea," he said.

"So did I."

"We can still do it, though I guess we won't be hiring Randy to drive it."

I acted affronted. "*I* was going to drive it."

His pretend attempt at a stern police chief expression didn't fool me. "You and I were going to take turns. We could have taught Randy to work in the kitchen and wait tables."

In addition to tourists that morning, locals crowded into Deputy Donut, and most of them wanted to discuss Randy's arrest. One woman told me, "We can all sleep now that a dangerous criminal is behind bars."

Her husband corrected her. "Most murderers kill people they know, like in this case." He puffed out his chest. "This Randy Unterlaw was no danger to you ladies."

Five of the Knitpickers arrived around nine. "Lois isn't coming," one of them said. "She's too upset about her great-nephew."

"And no wonder!" another exclaimed.

The first one added, "She says she doesn't like living up here anymore. She's thinking of moving back to Madison."

I hoped that when things calmed down and she got used to Randy's being in jail, she'd reconsider and stay. Despite Brent's warnings, I liked her, as a friend and as a neighbor.

A mother came in with a pair of twins, a boy and a girl who were about seven years old and had adorable matching gap-toothed smiles. The girl wanted a donut with pink sprinkles while the boy ordered chocolate sprinkles, and they both asked for chocolate milk. Smiling, their mother said, "I heard you have a different specialty coffee every day, and I knew I had to come in."

"Donuts, too!" her kids chimed.

"I'll stick to coffee," their mother said, "whatever you're featuring today."

"It's from Ethiopia, a light but very flavorful roast."

"I can't wait to try it."

When I brought them their goodies, the girl pulled up the sleeve of her ruffled pink T-shirt. "Look! I have a tattoo!" It was a pink and purple butterfly that appeared to have been drawn by a child.

Both kids were wearing shorts. The girl obviously loved pink. The boy, dressed in khaki and olive drab, turned sideways on his seat and showed me the tattoo on his knee, a red rectangle balanced on two black circles. "It's a race car," he told me.

"We made the tattoos ourselves!" the girl crowed.

I felt my eyes open wide. My mouth almost did, too. "How?" I managed.

"You draw a picture on the computer and print it on water slide paper."

I was lost. I swooped my hand down like a kid on a slide. "*Water* slide paper?"

The mother laughed. "That's what I thought, too, when we first heard about it on a crafty TV show. You draw a picture on your computer or on regular paper, and then you print or photocopy the picture on this special paper called 'water slide paper.' When you want a tattoo, you put the water slide paper ink-side-down on your skin. You hold a damp cloth over it, and the water causes the design to slide off the paper onto your skin."

The boy told me seriously, "You have to hold the tattoo very still for a half minute, or it gets all smeary."

"It's really fun," the girl said. "And it stays a long time! If you don't wash it off."

The boy's eyes went all dreamy. "I'm never washing mine off."

Their mother winked at me. "They're having loads of fun with it, but I told them they could each wear only one temporary tattoo at a time."

Temporary tattoos? That might explain how Frederick Aggleton could have worn a tattoo like Randy's early Monday morning. I didn't know if water slide paper had been available five years ago. If not, Fred could have written B.A.D. on his wrist with a marker. The man's face had been hidden in the five-year-old photo, and I'd seen only an unshaven chin in the videos from the previous Monday. I asked, "Where do you buy water slide paper?"

The mother answered, "Online or in craft stores. We found it right here in Fallingbrook, though, at that specialty grocery that used to be so nice but now has hardly any fresh food, Taste of Fallingbrook."

I could hardly wait to call Brent.

Customers kept me busy through lunchtime, and when I did catch Brent, he said he was in a meeting.

I rattled out, "Frederick Aggleton sells a type of paper in his store that can be used to make temporary tattoos."

"Thank you," Brent said formally. "I'll take that under advisement." He disconnected the call.

Take that under advisement. While Alec was still alive, a rookie cop had said it whenever one of his superiors corrected him, and Brent and Alex had begun teasing each other with what they called memo-speak.

Alec would ask Brent, "Would you like a coffee?"

Brent would say, "Yes."

Alec would answer, "I'll take that under advisement." Then they'd both laugh. They laughed hardest when Alec did not actually bring coffee or whatever he'd offered.

I wanted to interpret Brent's repeating the expression as code for, "Sorry I have to pretend I'm speaking to someone I barely know. I'm in a meeting with Yvonne Passenmath." But maybe my connection to Lois and her great-nephew was forcing Brent to distance himself from me. I should be okay with losing a friendship I'd almost single-handedly destroyed once before.

After all, it wasn't like I didn't have friends. Misty and Samantha stopped in together and sat at the stools at the counter. Samantha asked, "Are you okay?"

I poured her coffee. "Yes, but I'm surprised and disappointed that Randy changed for the worse instead of for the better."

Misty frowned. "Killers sometimes progress from smaller crimes."

"Yeah, but . . ."

Tom joined the conversation, "And they sometimes seem charming."

"I'm outnumbered," I admitted.

Unfortunately, Misty and Samantha left about a half hour before Scott and Oliver arrived for their afternoon coffee break, so I wasn't able to observe the progress of my matchmaking. Scott, Oliver, and I had basically the same conversation I'd had with Misty and Samantha, and with nearly everyone else in Deputy Donut that day.

Oliver shook his head. "I can't believe it. They must have the wrong person. Randy and I booked a golf game for this afternoon. I'll have to cancel it or find someone else."

Scott said mildly, "We knew what he was like in high school."

"I could have sworn he had reformed." Oliver turned to me. "I don't know whether Randy has savings, but I do know he doesn't have a job in Fallingbrook, yet. I interviewed him for a sales position at my construction equipment dealership, and was about to offer him the job. It'll be his if they drop the charges or he's acquitted. Meanwhile, I've started a defense fund for him at the Fallingbrook State Bank. May I put up a flyer about it on your bulletin board by the front door?"

Quickly, I said that he could. "And feel free to leave a stack of flyers here on the counter. I'm glad there's something we can do for him, but . . ."

"But what?" Scott asked.

Brent had told me about and let me see some of the evidence they'd collected against Randy, but I wouldn't compromise a possible trial by divulging any of it. "We get a lot of cops in here. From their body language, I'm guessing that the police have a strong case against him."

"That's too bad," Oliver said. "He had some good ideas, and I was looking forward to having him on my sales force, if you didn't snap him up first to drive your vintage delivery car."

I asked, "He told you about that?"

How could Misty possibly resist Scott? He had a breathtakingly winning smile. "He told us both, and that you and Chief Westhill were in competition to drive it." He looked at his watch. "Oops. My shift starts in ten. Unlike you, Rossimer, I don't get Labor Day off."

Oliver explained, "The self-employed can't always take time off, right, Emily?"

Wistful expressions on their faces, several women watched Scott stride out of Deputy Donut. I would have to find more ways to throw him and Misty together. Seeing each other during emergencies had not, so far, done the trick.

And Samantha could have the handsome man in front of me. "Guess what," he said.

"What?"

"I have a delivery vehicle that you might like. When do you finish tonight? I'll bring it around."

"We finish tidying about five thirty. What kind of vehicle?"

"You'll see." He held a finger to his lips. "Don't tell Chief Westhill. I'd like your reaction, first. How does after supper sound, like about seven?"

"Fine."

"Here, or will you be at home?"

"I need to catch up on some clerical work, so how about here?"

"Perfect. I don't have to worry about those mundane aspects of business. That's what employees are for. But you keep working hard, and you'll get there, someday." He paid for his donut and coffee, pinned a flyer to the bulletin board beside the front door, and left.

At four twenty-eight, the last three clients left. Tom and I locked and tidied the shop, and then we joined Dep in the office, turned on the computer, and ordered a few days' worth of freshly roasted coffee beans.

Tom opened the door leading outside to the parking lot. "See you tomorrow." Sitting at the computer with Dep purring on my lap, I watched him drive away.

I had to admire Oliver for setting up a defense fund for Randy, something that hadn't occurred to me. I told myself that his bringing a vehicle for me to see was more like a business meeting than a date. I hoped he saw it that way.

I'd been spoiled by my few years of being married to a nearly perfect man.

My cat, however, was far from perfect. She batted at receipts and bills, drastically slowing my spreadsheet entries.

At precisely seven, a car pulled into our parking lot.

It was a vintage police cruiser, complete with a rectangular red light on top that said POLICE.

It looked brand-new.

Chapter 32

❧

Barely taking my eyes off the gorgeous old police cruiser, I told Dep to stay. Why did I expect that to work? I bent over, blocked her with my open palm, and slithered out backward.

Oliver stood beside the driver's door of the black and white squad car.

"Wow," I managed. "What is it?" I pointed at the shield-shaped insignia on the front center of the hood. It looked like a medieval coat of arms, with the word "Ford" prominent above the gryphons, or whatever they were, rampant on red and blue fields. "Besides a Ford."

"A 1950 Ford. They called this model a four-door, spelled *F-o-r-d-o-r*. There was also a two-door model, which they spelled *T-u-d-o-r.*"

"Cute."

"I'm sorry to say that this particular one wasn't originally a police car, but I did put a one hundred ten–horsepower V-eight engine into it, like the most powerful engine they made in 1950 specifically for police cars. I'd just restored it when Randy said that Deputy Donut should make its deliveries in an old-fashioned police car. I'd already painted it black, so I repainted the doors and roof white and fastened a light to the roof. Isn't she a beauty?"

"It's perfect!" I was certain that Tom would like it, although he might prefer a few more horses under the hood. I wished that Randy could see it, wished that he weren't locked up, wished that Matthias and Georgia were still alive. Alec, too. Impossible wishes, all of them. I stifled a sigh.

Oliver asked, "Can you drive a stick shift? It's only a three-speed, plus reverse."

"Yes." My parents had always preferred standard transmissions. After I learned to drive standards, though, my parents switched to automatics. Alec had preferred standards for his personal cars, and I understood the satisfaction of accelerating while shifting cleanly.

"Want to drive her?"

I took a step backward and clasped my hands behind my back like a toddler who was told not to touch something. "I'm afraid to. It's beautiful." I was a good driver, but still . . . Maybe I didn't want to be tempted to buy it. Deputy Donut was doing well, but I was almost positive that we didn't need a delivery vehicle and wouldn't use one enough to justify owning it.

"Would you like to go for a ride? I'll drive first, and you can decide later if you want to try."

How could I resist an offer like that? "I'd love to!"

"Hop in." He slid into the driver's seat.

I opened the passenger door and climbed onto the passenger end of the bench seat. The car even had that new car smell. I automatically reached for a seat belt, but there wasn't one.

Oliver must have noticed my fumbling. "I didn't install seat belts because it would lower the value if I sell it as a classic car. But you should have seat belts in a delivery car, so if you want this beauty, I'll install them." He put the car in gear and pulled out of the parking lot. At the end of Deputy Donut's driveway, he turned right on Wisconsin Street and accelerated.

The Ford's engine thrummed. I was sure the nearly flat seat was a good copy of the original, but it wasn't as comfortable as new car seats. In addition, not wearing a seat belt didn't seem right, even though Oliver drove like a policeman, fast and capably.

He turned on the radio. "The dashboard is authentic. It's hiding the latest in car radios." Music nearly blasted me out of my seat. "I hid new speakers behind the grill."

I shouted, "This car has everything!"

He switched off the radio. "All it needs is your logo on the doors. I can have that done."

"And a big fake donut on top, like another light bar, I mean light circle."

He shuddered as if he didn't care for the whimsical idea that Randy had given me. "I'll leave that one up to you."

Maybe I wasn't going to fall for Oliver as I might have when I was fourteen, but I was rapidly falling for this car. I turned toward him. "How much do you want for it?"

His price was lower than I'd feared. If Tom and I needed to do a lot of deliveries, maybe we could afford the car and someone to drive it. "Or you could lease it, even month-to-month, and I'd take it back—without the fake donut on top—whenever you no longer wanted it." He told me the monthly payment. Again, it was less than I might have expected. "Also," he said, "let me know if you ever want to test-drive a front-end loader or a bulldozer."

"Could I use one to deliver donuts and coffee?"

He patted the dashboard. "Don't you think this baby would work better?"

Explaining that I'd been joking would have been lame. "Yes."

Beyond Fallingbrook's outskirts, Oliver turned west and stepped on the gas, and we raced down a two-lane highway bordered on both sides by dense woods. I was glad the road was smooth. With no seat belt, I was sliding around on the slippery vinyl. I asked, "What about trunk space? Would I have to put coffee urns and my cakes made of piled-up donuts on the back seat?"

"I'll show you." He signaled and pulled onto the road's wide gravel shoulder. "This baby was made back in the day when turn signals weren't standard equipment, but they were offered as optional extras on 1950 Fordors. So were heaters, windshield washers, outside mirrors, map lights, and lights in the glove compartment and trunk. I made certain that this car has every safety and convenience feature that was available in 1950 plus a few new ones."

He shut off the engine, opened his door, and his watch caught on the door handle. He took off the watch—an expensive gold one—and set it on the dashboard.

I clambered out and met him at the back of the car. He opened the trunk with a key. As promised, a light came on. The trunk was roomy enough for several coffee urns and cakes made of piled-up donuts.

Two other things drew my attention, however.

One was a white ball cap with a Green Bay Packers logo—a white capital *G* on a dark green oval outlined in yellow. I told myself that lots of people owned Packers caps.

The other thing was a white plastic supermarket bag with the words "Taste of Fallingbrook" on it. The bag was translucent enough for me to read the lettering on the thin rectangular package inside it.

Oliver Rossimer had water slide paper in the trunk of his pristine 1950 Ford Fordor.

Chapter 33

✿

Water slide paper.

Someone could have used water slide paper to make a temporary tattoo matching Randy's, which would come in handy if someone wanted to impersonate Randy while committing crimes.

My face heated, my ears rang, and I could think of nothing to say. Had I gasped at the sight of the water slide paper inside the Taste of Fallingbrook grocery bag? To cover my possibly obvious shock, I babbled, "You're right about the light inside the trunk! And didn't the old cars have spacious trunks?" There was room in this one for a medium-sized person, either dead or alive, and I didn't see one of those glow-in-the-dark trunk release pulls that were in newer cars.

I stepped back and couldn't help a quick glance toward the dense forest crowding the road. Even if I could make my way through it, I would never be able to outrun Oliver.

"These old cars were spacious everywhere." I was certain that Oliver was scrutinizing whatever he could see of my lowered face. He was undoubtedly wondering why I was flushed.

It was a coincidence, I told myself. Most Wisconsinites had at least one Green Bay Packers ball cap. Maybe Fred Aggleton was having a sale on water slide paper, and many people were buying it. I could understand why a mother of seven-year-old twins would want supplies for creating temporary tattoos, but Oliver? He did not, as far as I knew, have children. And he didn't seem like the playful sort who would apply tattoos for fun.

He reached in, put the cap on top of the bag so that it hid most of the label inside the bag, and then closed the trunk with more force than was required for present-day cars. He dusted his hands together. "The Chamber of Commerce is doing something different for Halloween this year. We're having a potluck dinner. Costumes are optional. We'll be sending out invitations soon, but I'm telling you early to give you a jump start on planning what to bring and wear. Everyone is hoping you'll bring donuts. Think I'll make a good pirate? Arrrrr!"

I exhaled. The pirate costume explained the water slide paper. Oliver was already planning his retirement, so why wouldn't he be getting ready for a holiday that was less than two months away? Oliver would be finicky about details like realistic tattoos.

I glanced quickly at his face. "I know you would!" Now I was gushing. "Weren't you Captain Hook when the high school put on *Peter Pan*, the musical?"

I couldn't read his face, but he didn't look evil. "Yes. And although you weren't in that musical, you would make a good Wendy."

If I'd heard those words from him when I was fourteen, my heart would have flown higher than Wendy did when she was following Peter Pan to join the Lost Boys. Now, however, I couldn't help being frightened. I was alone on a deserted country road with a man who might be a murderer. *Stop it*, I told myself. *You didn't suspect that mother and her twins of being murderers. Besides, many people would be intrigued by temporary tattoos.*

Oliver pointed toward the front of the car. "Want to try driving her now?"

"I'm going to have to talk to Tom first. If he's against the entire idea, maybe I'd better not know how much fun it is to drive it. Her."

"Okay." Oliver headed for the driver's door. I climbed into the passenger seat, which seemed higher than it had earlier, maybe because my knees and ankles had gone flimsy. *Oliver's not a murderer. Randy is, and Randy's locked up.*

Oliver turned the key in the ignition and then reached for his watch on the dashboard and slipped it over his left hand. Looking at his wrist, he tapped the face of the watch once with the index finger of his right hand, and then he adjusted the watch to place its face in the middle of the back of his wrist. He raised his left hand and shook it as if to let the watch slip down to a more comfortable position. He put the car in gear, and eased away from the shoulder and into the road.

My nervousness ballooned to panic, clogging my throat. In the surveillance video taken from the front of the post office on Monday morning, the man driving Randy's car had gone through the exact same chain of gestures with a wristwatch.

Could it be?

When I'd watched the surveillance videos, I should have noticed that putting on a watch was unusual for Randy. I had never seen him wearing one, not back in high school, and not recently. In high school, his tattoo had nearly always been plainly visible. Lately, I'd seen his left wrist many times as he pulled the cuff of his sleeve down as if trying to hide his tattoo. I would have noticed a watch.

Could Oliver have passed as Randy? They were both almost six feet tall and broad shouldered, with similar muscular builds. They both had dark hair. Unlike Oliver's, Randy's was flecked with gray. Oliver's hair was usually neatly combed, while Randy often looked like he'd just rolled out of bed. Oliver was always clean-shaven, but Randy usually had that five o'clock shadow thing going on. Early Monday morning, had Oliver imitated Randy, complete with bowlegged swagger, ball cap, bed head, unshaven chin, and long-sleeved shirt that didn't quite cover a tattoo? A temporary tattoo . . .

As far as I could tell, Oliver wasn't wearing aftershave or cologne at the moment, and I'd never noticed him wearing any. Randy's, however, was strong. Honey had said that the man who talked to her at the post office early Monday morning had been wearing a subtle fragrance, and I'd chalked up that observation to Honey probably being unable to detect anyone else's cologne over the smell of her own. If Oliver had been driving Randy's car, his clothes could have absorbed a hint of Randy's fragrance.

Besides, Lois hadn't noticed if her attacker was wearing cologne. That could have been because, as she'd said, she was scared. Or it could have been because her attacker was Oliver, and by that time, the aroma that he'd picked up from Randy's car would have worn off.

Belatedly, I realized that I should have accepted Oliver's offer to test-drive the vintage car. However, if Oliver truly wanted to prevent me from going back home, it wouldn't matter which one of us was driving.

Had Oliver murdered Georgia?

And Matthias, also? All along, Lois had insisted that the man driving Randy's car the evening that Matthias disappeared could not have been Randy because Randy would have stopped to chat. I'd believed that if the driver had been Randy, he had wanted to quickly distance himself from the spot where he'd buried Matthias.

Oliver would not have stopped, but only partly due to fleeing a crime scene. Back then, there was no reason for Oliver to have known Lois.

Enhancing the photograph, investigators had decided that the man driving up the hill toward Lois that day had raised his arm. Brent had said that the car's driver had waved at Lois, which was one reason that the police believed he was Randy. But another man could have been pretending to be

Randy, and he could have been making certain that if Lois's camera caught anything beyond the windshield, it would be a wrist sporting a copy of Randy's tattoo, made from water slide paper or inked on with a marker. Maybe he had deliberately hidden as much of his face as he could with his tattooed arm. He probably hadn't realized that reflections on the windshield had nearly obscured his face, anyway.

And then five years later, the same man could have created and worn a temporary tattoo matching Randy's simple homemade B.A.D. He could have dressed and walked like Randy, and then tracked down Georgia, the woman who owned the car he'd seen right after he'd killed and buried Matthias. He must have seen Lois aiming her camera at him, and he must have believed that Georgia, not Lois, had witnessed his leaving the scene of the crime.

Everything about the day that her son went missing must have remained etched in Georgia's mind. Before she succumbed, she must have told her attacker that she had traded her car for a minivan that day, but she would not have divulged Lois's name. For some reason, possibly the addressed packages stacked next to Georgia's front door, her murderer had gone to the post office in hopes of finding out whose van Georgia might have borrowed when she had to haul large boxes. He could have purposely parked in view of a surveillance camera. He'd made certain that the car and its license plate could be seen and identified, but he'd kept his face mostly hidden by pulling the ball cap down, bowing his head, and looking away from the post office and its cameras. His short conversation with Honey Bellaire could have sent him looking for Lois.

Why had five years elapsed between the two murders?

Woods streamed in a blur past the old car's windows. I fidgeted with the handle that would roll down the window next to me.

"Finding all the right knobs for this car wasn't easy," Oliver told me. "Didn't I do a great job on details?"

My left hand curled into a fist. My nails stabbed into the heel of my hand. "Yes."

Details. Five years between murders. Why? Randy had left town shortly after the first murder and returned shortly before the second one.

Five years ago, Oliver must have known that Randy was moving away. Oliver could have plotted that Randy would appear to have fled Fallingbrook to avoid being arrested for murdering Matthias. It could have worked. Randy might have been on Alec and Brent's suspect list, but his teenage history of violence and his moving away must not have been enough for them to build a case against him.

And then, shortly after Randy returned, someone killed Georgia. This time, Oliver's almost flawless impersonation and his planting of evidence in Randy's car had succeeded. Randy was in custody, charged with both murders.

How had Oliver driven Randy's cars without Randy's knowledge? To keep my hands still, I slid them, palms down on the vinyl, underneath my thighs.

Had Randy taken his cars to Oliver's father's dealerships for servicing? Five years ago, Randy could have told Oliver that he needed the car to be in good shape for the long drive to Wyoming. The car that Randy owned then was old, though, and probably long past its warranty. Why would he take it to a dealer, and not to a possibly less expensive mechanic?

Tom had told me that Randy and the son of a gas station owner had injured each other with knives. I was almost certain that, five years ago, only one of Fallingbrook's gas stations had a mechanic's bay. If the owner of that station was the father of the boy Randy fought, Randy might have continued to avoid taking his car to that station for servicing. The other mechanics in town five years ago had worked for Oliver's father, who had owned all of Fallingbrook's car dealerships.

Matthias had disappeared before an evening meeting with

potential hockey players and their parents. If Oliver had been overseeing the servicing of Randy's car, Oliver could have legitimately taken it for a test drive, a very long one. During it, Oliver could have killed Matthias and buried him near the Fallingbrook River, and then raced away from that valley while Lois photographed the setting sun. If Lois had produced the photo of the car right away, Randy might have been able to prove that his car was being serviced at the time the photo was taken. But she hadn't, and Randy had left for Wyoming. Now, five years later, if he even remembered that his car was being serviced that evening, he probably didn't have the receipts to prove it. He no longer had that car, for one thing.

Early Monday morning, Randy's car wasn't being serviced. Oliver had removed it from the parking lot outside Randy's apartment building. How had Oliver obtained a key without Randy's knowledge?

My mind seemed to spin faster than the tires on that isolated country road, and I came up with a theory. After Randy returned from Wyoming, he could have taken his car to one of Oliver's maintenance departments. Oliver could have secretly ordered an extra key for himself. When I'd asked Oliver how he accomplished so much, he'd claimed that he never needed much sleep. Around five last Monday morning, he could have parked his own car somewhere behind Randy's apartment building. He could have dressed like Randy, appeared near the back of the building, and taken Randy's car.

Starring in those plays and musicals back in high school, Oliver had been a good actor. As Captain Hook, he had swaggered around the stage. Imitating Randy's bowlegged gait would have been a cinch.

Randy's car was returned to the parking lot when it was just getting light, and the man I now suspected was Oliver had disappeared behind Randy's apartment building, probably to retrieve his own car.

On Monday evening, the man the police and I thought was

Randy had walked through Randy's apartment building lobby. He'd left around seven and had returned, carrying a white plastic bag, around ten. Lois had been attacked around nine thirty that night.

Watching the video, Brent and I had concluded that while Randy was gone that evening, he had attacked Lois, and then he'd brought the bag containing her photos, the bloodied rock, and the chisel into the apartment building. Later, in the wee hours of Tuesday morning, it had appeared that he'd taken the bag out through the apartment building's rear door and shoved it into his trunk.

"Smooth ride, isn't it?"

Oliver's question made me jump. "Yes. Are the springs original?"

"No." He gave me a long-winded explanation about searching for and finding springs.

Barely listening, I went back to my conjectures.

I'd assumed that the white plastic bag that the Randy look-alike had shoved into Randy's trunk was the one I'd seen Randy carry into his lobby, but maybe it wasn't. Maybe the man who showed up in Randy's lobby was Randy, while the man who came and went from behind the apartment building was Oliver.

And Oliver had killed Georgia and attacked Lois.

I remembered the sleeve that had been rolled up when the Randy look-alike talked to Honey Bellaire and when he parked Randy's car a few minutes later. Had the right sleeve been rolled up to hide blood? What had become of that shirt? Oliver would have known better than to shove it into Randy's trunk with the rest of the evidence. People constantly shed skin cells. Oliver's DNA would have been inside that shirt.

Randy's car had been in the parking lot of his apartment building early Monday morning, which implied, if he wasn't the one who took his car away that morning, that he'd been in his apartment while Georgia was murdered. Where had he gone between seven and ten Monday evening? Had he seen anyone either of those two times? If so, had he told the police, and they'd failed to corroborate his story? I pulled my hands out from underneath my jittery legs and folded my arms.

I wanted to be home. I would ask Brent to come over. I would tell him my latest theories. What would he say?

Probably that I was making up impossible scenarios in hopes of freeing my friend's great-nephew.

In a way, I hoped I was wrong about Oliver. If I was right, I could be in danger.

The road curved, and the woods fell away, revealing a heart-stopping view of the Fallingbrook River winding through a valley. The setting sun lit the clouds and the river below them with an apricot-tinted glow. Even if I didn't know that valley, I'd have recognized it from Lois's photos and painting.

Five years ago, on an evening very much like this one, Matthias had been buried in that valley.

Chapter 34

✻

"It's quite a sight, isn't it?" Oliver said.

"Yes." I hoped he would think that the catch in my voice was an emotional response to the beauty of the scene.

Cars and vans were parked on both sides of the road near the dirt track leading down to the river and, if I understood correctly, to where Matthias's remains had been found.

Without slowing the car, Oliver asked, "Can you tell what's going on?"

The vehicles were unmarked police cars and vans, and Brent was among the investigators watching the 1950 Ford police car speed past. For once, I was glad that Detective Yvonne Passenmath was fond of making her underlings toil over old trails and cold clues. Oliver couldn't take me down that lonely track and bury me near where he, or someone, had buried Matthias.

Reflections of the sunset on the passenger side windows could have prevented the officers from seeing me inside the black and white 1950 Ford, and I had trouble with the handle that rolled down the window. I opened it only a few inches, and then we'd passed Brent and the others. They couldn't have caught more than a glimpse of the top of my head, and I wasn't the only short person in the world with dark curly hair. I should have worn my Deputy Donut hat with the fuzzy donut. "It looks like a police investigation."

"Randy," Oliver said. "What a tragedy."

I didn't know how to respond without giving away my suspicion that Oliver was the actual murderer.

He accelerated even more. "Have you heard of anyone else missing?"

"No."

"I suppose not, now that Randy's in jail and we're all safe again."

We were heading toward Fallingbrook Falls. Although it was a popular tourist attraction, no one was likely to be tramping up and down the steep cliffs beside it after sunset. Oliver could shove me off the falls and claim later that I'd slipped.

If I opened the door and jumped out of the car, I might hurt or kill myself. Plus, there'd be nothing to keep Oliver from stopping and making certain that I could never tell the authorities my suspicions about him. With any luck, despite my wiggling and choppy breathing, he had no idea about the disturbing thoughts churning through my brain.

Maybe I was having that luck. Before we neared the falls, he turned the Ford around. "I'm a night owl, but you need to get up early, right?"

"Right." I was making a pleat in the knee of my black jeans. I slid my hands underneath my thighs again.

I was afraid that the officers might have left the road above the river valley, but although the sun had dipped below the horizon, it was still light, and the police vehicles were still there. Oliver slowed to the speed limit.

Brent was now on the right shoulder, his back toward us, striding toward an unmarked police car.

"You can drop me off here." I managed to sound calm. "Some of Alec's old friends will take me home."

"I wouldn't do that. You might be stranded for hours, waiting for them to finish." He sounded caring and considerate. He was a good actor, I reminded myself.

My handle turning had improved. I wound the window almost all the way down.

We were about to pass Brent.

He looked toward the Ford. I brushed my hair away from my forehead and then lowered my hand and pulled on my earlobe, hard, several times. It was a signal that Alec and I had worked out between us in case either of us ever wanted help from the other. It could have meant anything from "let's make our excuses and leave this party" to "save my life."

I didn't know if Alec had ever described that signal to Brent. And even if he had, did Brent see me give it? I wasn't sure that he'd recognized me. Turning my face to look back, I caught a glimpse of his frown, and then Oliver's wonderful car rounded a curve and left the Fallingbrook River valley behind.

Oliver fingered the dash. "The original car didn't have air-conditioning, but this one does. I didn't realize you were too hot. Most women don't like having their hair blown around."

I rolled the window up again. "I couldn't resist trying it. I don't remember ever being in a car with windows that work like this. It's fun." It was almost impossible to sound like I was having anything resembling fun.

I understood why Oliver had disguised himself before he committed murders. He'd had the means and the opportunities to carry out both crimes. He'd had a motive for killing Georgia. He would have wanted to eliminate her as a witness to his being near where Matthias was buried.

But why had he killed Matthias?

It wouldn't have been so that he could buy Matthias's grocery store cheaply. I doubted that selling groceries would appeal to him. And surely Oliver, who had no children, couldn't have been disgruntled by Matthias's Little League team's second-place finish, though I supposed it was possible that one of Oliver's father's companies could have sponsored the team.

Had Oliver blamed Matthias for food poisoning that Oliver or someone he loved had suffered? His mother? His wife? He and the head cheerleader, Nicole, had married right out of high school and, if I remembered correctly, they'd now been divorced for three or four years.

We hit a bump and the glove compartment door fell open and banged my knee.

Oliver reached over and slammed the door shut. "Sorry. I'll adjust the latch so it won't keep doing that."

Oliver's reflexes were fast, but not fast enough.

I'd caught a glimpse of a square of paper in the glove compartment. On it was a realistic replica of Randy's tattoo. B.A.D. I guessed that the paper was water slide paper and that Oliver had made more than one temporary tattoo like Randy's. Oliver had been prepared to impersonate Randy more than once, and on short notice.

Why were the ball cap, the water slide paper, and the temporary tattoo in this car? Maybe Oliver was in the process of taking them away from his own home so he could discard them. Or Oliver was preparing to plant them on someone else if Randy was somehow proven innocent. Tom, for instance . . .

Luckily, Oliver was again reciting the car's good points, and I didn't have to speak except to murmur a few polite words of praise. Inside, I was seething, with anger and with fear.

A sign welcomed us to Fallingbrook. Bright streetlights lined the road. Maybe Oliver really was taking me back to Deputy Donut. I would lock myself inside and call Brent and Misty. Even Yvonne Passenmath would be a welcome sight.

I ran my fingers through my curls, probably tangling them more.

Lois had said that she thought Randy had come back to Fallingbrook because of a woman, but she didn't know who. Had Randy been with the woman on Monday evening when Lois was attacked? What was in the bag he'd taken home— leftovers from a dinner he'd shared with his girlfriend?

If he'd been with someone, why hadn't he told the police

that he had an alibi for the time when Lois was attacked?

Maybe he was trying to protect the woman. Maybe she was married and he hadn't wanted to betray her secret.

I glanced toward Oliver, frowning as traffic became heavier, and suddenly everything fell into place.

In high school, most of the girls had been gaga over Oliver, and many had adored Randy, also.

I remembered one time when Oliver came off the football field after scoring the winning touchdown and had found Nicole talking to Randy. Oliver had put an arm around Nicole and guided her away, not gently. He'd taken his helmet off, and his eyebrows had been low in a frown like they were now.

What if Randy's secret girlfriend was Nicole and, although Oliver and Nicole had been divorced for several years, Oliver was still jealous?

Maybe Matthias hadn't done anything to Oliver. Matthias's only crime had probably been running out of gas and accepting a ride from a man he probably knew, at least by reputation. The Rossimers had been pillars of Fallingbrook society. Oliver could have explained why he was in Randy's dented-up old car—he was test-driving it.

What had Oliver planned? To frame Randy by kidnapping and killing someone while "test-driving" Randy's car? Oliver had probably expected Randy to be put away for life.

But it hadn't happened. Randy's departure for Wyoming hadn't appeared as suspicious as Oliver might have hoped.

And then after Nicole's divorce, Randy had returned, and Oliver still did not want Randy to have her.

Oliver's voice startled me. "Are we going back to Deputy Donut, or should I drop you off at home?"

"Deputy Donut. I left the cat there."

When Oliver pulled into Deputy Donut's parking lot, the night had darkened enough for the lights over our two back doors to come on. The car's movement would start our surveillance cameras recording. It would also send messages to

Tom's and my phones, giving us the opportunity to view the videos. An almost-inaudible *ding* came from my phone inside my backpack. I ignored it.

Maybe whether or not Tom heard his phone wouldn't matter. Almost before the Fordor came to a complete halt, I was out of it. "Thanks!" I put as much enthusiasm as possible into my voice. "I'll talk to Tom and let you know when he can see and drive this."

Although Oliver hadn't opened car doors for me that evening, suddenly he was a gentleman, escorting me to Deputy Donut's office. On the other side of the glass door, Dep meowed loudly, scolding me, no doubt, for leaving her alone.

I unlocked the door and bent down toward her. She swelled up into a giant fur ball, hissed, and swatted at my hand. I tried to edge into the office in a way that would keep her inside and Oliver outside.

I was only half successful. Dep stayed in.

But even though she was about twice her normal size, Oliver sidled around her and came into the office with us.

Chapter 35

My first impulse was to grab Dep and dash out to the parking lot and down the driveway to the street, but I doubted that I could successfully flee Oliver, especially with a squirming cat in my arms. Besides, if Oliver hadn't already guessed that I suspected him of murdering Matthias and Georgia, my sudden flight might clue him in. *Try to act normal,* I told myself.

Normal. Right.

Dep's domain was lit only by a night-light and reflections from outside.

The burglar alarm started beeping. I pretended I didn't hear it and dangled Dep's harness close to her. Still puffed up, she hissed.

Beep.

"Don't forget to disarm your burglar alarm," Oliver said.

"It won't take long to harness the cat and lock up again." I reached for Dep. She ran up the carpeted stairway toward the catwalks surrounding the room near the ceiling.

Beep . . . beep.

I wasn't going to be able to get us all out of Deputy Donut before the alarm went into full earsplitting mode.

Beep . . . beep . . . beep.

If that alarm blasted, I'd be petrified and unable to think or plan. Muttering, "Oops, guess I *should* disarm it," I turned on the office lights and typed in the all clear. I could have typed in a panic code that would have stopped the beeping but alerted our security monitoring company that something like a home intrusion was in process, but then both the landline and my cell phone would ring. If Oliver was still here, and it looked like he planned to be, he would figure out what was going on and I might not live long enough to tell any would-be rescuers about my suspicions.

Dep trotted down her stairway until she was at eye level with Oliver. She growled in a querulous but almost-musical way that would have made me laugh if I hadn't been mentally plotting our escape.

Oliver asked me, "Is it always this bad tempered?"

I'd never before seen her in such a snit. *Dep had been present when Lois was attacked.* "I've gotten used to her moods." That wasn't fair. Dep was normally a sweet and easygoing cat. "How about if you go out first, and when she calms down, I'll bring her outside."

Dep growled even louder.

"It looks like you could use my help with the cat." Apparently, Oliver didn't intend to go anywhere quite yet.

If he wasn't going to leave Deputy Donut, I had to get to the cash drawer and the switch that sent a silent message to 911.

What if he did leave, though, and managed to get away before I could set the police on his trail? He might end up murdering people in other towns, other states. The cash drawer was near the display case where we still had some of the day's donuts. . . . I offered, "Would you like coffee and donuts?"

"Sure."

Although I was certain that Tom was nowhere near, I opened the door into the dining area and called out, "I'm back, Tom!" Maybe Oliver would leave, and I could phone the police.

No such luck. Oliver glanced toward the parking lot. "There are no other cars out there besides the Fordor."

"Tom doesn't always drive."

That wasn't enough to send Oliver packing, either.

Dep was back on the floor again, crowding against me and butting her head against the edge of the door. I accidentally-on-purpose allowed her to escape into the dining room. In the gloom, it was spooky, with chairs upside-down on tables. Unfortunately, the Jolly Cops Cleaning Crew weren't due at Deputy Donut for about four hours.

Dep scooted underneath the nearest table.

Pretending dismay, I took Oliver up on his earlier offer to help. "Would you herd the cat back to the office while I start the coffee?"

" 'Herd a cat'—that's a good one. I don't think it likes me."

Neither do I. But all I said was, "Maybe she'll run back to the office, and you can shut her in."

I told myself that if Oliver had wanted to harm me, he would have driven me to Fallingbrook Falls or headed down a lonely side road into the wilderness surrounding Fallingbrook. He would not have brought me back to Deputy Donut. For one thing, about a dozen police officers had noticed the car he'd been driving, and it wasn't one they would easily forget.

Oliver was still chasing Dep from table to table. Cats could see better in dim lighting than we could. To continue giving Dep the advantage, I left the lights in the dining room off.

Could I slip outside from the storage room without Oliver noticing? Probably not, and I would face the same problem I'd have encountered by running outside from the office. Oliver was taller than I was, and would catch up easily. Besides, I couldn't possibly leave my cat alone with him.

I switched on the lights in the kitchen. Shadows shifted in the dining room. Oliver barged into an overturned chair and yelped.

One of our surveillance cameras was aimed at the serving counter near the cash drawer, which Tom always left empty and open at night. I reached into the back of the drawer and pressed the button that sent an automatic call to 911. Dispatch would conclude we were being burgled and would send police.

Having sent that signal, I didn't need to make a call on my phone.

I had a potentially better use for it.

I started it recording a video, and then leaned it against the side of an espresso machine where Oliver would be unlikely to see it. The phone would capture anything that went on in the rear of the kitchen, which was beyond the range of the camera trained on the cash drawer.

Oliver was on his hands and knees, partly underneath a table. "Here, kitty!"

Dep crawled farther away and swatted at him. I wouldn't have come, either, if someone had called me in that tone of voice.

I could do more to keep Oliver from getting too close to me while the police marshaled their forces.

First, I dipped a slotted spoon into one of the fryers—the oil hadn't cooled completely—and sprinkled a few drops of oil on our tile floor.

Second, I turned on the fryer and ratcheted it up to its highest heat.

Third, I filled a coffee carafe with water that we kept close to the boiling point. Even though the heat had been off for more than three hours, the water was still very hot.

I peered over the half wall. Underneath a table near the middle of the dining room, Dep spat and lashed out with a front paw. Oliver stood and put his hands up in surrender. "I give up. It won't let me catch it."

"Have a seat at the counter while I get out donuts and brew coffee."

Oliver perched on a stool almost directly underneath the surveillance camera. "Why did you wave at that police investigator?"

Technically, I hadn't. But I wasn't going to tell Oliver what

I'd actually done—tried to signal Brent that I could be in trouble. I set the carafe down and fiddled with the glass door at the back of the donut display case. "He was Alec's partner. I'm not sure he recognized me."

"People aren't as clever as they think. They don't always recognize who they think they're recognizing." Was he bragging about the way he'd impersonated Randy?

I put apple cider donuts on plates. Maybe, while he was underneath the surveillance camera, he would incriminate himself. "Like Randy." I tried to sound like I was merely making casual conversation. "The evening that Matthias disappeared, a woman took pictures of Randy's car leaving the valley where Matthias's remains were later found, but how can the police be sure, just from the car, that the driver was Randy? It's possible that someone else was driving his car."

"But not likely."

"He took his car to your father's dealership for servicing before his trip to Wyoming, right?"

"We serviced nearly everyone's cars back then." Oliver's lips twitched. "But we wouldn't have kept the records for a car that we never expected to service again." *Especially if the service manager made certain those records were destroyed . . .*

"Do you know if any of your mechanics had a grudge against Matthias? Maybe he was test-driving Randy's car and used it to kidnap Matthias."

"They said Matthias ran out of gas and thumbed a ride."

Matthias's car had run out of gas, but his gas can had been ditched beside the road. Finding that gas can, with her son's name written on it in black marker, was what had panicked Georgia. She reasoned that if her son had accepted a ride to a gas station, he would have taken the gas can with him.

Oliver bit into the donut. "Randy's in custody, and he's going to stay there for the rest of his life. Finally, five years later, he's in jail. Justice is done. There's no need for you or anyone else to make a different case out of it. Facts are facts. Randy killed both of those people. There were no violent crimes in or around Fallingbrook the entire five years he was in Wyoming." Oliver's dark brown eyes were almost black. "Randy was smarter than we would have thought, though. That woman you mentioned who took the pictures? He memorized her license plate and found her after he came back from out west. She'd parked her car here, outside Deputy Donut. He followed her home, made a note of where she lived, and went back to her home while it was still dark Monday morning, and attacked her."

A chill rippled down my back. Now I was sure that Oliver was bragging about locating Georgia and killing her. I realized that ever since he'd first come into Deputy Donut on Tuesday afternoon, he'd seemed to like boasting about himself. With luck, I could keep him talking—and not attacking me—until the police arrived. "But I heard that Georgia was not the woman who took his pictures when he was leaving the scene of the crime."

"Early Monday morning, that Treetor woman tried to save herself by telling Randy that she'd borrowed a friend's minivan that day. Whether that was true or not, she knew too much about Randy, and he had to kill her. But then he had to find out if the other old lady, the one who took the pictures and owned the minivan, existed. Again, he was surprisingly clever, except that he kept going in front of video cameras. Asking around, he discovered that she did exist, and that she was an artist named Lois who had recently moved back to Fallingbrook from Madison. He went to one of my car dealerships, of all places, searched our files, and found a customer named Lois who had recently started bringing her minivan for servicing again after a five-year absence. He went to her address and stole the incriminating photos she'd taken of him."

Did Oliver think I would believe that the police had let him in on secrets that only they, and a few witnesses, like Lois and me, knew?

I asked, "Did Randy tell you all this?"

"We were supposed to have a golf game this afternoon. Instead, I went to the police station and talked to him. He needs all the friends he can get right now."

Oliver didn't seem to have figured out that Lois was related to Randy, and I wasn't about to tell him. Instead, I shook my head. "It's barely believable. He seems completely reformed since his high school days."

"You're obviously wrong about that."

The person I'd been wrong about was Oliver. I picked up the carafe of hot water. "Randy can't have been as terrible as he seemed, even back then. Nicole seemed to like him."

"She married me for my money and divorced me for a settlement."

"Ouch. That must hurt, especially if she's dating someone else."

"I don't care. She chose a loser."

I tried to sound amazed. "Is Nicole dating *Randy?*"

The quaking of my voice must have given me away.

Chapter 36

❧

Oliver came around the counter into the kitchen and picked up Tom's favorite extra-large marble rolling pin. "Not now, Nicole isn't dating Randy. He's not in a position to date anyone." If I hadn't mentally built up a case against Oliver, his smug smile would have clued me in. He'd gone to extremes to put his rival out of commission, and he was proud of it.

Trying not to show my horror and keeping in mind where I'd dribbled oil on the floor, I took a step backward.

He kept coming. "How did you figure it out?"

I looked as bewildered as I could. "That Nicole might be dating Randy?"

"Stop playing innocent. You know what I mean. You blushed after you saw the inside of my Ford's trunk, and you've been acting strange ever since."

Edging away from him, I tried a smile. The full carafe was heavy. I rested it on one arm. My thin cotton shirt sleeve was not the greatest insulation against heat. "I've been strange all my life."

"You saw a water slide label through the bag, didn't you?" He probably couldn't help letting a tiny flicker of pride cross his features.

Maybe it was as close to a confession as I was going to get. Now that he was beyond the range of the video from the surveillance camera, I hoped that my phone was picking up both the video and audio, and that the playbacks would be clear.

The oily spot on the floor was a couple of feet behind me. I shuffled backward. "I also saw a temporary tattoo matching Randy's B.A.D. tattoo in your glove compartment. It's all pretty incriminating."

"It's all pretty circumstantial. Maybe Randy and I had a plan for Halloween that involved impersonating each other." He looked down at the rolling pin in his hand as if wondering how to pretend he wasn't thinking of using it on me. "You know, whatever you might make up about me and report to the police, it will be your word against mine, and I'm very respected in this community, while you couldn't hold down one job and had to inveigle your late husband's father to open a business and hire you."

I didn't bother explaining that Tom and I were equal partners in Deputy Donut. "I'm not making up your acting ability. I'm sure you could imitate Randy. If you wanted to get Randy out of Nicole's life, you could move like he does, do your hair like his, and not shave until it suits you. And you could make certain that his car was where surveillance cameras could pick up his license number while you were masquerading as him."

"Could. Didn't."

The police would be coming any minute. I took a chance that angering Oliver wouldn't cause him to attack me, but would make him say something he might later regret. "Randy and Nicole must have been seeing each other before he left for Wyoming."

"She was my wife then. She wasn't seeing anyone."

Having succeeded in needling him, I continued. "Or you suspected she was seeing him. She always loved him. He came back to be with her now that she's single again."

"You're making wild guesses."

About Nicole always loving Randy—maybe. But the rest

of my theories were totally believable. I tried to throw him off balance with flattery. "The temporary tattoos were a stroke of genius. I didn't know that water slide paper existed five years ago."

"Anyone can draw a tattoo on their wrist." Slowly, with that rolling pin in his right hand, he backed me toward the corner. "You've wrecked everything for yourself. I was going to continue dating you."

Be still, my heart. I didn't say it, except, maybe, with the scorn I was trying not to show.

He slapped the rolling pin against his left palm, probably harder than he intended. It must have hurt. "But now I'm afraid you won't live long enough to spin your tales about me impersonating Randy two different times, and managing to plant evidence in his car."

He was still bragging about what he, not Randy, had done. Oliver did not expect me to live much longer. Tom might not have noticed the signals that our surveillance cameras had sent his phone during the past five minutes, but where were the police officers our emergency switch should have summoned?

Oliver spoke with the suavity of a practiced salesman. "Even if I *had* ordered a spare key for Randy's car, it would be in the river where no one will ever find it."

That explained how he drove Randy's car and planted the plastic grocery bags in it, one containing the doll dress and the other containing the rock, the pictures, and the chisel. No one would ever say that Oliver Rossimer wasn't ingenious.

Becoming more desperate as seconds ticked by and the police didn't show, I needed to exercise a little ingenuity myself. "You can't get away with harming me. Alec's ex-partner saw us together this evening in a very memorable car."

"You admitted that you aren't sure he recognized you."

"I told Tom I was going out with you tonight."

"You're lying."

He was right. Oliver had asked me not to tell Tom. I shouldn't have obeyed him, but at the time, I'd had no inkling that Oliver was a murderer. Also, if it turned out that I liked the car, I wanted to surprise Tom. "No." I tried to sound convincing.

"None of that matters. You made a crucial mistake. You underestimated me. My plans never fail. You're going to have an accident. Just like that doll doctor and her son, you got yourself into the wrong place at the wrong time. I'll be the distraught date who tried to save you, and who eventually has to call 911. But it will be too late."

A strange thumping sound came from the front door.

The police?

No.

Rising onto my toes, I peeked over the half wall. I could just barely see the top of Dep, standing on her hind legs and pounding at the glass door with her front paws. An elderly couple on the other side of the door were smiling down at Dep. The woman squatted and touched the glass nearest Dep's swiftly moving paws.

I stared at the couple, willing them to see through the dim dining room into the brightly lit kitchen. I hoped they'd conclude that I could be in danger and, at the very least, they would distract Oliver.

The man helped the woman stand. Arm in arm, they walked away.

I transferred my attention to Oliver. He'd edged toward me and was almost close enough to swing that rolling pin at my head. Sliding my sneakers through the slippery oil, I backed up.

The filled carafe seemed to be getting heavier by the second. My hand shook.

I'd backed so far from Oliver that he'd cornered me between the building's rear wall and the office wall.

He raised the rolling pin.

I removed the lid from the carafe, gripped the handle more tightly, and tossed hot water at his face.

He hurled the rolling pin.

I ducked, but not quickly enough. The rolling pin slammed into the side of my head. Pain shot through my skull. My legs collapsed, and I fell back onto the floor. The back of my head bounced against the office wall.

Oliver was about to commit his third murder, and in my boneless, dazed state, there was nothing I could do to stop him.

Chapter 37

Crumpled like a rag doll in the corner, I couldn't breathe.

Oliver clawed at his face, red with rage, hot water, or both, and charged toward me. I willed my hand to find that rolling pin before Oliver could pick it up.

My hand refused to move.

Oliver slipped in the oil I'd sprinkled on the floor, went down heavily, and stared silently at the ceiling. For one horrifying second, I thought he was dead.

His chest rose and fell.

He was alive, and I was still in danger. Also, if I wasn't around to prevent it, he might date Samantha, marry her, and make her miserable with his jealousy. Maybe even kill her . . .

Cautiously, I braced myself on my hands and forced myself to stand.

Oliver was lying on most of the oil I'd spilled. I skirted around him and dipped the emptied carafe into the fryer I'd turned all the way up. In my panicky rush, I splashed hot oil on my right wrist.

Trying to ignore the burning pain and keeping my feet and ankles out of Oliver's reach, I stood over his head. "You stay right where you are, Oliver Rossimer, or I'm pouring boiling oil on your face."

He must have believed me. He didn't try to get up. His eyes seemed almost focused on my face, but he seemed slightly stunned. Maybe I wasn't the only one to have dented a skull during our short fray.

Through Dep's window between the kitchen and the office, I saw movement.

Tom was walking stealthily from the back porch into the office. Brent was behind him. Appearing to check everything at once, they turned their heads toward me.

I yelled, "I'm in the kitchen!" What a useless thing to say. "I could use your help!"

Dep galloped away from the front door toward the office and two of her favorite people.

Abandoning stealth and caution, Brent dashed into the kitchen. "What the . . . ?"

Oliver seemed to wake out of his stupor. "She attacked me."

"He has water slide paper in the trunk."

Tom asked, "What?"

"He killed Matthias and Georgia," I said. "He impersonated Randy both times."

Oliver thrashed on the oily floor but couldn't seem to get his feet underneath him. "She's hallucinating. You've got the right person in jail. But you'd better arrest her. She's threatening me with boiling oil."

Tom pried my fingers off the carafe of hot oil and set it on the counter.

Avoiding the slipperiest parts of the floor, I raced to the sink, turned the cold water on, set a big stainless-steel mixing bowl underneath the faucet, and thrust my right wrist into the stream pouring into the bowl. With my left hand, I pointed at the painful spot on my temple. "He threw your favorite rolling pin at me, Tom."

Oliver insisted, "She fell."

Tom looked into the corner. "My rolling pin is on the floor, and there's a major dent in the wall above it."

Oliver had an answer for everything. "She was throwing things."

"Em?" Brent asked.

"Look at Oliver's watch. I've never seen Randy wearing one, but the man in the post office video put one on like Oliver's when he got back into his car. Oliver's 1950 Ford is in the parking lot, painted like a police car. Check the trunk for a package of water slide paper and a white Packers cap like the one the Randy look-alike was wearing in the videos. Also, look in the Ford's glove compartment for a temporary tattoo that's a replica of Randy's."

"You need my permission," Oliver said. "And I'm not giving it. This is an outrage. She's raving. If she wants a lawsuit, she's going to get it. I'll talk to my lawyers tomorrow. Tonight."

He was probably right about that, but they'd be defense lawyers. "Get a search warrant." I blushed at telling Brent what to do. "And get them for his home and office computers. Look for a file he made, or even a drawing, copying Randy's tattoo." The cold water was numbing my wrist.

"Arrest her," Oliver said.

Brent refused. "We've been asking Randy about that watch. He doesn't wear one."

"He lies," Oliver said.

Brent informed him, "Randy's allergic to metal. That checks out."

Oliver scoffed, "He wouldn't be allergic to *gold*."

I was bursting to join the conversation, and I could tell that Tom was, too, but we both resisted, and Brent jumped on Oliver's comment. "How do you know it was a gold watch?"

"He borrowed mine. And gave it back."

"When?" Brent persisted in that steel-cored, controlled voice he used when he was angry.

"He borrowed it before that woman was murdered and her friend was attacked, and gave it back the day after. He thought he could pass as me. He'll deny it, of course, but what can you expect from that loser?"

My hand still in the bowl of cold water, I stared into Brent's face. He gave me a little nod. Brent had caught on that Oliver had incriminated himself by admitting he knew about the assault on Lois.

I brushed my hair back to uncover the rapidly swelling lump where the rolling pin had hit me. I asked Oliver, "Did Randy tell you why he didn't kill the second woman, the artist who you told me had moved back to Fallingbrook?"

"He wasn't certain that he hadn't, but he heard someone calling a deputy, so he couldn't stick around and make sure."

Again, Brent and I traded glances. Had Dep and I saved Lois's life that night, Dep by going into Lois's yard, and me by calling my cat? I was sure I'd called her "Deputy" at least once during those few minutes.

Brent told Oliver, "Randy confessed to something."

Oliver snapped, "Of course."

"Not what you think." I would never want Brent, or anyone else, to turn that laser-like gaze on me. "Randy's been spending time with your ex, but she didn't come forward about being with him in his apartment early Monday morning or being with him in her apartment Monday evening. I had a call while I was on my way here. Your ex is at the station now, explaining it all. Apparently, she was afraid of what you'd do to her if you found out she'd been seeing someone."

"I've known for years," Oliver muttered.

"Exactly," I blurted. "That's why you decided to ruin Randy's reputation and have him put away for life. So, you went out in his car, supposedly test-driving it, and you came upon Matthias Treetor. You didn't care who you killed, as long as Randy was blamed."

Oliver flailed, started to get up, slipped in the oil, and fell again. "Emily has a wild imagination. We all know that Randy killed those two people and came close to killing that other old woman."

Brent and Tom moved closer to Oliver. I warned them about the slippery floor.

"I noticed." Brent's eyes hadn't lost their grim expression, but I thought I caught a slight lilt of humor in his voice.

Tom shot me a quick grin.

The cold water on my wrist masked the pain of the burn. Oliver's face was still red, but the hot water had apparently missed him. Otherwise, he'd have accused me of scalding him. His flush must have been entirely due to his anger.

"We can talk about this in a more comfortable place, Rossimer," Brent said. "Em, Tom and I need to stay with this guy. Do you mind letting those folks in?"

Chapter 38

"Those folks" turned out to be Misty and three other Fallingbrook officers clustered outside the locked front door.

I opened it and turned on the lights in the dining room.

"Are you okay?" Misty asked me. "What was it—a burglar?"

"I'm okay." I wasn't. No longer in cold water, my wrist was hurting again. The good news was that the pain in my wrist was distracting me from the pain in my head. "But Brent could use your help. He's in the kitchen."

Equipment jingling and boots loud on the hardwood floor, the other three officers trooped toward the kitchen.

Misty laughed. "I'm not sure Brent needs much more help. Chief Westhill's looking very ferocious." She stared pointedly at me. "And so are you." Purring, Dep wound around our legs. "Who are they giving that death glare to?" The half wall prevented her from seeing the kitchen floor and Oliver, presumably still lying on it.

I picked Dep up and cuddled her. "Oliver," I said. "He fell. He did it."

"Did what?"

"Murdered Matthias and Georgia, attacked Lois, and would have murdered me, too, if I hadn't thrown scalding water at him."

"Emily! At Oliver? Your heartthrob! Why?"

"He stopped being my heartthrob years ago." I showed her the lump on my head. "Now you could call him my *head*throb. Tom's big marble rolling pin can pack a wallop, even if you duck."

"Need medical attention?"

"I should be checked out so the police can have official evidence for charging Oliver with assaulting me. And he might say the same thing about me and my pot of scalding water, except I think the water missed him." The warm cat made my wrist feel worse, but she was purring, and hugging her was comforting in other ways. "I did booby-trap the kitchen floor by sprinkling oil on it, but Oliver's to blame for stepping in the oil while he was charging at me, probably to pick up the rolling pin he'd bounced off my head so he could bounce it off my head a few more times."

"And the oil caused him to slip and fall?"

"Yes."

I could tell she was trying not to laugh. "Serves him right." She became serious again. "Want me to call an ambulance? Samantha's on duty."

"Not for me. I'll get to the hospital on my own steam." It wasn't a good word to choose, considering how my wrist felt. "After I give the video files to Brent."

"Video files?"

"From our surveillance cameras and my phone."

"Good for you." She was smiling again. "I can hardly wait to hear the details."

The three officers who had arrived with Misty escorted Oliver, now handcuffed, toward the front door. Oliver spat, "You're going to pay for your lies and for assaulting me, Emily Westhill."

"That's enough, Rossimer." Misty could be every bit as ferocious as Tom.

But Oliver only sneered. "Emily might have friends among the policewomen in this town, but you'll see who has the important friends. And which policewoman ends up out on the street with no job."

The other officers hustled him outside.

Misty winked. "This is going to be fun." She hollered toward the kitchen, "Brent, after you get Emily's statement, take her in for photos and a checkup!" She turned back to me and whispered, "I always wanted to order one of my bosses around." She winked again and then, handcuffs dangling from the back of her belt, she strode out behind the others.

I carried Dep to the office, shut her in, and returned to the kitchen.

"Let me see your wrist, Em," Brent demanded.

I held it out. "It's not bad." A nickel-sized blotch was an angry shade of red.

Tom plunked the bowl of cold water on the counter beside me. "It's not exactly good, either. Soak your wrist, Emily."

"I know." I parroted, "First Aid 101—for minor burns, ten minutes in cold water."

"How'd you get minor burns?" Brent asked.

"My fault. I was kind of in a hurry when I dipped the carafe into hot oil. It splashed."

Tom's voice was gruff. "Your quick thinking might have saved your life."

"Yeah, well. He wouldn't have gotten away with killing me."

Tom looked at Brent. "She didn't need the cold water. Ice runs in her veins."

I retorted, "No, it doesn't." I had proof. The tops of my ears were becoming very hot. "Oliver pretty much confessed, describing how the crimes were committed, all the while saying it was Randy who had done it all. The surveillance camera over the cash drawer will have caught some of it, and my phone over there will have caught most of it from a different angle." I told them about seeing Oliver put his watch on exactly the way that the Randy look-alike had, complete with a tap from his right index finger on the face of the watch.

"I'll capture the videos from all of our surveillance cameras for you, son," Tom told Brent.

I retrieved my phone from behind the espresso machine.

Standing close together, Brent and I watched and listened to the recording it had made. I didn't think Brent noticed putting an arm around my shoulders when the small screen showed Oliver hurling the rolling pin at me. Brent dropped his arm from my shoulder when the video showed me towering over Oliver with that pot of hot oil, but under his breath he murmured, "Way to go, Alec. You trained her well."

When my phone showed Brent, with Tom's help, handcuffing Oliver, we joined Tom in the office and watched the other videos. A pleased smile on his face, Brent e-mailed them, along with the recording my phone had taken, to Yvonne Passenmath. "We've got enough to charge him with assaulting you, Emily. And, as you told us, he came close to confessing to two murders and an attempted murder. We might even get him for attempting to murder you."

My knees were going all flimsy again. "Let's celebrate. Who wants donuts?"

Brent grinned. "Sounds good, but let's get you to the hospital and the police photographer first."

"Then can we come back for Dep?"

Tom pointed at the front. Misty was stringing yellow tape across the door. "This is now a crime scene," he said. "I'll stick around here to greet the investigators, and then I'll take Dep to your place, Emily."

Brent checked his phone. "Are you sure you want to stick around, Tom? Yvonne Passenmath will be here soon."

"I'll stay. I look forward to making certain she watches the videos."

I gave Tom the spare house key I kept in the office desk. "Why'd you come, Tom? Did our security system autodial you?"

"Yes, but I'm afraid I didn't have my phone with me, and I didn't get the message until about ten minutes after it was sent. I drove fast, though."

I hugged him, thanked him, and turned to Brent. "I know that our panic button summoned the patrol officers, but why did *you* come? You were out by the river."

He brushed a hand across his forehead and then tugged at his earlobe. "Alec told me about your secret signal. He and I had a variation of it."

Brent took me to the hospital. He stayed with me while a police photographer took pictures of my head and a doctor examined me and declared that if I had a concussion, it was slight. The doctor also said that no one needed to check on me during the night.

When Brent and I arrived at my place and greeted Dep, it was late. Brent was going back to Deputy Donut. "I'll try to get them to release your shop to you soon, Em."

"What about Randy?"

"I'm afraid he might spend the rest of the night in custody, but we should get those search warrants for Oliver's computers and his 1950 Ford first thing in the morning. We should be able to release Randy soon."

Four days later, Deputy Donut was open again, the red on my wrist had paled and stopped hurting, the lump on my head had shrunk, and Oliver was in jail, charged with the murders of Matthias and Georgia Treetor. Other charges were pending.

Lois served a delicious gourmet dinner to Randy, Nicole, and me. For some reason, Lois had also invited Brent.

I brought dessert. Donuts.

Nicole was as sweet as I remembered her from high school, and she and Randy were obviously besotted with each other. Lois beamed at all of us.

Afterward, Brent walked Dep and me home, and I didn't

mind his quick good-night hug. I even hugged him back. He hurried away, and I dead-locked the door.

"We're friends again," I told Dep. "I guess we always were."

"Mmp." She started toward the kitchen. Somehow, she seemed to know that I was about to open the can of sardines I'd bought the day before.

Survival
of the
Fritters
Recipes

Cranberry-Orange-Walnut Fritters

1 cup all-purpose flour
2 tablespoons sugar
2 eggs
¼ cup less 1 tablespoon milk
2 tablespoons fresh cranberries, chopped
1 tablespoon walnuts, chopped
2 teaspoons orange zest
¼ teaspoon orange extract
Granulated sugar
Vegetable oil with a smoke point of 400 degrees or higher,
    or follow your deep fryer manufacturer's instructions

Stir flour and sugar together with a fork.

Stir in eggs, milk, cranberries, walnuts, orange zest, and orange extract until blended.

When oil reaches 370 degrees, drop batter by large spoonfuls into the oil without crowding them. Fry until both sides are golden, approximately 1 minute per side, turning once. Lift basket to drain, then drain fritters on paper towels.

While still warm, roll in granulated sugar and serve.

Fudge Donuts with Fudge Drizzle

2 cups all-purpose flour
2 teaspoons baking powder
½ cup unsweetened Dutch process (alkalized) cocoa powder
1 egg, beaten
½ cup milk
¼ cup sugar
2 tablespoons unsalted butter, melted
Vegetable oil with a smoke point of 400 degrees or higher,
    or follow your deep fryer manufacturer's instructions

Sift flour, baking powder, and cocoa powder together.
Place beaten egg, milk, sugar, and melted butter into large bowl.
Stir in mixture of flour, baking powder, and cocoa powder.
Flours vary. If dough is too wet and sticky to form a ball, stir in flour, 1 tablespoon at a time. If it is too dry, stir in milk, 1 tablespoon at a time.
Form into ball. Optional: wrap and chill.
Roll dough to ½ inch thick.
Cut out with donut cutter and let cut donuts rest for 5 minutes.
Heat fryer to 360 degrees.
Place donuts, a few at a time, into hot oil. Fry for about 1 minute. Turn and fry for about 1 minute longer.
Drain on paper towels.
OR bake at 350 degrees for approximately 7 minutes on a cookie sheet lined with parchment paper or a silicone baking sheet.
When cool, decorate with fudge drizzle.

Fudge Drizzle

⅓ cup 35 percent butterfat cream
¼ cup corn syrup

⅓ cup demerara sugar
⅛ cup unsweetened Dutch process (alkalized) cocoa powder
4 oz. high-quality dark chocolate, coarsely chopped
¼ cup unsalted butter, coarsely chopped
1 teaspoon vanilla

Bring cream, corn syrup, sugar, cocoa, and half of chocolate to a boil in a heavy saucepan over moderate heat, stirring until chocolate is melted. Reduce heat and cook at a low boil, stirring occasionally, 5 minutes. Reduce heat again. Add butter and stir until butter melts, then remove from heat. Add remaining chocolate and stir until smooth. Add vanilla and stir until blended.

This can be made in advance and warmed (careful not to overheat or burn it) in the microwave oven until it's warm enough to drizzle.

Penuche Donuts

1 cup milk
3 teaspoons dry yeast
1 beaten egg
¼ cup unsalted butter, softened if you're not using a bread
   maker
1 cup brown sugar
3½ cups all-purpose flour
1 teaspoon salt
Vegetable oil with a smoke point of 400 degrees or higher,
   or follow your deep fryer's instruction manual
Brown sugar–coated pecan pieces (optional)

Raised donuts are a cinch if you have a bread maker. Simply place all of the ingredients in your bread maker and follow the manufacturer's instructions for dough.

If you don't have a bread maker, heat milk until just luke-warm (not hot). Place the milk in a bowl with yeast. Place dry ingredients in large bowl. When the yeast forms bubbles in the milk, add the yeast and milk mixture, the beaten egg, and the softened butter to the dry ingredients. Beat well. If the dough isn't stiff enough to work, knead in more flour, a little at a time. Cover and let rise in a warm place until doubled in size.

With or without a bread maker: Roll dough on a floured board to about ½ inch thick. Cut with a doughnut cutter. Cover and let rise until doubled in size. Fry at 375 degrees, turning when golden, about 30 seconds per side.

OR bake on cookie sheet lined with parchment paper or a silicone baking sheet in 350-degree oven for 10–13 minutes until tops are golden.

When cool, dip tops in penuche frosting and then (op-tional) in brown sugar–coated pecan pieces.

Penuche Frosting

1 cup brown sugar
½ cup granulated sugar
½ cup 35 percent butterfat cream
1 tablespoon corn syrup
2 tablespoons unsalted butter
½ teaspoon vanilla

Mix sugars, cream, and corn syrup in a heavy saucepan. Stir constantly over low heat. When the first signs of boiling appear (bubbles around the edge of the saucepan), stop stirring and allow to boil for only 1 minute. Remove from heat and place butter on top of mixture. Cool to lukewarm. Add vanilla. Beat to spreading consistency.

Brown Sugar–Coated Pecan Pieces

1 egg white
1 cup pecan pieces, chopped very small
¼ cup brown sugar

In small bowl, beat egg white slightly. Toss pecan pieces in egg white to coat. Stir in brown sugar until pieces are coated in sugar. Place on silicone baking sheet and bake at 250° for 20 minutes. Allow to cool.

Please turn the page for an exciting
sneak peek of Ginger Bolton's next
Deputy Donut mystery

GOODBYE CRULLER WORLD

coming soon wherever print and ebooks are sold!

Chapter 1

❧

The yelling began almost the second I started walking down the driveway between Deputy Donut, the café that my father-in-law and I owned, and Dressed to Kill, Jenn Zeeland's cute clothing boutique.

The loud argument wasn't going on inside Deputy Donut, where Tom was finishing the day's tidying. It was going on inside Dressed to Kill, where I was heading. I couldn't make out the words, but the women spewing them were obviously angry.

I almost turned around and went back to Deputy Donut.

However, it was nearly five. In ten minutes, Dressed to Kill would close for two weeks, and I needed the black jeans and white shirts that I'd ordered. Besides, what if Jenn was in danger?

I hurried to the front of Dressed to Kill.

I wasn't about to barge inside without peeking in first. Jenn's display windows were lovely, but I couldn't see beyond her hand-knit sweaters, mittens, scarves, and hats, and the cords and down-filled vests that went with them. The clothes were draped over antique skis, sleds, skates, and snowshoes. In one window, an electric fireplace sent warm hues rippling over the entire scene. It could have been very welcoming if the women inside the store hadn't been screaming at each other only seconds before.

A red-faced woman burst out of Dressed to Kill. She muttered, "Don't go in there," budged past me, and raced south on Wisconsin Street.

My training kicked in. *Get a description, Emily.*

I guessed she was in her mid to late forties. She was tall and angular with straight brown, flyaway hair. Her mid-calf, flowing dress, a floral print in blue and white, hung several inches below an unbuttoned navy wool coat. She hadn't zipped up the sides of her tan, knee-high leather boots. With their tops flapping and threatening to trip her with each step, she ran past the bookstore and the artisan's co-op, and then she turned right and disappeared. For a few seconds, I heard the *clap, clap, clap* of those unzipped boots.

I had never seen her before.

I again considered returning to Deputy Donut. Before Tom and I opened our coffee and donut shop, he had been Fallingbrook's police chief. Tom could handle whatever had gone on inside Dressed to Kill.

And so can you, Emily.

I pulled the door open. Tiny bells jingled.

Usually, unless Jenn was busy with a customer, she heard the bells, peeked around racks of clothing, and greeted me.

This time, she didn't. I was getting twitchy.

That shouting I'd heard earlier . . .

And now, this breathless quiet . . .

I told myself I was being overly dramatic. Jenn knew I was coming. Besides, she was probably immersed in wedding preparations.

I tiptoed into the store. I couldn't help touching, with one tentative finger, an emerald green velvet cocktail dress. It would be perfect for Jenn's reception the next night, but I was attending the reception late, only to keep the donut wall stocked, and I would be wearing my Deputy Donut uniform. The black jeans and white shirt would be new, though, if Jenn was here to give them to me.

"Jenn?" I called.

No answer.

I walked farther into the store, past a table of neatly folded sequined sweaters. "Jenn?"

Near the back of the store, a door slammed or something fell.

"*Jenn!*" I sounded a little frantic. "Are you here?" If she didn't answer by the count of ten, I was going back to Deputy Donut for Tom.

I got to eight, and then footsteps approached from the office beyond the dressing cubicles. Someone vigorously blew a nose.

Tall and slender, dressed in tight jeans and a luscious coral sweater that she must have designed, Jenn came out from between the dressing rooms. Her head was bowed, and her long blond hair hung down like curtains, concealing the sides of her face. "Hey, Emily," she mumbled toward her sweater. "I'll get the things you ordered." She walked away quickly, like she didn't want me to get a good look at her.

It was too late.

I'd already noticed her red and swollen eyelids.

The poor thing. She was only a little older than I was, in her mid-thirties, but the sad eyes aged her, and in less than twenty-four hours, she was scheduled to wow everyone with her long white dress and the radiance that wedding guests expected from brides.

She returned, holding the clothes, which were on hangers, high, as if she were hiding behind them. She walked to the cash desk at the front of the store and hung the garments on a rack. I followed. Fiddling with receipts and invoices, she didn't meet my gaze. "These should fit," she said. "Teensy for you and muscular for Tom."

I tried to prolong the joking atmosphere. "You've changed the names of sizes?" She raised her face, and I couldn't ignore the tear rolling down her cheek. "What's wrong, Jenn?"

"*Everything*. I wish I had your curls."

I couldn't believe she was crying because she didn't have a crop of unruly dark curls.

"AND those vivid blue eyes."

"Don't be ridiculous," I said. "Nearly everyone wants straight blond hair like yours, and your hazel eyes are beautiful. Besides, curls seldom behave the way I want them to." Plunking a hand on my Deputy Donut cap, a police hat with a faux-fur donut attached where the badge would ordinarily be, I accidentally pushed the cap down. It nearly covered my eyes. "It's a good thing I designed a hat to hide my hair at work." I shoved the hat up again. "The bad news is that when I remove it every evening, I have a bad case of hat head."

"The blond is out of a bottle, but the straight is real. Without the help of chemicals, my hair is mousy brown. Like my sister's. Do you know Suzanne?"

She was jumping so quickly from subject to subject that I couldn't do much besides shake my head and clench my teeth to prevent my mouth from gaping open.

"She just left," Jenn said. "I thought maybe you saw her. She's my half sister, really. We had different fathers. She's ten years older, and when our mother got sick, Suzanne promised to look after me. I was only nine. Looking after is one thing, but . . ." She blew her nose again. "Smothering is quite another. I mean, we work together *here* all right."

"Here? I never saw her before today." I didn't mean to sound skeptical.

"We own Dressed to Kill together, fifty-fifty. She does the books, usually at night, long after you've closed Deputy Donut. She doesn't like dealing with customers or ordering clothes, so I do all that. She says it would be different if we sold shoes. She loves shoes and knows just about everything there is to know about footwear."

Maybe wearing boots unzipped and flopping around one's ankles was the latest trend. Would knowledge about footwear make someone cry? "Did she upset you?"

Jenn wailed, "She told me to cancel the wedding. *Told* me!"

All I managed was, "Oh." Did Jenn's half sister want Jenn's fiancé for herself?

Apparently not. "She *hates* Roger! She always has. She never gave him half a chance."

Still not knowing quite what to say, I mumbled something meant to sound sympathetic.

"I never should have agreed to marry him in the first place, but the wedding's tomorrow, and now it's way too late to change my mind."

Seriously confused, I held up a hand. "Wait. Don't you want to marry him?"

"Yes. No." She strode to the cash desk and grabbed a fresh tissue. "I don't know. To make matters worse, I haven't told Roger that I invited my old boyfriend to the wedding and reception. There was never a right time to tell Roger. And my old boyfriend and I are just friends, really, but he's one of my best friends."

I saw where this could pose a problem. "Maybe you should tell Roger before tomorrow. Or, wouldn't a best friend understand if you uninvited him?"

She clicked long and shapely nails against the cash desk. "I couldn't do either of those things. Uninviting someone would be just too rude. And I don't want to make Roger angry tonight, the night before our wedding. I'll just have to trust that he won't make a scene tomorrow."

Some people were really good at causing problems for themselves. I suggested, "If you're not sure about marrying Roger, maybe you could postpone the wedding until you know what you want to do."

"I do know. Marry Roger. I'm just having pre-wedding jitters, I guess. They say every bride has them."

I'd never had the least doubt about marrying Alec.

As if I'd said it aloud, she apologized. "I shouldn't be reminding you. You must miss your husband."

"That's okay. I've finally reached the stage where thinking

about him brings back wonderful memories." Still, I couldn't help remembering the night that my detective husband was killed while on duty, and it still hurt. "Why did your sister wait so long to tell you to cancel the wedding?"

Jenn bowed her head again, letting her hair fall in front of her face. "She's been saying it all along. She told me to stop seeing him when we were first dating. Like it's any of her business, you know? And this afternoon, she went ballistic on me, screaming, yelling, the whole nine yards. For no reason, other than this last-ditch attempt to get me to drop Roger."

"Is she married?"

"No. Never has been. And I know she cares about me, really. It's just that . . ."

"Smothering," I repeated.

"She doesn't want me to move away from Fallingbrook, either."

"Are you going to? We'd all miss you—and your wonderful shop. I love how you turned your online knitting and knitwear design business into a bricks-and-mortar store." And I'd been buying a lot of sweaters . . . "But you can run your online store from wherever you live, can't you?"

"I don't plan to close Dressed to Kill, but Suzanne says that Roger won't let me stay in business, period. She thinks he's jealous of my success. But how could he be? He's doing great as a life coach, even though he inherited so much from some distant relative that he doesn't have to work. Suzanne says that Roger has always moved around, and he's not going to want to stay in Fallingbrook. She even uses his wealth against him, saying it will allow him to live anywhere." Jenn's face crumpled, and tears welled in her eyes. "Just now, she accused me of being a gold digger."

"That's nonsense." Jenn seemed too sweet to marry a man only for his money. She had to care about him. "He used to live in Fallingbrook, didn't he? And he came back, so maybe he's ready to settle down, with you, here."

"I hope so. I don't think I could bear to part with Dressed to Kill." She gave a resigned little shrug. "But I might have to. The things we do for love." Her half-hearted attempt at a smile didn't reach her eyes. "And the things we do because we've already planned a wedding. Maybe I could have canceled it a year or even six months ago, but now it's too late. For instance, you and Tom—you wouldn't let me put down a deposit. You built that donut wall and you're planning to stay up tomorrow night to provide late-night snacks for our guests. You've probably ordered tons of extra ingredients for the donuts and crullers. I can't ask you to cancel *now*."

"It wouldn't be a problem. We can use that donut wall another time, and the ingredients will keep. But you'd lose your deposit on the banquet hall rental and the meals you ordered, and you probably can't send your dress back, and . . ." Why was I giving her excuses to marry someone who, I was beginning to suspect, might make her unhappy?

"Yeah, it's definitely too late. And I want to marry Roger. I do." She gave me a watery smile. " 'I do.' See? I'm already practicing my lines for tomorrow."

Connect with U s

Visit us online at
KensingtonBooks.com
to read more from your favorite authors, see books
by series, view reading group guides, and more.

Join us on social media

for sneak peeks, chances to win books and prize packs,
and to share your thoughts with other readers.

facebook.com/kensingtonpublishing
twitter.com/kensingtonbooks

Tell us what you think!

To share your thoughts, submit a review,
or sign up for our eNewsletters, please visit:
KensingtonBooks.com/TellUs.